Silent Kill

David Fingerman

L & L Dreamspell
Spring, Texas

Cover and Interior Design by L & L Dreamspell

ISBN: 978-1-60318-230-0

Library of Congress Control Number: 2010922596

Visit us on the web at www.lldreamspell.com

Published by L & L Dreamspell
Printed in the United States of America

Acknowledgements

I'd like to thank The Minneapolis Writers' Workshop and The Southside Writers' Group for their constant encouragement and critiques. Thank you Ed Stackler, Cindy Davis, and Helen Montgomery for your keen insight. Thank you Dep. Dave Kohler for letting me ride along and showing me a day-in-the-life of a Sheriff's Deputy. A big thank you to Lt. Steve Burke who showed more patience than I deserved while I barraged him with questions on a daily basis. And thank you to Lisa Smith and all those at L & L Dreamspell who made this book possible.

Any mistakes, miscues, and inconsistencies regarding the Minneapolis Police and Hennepin County Sheriff's Departments are to be blamed strictly on myself. They were made either because of my lack of understanding or creative liberties to advance the story. To my knowledge there has never been any sort of hazing to rookie cops or deputies.

For Joan & Sol

One

Monday, 11:45 a.m.

The flashing lights of the black and white filled the rearview mirror as it kissed his rear bumper. Dr. Leonard Hout swore under his breath. The red light switched to a green arrow. Looking both ways with exaggerated movements, the doctor made a slow left turn and, only six blocks from home, pulled his Lexus to the curb.

Again the police car tapped his bumper.

"What a prick," Hout muttered.

The door swung open from the car behind and a skyscraper with mirrored sunglasses stepped out. A bulletproof vest, worn outside the uniform, eclipsed the sun as the policeman approached the side window. Leonard pressed the button and the driver's window whirred down. The August heat poured in, making him sweat almost instantly.

"License and proof of insurance."

"Yes sir." Dr. Hout unbuckled the seatbelt, reached into his back pocket and removed his wallet. Fumbling through the credit cards he found his driver's license and handed it to the officer.

"Do you know why I pulled you over?" The huge policeman looked at the license. "Mr. Hout." It didn't sound like a question.

"No, sir."

"You a doctor?"

Leonard heard a challenge in the policeman's deep voice. "Yes, sir."

"Psychiatrist, huh?"

Leonard frowned and then noticed the copy of *Psychiatric Update* lying on the passenger seat. "Yes, sir."

"I've seen a couple of shrinks in my day," the officer said.

I'm sure you have.

"So you think that just because you're a doctor, you don't need to obey the traffic laws?"

Leonard shook his head. "No sir. Absolutely not."

The cop bent over, hands on his knees and stared through the open window. "Do you think just 'cause you're some head shrinker, you're better than everyone else?"

Something didn't feel right. The cop's words, his stance, his tone of voice… A knot formed in the pit of Hout's stomach. A drop of sweat rolled down his cheek and he gripped the steering wheel tighter to keep his hands from shaking.

"No sir. Not at all."

"Do you know the speed limit, Doctor?" The officer spit a wad of tobacco. It splattered on the hood of the Lexus.

"I thought it was thirty miles an hour." Hout knew the speed limit well, and he knew that was the speed he'd been driving. He'd seen enough cars pulled over this week to know about the trap. He had been careful.

The officer straightened up. "Do you know how fast you were going?"

Hout wanted to look into the policeman's face but the man's stomach took up the window. A swallow caught in the doctor's throat. He'd noticed it before, but it didn't register. Cops don't wear their bulletproof vests on the outside of their uniforms. Two small, circular dents had been punched into it. *My God!*

"I honestly thought I was going thirty, Officer."

"I clocked you at thirty-one. I'm going to have to give you a citation, sir. Oh, excuse me…Doctor."

"Thirty-one!" Hout's face steamed. He instantly forgot about the dents in the vest and the size of the authority. "I'm getting a ticket for going one mile an hour over the limit? I'll see you in court, Officer."

Even before his words spilled out, Dr. Hout regretted losing his temper. But this was nuts! Never had he heard of anyone getting a ticket for going one mile an hour over the limit.

An angry fist smashed against the roof of the Lexus.

“That’s it. I don’t have to take this abuse.”

The driver’s door flew open and a giant paw reached in and caught the doctor by the collar. Playing a rag doll, Dr. Hout flopped out of the car. Arms and legs flailed in midair. Lightning shot through his legs as they smashed into the front fender, but from the waist up he kept moving. Metallic thunder crashed in his head as the cop slammed it onto the hood of the car. The doctor felt something wet on the side of his face. He thought he might be bleeding.

A moment later the sickly sweet smell of tobacco filtered through his nostrils. The damn wad of tobacco. He tried to squirm out of the grip but a heavy hand at the base of his skull held him in place.

“I just try to do my job and all I get is some higher-than-fucking-God psychiatrist telling me to go fuck myself.”

Hout tried to shake the static from his head. “I didn’t say that. I’m sorry if you got that impression.” It was hard to speak with one side of his mouth pressed against metal.

“Did I say you could talk?” The cop grabbed a handful of Leonard’s hair, lifted his head a few inches, and slammed it back onto the hood.

Leonard’s knees buckled, his lips smacked into the gob of brown juice. He tasted blood and tobacco and car. Nausea churned in his stomach, ready to erupt.

Fresh pain shot through his shoulder as the policeman jerked his left arm and twisted it up behind his back. A click and then a new agony of metal bit into his wrist. Before he could move, the cop yanked Leonard’s other arm behind him and the other cuff snapped off the circulation of his right hand.

As if he were nothing more than a child’s toy, the giant cop flung Dr. Hout toward the police car. Hout lost his balance and landed hard on his backside, barely avoiding crushing his hands.

Sitting on the ground, he noticed the cop's white socks and sneakers spotted with blood. The uniform slacks hiked well above the ankle, cuffs hugging massive calves.

The doctor frantically searched the sidewalk for help. The noonday sun reflected off the house windows so he couldn't see inside, but he prayed someone, somewhere, might be watching, and hopefully filming this on their camcorder. That might help later. For now Dr. Hout had to rely on his own wits.

The policeman walked up and stood over him, blocking out the sun. He reached down and lifted Hout off the ground by a handful of his thinning hair. Dragging him across the pavement like a sack of laundry, the giant opened the door to the squad.

Leonard Hout choked back a cry; vomit bubbled up his throat. A man lay crumpled on the back seat, his dead eyes staring at the roof. He wore a blood-soaked T-shirt, shit-filled briefs, and black socks. In a grotesque comedy, a police badge had been pierced through his nose. The man, who had obviously been a police officer until earlier that day, would have been considered large until compared to the one who now wore his uniform.

The doctor opened his mouth to scream but a fist in the stomach stifled that. He doubled over as the air spewed from of his lungs. A knee caught him hard into his ass, shoving him in the squad.

"Watch your head, sir…er, excuse me. Watch your head—Doctor."

Hout landed on top of the body and the door slammed shut.

Two

Monday, 3:15 p.m.

Louise Miller clocked the on-coming Honda Civic at 43 in the 35 mph zone. She let it slide. Eight miles an hour over was where she drew the line. Depending on her mood, it could go either way whether the driver got a citation. This afternoon she felt good. A hot spell of 90-degree temperatures that had plagued Minneapolis for the past week and a half was finally abating as the clouds rolled in, dropping the temperature into the mid-eighties. Maybe a good downpour would lower it even farther—into the seventies.

In another few weeks the leaves would start changing colors and she'd have to listen to her brother yap about the cycles—how winter would be here soon, but that just leads to spring which in turn leads back to summer. She'd playfully slap him upside the head and remind him he lived in Minnesota. It is what it is. It had become their yearly tradition.

The radar flashed 53 at the oncoming Dodge Neon. Louise looked in her rearview mirror as it passed and saw the brake lights come on. She flipped the switch so the radar now read the speed of cars behind her. The Neon had slowed to 36. She let it go. She had more important things to think about. Like what to feed her brother for dinner.

To plan the celebratory dinner for Andrew, a country theme might be appropriate. That would relate well to his first shift patrolling rube country. As a Deputy Sheriff, Andrew was responsible for all of Hennepin County, which would mean patrolling mostly the northern suburban cities where cops were in shorter supply. He said he liked the idea of working with a variety of people. There he'd be dealing with farmers, rich businessmen and families that wanted to raise their kids away from crime and pollution. Andrew already knew of a couple Minnesota Twins, a T-Wolf, and a Viking living out there. As far as he knew, all of the Minnesota Wild still lived in Canada or Europe in the off-season. Of course there were those who weren't as fortunate, populating the trailer parks that separated the farms and the townhouses and small groups of homes where everybody knew their neighbors. No privacy.

Louise looked at it this way: once you leave Minneapolis—she begrudgingly admitted the immediate suburbs—you were in the boonies where everything became farmland. So much open space made her tense. She liked the idea of houses stacked next to each other. As a kid one of her favorite activities had been to climb up on the roof of her house and jump across to the neighbor's. She never fell.

Okay, we'll do corn on the cob. Andrew didn't eat red meat so she would buy a chicken. Now that he worked out in the sticks patrolling cornfields, she wondered if she could buy a live one and make Andrew chop off its head, then pluck and gut it, just like they do on the farm.

A tan Buick Rainier passed by and swerved in front of her squad. It drifted onto the shoulder before straightening out and driving away at over 50 miles per hour. Louise activated the lights and siren and radioed in her location for backup. The driver would probably end up being some drunken idiot, but Louise didn't want to chance somebody wanting to challenge a cop, especially a female cop. There were rumors, too, about a new gang initiation. Offing a cop brought instant respect. She hadn't been able make out the driver's race through the tinted windows.

The Rainier pulled to the curb. Louise stopped her car about fifteen feet back. She keyed in the license plate number and eyed the data. The owner had previously been revoked for a D.U.I. He didn't have insurance, either.

Louise put on her hat, tucked her rat-tail under her shirt, and slid out of the squad. As she walked toward the Buick, its driver's door opened. A white man a head taller than Louise staggered out.

"Get back in the car, sir, and place your hands on the steering wheel!"

"What's the problem, officer?" he slurred and took a step toward her.

"I said get back in the car!" She placed her palm on the handle of her gun.

The man smiled but made no move to retreat. "I'm sure we can work this out amicably." Without taking his eyes off of her he reached behind him.

Louise had her gun out and aimed at his head before he could wipe away that oafish grin. "Get on your knees and put your hands on top of your head!"

Louise guessed the man had never had a gun pointed at his head before. At least he had enough sense to show the proper reaction. He appeared scared.

"What's wrong with you?" His voice and manner sobered instantly as he dropped to his knees.

"Cross your ankles!"

Another squad whipped around the corner, lights flashing, siren off. It boxed the Rainier in. Officer Paul Handley smiled as he got out of the car. "Leave it to you, Miller."

"I've got a gentleman here who doesn't like to follow orders."

Handley stood above the man and told him to get to his feet and keep his hands on his head. The man complied. He told him to put his hands on the roof of the car and to spread his legs. Again the man did as told.

"He seems okay to me. Maybe it's you."

"Nope, it's not me. Maybe it's a gun thing."

Louise holstered her 9mm and patted the man down. Clean. "Take out your wallet and give me your driver's license."

He reached in his back pocket. "That's what I was trying to do before."

The wallet bulged with a wad of cash. He looked at Handley's steel blue eyes glaring at him, and then at Louise.

"You blew it, officer." He handed her his license.

Louise narrowed her eyes in suspicion. "Were you going to bribe me?"

Again, the man's eyes flickered to Handley. "Of course not."

"Have you been drinking, sir?" Louise glanced at the name on his license: Walter Farkos. The I.D. verified that he owned the vehicle; his picture matched.

He still kept his eyes on Handley. Like a poker player, Handley stared back, giving him nothing. Louise loved the guy like a father. Unlike so many other cops, Handley had nothing to prove in the macho department and felt no need to take over for the little lady. He came as a backup and that's how he would stay. Louise did not look forward to his upcoming retirement.

"I had a couple of beers," he told Handley.

"I wasn't the one who asked," Handley replied.

"Really? I thought you were the ventriloquist and that was your dummy." He chuckled, impressed with his witticism.

Handley raised his eyebrows at Louise. She shook her head.

She opened a small plastic bag, pulled out a disposable mouthpiece and attached it to a handheld breathalyzer. "I want you to blow hard into this." She held it up to his mouth.

"If I refuse?"

"Then I mark you down as a refusal. You still get busted for D.U.I. and about a dozen other charges I'm going to tack on. You lose your license for a year."

"Which makes more paperwork for you."

"No sweat off my nose either way. I get paid the same whether I'm writing up your report or someone else's."

"I think I should talk to my lawyer..."

"You'll be able to do that later."

Walter Farkos gave her an evil glare then blew into the tube.

He registered a 0.18. Louise placed him under arrest, read him the required advisories, then cuffed him and escorted him to the back of her squad. She then called to have his vehicle towed.

"I was all set to hold him down while you kicked the crap out of him," Handley said.

"I'm working on my restraint. I was tempted, though."

"Well, I'm impressed. By the way, you're coming to my retirement party, aren't you?"

"You're retiring?" Louise grinned and playfully punched him in the arm. "Wouldn't miss it."

With Farkos safely inside, the two officers leaned against her car, enjoying each other's company. "So, what are you going to do with your time?"

After twenty-seven years in the department, Handley had only two months left before retirement. Gray hair, but still in good shape for a cop in his fifties, Handley gazed at the cloudy sky, contemplating her question. "Hmm," he said it like no one had ever asked that question before. "Definitely do some fishing."

"That'll take an afternoon. Then what?"

Handley smiled. "Always liked you, Miller. Gonna miss kicking ass with you."

"Yeah, me too. Not going to be the same without you there holding some junkie down while I smash his skull."

Handley laughed before turning contemplative. "Seriously though, I am going to miss you."

"So what else are you going to do?" Louise tried to keep her voice level. She didn't want to become emotional.

"Sara wants us to move up north. A little souvenir shop not too far from Ely went up for sale. We're thinking about taking it over. She really wants to do it. Said she's had enough of the city."

"That sounds great for her, but what about you?"

"Honestly? I think after the novelty of fishing everyday wears off I might die of boredom. What do you think?"

Louise pondered. "I suppose it sounds like a dream for some people, but not the lifestyle for me."

"I don't want to know your lifestyle. Don't ask, don't tell, right?"

Damn, she was going to miss the big galoot. "I think you need to follow your heart. Do what's right for you."

"Typical woman answer." Handley chuckled.

"Hey, what can I say? 'I yam what I yam,'" she said in a perfect Popeye imitation.

They both laughed then stopped at the same time, each looking away from the other.

"I don't know," he said.

"All right, asshole. You want my opinion? Here it is."

"That's Officer Asshole to you. You never did learn to respect your elders."

Louise smiled. "You love your wife, buy the shop. Give it some time. If it works out, great. If not you can always move back."

"Good point. That's why I like you. No bullshit."

"Hell, you just need a woman to tell you what to do."

They stood in companionable silence for a while longer.

"I suppose we've wasted enough taxpayer money for one afternoon," he said.

Handley got in his cruiser and drove off while Louise sat in hers waiting for the tow truck. She started writing her report, paying no attention to the radio until she heard someone at dispatch issued an APB for Officer Mark Lone Bear. Earlier they'd been covering all of the channels, asking him to report. He hadn't answered. Now, he was missing.

A chill ran through Louise as she thought about her friend from long ago.

The sweat poured down her face as Louise finished the obstacle course. She smiled as the DI called out her time. She had beaten more than half the guys in her class.

She wandered away from the crowd for the drinking fountain that sat on the other side of red brick structure housing the restrooms. Two of her fellow recruits followed. She didn't notice them until she turned the corner.

"Hey Miller, drop your pants. With a time that good we figure you gotta have a dick and a set of balls on you."

His name was Johansson, a typical blond haired, blue-eyed Minnesota Swede who had probably been captain of his high school football team, dated the head cheerleader, and relentlessly teased and beat up nerds. Next to him stood Ross. He followed Johansson around like a lap puppy.

"I'll show you mine if you show me yours, but I'd be willing to bet, mine are bigger," Louise said.

The smirk disappeared from Johansson's face. He pounded his fist into his open palm. "Just because you might *have a tiny pair of titties hiding under that shirt, don't think I won't kick your ass."*

"Bring it on." Louise crouched into a fighting stance, her fists ready for damage.

Johansson smirked at his friend. "This is gonna be fun. You want in?"

"I want in."

The deep mellow voice startled Louise. She spun around. A man with a chiseled square jaw, Roman nose, and black hair parted down the middle and tied behind him, Mark Lone Bear stood ready to back her up. Johansson was big, maybe six-one. Lone Bear towered over him.

"This has nothing to do with you." Johansson's voice held a note of fear.

"Doesn't he look a lot like Custer?" Lone Bear asked Louise. "Looks like he could use a haircut, too."

Johansson elbowed Ross in the arm and started to walk away. "Screw it. They're not worth getting thrown off the force for."

When they were gone, Louise held out her hand. "I don't think we've formally met. Louise Miller. And just for the record, I could've taken him."

He buried her hand inside his. "Mark Lone Bear. And just for the record, I believe you."

Louise smiled up at him. "I appreciate you having my back, though."

She leaned over the drinking fountain, letting the water splash on her face, letting some of it get in her mouth.

"Nice braid," Lone Bear said. "Eat your vegetables and one day it will grow big and strong, like mine." He turned around and showed her his black hair, braided in the thick cord, hanging down to the middle of his back.

"I'm surprised they didn't make you cut it off," Louise said.

Lone Bear chuckled. "I'd play the race card and they knew it."

That was the point Louise knew that she had a friend and kindred spirit on the force.

"Wanna get a beer after this?"

"Don't drink. I'd be willing to do a coffee."

They stayed best friends through training, but afterward they got assigned to different precincts and drifted apart. Each had sworn to stay in contact but neither one ever did. She had seen him once, maybe twice since they graduated rookie school together.

The tow truck passed Louise and parked in front of the Buick. Before she made it out of her car the driver was already at work hitching up the Rainier. A young kid, Louise liked him, although she could never remember his name. He worked with a calm efficiency and seemed to enjoy his job. She'd also seen him interact with other cops and he treated her just like he treated them, like she was one of the guys. She kept reminding herself to write a complimentary letter to his supervisor but, like getting in touch with Lone Bear, she never found the time.

"Nice car." The kid pulled the lever, and the car rose onto its back tires.

"Feel free to nick and dent the hell out of it," Louise said.

"Asshole, huh?"

"Big time," Louise answered.

"I'll be real careful." The kid winked and got in his truck. Louise sat back behind the wheel of her car, twisted around and smiled at her captive through the cage separating him from the front seat.

"Is something funny, Officer Dummy?"

"Right now I'm your only audience and I don't think you're funny. Stupid—yes. Funny—no. I can change that, though." Louise pulled a can of pepper spray from her belt. "Do you know what this is?"

"You wouldn't dare! Do you know the kind of lawsuit you'd have macing a man in handcuffs?"

"That's what makes me so clever. I get to smash your face against the cage a few times first. My report will say you went crazy and I maced you for your own protection. I'm sure Officer Handley will verify that you seemed very volatile and emotionally distraught."

Walter leaned back in his seat and kept silent.

Driving back to the precinct, Louise heard Mark Lone Bear's name once again over the radio. He hadn't reported in. No one had spoken to him, or heard from him, since roll call. Both he and his car were missing. A swallow caught in her throat. News like this never turned out good. Even her backseat occupant seemed to show concern.

"Are you all right?"

Louise ignored him. On automatic pilot, made her way back to the station. She walked through the motions as Mr. Farkos went through processing.

"Hey, Miller."

Louise found herself standing face to face with her sergeant.

I really don't need this now. "Yes, sir."

"We're offering voluntary overtime to search for Lone Bear. You in?"

The light in Louise's mind flickered. "Damn straight."

"We're searching every street and every alley in the city. Anything suspicious, I want to know."

"You can depend on me, Sarge."

With renewed energy Louise finished with Walter Farkos and got back in her squad. She had an acquaintance to find that she wanted to turn back into a friend.

As the shadows lengthened, Louise concentrated on the alleys in her precinct. She realistically knew the odds of finding Lone Bear, or his car—especially since he cruised in the precinct next door—were close to nil, but the odds were even worse on the street. At least they were paying her time and a half.

Commotion caught her attention two blocks down, a gang congregating in the middle of the block. Louise cut back onto the street and radioed for backup. If they were dealing she wanted to trap them, box them in, and also have a couple of cars on the street for when they scattered.

Within minutes the cars were in position.

"Now," Louise said into the radio.

As she pulled into the alley Louise could only assume her counterpart did the same on the other end. She stepped on the gas. A Hispanic teen raised his head; a second later the entire group took flight, running toward the streets. Louise counted eight but there could have been more. It didn't matter. All they needed was one. If they were dealing, and they weren't juvies, especially ones familiar with the system and looking at real jail time, they'd turn on their friends.

Shadows from a garage covered the alley but not enough to hide a pit bull and a rottweiler struggling where the gang had stood. Louise flipped on her headlights. The oncoming squad did the same.

The pit bull, a brown dog with thin black stripes, had his jaws clamped on the rotty. The brown shook his head vigorously, sending a spray of the weaker dog's blood across the cement. Louise felt revulsion. Not at the blood, but that human beings trained animals this way. She called for animal control while her counterpart stepped out of his car.

A shot echoed in the confines of the alley and the victor lay dead. A perfect shot to the head had scattered his brains. Louise ran to the rottweiler and bent over him, checking his front paw, and shook her head. Blood flowed from his neck as she examined the wound. Too weak to attack her, the dog let her pet his head.

"You'll be okay," Louise whispered. "You deserve a good life. I'll take care of you."

"Back away, Miller."

Behind her, fellow officer, Todd Huffman had his gun pointed at the downed pooch.

"What the hell are you doing?"

"Putting the mutt out of his misery. Get out of the way."

Louise lurched to her feet and put herself in between the gun and the dog. "Don't you dare. I'll take care of him."

"Are you crazy?"

"No, are you?"

"What's your problem, Miller?"

"I told you I'll take care of him. He's not that badly hurt."

Huffman lowered his gun. "Even if he lives, once they're trained to fight you can't change them."

"Bullshit," Louise said.

The animal control truck turned into the alley and pulled up behind Louise's car. The door opened and the AC officer got out. Louise went over to greet him. Before she could tell him to take the dog to the shelter another gunshot reverberated down the alley.

Louise spun around, stricken that her new pet had joined the realm of the winner. Huffman holstered his gun.

"You bastard!"

Louise charged, her head down. The 5 foot 4 inch, 145-pound spitfire connected into the gut of the 6 foot, 235-pound policeman. Braced and ready for impact, Huffman still flew into the grill of his car. Louise aimed for the face, knowing that a gut shot would do nothing but bruise her knuckles while he wore his vest.

Huffman easily blocked her punches until the animal control guy pulled her off. She struggled to break away but he'd caught her in a full nelson.

"Lock *her* in a cage," Huffman spat.

With her arms raised and locked Louise saw neighbors exiting their back doors. Now that cop cars were in sight, they felt safe. Who knew? One of them might even be recording. She quit struggling. "I'm fine."

The AC man broke the hold. "You'll pay for this, Huffman."

"You crazy bitch, I was doing the dog a favor."

"I'll be sure to return the favor."

"Is that a threat, Miller?"

Still seething, Louise got back in her car. With Huffman's squad in front and the animal control vehicle behind, Louise wasn't going anywhere soon. She worked on her report as Huffman canvassed the neighbors and the AC officer started his cleanup of the alley. Over the radio she heard that one of the perps had been caught. He had screamed the dog's name—Louise assumed it was the dog's name—and bawled his eyes out when he heard the first gunshot. A strange kind of love. He didn't mind his dog being torn to shreds, but a quick painless death and he went to pieces. Other than wishing the scum a slow and painful death, she didn't care anymore.

Three

Monday 7:50 p.m.

Over the radio, dispatch called out a drunk and disorderly at Happinin's Bar—widely known as Hap's—on 104th and Pike's Crossroad, in the city of Kenowa. The small community of about 2500 residents stretched between Corcoran and Medina. Hap's got about fifty percent of the city's calls.

Andrew Miller's stomach tightened; adrenaline began to pump. Just coming on 8:00 p.m., he prepared for his first call as a deputy sheriff patrolling the streets. After issuing a couple of speeding tickets and a few warnings, he couldn't think of a more perfect call. It could turn dangerous, but most of the drunks either cooperated once the law got there, or they couldn't fight worth a damn. Andrew hoped for cooperation.

Sergeant Carlin Rivers glanced at him from behind the wheel and pulled a U turn at the intersection. "Think you're ready?"

Andrew smiled, remaining calm on the outside, his nerves tingling underneath the skin. "No sweat." All 5'11" and 190 pounds were ready for action.

He'd remember this one, like the first paycheck he received from his first job. A $164.00 check from Dayton-Hudson sat enclosed in a frame on his desk at home. Andrew would make an extra copy of this incident report and frame it next to that check.

After a year of babysitting juries and escorting prisoners from the jail to the courtroom, and back to the jail, Andrew felt elated when they told him his bid for an assignment on patrol had been granted. At 23 years young, and as corny as it sounded, he wanted to make a difference—a thought he kept to himself.

His Field Training Officer was twenty-year veteran, Carlin Rivers. Tall, laid-back, and unassuming, everyone knew Rivers as a fountain of information and experience, and not above some rugged practical jokes. For the next couple of weeks Rivers would teach Miller the demographics, procedures, and paperwork.

Rain sprinkled the streets as the two deputies cruised through red lights and sped around cars whose drivers were either unaware, morons, or both.

"I'll bet ya twenty bucks it's O'Dell," Rivers said.

"Who's O'Dell?" Andrew asked.

"A mean S.O.B., and that's before he starts drinking. Once the bars open and he's had a few, then he starts to get really nasty. Plastered, he turns into a whole 'nother animal"

"Great. And he's been drunk for about eight hours?"

"Don't worry, a smooth tongued college boy like you should be able to sweet talk him right into the back seat. Consider this your first test."

Carlin pulled in the parking lot. The two got out of the car and walked into Hap's.

Dim lights covered by stained glass shades on golden chains hung from the ceiling. A rainbow of colors cast an atmosphere of intimacy. Straight ahead, past a few tables, the bar stretched from wall to wall. Behind the bar, a huge mirror reflected the dark images of the room. In front of the oak counter, slumped over with his head tucked in the crook of his arm resting on the bar sat Otis O'Dell.

"It's about time you got here," the bartender said, his voice just short of a shout. "I called over twenty minutes ago."

"Hey Ted," Carlin said. "This is Andy. Andy, that's Ted, the best barkeep in town. And that fat ass sitting at the bar is Mr. O'Dell."

"Andrew, not Andy," Andrew said without taking his eyes off the drunk. The man was huge.

"New to the streets," Carlin confided. "Good man, though."

Carlin clapped a hand on Andrew's shoulder. "All yours, rookie. Shout if you need help."

Andrew took a deep breath and walked up to O'Dell. The crack of a cue ball smashing into a triangle of others shattered the silence, making Andrew jump. Off to the right, a small adjacent room lit in fluorescent blue held two tables, one with green felt, the other with red. The green one was in use. A few bills rested next to a schooner half-filled with beer as a blond haired man with a black beard leaned over, lining up his next shot. A shadow stretched across the floor, telling Andrew another person was in the room. They seemed oblivious as to the goings-on outside their realm.

Andrew turned his attention back to O'Dell. "How ya doin' tonight, partner?"

The man didn't move. Andrew put his hand on O'Dell's shoulder and gave it a shake. "Think you can talk to me for a minute?"

Slowly, the drunk raised his head. Big and round, it reminded Andrew of the pumpkins in his grandmother's garden when he was a boy. O'Dell opened red, watery slits that vaguely resembled eyes. Thin strands of greasy gray/black hair stuck to his face, glued there by old sweat. Two or three day's growth of stubble dotted the acne-scarred face. He gazed at the deputy, then, squinting, moved close until their noses almost touched. Andrew looked into O'Dell's eyes. The guy could have been anywhere from forty to sixty-five. He had one of those faces that years of abuse demolished with time.

Otis grunted and Andrew took an involuntary step back as the man's breath attacked his nose. It reminded Andrew of dead skunk. O'Dell turned back to the bar, looking for a glass of beer that had already been taken away. Finding none, he let out another grunt and plopped his head back down. Andrew pulled up a stool and sat next to him, placing his arm around the big man's back. "How about we give you a ride home, Mr. O'Dell?"

Otis raised his head again and this time registered that someone sat beside him.

Quite unexpectedly, Otis roared then sprang off his stool into the deputy. Too surprised to react, Andrew flew off his own bar stool, landing hard on the floor. Andrew tried to roll away, and made it to his side before O'Dell landed square on top of him. For a drunk that weighed well over 300 pounds, Otis O'Dell moved with amazing speed and agility.

Andrew avoided the brunt of O'Dell's weight, but still took a good clipping. Pushing off the mountain of flesh, Andrew rose to his hands and knees and tried to shake the cluster bombs out of his head. He heard another scream as O'Dell jumped on his back. He clapped his hands around Andrew's head and twisted. The tonnage almost crushed him, but the deputy kept his own weight distributed.

Andrew dipped shoulders forward and Otis slid off. Just as the deputy lifted his head, O'Dell, with his back on the floor, reached up and grabbed him by the ears. Andrew yelled, Otis shouted incoherent curses. They tumbled into a vacant table, knocking it over and sending it rolling into the poolroom. The two fighters managed to make it to their knees. Otis grabbed Andrew by the head, wrapped his arm over Andrew's neck and applied an excruciating headlock.

Andrew twisted his body and tried to grab Otis in a bear hug, but found he couldn't come close to getting his arms around the giant. As red heat blazed in his head, Andrew reached down into his belt and pulled out the baton. He flicked his wrist, and like a TV antenna, the baton extended.

Andrew whipped at the drunken man's thigh. It should have stung like hell, but the only reaction he got was the vise tightening around his head. If only the mad man would get up off his knees, Andrew could shatter a kneecap. No amount of alcohol would suppress that pain. Unfortunately, Otis O'Dell seemed perfectly content to stay in that position until the deputy's head popped open like an over ripe melon. *Where the hell is Carlin?*

Miller finally dropped the baton. He could tenderize that thigh all night. O'Dell would be in a lot of pain, but he wouldn't realize it until he woke up the next morning. Black spots danced before Andrew's eyes. Losing it. Another second. He shot his fist in the drunken man's crotch, then grabbed his balls and squeezed, tightening his grip to match the pressure on his head.

Otis wailed a high-pitched scream, let go of the deputy's head and grabbed for his arm. Andrew's head swam at the release of pressure as he tightened his grip even harder, and twisted. Otis let go of Miller's arm and clutched his own head, shrieking. As the dizziness faded, Andrew reached behind and pulled a set of handcuffs off his belt.

"Stick out your arm," Andrew shouted.

"Lemme go!" Otis screamed again.

Andrew tightened his grip and twisted a little more. O'Dell's pitch raised another notch as he grudgingly brought out his arm. With one hand Andrew snapped on the cuffs. The bracelet barely fit around the man's chubby wrist. Tears streamed down O'Dell's face. Andrew released his balls. Otis doubled over, his face kissing the floor.

"Give me your other arm," Andrew panted getting to his feet.

The fight had drained out of Otis, and he did as he was told.

The blond pool player and his friend stood at the doorway of the small room. Both raised their beer in salute. Fellow deputies Jesse Campbell and Reggie Davis had joined Andrew's partner at the door. Andrew had no idea how long they'd been standing there. All three laughed hysterically. Jesse Campbell wiped away tears he'd been laughing so hard. "Bravo, New Age," he shouted.

Anger welled up in Andrew's stomach and boiled over into his chest. "I could've used a little help!"

Carlin, still smiling, shrugged. "I told you to shout if you needed help."

That brought on a new fit of laughter by the other spectators.

"Assholes," Andrew muttered. He wasn't real fond of his new nickname, either. He pat-searched O'Dell then pushed him past the deputies and out into the rain. He shoved the drunk into the back of the car, slammed the door shut, and then slid in onto the front passenger seat. Feeling sullen and betrayed, he yanked out the clipboard from under the seat and wrote his report. Though the car still felt cool from the air conditioner he wished he had the keys so he could crank it up.

The rain drummed rhythmically upon the squad car while Otis whimpered from the back seat. Pausing to rub his throbbing head, Andrew saw the three deputies walk out of the bar. Joke over. Campbell and Davis strolled to their own squads as Rivers opened up the driver's door and got in. Andrew ignored him, concentrating instead on his report, pushing the pencil harder onto the paper.

Rivers stared at him a long time. Finally he spoke. "Lighten up, kid. You did pretty good in there. You passed part one of your test with flying colors."

Andrew stopped writing. "Test? Part one?"

"Show me your report before you turn it in and I'll let you know how you did on part two."

The pencil snapped, sending shards of wooden slivers throughout the front seat. Rivers backed the car out of the lot and pulled into the street. Miller pulled out his pen and focused on the report, letting the steady rhythm of the windshield wipers calm his nerves. Otis seemed to have already forgotten his fight and hummed a tuneless song to himself.

The rain faded to mist and inside the car silence between the deputies kept the atmosphere tense. Andrew refused to look up from his report. He forced himself to think of meditative verses to keep from exploding. Rivers had yet to open his mouth—no apology, no nothing. Andrew wondered if this was what the next two weeks were going to be like. What would happen if he asked for a transfer after the first day? While pondering his suddenly grim future, Andrew noticed they were heading the wrong direction to drop off their prisoner.

Otis had stopped humming. His heavy breathing kept time with the wipers, a kind of grunting, mechanical, two-part harmony.

"Where the hell are we going?" Andrew asked, breaking the silence.

Carlin pulled the car to the curb. "Nowhere. We're already here." His voice betrayed no hint of friction between the two.

The houses along the street were old, small, and cheap. But even in the darkness Andrew could tell that most of them were well kept. It made him think of his parents, people who'd had little, at least materialistically, but proud of what they did own.

Rivers opened the door and stepped out. A blast of warm, humid air rushed in and Andrew instantly felt like he was suffocating. He rolled down his window to get the air moving. The streetlights sparkled in the misty night. The back door swung open and without opening his eyes, Otis turned his back on Andrew's partner. The handcuffs clinked open and O'Dell rubbed his wrists as he got out of the car. He no longer moved like the drunk in the bar.

"What the hell is going on here?" Andrew demanded.

Rivers pulled out his wallet and stuffed a fifty in Otis' meaty palm. "Better put some ice on that leg. It's gonna hurt like a son-of-a-bitch in the morning."

"Yeah, yeah." Otis staggered up to his house and threw up his hand dismissing the sergeant.

Carlin got back in the car and waited until Otis made it safely inside. He reached out to put the car in drive but Andrew grabbed his arm.

"You going to tell me what's going on?" Anger crept back into Andrew's face. His fingers pressed hard against his partner's skin. He wanted to break Rivers' arm.

"Let's see your report," Carlin said. If his arm ached, he didn't show it, but his smile disappeared.

Andrew relaxed his grip. "I'm not done yet."

"Show me what you've got."

Andrew released Carlin's arm, took a deep breath and handed him the paper. He stared into his FTO's eyes, curious of his reaction. Carlin returned the stare and without even glancing at the paper, tore it in half. His smile returned growing a little wider each time he tore another strip from the report. With the paper shredded, he wadded it up into a little ball and tossed it out the window onto the wet street.

"It's all about trust," he said.

Andrew's jaw dropped, the anger dimmed in his eyes, replaced by confusion. "I give up. Other than totally messing with my head, I don't have a clue as to what it is you're doing."

Carlin laughed. This time he put the car in drive and pulled away from the curb. "Did you ever watch pro wrestling when you were a kid?"

"Sure. What kid didn't?" Andrew said.

"Remember a guy called the Mexican Beast? Wore a mask, screamed in Spanish, used to belly-flop off the top rope and crush his opponents?"

Andrew thought for a moment. "Vaguely. I think he was mostly before my time."

"He can still handle himself pretty good, don't you think?"

"What do you mean?" As soon as the words were out of his mouth, Andrew slapped his hand against his forehead. "You mean I was fighting a pro wrestler? I was fighting the…" He stopped and cleared his throat. "Otis O'Dell is the Mexican Beast?"

"Doesn't look Mexican, does he? That's why he wore the mask. He had about five different identities throughout the seventies and early eighties. He wanted to be champ. Every time he took a few losses, he'd come back as somebody else. Then came the bodybuilders and steroids and they just phased him out. They made him the loser to all the up-and-comers until he called it quits. Then he discovered drinking full time."

"He didn't seem too drunk at the end," Andrew said.

"Don't kid yourself. He would still probably blow a .20 if we tested him now."

"So now what? You bet on fights with new deputies and he gets a cut?"

Rivers chuckled. "I'm glad I didn't bet. I thought he was going to kick your ass."

"Thanks for the vote of confidence." Andrew clenched and unclenched his fists, still mad as hell, and now he could throw hurt onto his heap of emotions.

"I was impressed, kid. You were a little raw, did a couple of stupid-shit things, but overall, you did okay."

"What would you have done if I killed him?" Andrew asked.

Carlin laughed. Every time he tried to speak, he burst into laughter again. "I was more worried about it going the other way."

"I'm serious. You don't know how close I came to pulling my gun and blowing a hole in his gut."

"Would've never happened." Carlin wiped his eyes dry. "We were watching. If your hand even came close to your holster, the three of us would've been on top of both of you faster than stink on shit."

Andrew focused his attention to the landscape as it crawled silently through the dark streets of northern Hennepin County. The part time cops were off duty, which left Kenowa, Corcoran, Medina, Greenfield and other small 'burbs in the hands of the Sheriff's department. A lot of farms and strip malls fought for space while Town homes sprang up overnight, bringing in city traffic and city crime.

"So, does every new deputy have to take this test?" Renewed anger made Andrew's words sharp.

"The ones that ride with me do," Carlin said. "And I must say that you did better than most."

"Funny, I never read anything about this in any of the manuals."

"Miller, there are rules you follow that keep your Captain and

Lieutenant happy; rules you know inside and out when you want to get promoted. Then there're the unwritten rules that keep your ass alive out on the street. It's good to know both sets."

Andrew let the words sink in. In a twisted sort of way, they made sense. "So this whole thing was a setup. Dispatch, the bartender, all of it."

Rivers didn't look at his partner. Staring ahead at the road, he said, "In a week or two you're gonna be on your own. A situation might come up, especially if you're working dog watch, where it might get violent and backup might be ten to fifteen minutes away. Ain't no manual or lecture that can prepare you for that. Now, do you want me to start off with what you did wrong, or what you did right?"

Andrew leaned his aching head back against the cage that divided the front and back seat and slowly let out his breath. He tried to clear his head of all negative energy. Finally relaxed, he said, "You might as well start with the bad."

Four

Monday 10:45 p.m.

Darkness covered his body so completely he felt it seep into the skin. Air, damp and humid, made sweat feel like worms slithering down his face, his arms, his back. He wanted so much to swat them away. He tried again to move one arm then the other, but his body could hardly twitch let alone move.

Leonard Hout had become a statue, lying spread eagle on his stomach, the bindings dug into his wrists and elbows. Bands stretched across his shoulders and waist; leather straps cut into his thighs, knees and ankles. Only his head had not been anchored into place. He lifted the side of his face from a wooden slab that smelled of rot. Tears rolled across the bridge of his nose, dripping silently onto the board.

He'd been unconscious, but had no idea for how long. *Long enough to be carried somewhere and strapped to this contraption hardly able to breathe.* The loss of time felt like a mystery. Hell, he couldn't even be sure if it was still Monday. He remembered trying to scramble off the dead body. The giant cop had grabbed him by the belt and yanked him back out of the car. The ache in his jaw reminded him of the fist flying into his face as he was spun around. Then nothing. Now he was here, and thinking about that made his jaw throb even worse. If he weren't careful, panic would soon take control.

He shifted his mind, trying to remember what Cindy had

been wearing when he left for work, and praying they might see each other again. Their fifteenth wedding anniversary was just three months away. *Please let me make it to that. Let me tell her again that I love her.*

But his restricted position occluded most of his free-ranging thoughts. Now all he could imagine was being able to move. He'd sell his soul to just be able to bend an arm or lift his leg. Straining to see through the darkness, Hout tried to grab a clue as to where this hell might be. Then the worms of sweat began crawling again. He tried to think about the last time he and Cindy made love, but the worms kept coming back, taking less and less time between attacks.

The board vibrated at Leonard's cheek, making his teeth tingle. He heard the thump of footsteps. He lifted his face off the plank, just a speck, but a cramp in his neck made it too painful. Squeaking hinges screamed at his exposed ear as a curtain of light grew on a room of horrors.

Past the shadows, the doctor found himself staring at a giant X attached to the wall. Loops of thick rope dangled at the four ends of the crisscrossed beams of wood. He twisted his head. In the corner, just below the ceiling, a piece of plywood covered what might have been a window. Below that, stocks, with a large hole in the middle, and two smaller holes on each side. He had tried one out for about half a minute once, when he and Cindy had gone to Salem, Massachusetts for a vacation. They toured what was proclaimed to be a real pilgrim village. She locked him in to take his picture, and then threatened to leave him there. She'd started walking away. He laughed, trapped in the wooden device, but inside he screamed needing to get out. Now he screamed out loud, fighting against the leather binds, and losing.

"Admiring my toys, I see."

The voice chilled like ice on Leonard's skin. Heavy footsteps on creaking stairs approached slowly.

"I've got money. Please let me go," the doctor pleaded.

"Particularly nasty, this one," the voice said. He tapped the board with the toe of his boot. "Back at the zoo we called it the surfboard." The voice spoke softly, deep and menacing, like tightly controlled anger looking for an escape. There was no mistaking it for the insane cop.

"The keepers used to torture us with it. Its genius is its simplicity, don't you think? I made this one in less than an hour."

The giant bent over at the waist and smiled down as Leonard clamped his jaw so he wouldn't whimper.

"They tried to break me on it, but they never did. You would be easy to break."

"Oh God." Leonard closed his eyes, and for the first time since appearing before the three-member panel for his board certification, the doctor prayed.

"I could have killed you. I considered it. I still might. You do what I want, and just maybe I'll do what you want. Just maybe I might let you go. We'll have to see how good of a boy you are."

"What do you want?" Deep inside Leonard knew the lie for what it was. Logic told him the man had no intention of ever letting him go. Leonard had seen it in his face. Maybe he could out think him. "I'd be more apt to do what you wanted if we could speak face-to-face like civilized human beings."

The big man's knees cracked as he squatted, and then laid forward until his face rested on the board, his nose almost touching Leonard's. The smell of chewing tobacco made Leonard gag. Seeing the brown juice dripping off of his lips made Leonard struggle not to vomit.

"Apt? You'd be apt?" The man stretched over and licked a tear off of Leonard's cheek. A wad of tobacco drooled out of his mouth and onto the doctor's face, rolling into his ear. "Is this face-to-face more to your liking?"

"It means I'll be more cooperative, more willing to help—"

"I know what it means!" The man boosted himself onto his knees and slapped Hout on the ear.

With Leonard firmly planted on the board, his body had no give. The smack echoed in his head, pain reverberating to his teeth.

"Don't talk to me like I'm stupid! Just for that, I'll have to think up some games for us to play while you're still my guest. You'll cooperate no matter what! I'll let you 'apt' on that for a while."

As the footsteps faded, Hout fought the restraints. All he accomplished was a deeper bite of leather into his skin. Psychiatry deserted him. "Anything you want!" he shouted after the footsteps. "Anything!"

"We'll see." The voice sounded so calm it almost floated to him.

He heard a click and the lights went out.

Five

Monday 11:55 p.m.

His watch read almost midnight by the time Andrew reached his sister's apartment. Once again someone had propped open the outside security door, making it easy for anyone to walk right in. He closed the door behind him, making sure the lock clicked home before he climbed the three flights of stairs. Andrew knocked on her door and heard a pair of clogs clomp across the hardwood floor. Two deadbolts and a chain lock disengaged.

Louise Miller opened the door and with no show of emotion, kissed her brother on the cheek. Without a word she walked back into the apartment, leaving the door open. Puzzled, Andrew followed her in and redid the locks. Something was wrong.

Her short red hair, cut stylishly punk, as she called it, lay on her neck except for a braided rat-tail that trailed down to the middle of her shoulders over her Minnesota Vikings t-shirt. Her broad shoulders rolled as she walked, like she was working out tension. It reminded Andrew of a cat.

"Talk to me," he said.

Louise turned around and rubbed her face. Andrew noticed the darkness under her eyes. They were red. If Andrew hadn't known better, he would have guessed she'd been crying. But Louise Miller didn't cry. Everybody knew that. That meant either she had been drinking, or she was very tired. He hoped the latter.

"I'm sorry," she said. "This should've been your night. How was it?"

A Felix the Cat clock chimed loudly on the wall. Its tail swished back-and-forth while its eyes veered left and right in unison. Louise fell onto the tan leather sofa and plopped her legs on the coffee table, bouncing cigarette butts out of the ashtray. Her uniform was draped over the back of the chair next to the couch. Her purse and gun rested on the seat cushion beside her. A pack of smokes lay on the table. Louise shot him a challenging glare, daring him to open his mouth. Just last week she bragged about her three-month anniversary of being smoke free.

"It was an interesting evening," he said. "A real learning experience."

Louise took a cigarette and flicked her lighter. She stared at the flame for a moment before touching it to the tobacco. Sucking the smoke deep into her lungs, she leaned her head back over the couch and blew rings toward the ceiling. "I'm sorry," she said again. "It's been a bad day all around. Just got home about a half hour ago. Put in a double shift. I think there's a TV dinner in the freezer. It's yours if you want it. It's not the celebration dinner we planned, but what can I say?"

He walked past her and into the kitchen, found one clean glass in the cupboard, went to the refrigerator and pulled out a pitcher with one last gulp of orange juice. Even living alone, she refused to take the last swallow. Andrew reminisced back to when the rule of the house was, you finish it, you clean it. Whether it be the last bite of cake or the last swallow of orange juice, Louise always made sure she never had to wash the plate, bowl, pitcher, whatever. Louise hated doing dishes.

"Tell me what's wrong," he said.

Andrew walked up behind the couch and stood looking down on his sister. She blew a cloud of smoke in his face and smiled as he tried not to choke. "That bastard, Huffman, shot a dog. I was going to keep him as a pet."

"Huffman or the dog?"

Louise showed him her middle finger. "It was injured in a dog fight. I wanted to bring him home. I could've nursed it back."

"How bad was it hurt?"

"Bad."

"So he put it out of its misery."

"That's what he said. But he just shot it for fun."

"You're still hung up on Sparky, aren't you? How long has it been now—two years? Let me guess. You checked the dog's paw for the white star, didn't you?"

"Damn, that was the coolest marking I've ever seen." Louise had a far away look in her eyes.

"I still say it's possible he just ran away," Andrew said.

"Not unless he knew how to open a car door."

"You need to get over it."

"I loved that damned dog. Somebody stole him. Probably abused the hell out of him, tortured him into a fighter."

"Let it go. I'm sure he went to a good home."

Louise didn't want to talk about it anymore. She changed the subject to another sore topic. "It's also missing persons' day. Have you ever heard of a doctor named Leonard Hout?"

"No. Should I?"

"He's some hot shot shrink that allegedly got kidnapped."

"Damn," Andrew said.

"That's not even the big news. One of our cops is missing." She let the words hang in the air and watched his reaction.

"What do you mean, missing?"

She sighed. "Missing, as in he and his car haven't checked in, and nobody can find either one."

"I would guess he's still with his car."

"My god. And they haven't promoted you to detective, yet?"

Andrew blushed. "Who is it?"

"Sorry. I didn't mean to snap." Louise snubbed out the cigarette and reached for another. "Mark Lone Bear." She flicked the lighter and only got a spark. After the fourth attempt, "God-damn it!" She threw the lighter across the room. It bounced off the Dali print and chipped the glass covering. As the lighter fell to the floor, so did the painting. Glass shattered as the frame broke. The melting clocks landscape slid onto the floor.

"Shit." Louise stared emotionless at the blank wall.

Andrew walked over and started picking up shards of glass. "Did you know the guy?"

Louise pressed her palms into her eyes. Uncharacteristic, Andrew thought. This was the girl who sat stoically through their parent's funeral, who prided herself on concealing emotion. Better than any guy, she'd claimed.

"We went through rookie school together. He was the only Indian; I was one of three females, and the only one of the three who could ace the physical shit. We both took a lot of crap. We were there for each other, got sworn in together. We got assigned to different precincts, kind of drifted apart over the years. He's an all right guy. Not the type to just up and disappear. I'm surprised you didn't hear anything over the radio."

"We stuck to one channel for what was coming into our area. My FTO said he didn't want to over-burden me. So, unless it came over as an emergency, we wouldn't get it."

"It's probably all over everything by now." Louise reached over to the chair and grabbed her purse, the cigarette still dangled from her lips. "Wouldn't be surprised to see it on the news tomorrow morning."

Andrew set the pieces of glass in a wastebasket then sat down on the other end of the couch and watched as Louise rifled through her purse, then dumped the contents on the coffee table. She grabbed the matches like they were gold and held the flame to the cigarette with shaking hands. When her lungs filled with smoke she leaned back and blew out a cloud with her words. "I've got a bad feeling about this."

"What do ya think happened?" Andrew asked.

"I wish I knew. I can't believe he's done anything illegal. It might be a family emergency. He's got folks on the Pine Ridge reservation in South Dakota, and I know they were having health problems back when I saw him all the time. Maybe something happened and he had to get over there, quick. Family was his top priority."

"In a Minneapolis cop car?" His sister should've know better.

She let out a half chuckle, half grunt. "All right, it's stretching a little bit. I just hope he's okay."

Louise took one last drag from her smoke then snuffed it into the ashtray. She took all of the others that had bounced out and neatly brushed them back in. Looking up at him, Andrew saw her eyes bright and vibrant. Healthy color spread throughout her face.

"So." Her voice shifted to a more lively tone. "Tell me about your first night on the street. Is it safe for Goober to walk through his cornfield at night?"

As many times as Andrew had seen the transformation in his sister, he still had no understanding as to how she did it. Depressed as hell, then one second later she acted like she'd just won the lottery. The first hundred times, he thought she had put on an act, but now he truly believed that somewhere in that brain of hers, some chemical imbalance played with her personality as easily as flipping on and off a light switch. No wonder she couldn't hold onto a boyfriend.

"If you're referring to me working out in the suburbs, then yes. It beats busting a dealer only to find ten others taking his place as soon as you get him in the car."

"Ooh, you sure told me," she said.

He had to admit it was a lame comeback. He'd come up with a good one eventually. Unfortunately, it probably wouldn't come to him until tomorrow. "I'm starved. How about we order a pizza?"

"Good idea." Louise got up off the couch and walked toward the kitchen. "There's a coupon on the fridge."

She called in the order then turned to her brother. "I'm going to take a shower. Feel free to flip on the tube. Can't find the remote. It's probably in the couch somewhere."

She closed the bathroom door. Andrew bent down and returned to the task he started, picking up more glass all the while meditating to the ticking of the clock. Louise emerged from the shower seconds before a knock on the door.

"Great security in this building," Andrew noted.

Louise shrugged. "No big deal. Someone breaks in when I'm home, well, I'll be saving the taxpayers some money." She patted her gun as she walked by. "There won't be any trial. If I'm not home; you see anything in here that can't be replaced with something nicer?"

As they ate the half-veggie, half-pepperoni and sausage pie, Andrew told her about his day. She smiled and nodded as he talked, occasionally interrupting with advice or observations. But the story about the bar fight drew her ire. She mumbled something about macho pricks.

"If they tried that bullshit on the police force there'd be hell, and lawsuits, to pay. You gonna report him?"

"I thought about it, but I'm not ready to be ostracized by the entire force just yet." He finished the last slice of his half of pizza and grabbed one of his sister's. Plucking off the meat and throwing it back in the box, he added, "Besides, in a warped sort of way it kind of made sense."

"Whatever. As long as you can live with it." Louise placed the discarded pieces of meat onto her last slice, folded it over, and crammed the whole thing in her mouth.

Andrew shook his head in disgust as he got up off the couch and threw his sister a napkin. "It was a good dinner, thanks."

"I slaved at it all day," she said, her mouth still full.

Andrew stood up and stretched. "Well, it's getting late. I should probably get home. Corwin might be getting worried."

"You haven't put that flea bag to sleep yet? Toss me the scissors, will ya?"

Andrew picked up a pair of scissors on top the stereo speaker and walked over to his sister, giving her the shears handle first. Louise began to cut out the picture of the fat little Italian chef on the pizza box. Andrew looked at her quizzically.

"Target practice," she said.

Andrew rolled his eyes as he opened the front door. "Good luck finding your friend."

The scissors stopped cutting. Andrew felt her eyes burn into him. She had been in a pretty decent mood, and now he just ruined it.

By two a.m., clouds split apart like curtains being drawn open. The crescent moon hung in the sky like a sideways smile shining down. Andrew drove down the wet street in silence, listening to the hum of tires roll against tar. His mind jumped from the bar fight to the missing policeman to events with his sister. So much to think about. He focused on each topic and let things fall into place. With mind and body wide awake, he figured exercise before meditation would help him sleep.

Fog settled in and enveloped the night in a surreal sort of way that made Andrew imagine he was driving into another world. From the boulevard, elm trees branched out high above the street, their leaves cloaking the ground from the sky. Traveling through nature's tunnel, Andrew thought as he followed the misty glow of streetlights pointing the way.

The netherworld became Minneapolis again as Andrew banged his palm against the side of his head. "Yes!"

Inching the speedometer past thirty miles an hour, Andrew hurried home. He smiled while pulling into the parking lot, got out, almost forgetting to lock the door, and raced up the three flights of stairs to his apartment.

Corwin meowed annoyance from the couch, irritated from the sudden burst of light that filled the room. The cat squinted at his roommate then arched his back and stretched his legs before curling up in a ball and going back to sleep.

"Good evening to you too," Andrew said, on his way to the telephone.

"Hello," Louise groaned after the seventh ring.

"Goober still has to be careful of stalkers. Get it? Corn stalks?"

Snickering like a school kid after a crank call, Andrew hung up the phone before his sister could slam down hers.

Six

Tuesday 1:00 p.m.

The doctor awoke to the touch of a soft wet tongue lapping the exposed side of his face. The stench of warm moist breath triggered his gag reflex in a belch that stopped in his throat.

"S.K.! Back off. Sir Knight!"

One last taste of the doctor's ear and the smell vanished; its host silently disappeared.

"Good afternoon, sleepyhead. Did you sleep well?"

Locked in pitch blackness, Leonard hadn't known when he'd been awake or in a nightmare.

The sound of tearing Velcro, and Leonard broke into tears. He wanted to jump up and scream, run around the room like a little boy. Instead, he could no longer feel as each leather strap fell free of his body. Freedom, and all he could do is lie there as if invisible binds still tied him down. Lesions burned at his hipbones, elbows and stomach. Raw skin sent bolts of pain as it grated against his shirt and pants. A giant claw gripped the back of his neck and jerked him off the board. Every muscle screamed as he was hoisted to his feet.

The pressure eased off his nape and he stood swaying for a moment, and then toppled over. Unable to bend his legs or use his arms, Leonard slammed onto his back. A thunk sent shock waves through his head as it connected with the cement floor. A small chuckle from above sent a shiver like electricity roughly throughout his body. The hand reached down and grabbed his collar, pulling him to his feet once more.

Dr. Hout took in the room, straining the muscles in his neck just to turn his head. The fist holding his shirt and leaning into his throat hindered the movement even more. Physical pain, coupled with what he saw, assured him this nightmare was no dream. On the other end of the room, the side he couldn't see earlier, nailed to a blank cement wall, hung an oak cabinet no bigger than the medicine cabinet in his bathroom. A small lock and chain through the black metal handles secured the doors shut.

"I have to apologize to you," the captor said. "I was hoping to spend time with you today, but something came up and I've got business to take care of. But just to show you I'm not all bad, I'll let you stretch a bit. Get some feeling back in those bones."

Listening to that voice made Dr. Hout's hair tingle at the root. A shiver traveled down his back, jetting throughout his limbs. A tear welled up in Leonard's eye.

"Why?" His voice sounded as raw as his abraded flesh.

"Because you were there." Silence followed, eerie and thick as the captor looked down at his prey. Moist brown eyes returned the doctor's gaze as the man's sneer slowly widened into a smile. The smell of tobacco would haunt Leonard for the rest of his life. He had no idea how long that would be.

"And because I can."

A powerful arm pulled Hout close, pressing his face into the kidnapper's shirt, just under the armpit. Leonard gagged, smothered by the old sweat. He thought about the comfort of passing out.

"I have to go," his captor said, almost lovingly while dragging Leonard across the floor.

A banging snap shattered the quiet and echoed off the walls. Leonard jumped at the sound and tried to look around. A headlock stronger than a vice kept it in place until things were ready.

The pressure released and his head became free—swimming in pain, but free. In front of him stood the stocks. He tried to struggle but his body, still stiff and numb, wouldn't allow it. With no warning, Leonard was shoved down. His knees buckled and a thrust rammed his throat into the small semicircle cut in the wood. Gasping for breath, his arms were jerked up, and before he could draw air, another slam crashed on the back of his neck and he was trapped again.

Footsteps clacked across the floor. Terror flooded through Leonard as he struggled in the stocks. His wife wouldn't be there to free him this time.

"I have to go to the bathroom." It wasn't a lie.

"Then go," his tormentor said as he disappeared up the stairs.

The door banged shut. Left alone in the miserable solitude, Leonard screamed. He screamed until all the air had drained from his lungs. Gasping for breath, a new chill froze his spine. He was not alone.

Straining, Leonard twisted his head. Sitting with his rump and hind legs on the bottom step and stout front legs planted firmly on the floor was the biggest, meanest, ugliest, most muscular rottweiler Leonard had ever seen. The dog stared at him, its black gaze implacable. It growled deep in its chest and glided its tongue across fangs while an elongated drop of drool silently splashed on the floor. Maybe the light had played a trick. Leonard prayed that it was the light. It lasted only a second, but the dog's eyes had glared red. Leonard Hout was in Hell.

~

Another cloudy day and another day ruined for the beach. An unexpected afternoon off and it would be wasted. Melanie Cartier stared longingly out the window of her twenty-third story office. She caught her reflection in the glass and noticed her tired and sunken eyes. Dark brown hair that usually bounced with body hung raggedly down her shoulders.

Mental note: stop at the salon on the way home and pick up conditioner.

Below her, downtown bustled. Off in the distance she could hear Cedar Lake calling her name. On a weekday afternoon such as this, the beach, only three blocks from her condo, would be almost deserted. For a few moments around lunchtime a break in the clouds allowed the sun to poke through, giving Melanie hope. But by dessert, the threat of rain again hung over the city. Melanie cursed under her breath. Only two more weeks and it would be September—the end of tanning season.

Papers scattered across her desk seemed to have no order or rhyme any sane person would be able to figure out. Yet if someone came in and asked for the motion for discovery, she would be able to reach in that mess and pull it out with her eyes closed.

Paul Handleman, a new associate in the firm, walked by her office door. "Hey Mel, I thought you had a depo this afternoon."

"Cancelled. Again."

The deposition of Dr. Leonard Hout had been scheduled months ago. It had already been continued once because of his schedule. The judge would have a fit when she asked for another one. "He just up and disappeared. Nobody's seen him. He took off for lunch yesterday then never reported back. His wife's worried sick." She shrugged. "You'd think he was the one on trial. Who knows, maybe he is guilty of something, thought we might find out, and skipped town."

"What was he going to testify to?" Handleman asked.

"The most damaging would be that his ex-partner committed a serious breach of conduct. Specifically, he gave the plaintiff antidepressants and then seduced her. Two days later she sliced her wrists. Her thirteen-year-old son came home from school and found his mom dead in the tub."

"Ouch. Maybe the partner rubbed him out."

"I thought of that, but he's not even that big of a witness. He's mostly there to substantiate the more serious allegations. It's the kids themselves that will talk of how bad their mother looked after her visits to the doctor, and how the drugs made her worse. Nothing affects a jury more than a crying child. If that testimony holds, which there's no way it won't, the jury will give me whatever I ask for."

"I meant it as a joke," Paul said with and wink and a smile. "I didn't want your whole recitation." He disappeared down the hall.

"Twerp."

Releasing a heavy sigh, she wiped her sleeve across the desk, shoving the papers inside her briefcase. It made her think of Marlon Brando clearing the table in "Streetcar Named Desire." She would sort them out again on her kitchen table, tonight. The day might be wasted but at least now she could beat the traffic and get home at a decent hour. Maybe even catch Oprah on TV.

As Melanie left the building, the first drops of rain started to fall. She cursed under her breath. "Thanks for waiting." She had to walk two blocks to a public ramp because she left her parking card in her other purse. She couldn't even sweet-talk the attendant. What kind of lawyer was she that a pimply faced, uneducated, loser couldn't be swayed to let her park her car in the private ramp? Despite the fact that she was one of the few women in the firm pulling down a six-figure salary siding closer to seven figures, she was second-guessing her talent as a litigator, and a woman. Christ, she couldn't even charm her way in with a kid who was ninety percent hormones. Her therapist would have a field day with that one.

Wet, tired and angry at the world, Melanie managed to maneuver around the road construction and finally get onto I-394. It always seemed to rain harder on the freeway, she thought as she flipped on the windshield wipers and the lights. *Must be all that road spray.* Her mood lightened some in thinking that in ten minutes bath water would be running, Copeland's Rodeo would be filling her home and Sing's Kung Po Chicken and Lo Mein would be on the way.

In the rearview mirror, she saw a red car riding her bumper. "Jerk." She thought about stomping on the brakes, then suing the bastard for whiplash when he rear-ended her. But with the kind of day she'd been having, she probably would get whiplash. Instead, Melanie slowed the car to let him pass. He didn't. The asshole rode her tail, his wipers swishing back and forth across his smiling face.

The exit to Penn Avenue approached—her exit. A shudder trickled through her as the red car followed her up the ramp. The fact that he'd given her a little more room was no comfort. She turned left and crossed the bridge over the freeway then signaled right. So did he.

"God damn you." Melanie bit her lip as she glanced in the rear view mirror. "Of course he'd signal right." If he'd turned left, he would've been back onto the freeway heading the way he just came.

"I'm getting paranoid."

Concentrating more on her rearview mirror, Melanie didn't see the squirrel dart across the street until the last second. She stomped on the brake. Her tailgater did the same, only a moment too late. She felt a tap as their cars met.

In the mirror she saw him shrug then give himself a kind of slap on the head. With an apologetic look on his face, he pulled over and motioned for her to do the same.

Drive to the fourth precinct and let him follow you there. Melanie ignored the voice and pulled over. She reached into her purse and searched for her wallet. The door to the car behind opened and the man stepped out into the rain.

My God, he's huge! She dropped the wallet and felt around the purse until her hand wrapped around the small metal canister. Pepper spray didn't differentiate sizes. *Get the hell out of here.* Yet her eyes were glued to the rearview mirror, her knuckles white around the canister. The man reached into his coat pocket. Melanie finally listened to the voice and put the car in gear as the man pulled out a wallet. With a flick of his wrist he snapped it open so she could see the badge.

Melanie put her car back in park, closed her eyes and let out a long sigh of relief as the cop approached. She didn't know how long she had been holding her breath, but from the exhale, she guessed about an hour. *Cops I can handle.* She dug through her purse for her driver's license. She gave herself a comforting smile as the canister of pepper spray rubbed against her hand.

She wondered if they were like fire extinguishers and needed refilling or repressurizing. She couldn't remember if it had been sitting in her purse for one year or two. She made another mental note to just buy a new one.

"Geez lady, I'm sorry. I'm off duty and just finished a double shift," he said, tapping on the closed window. "I've been looking for that missing cop. Did you hear about it on the news?"

Melanie prepared her most cooperative smile as she lowered the window. Before she could deliver a word his arm shot through the open window like a cannonball. His massive paw grabbed her by the throat and squeezed. Instinctively, her left hand hung onto his forearm, her expensively manicured nails digging into his skin. Her mind tried to process the situation. Policemen didn't act like this. The clamp tightened around her throat. It felt as if the blood were beginning to boil in her head. The oxygen to her brain had hit a snag and stopped.

Fog filled her head. She became woozy as her thoughts muddled. In her last moments of clarity, Melanie grappled for the canister and grasped it in her right hand. Fighting back with all the strength and concentration she had left, Melanie aimed at the man and pressed the button. As she lost consciousness, Melanie Cartier's last vision was that of the man looking at a thin jet of liquid shooting over his shoulder.

Seven

Tuesday 5:30 p.m.

Louise Miller stepped out of the Native American Center on Franklin Avenue even more frustrated than when she went in. She hadn't expected much, but she also hadn't expected such a cold reception. She got the impression they were blaming her because the police weren't doing enough to find Mark Lone Bear. Who cared about another missing Injun, even if he was a cop? No, no one in the Center had seen Mark Lone Bear since the last week's game. They had expected to see him last night. For the first time since he began volunteering his services he hadn't shown up. Not even a call. His kids got trampled in basketball because their coach wasn't there. And no, he didn't answer when they tried calling.

She walked to her car, the sun beating down on her already aching head. The clouds had dispersed, but the humidity remained. The air conditioner felt good and Louise sat in her squad letting the coolness dry the sweat before pulling out of the lot. She decided to make one more stop, but first tried a couple of the deep healing breaths that her brother had taught her. Feeling a little better, she drove two blocks down to the bar.

Lacey's Bar & Grill was a Native American hangout that cashed welfare checks. They also had an underground reputation for collecting AA medallions in exchange for free drinks.

Trepidation itched at Louise's skin as she sat in the car. She could get reprimanded for doing what she was about to do. It could also mess up her chances for sergeant. Brass would probably look at it as overstepping boundaries. "Detectives should have done this," she whispered under her breath. Hell, maybe they already had, but if so, she hadn't heard anything about it. Not that they ever bothered to tell her anything.

The other factor she considered, but chose to ignore: her personal safety. This could turn into a very bad situation if she didn't handle things just right. A lone cop; a woman cop at that, and with no backup? Even Louise had to admit that she had brighter moments in decision making. But Mark Lone Bear had few friends on the force and Louise felt that she was one. Maybe the only one. Another downside she thought as she stepped out of the car—she might be taking this a bit too personally.

The sun brought back her headache as Louise approached the door to the bar. Glass painted black served twofold. It kept out the light and it kept out prying eyes. She pushed the door open; light flooded the bar to a roomful of groans. To exert her authority Louise kept the door open, giving her eyes time to adjust.

The chatter stopped and all heads turned toward her. Louise let the door swing shut and, as casually as she could, walked up to the bar. She sensed every eye watching as the ceiling fan circulated the smell of beer, cigarette smoke, and old sweat. Her headache surged. "Is this place exempt from the smoking ban?"

Behind the counter, a heavyset man with a pock-marked face and slick black hair tied in a braid approached her.

"What can I get you, officer?" With an emotionless voice he placed a paper napkin on the bar.

"Information," she said, loud enough for all to hear. "I'm looking for Mark Lone Bear."

"He's fucking your momma," a voice in the back called. The response elicited only a couple of chuckles.

The muscles tensed in her neck. She squinted toward the voice and recognized the scumbag. "Is that you, Freddie Thunder Cloud? Hey, thanks for the tip the other day. The bust went down without a hitch."

"What are you talking about you fucking cunt? I ain't no snitch! You don't know what you're talking about."

She gritted her teeth, wanting to go back there and smash his head open on the table. *Choose your battles, Louise.* She turned back to the bar.

"You might have just gotten him killed, officer," the bartender said. "He's just a little drunk. He didn't mean nothin' by it."

"Just jerking his chain. You can smooth it out after I'm gone. Hell, if somebody caps him, no loss."

The barman stared holes through her. Louise took a deep breath. This could get out of hand too easily. "Listen, I'm sorry." She massaged her temples. "It's been a long day."

"You're one wound up cop, Officer Miller."

She stopped rubbing her head just in time to catch the last glimpse of the bartender's eyes dart away from her nametag.

Louise let out a long breath. "Listen, Mark was a friend of mine. *Is* a friend of mine."

The bartender smiled an unhappy smile and sucked on his tobacco stained teeth. "Haven't seen him. We've seen the news. Nobody here knows nothing."

Around the bar, a couple of guys had moved closer to hear the conversation. She glanced at them. They immediately shifted their attention away from her. The rest of the customers seemed indifferent.

She slipped a card out of her pocket and slid it across the bar. "Call me if you hear anything."

The bartender eyed the card but didn't pick it up.

"That goes for everybody," Louise called out. "We're trying to find him, okay? Believe it or not, we're on the same side this time."

With no response but cold stares, Louise walked out of the bar.

Outside, Louise cursed herself once more for forgetting her shades. The sun burned into her eyes as she walked back to her squad. Still, she preferred heat outside to the frigid atmosphere inside the bar. Even considering the exhaust fumes from the street and the trash from the dumpster, the air smelled cleaner.

"Pssst."

She froze, one hand on the door handle of the squad.

"Hey, lady." A loud whisper came from behind the dumpster, around the corner of the building. Her adrenalin shot up again.

"Come out where I can see you."

"Can't," the voice came back. "Can't let them see me talking to you."

Ambush. But it could also be some needed info. She cautiously stepped away from her car and unsnapped her holster. With one hand on the butt of her gun, she searched for cover options. Bullets could rip right through the cheap metal dumpster. She could pull the car up, but they could get her before she got the door open. Calling for backup would give whoever plenty of time to slip back inside the bar. If the owner of the voice knew something, she wanted to know it too.

Louise decided to give faith to her vest and pray that if it was a shooter, he wouldn't aim for the head. She walked around the car, opening space while drawing her revolver. With the safety off and the gun raised Officer Miller snuck around the corner.

The kid stood about 5'4", wiry build, and a smooth dark complexion with peach fuzz growing under a hooked nose. Other than a dream catcher tattooed on his left forearm and the reek of marijuana on his breath, he shared a lot of traits with Mark Lone Bear, a well-groomed Oglala Sioux. He didn't look old enough to be hanging in a bar, but the older Louise got, the younger all the kids looked; especially the Indians.

"Jesus fucking Christ!" His arms flew into the air.

With a shaking hand Louise holstered her revolver. "Sorry." She had no conviction in the apology. "Didn't know what I was up against."

"I told you I can't let anyone see us together." His panting outweighed hers.

"What's your name?"

"You don't need to know my name," he said, still recovering from a gun pointed at his head. Sweat trickled down his cheek.

"Talk to me."

The young man looked around for spying eyes. "I know Officer Lone Bear. I like him. He always treats me good."

"He's a good cop."

"Yeah. Anyway, yesterday I was hanging around and I saw his car."

"How do you know it was his car?"

"It's always him cruising the neighborhood. He has a routine, ya know? Anyway, he pulled this guy over. Some white guy with a fancy car. I was going to go over and say hi. Ya know, when he got done—"

"Where were you?"

"In the alley. About three or four garages in. Anyway, I know most of the cops around that neighborhood, and it wasn't Lone Bear. I never seen this guy before. A white guy. Huge. Beat the shit outta this other guy and threw him in back of the cop car."

Despite the heat, the blood in Officer Miller's veins turned cold. Goose bumps dotted her arms. She tried to keep the excitement out of her voice. "What did he look like?"

"Dunno. He wore these big sunglasses. Don't ask me to look at mug shots. All you people look alike. I'd never be able to pick him out."

A door in the back of the building swung open. Her witness tensed, ready to bolt. "Oh shit!"

Louise shot out her arm and grabbed him by the collar and shoved him against the wall. "You have the right to remain silent…" she recited as she twisted one of his arms behind him while reaching for her cuffs.

The man walking through the door with a plastic bag full of trash momentarily froze. "I can do this later." He hurried back inside, pulling the door shut behind him.

Louise escorted her prisoner to the squad car and guided him into the back seat.

"Thanks," he said as the car pulled out of the lot. "That was quick thinking."

Her eyes met his in the mirror. He was sweating. "It wasn't an act. I'm taking you in."

"What? No! I told you everything I know."

"You need to talk to some people. People that might be able to jog your memory. Help you think of things you might've forgot."

"Uh uh! No way! You take me in, I didn't see nothing."

"I thought you wanted to help," Louise said.

"I told you everything I know!"

"What time did it happen?" Louise asked.

"I dunno. Around lunchtime, I guess."

"See. You didn't tell me everything."

"I'm not talking to anybody else." He stared resolutely out the window.

They drove around the neighborhood while Louise thought. The air conditioner blasted and her passenger basked in the coolness. Finally, she said, "I'll make a deal with you. Will you at least talk to me?"

After a few seconds of grudging silence, "Yeah, I guess so."

"Okay then. First off, what's your name?"

Again some hesitancy. "Bill. Bill Johnson."

"Oh c'mon. I'm going to need some trust here."

"Seriously. My stepdad adopted me."

Louise sighed in resignation. "Okay, Bill Johnson. What's your address?"

"What's yours?"

Louise glanced in the rear view mirror at a young Indian boy with a huge grin.

"I'm going to need some trust here," he said.

"Don't push your luck, Mr. Johnson. I bet if I searched you I'd find an illegal substance or two. What's your address?"

It was Louise's turn to smile. This hadn't gone as smoothly as he planned.

"How about I give you my cell number? I'm not around the house much anyway."

Louise stared back at him through the mirror. "You got

moxie, kid. I'll give you that. Okay, give me your cell number." It wouldn't be too hard to track the address with a phone number. She jotted down the number he gave her.

"Now where do you want me to drop you off?"

"Any place we won't be seen. And don't forget to take your bracelets back."

Louise called in. "If nothing is going on, I'd like to do a little community relations; take a kid to lunch, and then home. I'll have to cross the border. He's in the fifth."

"Go ahead," came the reply. "It's a slow day."

Officer Miller drove across the bridge over the freeway that separated the third and fifth precincts. She drove to the spot where Dr. Hout's car had been found abandoned and turned into the alley. She let Bill Johnson out of the car and released the cuffs.

"Okay, I want to know where you were, and everything you saw."

Eight

Wednesday 9:45 a.m.

Sarah Markham poked her head in Paul Handleman's office. "Have you seen Mel?"

"She had court this morning." Handleman didn't bother to look up from his desk. "She rarely comes in the office first when she has a nine o'clock."

"That's what I thought too. But the judge's clerk called, asked where she was."

"Really? That's uncharacteristic. Did you try her at home?"

"Yeah, no answer."

"Her cell?"

"No answer there either."

Paul finally took notice. The only time Melanie couldn't be reached on her cell phone was when she had to be in the courtroom. "She must be stuck in traffic or something. I'm sure she'll be bitching about it when she comes in."

Six months as Melanie's paralegal, Sarah had never known Melanie Cartier to be late for anything.

Sarah walked into Melanie's office looking for her appointment book when a ringing phone interrupted her. She picked up the receiver. "Melanie Cartier's office, this is Sarah."

"Is she in?"

Sarah recognized Gary Warren's voice. He represented the

drunken doctor and had been badgering Mel to get the missing doctor's deposition.

"She's in court this morning, can I take a message?"

There was a pause before the lawyer responded. "This is Mr. Warren. Just tell her I intend to make a motion for dismissal for failure to proceed if she doesn't get that doctor's deposition set before Friday."

Sarah forced herself to sound pleasant. "I'll give her the message."

"Get in touch with my secretary to set up a time."

"I'll let her know." Sarah hung up the phone and stood for a moment staring at the receiver. "You pompous oaf."

~

Dr. William Gillespy sat across the desk and watched Gary Warren hang up the phone. He felt every day of his 65 years as he ran his bony fingers through the few strands of gray that were left of his hair.

"This case keeps getting better and better." Warren sat back in his plush leather chair and steepled his fingers as he used his professional smile to comfort his feeble client.

Dr. Gillespy didn't share his lawyer's enthusiasm. "I thought Leonard was just a minor witness."

"He's not all that minor. Definitely a piece to the puzzle that will be noticed if he's not there."

The doctor fidgeted in his chair. "Do you really think the judge will dismiss the case?"

Warren laughed as he leaned forward. "Highly doubtful, but I might be able to get some costs out of the other side for our inconvenience."

"What, I'm not paying you enough? You run quite a racket, Mr. Warren."

"Don't kid yourself, doctor. The money you're paying will be a drop in the bucket compared to what I'll save you. You'll find I'm quite worth the price. I'm not fond of Ms. Cartier, but I have to admit that she's almost as good a lawyer as I am. Almost."

"I pay malpractice insurance to pay off legal suits."

"What if they refuse to pay? There is legal precedent. They may fight you on this. They might even win. You were allegedly drunk when you were treating that woman, plus you had sex with her, during a session I might add. That could put quite a snag in things."

"You told me that since they didn't have enough evidence to charge me criminally, and that the family probably wouldn't go after me civilly."

The lawyer rose from his chair and crossed the room to an earth globe resting on a pedestal. He flipped open the top of the world and pulled out a bottle of scotch and two glasses. He walked back and sat on the corner of his desk. The doctor took one of the offered glasses.

Warren poured them each a couple fingers of scotch and smiled. "It's rarely as successful, but plaintiff attorneys urge their clients to sue. It's the American way. God bless us. For their clients it's a no-brainer. If they lose, no big deal, they only wasted their time. If they win, or even settle, it's free money. That's why you hire me. You want to make sure that all they get is time wasted."

The doctor enjoyed the alcohol burn as it slid down his throat. He closed his eyes, wishing the world would go away. When he opened them he was staring at his empty glass. "I don't know. Maybe we should settle." Dr. Gillespy sipped his drink. A tinge deep inside sparked off a feeling of guilt. He smothered it, blaming the alcohol.

"Well, of course the final decision is yours, but for now I strongly recommend against it. Right now things are falling in our favor. Let's see how it plays out before you make any rash decisions you might regret later. Why don't you go home and sleep on it?"

Gillespy let out a sigh and stood up. "Thank you counselor." They shook hands and the doctor left the office.

The meter had expired; a ticket was stuck under the wiper blade of his white Lincoln Continental. He removed the citation and tossed it on the front seat, paying it no further attention. He couldn't keep his mind off the court case as he cranked the engine and pulled away from the curb.

A woman died and they're trying to blame me. It's not fair. Then he thought of her breasts and the way they jiggled when he unhooked her bra...

Screeching brakes and the crash of metal against metal jolted him back to the present and his head to the steering wheel. He grew suddenly sober as he saw in his side mirror the Toyota door behind him fly open and a man leap out.

"What the hell were you thinking?" the man shouted. "You didn't signal. You didn't even look!"

The doctor thought about the drink he just finished in his lawyer's office, and the half flask of gin he downed before the meeting. He closed his eyes for moment. He had to think. He pressed the button and the window slid down. The man panted, swearing under his breath, and a bubble of bloody snot hung from his nose.

"I'm having a really bad day." Gillespy checked the street behind him, signaled, and to a flurry of obscenities, drove away.

Nine

Wednesday 11:00 a.m.

Knowing it to be a futile effort, Dr. Hout kicked at the post that held up the stocks and kept him locked in place. Each shot vibrated up to his neck and wrists. He ignored the pain. The board felt tighter around his throat with every shout, every curse. At least the dog had gotten bored sniffing his crotch. Enough time had passed that the urine stain should have mostly dried.

The door opened. Heavy footsteps slowly plodded down each step. The doctor's screams faded. Reasoning hadn't worked. Maybe it was time to build up the man's ego.

The dog danced in circles, awaiting his master. The doctor's neck hurt too much to look higher than his captor's waist. The man walked by him and a loud thump sounded as something hit the floor.

The doctor ignored it. "You did a hell of a job. I'm ready to work with you. My wife says it takes her weeks to get me to change my mind." *Now he knows I've got a wife. I'm a human being, not a sack of meat.*

Footsteps approached.

Please, please, please, please, please, the doctor prayed.

Thunder and lightning exploded in his head as something connected to his nose. Blinded by pain, he heard the crunch of cartilage and tasted blood as it flowed over his lips and down his chin. Through tears he saw a giant hand massaging a giant fist.

"Don't try that psychobabble bullshit on me. I've been worked on by the best." He grabbed Hout's chin and bent the doctor's head back. Hout thought his neck might break.

"It's not all about you, doctor. The fucking world doesn't always revolve around goddamn doctors." The sadistic tone from the previous visit had vanished. Hout recognized this voice as the vengeful one that pulled him over.

"I think I cut my knuckle on your tooth."

Tears mingled with blood, salting the coppery taste.

Keys rattled and after a clank, the bar lifted off Hout's neck. He snapped upright and felt something give in his back. He dropped to his knees, weeping. A hand grabbed the collar of his shirt and dragged him across the room. Hout landed next to a body lying on the surfboard, covered by a blanket. A rasping sound came from underneath the cloth. His captor lifted if off and Hout saw a woman in a tan pantsuit, unconscious, and struggling to breathe. The dog silently crept up and sniffed her hair, licking her face before losing interest and walking away.

"Fix her. I watched her all night and all morning and she hasn't gotten any better."

"You said you were worked on by the best; who was that?" Hout thought that if he knew the psychiatrist, he might be able to figure out the method of how this man had been treated, and how to break through.

Instead, he got a kick in the ribs and pushed face-first on the surfboard. The sound of the Velcro fasteners being undone finally broke him. "Please don't tie me down again!"

The big man grabbed the doctor by the hair and jerked him to his feet. "Fix her. If she dies, you die. Understand?"

"Please," Hout gibbered, falling to his knees. "I'll do whatever you want. I can't be tied down again. Please."

Knees crackled as the captor crouched down and took the doctor's chin in his hand tilted his face so they were looking eye to eye. The doctor's blood lubricated the grasp, smearing red over his cheeks. With blood and snot clogging his nose, at least the doctor couldn't smell the tobacco.

"Concentrate. She needs a doctor. You need to help her." He released the doctor's face and wiped the blood on his hand off onto the doctor's shirt.

"I'm not a medical doctor, I'm a psychiatrist."

"If you won't even try to save her life, I'll kill you now."

The doctor listened to her labored breathing, and tried to comprehend what was wrong with her. It took some time, but pain, fear, and humiliation slowly gave way to medical training from all those years ago. He rotated the woman on her back.

Hout choked on his breath. He knew this woman. Bruises covered her swollen throat as she struggled for oxygen. He laid his fingers on her neck. The pulse was strong and steady. The Velcro straps from the board caught his attention again. He shivered as he tried to block them from sight.

"She needs to go to the hospital." He tilted her head back trying to clear the airway.

"You fix her here."

"She might need a tracheotomy."

"So? I have a lot of toys."

Dr. Hout turned to Jell-O as a smile ooze across his captor's face.

"She could die."

Again, the man took Leonard's face and held him at eye level. "Your life depends on it that she doesn't." This time when he released Hout, the man grinned and licked his blood soaked hand, an action that made Hout gag, but in spite of that his stomach rumbled. How long had it been since his last meal? He ignored the pangs.

Dr. Hout leaned over the woman and tried to remember where he knew her from.

A patient? Possibly, but not likely. He studied the swelling of her neck. Edema around the trachea was serious, but probably not fatal. The labored respiration came from her uneasy breathing by the swelling, but she was getting air. He guessed she'd be breathing normal within another day.

Again, the straps from the surfboard came into his vision causing him his own labored breathing. *I can't be tied down again.* "I'll have to sit with her," he told his captor.

The man glared at him suspiciously.

"If she stops breathing I'll need to do an emergency tracheotomy. I'll need a scalpel and some tubing." Never a good poker player, the doctor prayed his captor wouldn't call his bluff.

"Not a problem."

Dr. Hout ignored the menacing tone and fought to hide a surge of excitement. Not only would he not be bound or stocked, but he'd have a weapon. A quick slice on the carotid artery, go for the femoral artery, cut off the bastard's balls in the process, whatever was most convenient at the time, the sadist would bleed to death in minutes. Then slash out his eyes.

Hey! Don't get too far ahead of yourself, Leonard.

A shudder suddenly ran down the doctor's spine. Could he bring himself to do unnecessary surgery just to get a possible weapon? Could he actually kill another human being, even if it were in self defense?

Drops of blood dripped from his nose onto the woman's suit. He watched the fabric absorb his blood. Maybe he wouldn't have to cut her. He'd hold the scalpel to her throat, and just before making a cut he would say he needed help. When the sadist got close—zap, right across the throat. He heard Margaret Hamilton's voice in his head. *And your little dog too.* Leonard smiled at the thought.

"She's going to live, right?" Leonard heard relief in the man's words, and was surprised at his tone.

Why is this woman so important? Why is she more important than me? "I don't know. She's in rough shape," he said.

The captor grabbed the doctor's shirt and hoisted him to his feet once again, and this time slammed him against the wall. "Then what were you fucking smiling about?"

Blood from Leonard's face splashed on the man's arms. This time the *thunk* from the cement wall to the back of his head nestled him into unconsciousness.

Ten

Wednesday 2:45 p.m.

Andrew pulled into the headquarters lot fifteen minutes early. Carlin was already seated in the Crown Victoria, its engine running. "You're already signed in. Let's go," Carlin called out. "It's serious tonight."

Technically, Andrew's shift didn't start until 3:00. The chicken and rice he had for lunch hadn't sat too well. He grabbed a couple antacids from his pocket, and climbed into the cruiser.

"What's up?" Andrew asked.

"Missing cop, Minneapolis. Been missing since yesterday."

"Mark Lone Bear."

Carlin looked over at his trainee. "What do you know?"

"That his name is Mark Lone Bear and that his squad is missing too. My sister knows him."

Carlin grinned. "Your sister one of them cop groupies or something?"

"Or something," Andrew said, ignoring the bait. "She's been a cop for about five years. I guess they were pretty good buds in rookie school."

"That so? She got any ideas?"

"Not really. Just that he's got family on the Pine Ridge reservation. Still doesn't make sense, though. She said he's a responsible guy. If there were a family emergency, he'd call."

"You ever been over there?" Carlin asked.

"Been where?"

"Up on the res."

"No." Andrew shook his head.

"In-laws live in Montana. Drove through a couple times. Talk about poverty, Christ, a lot of those people don't have phones let alone electricity. Besides, he wouldn't be stupid enough to take a squad. That just don't make sense."

"Yeah. I think she fears the worst."

"Her and everyone else," Carlin said. "Tell you what. MPD will have the city covered. We'll stick to the northern 'burbs and keep our eyes sharp. If it's a slow night maybe we'll slip across the border into Anoka County and take a look around, see if anything looks suspicious. There's a few Indian hangouts we can check. You never know, we might come up with something, huh?"

Andrew let the breeze from the open window wash over him as they drove out of Brooklyn Center and past the first cornfield. What were the chances of them locating the car, or the cop? "Maybe I should have bought a lottery ticket. I think the odds are better."

"Hey smartass, do you know how many crimes were solved just because a deputy happened to run across some tiny detail that looked like just maybe it might be worth investigating, or even just happened to be in the right place at the right time?"

"No, how many?"

"How the hell would I know? But I bet there were some. Keep your eyes peeled."

~

Nathan Rogers and Joshua Johnson let the canoe idle in the still water. Perch Lake resembled a large plane of glass. They'd had a lazy day, rowing, drinking beer, and catching rays. They roped the coolers inside the seats so they could lie back to get the maximum exposure from the sun. Nathan sat up and reached into his cooler for another beer. Squinting across the lake he saw the public beach active with swimmers. Otherwise, they only had to share the water with three sailboats and one other canoe.

"One more brewski and I think we'll have to head back," Nate said.

"Yeah, whatever," Josh replied, his eyes closed and body smelling of tanning lotion. He dipped his hand in the cool water, scooping a handful and pouring it over his face.

"My grandparents are coming over for dinner tonight. Folks said I better not be late."

"That's fine. I'm getting cooked anyway." Josh sat up and reached into his cooler grabbing another brew. "So, what's up with your grandfolks?"

"I dunno. I think it's because Frank has cancer and he wants to discuss his will."

"You call your grandparents by their first names to their face?" Josh asked.

"Yeah, right. And your dad pays me to have sex with your mom while he watches."

Josh grabbed the sides of the canoe and started rocking side-to-side pushing the small boat far enough that water edged over the rim.

"God damn you!" Nathan grabbed the sides of the canoe trying to stabilize it. "Don't tip us over, asshole. I don't want to smell like dead fish and algae."

"Don't be such a pussy. You're going to have to take a shower anyway to wash off all that lotion you slathered on."

"Just don't tip us over, okay?"

"Fine," Josh chugged the rest of his beer. Throwing the empty can back into his cooler.

"Wanna head back?" He grabbed the oar.

"Yeah."

Nathan threw his empty into the lake. Josh gave him a pointed glare. "Why do you have to be such a dick?"

Nathan smiled as he picked up the other oar and started paddling. The prow of the canoe cut through the water. The two boys listened to the splash as the oars rhythmically dipped into the lake. About fifty yards from shore, a pair of ducks landed not twenty feet away, their wings outstretched as they glided into the lake making a miniature wake behind them.

With an evil grin, Josh stopped paddling.

"Don't." Nathan said with a look of irritated anger.

"Sorry, Dude, I just can't help myself."

Before Nate could say another word Josh flipped the canoe. With a great splash both boys tumbled into the water. When they broke the surface the two ducks quacked insults before flying off.

"You asshole," Nathan spat out with a mouthful of water.

"I had to do it. It's a rule."

One of the coolers had gotten loose and floated away. Nathan swam after it while Josh grabbed the oars and righted the canoe. After successfully rolling back in, Josh held out a paddle to his friend.

"Fuck you. I'm swimming in. Knowing you, you'll flip the thing again."

"C'mon. I'll be good. I promise." Josh urged Nate to grab hold of the paddle.

"You're such an asshole." Nathan kicked his way to shore using the cooler to help keep afloat.

"I said I'm sorry already. How many times do I have to apologize?" Josh kept the slow pace next to his friend just in case Nathan changed his mind.

"You never learn," Nate said. "You always do this. Sometimes no means no."

"Oh c'mon, don't be such a girl. You knew it was going to happen. That's why you always invite me."

Nathan turned his head away to keep Josh from catching sight of his smile. Yeah, he knew it would happen, and he looked forward to the swim.

Close to shore his smile vanished when his foot kicked against something hard. "Son-of-a-bitch," Nathan yelled. He let go of the cooler and went under.

"What is it?" Josh waited for Nate to surface. Nothing. It could be a practical joke; something to get back at him for flipping the canoe. “Nate?” Fear tinged his voice. What had happened? Just as he decided to jump in, the surface of the water broke, and Nate emerged, gasping.

“Dude, you have to see what I found.”

“Very funny,” Josh said, but relief was evident in his tone.

“No really, you’ve got to see this.”

“Let’s go, asshole. You’re going to be late for your grandparents.”

Nathan grabbed the side of the canoe and tipped it. Joshua toppled over into the water. Before he could utter as much as a ‘fuck you,’ Nathan grabbed his arm and pulled him under.

~

The dispatcher’s voice crackled over the radio calling for any cars near Perch Lake. A couple of boys had found a vehicle driven into the water.

“I guess that would be us,” Carlin said. “We’re only a mile away.

Andrew spoke into the receiver on his collar, saying that they would respond. Their ETA would be about five minutes.

“South side of the lake,” dispatch informed them.

“I’m guessing a stolen car,” Carlin said. “Any bets?’

Rivers and Miller cruised Perch Lake Parkway looking for two boys. During the summer months Perch Lake had become a Mecca for drug dealing and underage drinking.

“Keep your eyes off the babes,” Carlin chided his trainee.

Andrew smiled, knowing he’d been caught staring at the tan girl in the purple thong bikini. “Just a momentary lapse, sir.”

“It better be more than momentary or I’ll begin to worry about you.”

“Next time I’ll make sure it’s more than momentary.” For the first time Andrew wondered if maybe he could be one of the guys. A weight seemed to dissipate off his shoulders. Even his upset stomach eased a little bit.

“After we finish up here, I’ll take you to some of the Indian dives in Kenowa and Corcoran and teach you the art of community relations."

Well past the beach Carlin pulled the car up over the curb toward the two boys who were frantically waving their arms.

"What's up gentlemen?" Andrew asked as he stepped from the car. Outside his peripheral vision, he saw Carlin nod, and knew Carlin wanted him to take the initiative.

"You're not going to believe what we found," the boy to Andrew's left said.

"You found a car. We know," Andrew said.

The other one grabbed his friend's arm. "Shut up Josh. Let me handle this. I found it." The kid paused and gave the deputies a smug look. "You guys lose something?"

A chill coursed through Andrew's blood. "If you've got something to say, spill it." He could sense his sergeant smile.

"Just wondering if there might be a reward or something."

Andrew hid a smile as his FTO glared at the boy.

"Cut the smarmy attitude shit and start talking," Carlin ordered.

The kid, Josh, spoke up with no more urging. "About twenty feet into the lake we found a cop car. I bet it's the one from the news."

"I dove down and found it," Nate said.

"I helped!"

Andrew froze and his stomach knotted. The kid wasn't making this up. Carlin had an unreadable expression on his face.

"See anyone in the car?" Carlin asked.

"Couldn't see. It was too dark," Josh answered.

Deputy Rivers spoke to Andrew with a hushed voice. "Call it in. Use the non-comm line. Let's keep the press out of here as long as possible."

"Yes sir." Andrew headed back toward the car.

"Call Water Patrol. We'll need some divers. And call the crime lab."

"Yes, sir."

"And Miller," Carlin muttered under his breath.

Andrew stopped and turned around, tossing a questioning gaze back at Carlin.

"Today might be a good day to buy that lottery ticket."

Miller went to the car and radioed in the information on a secure line then brought out the bright yellow crime scene tape. He scoped out the area looking for trees, or anything else to wrap the tape around.

"Why don't you hold off on that for a couple of minutes," Carlin said. "Right now we're just a couple of cops talking to two boys. As soon as that tape comes out, it's an instant invitation for every jerk and their uncle to come down and see what's going on. Enjoy the quiet. In about ten minutes it's going to be a circus around here, and guess who's going to be in charge of crowd control?"

One of the kids twitched impatiently. "Excuse me, officer?"

Carlin eyed the kid with the smart-ass mouth who had asked about a reward.

"I have to get home. My folks are expecting me for dinner."

"You're going to be late." Carlin pulled out his notepad.

"But it's important. My grandparents are going to be there. My grandfather is dying of cancer."

"How bad is he?"

"I dunno. Bad enough, I guess."

"Are your grandparents from out of town, like you might never see them again?"

"No, nothing like that. They live in Bloomington."

"You're going to be famous, kid. Every news station is going to want to talk to you. Enjoy your fifteen minutes. I'm sure your grandfather will understand." Carlin rubbed his eyes and reconsidered. "Aw, what the hell. Go on home if you want. You sure you want to miss being interviewed on the news? I'm sure your friend won't mind getting all the credit."

Nate pretended to give it some consideration before answering. "I'm sure they'll understand if I'm a little late."

"I'm sure they will. Now let's start with the basics. What's your name?"

Andrew took that as his cue to take the other boy aside and start his own interrogation. Shadows grew longer as he pulled more details from Joshua. Wearing only a pair of cut-off jeans, the boy soon began to shiver. Andrew glanced at his partner. His interviewee showed a fair amount of goose bumps too.

"Think we can get these guys a blanket?" Andrew called out.

Carlin nodded and as Andrew walked to the cruiser a Blazer rolled up. Two deputies from the Water Patrol stepped out. Andrew opened the trunk of his cruiser and grabbed a couple of blankets and tossed them to the kids. He walked over where the new arrivals were conferring with each other.

"We got a volunteer on the way," one of deputies said. "He should be here any time now."

Onlookers, noting the police activity, took an interest.

"Might be time to seal the perimeter," Carlin told Andrew. "Why don't you put up the tape?"

Feeling like little more than a toady, Andrew carried out the order silently. It had to be done. What had bothered him was being dismissed without a second glance.

"What's going on?" a voice shouted from the crowd.

Andrew had been so lost in his thoughts and wrapping the tape around trees that he hadn't noticed the crowd gathering on the other side of the barrier. "Not sure yet," he replied. "Kids in a canoe found a car in the lake."

"Was there a body in it?"

Andrew realized he'd said too much. "Nothing that interesting," he tried to recover. He ignored questions that now peppered him and unrolled the yellow tape to another tree.

A Dodge Neon pulled up next to the Blazer and small man with short cropped hair stepped out. He ducked under the tape and walked straight to Deputy Miller. "Chuck Marks." He held out his hand. "I'm your diver."

Andrew shook his hand and led him to the other three.

"Mike, Neil." Chuck acknowledged the two Water Patrol deputies. Andrew felt a little vindication that he ignored Carlin.

"Ready? Let's do this," Neil said to the volunteer.

Chuck returned to his car, got his gear and then followed the deputy into the Blazer.

The three deputies chatted while the other two changed.

"I can't believe you guys don't pay those civilians," Carlin said.

"That's why they call them volunteers," Mike answered. "God bless 'em, though. They save our budget from going in the red."

The two men stepped out from the Blazer in full scuba gear and motioned for the two blanket-clad boys. The four of them walked to the edge of the lake. Nate pointed out the area where they found the car. The deputies waded in then disappeared under the water.

Andrew headed down to the shore where the kids were standing. "You guys are going to be here a while. Want to call your folks?"

"I left my cell in the car after I called you guys. Can I go get it?" Josh glanced off in the direction of where he'd parked his car, and saw a throng of people on the other side of the tape blocking the way. "Whoa! Where did they all come from?"

"Here and there. Come on, I'll go with you. Don't say anything to anyone," he said and then added for Nate, "You wait here."

Andrew broke a path to the car for Josh like an offensive lineman opening a hole for a halfback. Questions came at them from all sides, most asking what was going on. The kid obediently kept his mouth shut as they reached his car. He looked around nervously as all eyes stared.

"Aw shit." He reached under the rim over the front tire and pulled out a magnetic box holding the key. "Guess I better find a new hiding place, huh?"

Andrew grinned as Josh leaned into his car. "Probably a good idea. Besides, that's one of the first places car thieves look. Best to keep the key with you. You can even use a safety pin and pin it to your shorts if you're going swimming."

"Then I'd look like a dork."

"Pull your pocket inside out and pin it on the inside," Andrew suggested.

Josh raised his eyebrows. "I'll have to remember that one."

They made their way back through the crowd. Josh took a seat on the ground next to his friend. Andrew joined his partner and the other deputy down by the shore. They were talking about the Vikings and if they could take the division this year when the surface of the water broke. The two divers emerged, water cascading off of their bodies. The deputy took off his mask. "Call Crime Lab and tell them to bring a tow. Might want to inform MPD also and have them send someone out."

Carlin sighed. "Damn, kids weren't bullshitting, huh? Did you see a body?"

"Didn't see one, but it's pretty dark and muddy down there."

"Crime Lab should already be on the way." Carlin glanced at Andrew; the young deputy nodded. "Well rookie, tonight's test looks like it will be honing your report writing skills. I'll call it in. You get a formal statement from the kids. I'll join you in a minute."

Andrew nodded and headed toward the boys.

"And Miller." Andrew turned around. "Be thorough. This case has media written all over it. No mistakes."

It took less than twenty minutes for the Crime Lab van and a tow truck to arrive. Close behind, the media crowded in. All of the local TV news stations were present and setting up. Even at dusk lighting wouldn't be a problem.

Jesse Campbell pulled his cruiser up next to Carlin's.

Andrew closed his eyes and massaged his temples. "What's he doing here?"

Carlin chuckled. "When I called in I told them we might need some extra help with crowd control."

"Hey Sarge. How ya doing, New Age?" Campbell approached

and patted Andrew on the shoulder.

The tow truck backed up to the lip of the water. The two divers carried the cable into the lake. A few minutes later one of them bobbed to the surface and gave the thumbs up. The cable churned. Lights from the television crews lit up the area as reporters started talking into cameras, each one volleying to make sure that they got the live story, and a good angle of the action.

"It's like they already know what's down there," Andrew said. "How would they know? I thought we were using closed channels."

"Easy enough to slip up in the chain," Campbell said. "Somebody uses the wrong channel, the press has the scanners manned twenty-four/seven. It's an easy enough mistake."

Andrew thought that maybe Deputy Campbell might be defending himself.

"Most likely an anonymous tip," Carlin said. "They've all got moles in the department."

As the cable rewound, the tow truck pulled forward. The red and blue lights on top of the car surfaced ending any speculation. As the rest of the car emerged questions from the reporters flew at the deputies.

"Is that the missing police car?"

"No, that one's still missing, this one just decided to take a swim," Campbell muttered under his breath.

"Be professional," Carlin chided. "The cameras are rolling. Who knows how sensitive those mikes are."

"You're right, Sarge, sorry. But what a stupid-ass question."

The crowd stood compliantly behind the yellow barrier, but one reporter with the logo for WMLS Channel 6 sewn into her blazer lifted the tape and tried to sneak under with her cameraman.

"One more step and I'll arrest you for obstruction," Andrew yelled.

The reporter shot him one of those shit-eating, it-was-worth-a-shot grins and ducked back under the tape.

"Good catch, New Age," Campbell said.

"Knock that New Age shit off. It's getting old," Carlin said.

"I didn't mean nothing by it," Campbell said.

"No big deal." Andrew turned to Carlin. "Thanks. I appreciate your sticking up for me, but if it bothered me I would've dealt with it."

Carlin smiled and held his hands up in surrender.

Two deputies from Crime Lab were examining the police car. When one opened the front door, water cascaded to the ground. No bodies, or anything else, occupied the front seat. With latex gloves on he carefully took the key out of the ignition. Touching only the sides of the key he slid it into the trunk lock.

Eleven

Wednesday 5:45 p.m.

Louise didn't volunteer for another double shift. Tired and depressed, all she wanted to do was go home and crash. Maybe a hot bath first, then fall asleep. She got in her Saturn, switched on the ignition, flipped on the air, and stuck a Melissa Etheridge CD into the slot all in one swift motion. Cranking the volume as high as it would go, she maneuvered her sound machine through traffic. No matter the time of day, between road construction and the influx of more families moving into her neighborhood, wonderful urban sprawl, the route home always seemed like rush hour.

With only moderate use of her horn and middle finger Louise made it home somewhat sane. Some of her tension vanished as she trudged up the stairs and heard Chick Corea through the other side of the wall jazzing away at the piano. Keys dangled from the lock, a bad habit Karla had when she came to visit, especially when carrying groceries. But if she were carrying groceries, at least there'd be a good meal tonight.

A wispy trail of smoke rose from the coffee table permeated the air as the tip of sandalwood incense glowed. On the couch, eyes closed, Karla Spire lay soaking in the music. Louise tiptoed over and stood above her gently blowing on Karla's blonde bangs while jingling the keys.

Karla opened her eyes and grinned. "Hey, you. Did I leave them in the door again?"

Louise nodded.

Karla reached up and pulled Louise down. As they kissed, an unfamiliar urgency came from Karla's lips. Their lips parted and before she could ask what was wrong, Karla said, "I'm so sorry."

"What?" Confusion blanked Louise's face as she rolled off her lover and onto the floor.

Karla stared at her with shock mixed with sympathy. "Don't tell me you haven't heard?"

"Heard what?" Impatience crept into her voice, along with a little fear.

"They found Mark Lone Bear. At least they think it's him. It's been all over the news."

"When? Is he all right?" *What a stupid question. At least they 'think' it was him meant the body must have been a mess.*

Louise let the depression overtake her. She knew Karla felt it too. No point trying to mask it.

"About half an hour ago. They interrupted Jeopardy."

"I've been stuck in traffic for the last half hour. Where'd they find him?"

"North of here," Karla answered. "They found him in Perch Lake, in the trunk of the police car."

That was an area where her brother patrolled. Louise reached for the phone and called him on his cell. No answer. Chick Corea went silent as Karla turned off the stereo and flipped on the TV, keeping the volume low. Louise called the Sheriff's Department and asked for Andrew. No luck. Karla surfed the channels looking for the story on the news. No luck there, either.

"Where's Perch Lake?" Louise asked.

"I think it's in Kenowa."

"Where the hell is that?"

"I have no idea."

"Wanna go for a drive?" Hoping Karla would say no.

"Do you want me to?"

Louise took a deep breath. "I would guess that about ninety-nine percent of the off duty cops will be there. Probably not the best time for me to come out of the closet."

"Why don't I stay here?"

"Damn, I love you." Louise felt her depression fade just a speck.

Karla stood a good two inches taller than Louise. Louise walked over and reached up, brushing the bangs of Karla's stylish haircut away from her eyes, and stroked her cheek before kissing her lips long and hard.

"Why don't I MapQuest Perch Lake for you so you don't have to fumble with a map while you're driving?"

"You are way too good for me."

"I know." Karla smiled and stroked Louise's cheek.

Louise followed her into the bedroom and stood behind while Karla sat at the desk and logged onto the computer. "One of these days you're going to have to come out, you know."

"Like it's a big mystery now." Louise massaged Karla's shoulders. "I look about as butch as I can get, don't I? I think the rat-tail is a dead giveaway. Half of the department already knows. I'd be willing to bet a paycheck that the other half suspects. They're just nice enough to keep their comments behind my back."

"Your brother doesn't know, does he? And I like the rat-tail. Makes you look sexy."

Louise smiled. "Andrew is in deep denial. Somewhere in that thick skull of his, he's got to be aware of it."

"We've been a couple for three months. Why don't you tell him? From what you've told me, he doesn't seem to be a homophobe."

"He's not, but when it comes to family you never know how views might get skewed."

A map materialized on the screen. Karla pressed the button and the printer came to life. "There you are." She handed Louise the directions. "Please don't be out there all night."

Perch Lake rested on the northern border of Kenowa near Corcoran. Louise took the paper and studied the map. "Good God, I can't believe people actually live out there."

"What's wrong with the suburbs? I hear they even got indoor plumbing and everything now."

"Maybe, but I bet you still can't get cable."

"They've got this thing called satellite. I hear it's just as good."

Louise kissed Karla on the cheek. "As soon as I know what's what I'll come home. Promise."

"Tell Andrew about us," Karla said.

As Louise stepped out of the apartment, she said, "Why don't I invite him over for dinner this weekend? Maybe we can show him."

Karla laughed. "You are so evil."

Louise winked as she left.

Knowing Karla wouldn't, Louise locked the door behind her. As she walked away she heard the TV die and Chick Corea come back to life.

By the time Louise arrived at Perch Lake the sun resembled a large yellow balloon sinking toward the horizon. She parked her car and pushed her way through the mass of onlookers and media on foot. On the other side of the yellow tape, the Hennepin County Crime Lab scoured the area with the Kenowa police and the Sheriff's department intermixed. Closest to the scene Louise found many of her fellow officers. She didn't know a lot of the cops from Mark's precinct, but hoped that he did have some actual friends among them. The few from her precinct were there strictly to show solidarity. Still, she wondered if they'd be there if it were her body that was found.

Standing behind the tape and exchanging greetings with a few of her coworkers, Louise sought out and found her brother sitting in his car writing a report. "Hey, Deputy Dawg."

Four deputies looked up. Only Andrew smiled. He came over, lifted the tape and invited his sister into the inner circle. The other officers grumbled as they obediently stayed behind.

"Didn't know that's all it would take," one of the officers called out.

Louise winked. "Now you know for next time."

The police car had already been towed. Mark's body was probably resting on a slab at the morgue. Many of the Crime Lab crew were wrapping up their work. A couple of news stations had stayed but the cameras and lights were off. She recognized Bianca Skylar from Channel 6 News. That bitch would stick around until the end. The mini towers on top of the vans were down. Louise guessed that the reporters, especially Skylar, had convinced the station brass they should stick around to do a live shot for the 10:00 news.

"Tell me," Louise said.

"A couple of kids canoeing found the police car. Crime Lab towed it out and found Officer Lone Bear in the trunk."

Louise admired the way her brother used the formal term for her friend. "Positive ID?"

"Yeah. Detective Iverson from MPD ID'd him. His body wasn't in the water that long so it was still in pretty good shape. Preliminary speculation is that he took one shot to the chest. That probably did him in, but the autopsy will show for sure."

"Why wasn't he wearing his vest?" Louise muttered.

"We don't even know if he was in his uniform. Clothes are missing."

Louise stopped for a moment, not realizing she had been thinking out loud. Another deputy approached them.

"Officer Louise Miller, this is Sergeant Carlin Rivers; Carlin Rivers, Louise Miller," Andrew announced.

The two shook hands. Rivers stood a little taller than Andrew, but not as filled out. Still, his features were hard, like he could handle himself in any situation. All-in-all, he looked like a cop's cop; the kind little kids could trust and come running to when they're lost. But also the kind who would not hesitate to mix it up and crack a few heads.

"Andrew told me you and Lone Bear were friends. I'm sorry for your loss."

He told me you broke every rule in the book and put him in a fight, Louise thought, but this time consciously kept her mouth shut. "Thank you."

"If you'd like to view the body, I'm sure you'll have no problem at the morgue."

Louise didn't trust Rivers any farther than a baby could projectile vomit, but she was impressed by his sincere demeanor. "Thank you, I'll do that."

"Just a heads-up though. He's not a pretty sight. The water bloated him some, and there's a lot of bruising."

Again, Louise nodded her thanks. He did have a certain charm, and the kind of personality that could diffuse a possible hostile situation. Maybe her brother had been right in not reporting the bar fight.

"Any clues you can talk about?" Louise asked.

"Not really," Carlin answered. "Uniform, gun, and badge are missing. I'm sure the water took care of any possible evidence, but the tech guys might be able to come up with something. I'm sure we'll be working together on this."

Part of Louise hoped he was right. The other part feared machismo would get in the way of cooperation, each side holding back in order to outmaneuver the other to make the bust. *Fuck that.* Andrew wouldn't play that game, and neither would she. Together they'd make sure both sides had all the pieces.

She suddenly felt uncomfortable under Rivers' gaze. "Well, I know you've got your reports to write, and I'm just in the way here. I think I'll go to the morgue and say good-bye."

Louise and Carlin exchanged their pleased-to-meet-yous and she headed back to her car.

"Call me," Andrew shouted after her.

"Dinner at my place, Saturday night. Be there," Louise called back.

She pulled away from the scene hoping the smell of fish and algae wouldn't stick. She had the rest of her evening planned out. First stop, the morgue. Then she'd go home, smother herself in Karla, let down her guard and cry.

Twelve

Wednesday 11:10 p.m.

Despite his lawyer's assurances, the world unraveled around Dr. Gillespy. Sitting at the desk in his study, he pressed a button on the remote control and Chopin's Piano Concerto No. 1 in E Minor filled the room. He poured himself a glass of sherry in a leaded crystal goblet, and walked to the window. Beyond his reflection, Gillespy stared out past the highway into a neighboring cornfield. At this time of night only an occasional semi sailed by, breaking the silence of his suburban serenity. He loved this area. Million dollar houses like his abutted against farmland, creating true diversity.

A small telescope on a tripod invited the psychiatrist to spy on the planets. Unlike the telescope at his apartment in Manhattan, this one pointed at the sky. Gillespy missed his weekend trips to New York. He'd lost his one bedroom hideaway when his practice diminished to nothing. Even his colleagues had betrayed him. Most of all, the partner he'd mentored had spoken against him and stolen most of his patients. Hout said he'd changed over the years. How his drinking went out of control; how it changed his entire personality. That was bullshit! Gillespy admitted he might have a nip or two too many every once in a great while, but it never affected his work, or his judgment.

"How are you doing, Leonard, you traitorous bastard? Sitting in your smarmy office delighting in how you're going to screw me over in court? You sanctimonious son-of-a-bitch." Gillespy grimaced as he gazed at the fields beyond the highway.

He walked back to his desk and sat in his leather Executive Supreme chair. It occurred to him that his study somewhat resembled his lawyer's office. A little cozier here, but both rooms had oak paneling with bookcases overflowing. Instead of law books, these walls were lined with medical and psychiatry books and psychology journals.

Gillespy downed the sherry in one gulp, poured himself another and opened his desk drawer. He stared down at the syringe and vial of acetomorphine. If he did this right, his breathing and pulse would shallow to nothing. No pain, no worries. With his death, maybe the Palmers would drop the lawsuit and his grandchildren would have something left to inherit.

As the concerto moved from the allegro maestoso to the larghetto, the doctor unbuttoned the cuff of his shirt, rolled up his sleeve, and downed his second glass of sherry. *One more won't hurt anything.* He poured himself another. This time he took a small sip and savored the flavor, swishing the liquid around in his mouth.

The doctor set the glass down and lifted the vial. He leaned back in his chair and held the drug up to the light as if studying its composition. A sudden pang stabbed at his heart as he picked up the needle and stuck it in the tiny bottle. After staring at the empty syringe for a few moments he pulled out the needle and carefully laid the equipment on his desk, his hands shaking.

"I can do this."

Instead, he picked up the telephone, pressed speed dial, and listened while the phone rang on the other end. "Hello?" a tired voice answered after the fifth ring.

All of a sudden Dr. Gillespy wasn't sure what to say.

"Hello?" The voice, that of a young man, became agitated.

"Hello, Michael. How are you?" the doctor asked.

A stiff pause. "Dad, is that you?"

"Yes, it's me."

"It's after eleven. What do you want?"

"I just called to see how things are. See how my grandchildren were doing."

Silence.

"I wanted to talk to you," the doctor said.

"You've been drinking?"

Not so much a question, a statement, the doctor thought. "No." He raised his glass and took another sip.

"Bull." The connection was broken. The doctor could still hear the anger over the dead line.

"Bullshit," Gillespy shouted into the phone. "Bullshit, bullshit, bullshit!" He tossed back glass number three and slammed the phone down. The sherry bottle was still almost a third full instead of two thirds empty. "What an optimist you are, doctor." He forced a small chuckle.

Grabbing the phone once more he pressed speed dial again, a different number this time. Only two rings before his son-in-law answered.

"Good evening, Paul. May I speak to Judy please?"

Paul hung up. The doctor pressed redial.

Before Paul could even say hello, Gillespy shouted, "I have the right…" The phone went dead. "…to speak to my own daughter." The last came out in a whisper.

He pressed redial again but now got a busy signal.

"You'll all be sorry when I'm dead." *No they won't, they'll probably rejoice.*

Gillespy stared at the bottle, his only true friend, while part three of the concerto commenced. *Why even bother with a glass?*

"Because you're a man of class." He filled the goblet to the rim, trying not to spill any as he raised it to his lips.

Maybe I should just burn the will. It would be fun to think of the ensuing battles between brother and sister. Having to go through probate court would make it all that much more interesting. It's not that Judy would really care, she's never been very materialistic, but that husband of hers would fight. Michael would fight just on principle, squandering their children's inheritance on attorneys' fees.

He took a gulp from his glass letting the day's alcohol work its magic as the concerto ended. *No, forget that. I can add another codicil give them one dollar each and leave the rest to charity. Now which charity would they hate the most?*

Gillespy refilled the goblet emptying the bottle. "Not enough of you left to save," he said to the glass.

On his desk in a silver frame was a family portrait. He remembered the forced smiles he made his children wear. At only thirteen, Michael had already developed worry lines. The doctor squinted. *Could his hairline have been receding then, too?* He frowned, shifting his attention to his daughter's image. Even the smile could not hide the eleven-year-old's pain. His then wife, doped up on antidepressants and alcohol looked as if she came from Stepford. *What was her name?* Martha? Margaret? It didn't really matter. Not anymore. She'd left him over a decade ago.

"To hell with you all," he toasted merrily. "Do whatever you want with my money."

Silence enveloped him as he raised the sherry to his lips one last time. In three gulps it was gone.

Was the bottle full this afternoon, or was it yesterday? He picked up the vial and peered through it, rolling it back-and-forth between his thumb and forefinger. He stared hypnotically through the clear liquid warping the images of a Monet print on the far wall. After the fascination of that wore off, he reached for the syringe and once again stuck it in the soft top of the bottle. Slowly and meticulously he filled the tube.

Opening his desk drawer, Gillespy found a large rubber band. "You'll do." He slid it up his arm and clenched his fist. He thumped the crook of his elbow until a vein bulged.

Checking one last time to ensure the bottle of sherry was empty—God forbid it go to waste—Dr. William Gillespy closed one eye, took careful aim for the vein and stuck the needle in his arm.

Thirteen

Thursday 8:00 a.m.

Leonard regained consciousness with his head pounding. It rested peacefully on the other captive's breast. He had no idea as to how long he'd been out, but it had been the first rest without the nightmares since he'd been kidnapped. Glancing around, he found that his tormentor had left a pot within reach. The doctor used it to relieve himself, hoping not to awaken his partner.

A trickle of blood oozed from underneath the handcuff. The sadist had clamped it too tight. Grateful, Hout had at least talked his way out of the stocks, and more importantly, the surfboard. Attached at the wrist to his co-prisoner by the handcuffs, the doctor, on his knees, stared down at the woman's face. He knew her from somewhere, but she wore the bruises like a mask. He taxed his mind trying to remember where he knew her from. He shifted his gaze to the cabinet and the small lock securing it. *It shouldn't be too hard to break into.* What might be more difficult would be to carry the woman across the room.

Hungry, with only one meal of water and stale bread in only God knew how long, a tired, weak, and sore Leonard Hout maneuvered his arms under and around the woman. Her cuffed hand twisted behind her back as he did. Getting on one knee and his foot planted firmly under him he struggled, but finally managed to hoist the woman on his shoulders.

He froze at a low growl at the foot of the stairs. The rottweiler had risen up off the bottom step. Its fangs glistened in the dim florescent light. The psychiatrist gulped, gently put the woman down, and resumed his kneeling position. The dog also resumed his position, quietly planting himself back on the step. The woman's breathing sounded a little less raspy. Hout touched his free hand on her neck to check her pulse. The bruises were more pronounced and there was still quite a bit of swelling, but the beat felt strong and normal.

She stirred, not for the first time since before he fell asleep. This time her eyes fluttered open. She squinted as the fluorescent light burned her eyes, and tried to speak only managing to push a whimper through dry lips.

"Shhh, don't try to talk. My name is Leonard Hout."

Her eyes widened and she tried to sit up. The psychiatrist tenderly pushed her back.

"Where am I?"

If frogs could talk, that's what they might sound like.

Chamber of horrors? The valley of death? Hell? All of the above? "I don't know," he said honestly.

She raised her cuffed hand to her throat, the doctor's hand followed. She then noticed they were bound together. Her eyes told Hout that if she were able to scream, she would have.

He brushed the hair out of her eyes, deciding on the direct approach. "You were choked. You'll be fine, but you were hurt. There's still some swelling. At least you can breathe. You'll have a sore throat for a while." The doctor didn't know how far to take her. If it were him, he'd want to know everything. "We've been kidnapped. I don't know why."

"Gillespy," she rasped.

His eyes sprang wide as his jaw dropped. "That's where I know you from!"

The dog let out a menacing growl.

Hout lowered his voice to just above a whisper. "You're the

lawyer that's representing that family who's suing Gillespy. We're supposed to meet for a deposition. I knew I recognized you. What is it—Cartier?"

The jumble of pieces started to form a picture. Hers wasn't a random kidnapping. And if hers wasn't, neither was his. There was a direct link between them. How did this relate to his ex-partner? And how did it related to this sadist? Gillespy was a drunk, not a kidnapper and killer. Despite how his partner deteriorated over the last couple of years, Hout couldn't imagine him plotting something so despicable.

The familiar footsteps from above caused goose bumps to erupt on Leonard's arms. "He's back," Leonard whispered. "I've got a plan. No time to explain. Just play along. Keep pretending that you're unconscious. I'll get us out of here."

The rottweiler seated on the stairs cocked his head to look up at his master. The lawyer closed her eyes and went limp. *Good,* Leonard thought, but he could see the pulse pounding in her throat.

"Have you been good company, S.K.?" the giant asked.

The dog stood up at attention. With only a stub of a tail the canine's rear end wagged back and forth in appreciation of his master's company.

The sadist went over to his prisoners. He carried a tray holding a glass of water, a bowl of strawberry ice cream with a plastic spoon, and a cheese sandwich sliced in two. He threw half of the sandwich to S.K. who swallowed it whole.

"I was hoping she'd be awake by now." The kidnapper looked down on the pair. "The ice cream is for her. The sandwich is for you. Eat. You need to keep your strength up."

Compassion? Hout couldn't believe that the man capable of it. Now would be the best time to try and get that scalpel.

Hout gobbled the sandwich with his free hand. "She's having more trouble breathing than she should. I had to give her mouth-to-mouth a couple of times."

"Lucky you. She could do better."

"What if I need to do a tracheotomy and you're not here? I really need that tube and scalpel."

The kick came swiftly into his ribs. The doctor fell to his side, curling into the fetal position in agony.

"Do you think I'm stupid? Do you?" He kicked him in the back and this time Leonard cried out. The lawyer flinched, every muscle going stiff. "Well, well, well," the monster's voice instantly calm. "Do we have an actor in our midst?"

He knelt over the lawyer, placed his hand on her throat, and squeezed. Her eyes shot open, filled with terror. He chuckled.

"You seem to be making a miraculous recovery."

Rising to his full height the sadist turned his back on the couple. As his breath returned, Leonard uncurled and saw him move the board with Velcro straps, turning it to a new angle. Coming back to his prisoners, he reached into his pocket and pulled out a keychain. Leonard estimated at least ten keys dangling off a metal four-leaf clover.

Unlocking the cuffs and putting them in his pocket, the man dragged his prisoner back to the surfboard. Leonard struggled uselessly.

Making sure the shrink would be able to see the giant X attached to the wall, the giant strapped him in. Then he walked over to the lawyer, easily overcoming her struggles, and hefted her over his shoulder. He carried her over to the X and tied her wrists and ankles to the beams.

Fully awake and spread eagle she struggled but the thick ropes held her tight.

"I told your friend you could do better than him."

In one quick motion he hooked his finger over the top button of her blouse and ripped it open. Buttons flew off and bounced in all directions as he admired a white lace bra cupping small breasts.

Her face went ashen as tears welled up and poured down her face. "Please."

"Is that a please do me?" he asked in a sultry voice. The madman gently breathed in her ear, then stiffened his tongue and lapped the salt water off of her cheek.

"Leave her alone, you sick bastard!" Leonard screamed.

He gave the doctor a lopsided grin. "I'm sick, huh? Then it's a good thing I have my own private shrink, don't you agree?" He focused his attention back to the lawyer, this time staring at her breasts.

She battled to breathe. Only small gulps of air made way to her lungs.

The captor gave a quick laugh and bit his lip. He traced his finger along the path of her tears down to where they fell to the floor, then ran his thumb across her swollen neck, down her throat to the edge of her bra and caressed her breast.

"Well kids, it's been fun. But I've got places to go, people to see." He sighed as he reached inside her bra and pinched her nipple before heading for the stairs.

The attorney lashed against the binds and burst into sobs. She went rigid again when she saw his grin. "Oh hell doc, I can't stay mad at you."

He picked up the glass of water and set it next to Leonard's hand, then undid the Velcro attached to the leather straps securing his left arm.

"In case you get thirsty."

What's his angle, the doctor wondered. I *just don't get it!* Get it or not, he went cold at the sadist's smile.

"Oh, and, uh, I need a favor from you. You need to give me your ATM pin number. It's time you start paying for your room and board."

Before he could stop himself, Leonard spat out the numbers, hating himself for his weakness.

"Thank you," the big man said, exuding civility.

He picked up the glass and in two gulps downed half of it. Leonard's throat went dry. His captor smacked his lips. "Ahh, nice and cold." With a menacing grin, he then took the pot of urine and carefully refilled the glass, setting it within reach of the doctor. Throwing his head back with laughter, he started up the steps.

Halfway to the door, he stopped. "And just in case you lied, or have any notion of taking advantage of my good will and freeing yourself..."

The doctor cringed in the waiting silence, his pulse thudding behind his eyes, which carefully avoided those of the attorney. The captor pointed at the dog. "Silent Kill."

The dog jumped from his step and lunged toward Leonard. His teeth bared in a noiseless snarl, drool hung from his mouth as his clawless paws galloped on the cement floor. Leonard let out a scream as he raised his arm to protect his face from the oncoming carnage.

"Sir Knight!" the captor snapped.

The dog skidded to a halt inches from the doctor's face. As if nothing at all had happened, it swung around and trotted nonchalantly back to his place on the step.

"He only responds to my voice. Just something to think about." A malicious sneer spread across his face.

The door opened then clicked shut. Drenched in sweat Leonard tried to restore his breathing and pounding heart to normal rates. For a moment he'd forgotten about the pain in his side and back as the fluorescent light flickered. But now that peace and quiet temporarily prevailed, the echo of each kick returned in full force.

"That wasn't a very good plan," Melanie rasped.

Leonard turned his head away from the lawyer. He didn't want her to see him cry.

Fourteen

Thursday 10:45 a.m.

The persistent ringing inside his skull finally stopped but the throbbing continued. Gillespy raised his head from the desk. Bright light stung his eyes. His arm ached; he saw scratches and a needle, broken from its syringe, jammed in the crook of his elbow. Next to him lay the syringe, and next to that an empty bottle of sherry, and the dried liquid staining the mahogany desktop.

"How the hell did I do that? Can't I do anything right?"

Gillespy winced as he pulled the needle from his arm. He applied pressure with his thumb until the bleeding stopped. The same ringing he'd heard in his dream started up again, but this time in the conscious world. The doctor picked up the phone and held it to his ear.

After a long silence, "Dad? Is that you?"

"Michael?" His voice, along with his mouth, felt dry.

"Are you okay? I've been calling all morning."

"I think I've got a touch of the flu," Gillespy said. "I took some medication and it really knocked me out."

"Medication, huh?"

"What do you want, Michael?"

"I started to worry after you called last night."

Did I call you last night? The doctor couldn't remember. "It wasn't anything important," he finally said.

"It never is—is it, Dad?"

Gillespy couldn't think of a retort. He sighed into the phone. "What do you want from me, Michael?"

There was a laugh at the other end. "Nothing. Not anymore."

The line went dead.

The doctor hung up the receiver and walked across the room to a finely carved black onyx liquor cabinet with a Chinese garden gilded in gold decorating the doors. He opened it up and pondered which bottle would make the better breakfast. Feeling in the mood for something sweet, he pulled out the Bacardi. *Who am I trying to fool?* Expecting no company and feeling like he had no class, not anymore, Gillespy didn't bother with a glass.

The farmland across the road looked lush. A line of thin clouds wisped across the sky like vapor trails. Just before turning away from the window, the doctor saw a lone red car speeding down the road. It slowed as it approached the house, stopped, then pulled into the driveway. Alarmed, Gillespy stepped back, taking cover behind the drapes.

The sunlight reflected off the driver's windshield, giving it a mirror-like sheen. Every muscle tense, Gillespy waited for the driver to get out. The car door remained shut.

Salesmen and Jehovah's Witnesses didn't travel out this way randomly. Maybe it was someone from the press. "Bastards," he spat. Still, the door did not open.

"What are you waiting for, you fool?" The doctor cloaked himself with the curtain.

As fast as it had arrived, the red car squealed its tires in reverse, flew back down the driveway, and then shot out of sight.

"How very odd." Perplexed, the doctor lowered the drape. Taking a thoughtful sip from the bottle, he wandered back to the desk and promptly blocked the incident from his mind and contemplated instead on cutting his son out of the will. He pressed a button on the remote; the music of Chopin again filled the room. Disgusted, he turned it off. "Just not in the mood for you today, Frederic. In fact, I'm not feeling at all classical today." He opened up his desk drawer with the CDs, trying to figure out just what kind of mood he *was* in when he heard an engine revving in the driveway.

"You again!" He stomped across the room toward the window.

The rum exploded in his stomach sending a burning chill throughout his body. Gillespy cowered behind the drapes trying to make himself invisible as sweat trickled down his forehead. "It was just a little accident. Nobody got hurt. Why can't you leave me alone?"

Since the little mishap outside his lawyer's office, they had been calling, leaving messages for him to come down to the station, but this was the first time that they came out to visit.

A Sheriff's Deputy got out of his squad and approached the garage, looked it over, and then came to the front door. Gillespy was grateful the garage door had no windows.

The doctor dropped to the floor, resting his chin on his knees when the doorbell chimed. His hand shook as he took a long pull from the bottle. He waited silently; the doorbell rang again. Gillespy sat as still as a statue as the bell went off for the third time.

After waiting what seemed a suitable amount of time, Gillespy rolled onto his knees and peeked out of the window. The car was still parked in the driveway. A human shadow stretched across the ground approaching the window. The doctor moved faster than he had in years as he rolled back against the wall. Off to the side he could almost feel the eyes of the deputy staring in.

Long moments passed during which Gillespy hardly dared breathe. He didn't move, didn't twitch a muscle. Finally he heard the sound of the motor starting up. Taking a deep breath he dared to peek out the window. He carefully crept back to the window and using the curtain as a veil, he peeked outside. The shadows were gone. It took both hands to steady the bottle as he raised it to his lips and watched as the sheriff's car backed out of the driveway.

~

Full of rage, he grasped the steering wheel so tight it seemed his knuckles would pop out of his skin. He'd had the scanner. He congratulated himself for being so smart. The cops were foolish, broadcasting their move, giving him warning to get out of the doctor's driveway. He thought of the movie *Terminator.* "I'll be back," he said in his best Schwarzenegger voice.

They wouldn't take him in, would they? Not for a hit and run. Besides, Gillespy would be too smart for them.

Static chopped up the conversation on the police scanner as he strained to hear. Were they talking about the doctor? Nope. Black male. Stolen car. He relaxed. He drove past farmland, blocks of townhouses, and even through the trailer park. No word about the doctor came over the scanner. He sent the doctor a telepathic message.

"I really need to talk to you."

"I would like to see you too, Elias," came a stern reply.

The big man smiled as he circled the trailer park and headed back toward the doctor's home. Only a few miles away, a voice crackled over the scanner.

"Gillespy's not home, we'll try again later this afternoon."

He slowed to let a truck pass while he thought about the scanner update. What would be the point of going there now?

"I'd like to see you too, Elias," Elias mouthed the words trying to find a hidden meaning. He couldn't.

A deputy's car approached from the oncoming lane. Elias slid low in his seat, reaching for the comfort of the .357 magnum resting between the seats. No one in sight either, no witnesses that might also need to be taken care of.

The squad care grew larger on the road in front of him. He held his breath and stared straight ahead, trying to look nonchalant. The car passed. He let out a breath and glanced in the rearview mirror at the receding vehicle.

"Are you the pig that told me the doctor wasn't home?" He waited for the car to make a U-turn. It didn't.

He drove back to the doctor's house and pulled into the empty driveway. Turning off the ignition, he sat in his car staring at the house with its long picture windows and gold plated knocker on the door. The curtains were closed. Maybe it was only his imagination but Elias thought he saw the curtain move.

"What should I do? It's so dangerous right now."

"Go home now, Elias, we'll meet another time; a safer time."

The big man smiled as he started the car and backed out of the driveway. As clouds thickened and rolled between sun and earth, he decided to go home and check up on his guests.

Fifteen

Thursday 11:35 a.m.

The ice cream had melted into a sticky pink puddle in the bowl. Leonard's stomach grumbled as he lay bound to the surfboard unable to move any more than a statue while staring at the attorney. Trying to maintain a façade of civilization under the bizarre circumstances they found themselves in, Hout and Cartier had introduced themselves. For a few minutes they tried to surmise as to why. At first, Hout defended Gillespy. At one time he'd been an excellent psychiatrist.

"He taught me so much in the beginning," Hout said. "It wasn't until after the drinking started that things fell apart for him. It was like watching Jekyll turn into Hyde."

Now he had to agree, Gillespy was an incompetent drunk. Neither one would have guessed he would hire a murderous thug to kidnap them. Leonard concentrated on the question, trying to ignore the painful position he was bound in.

"It's logical he'd kidnap me. I'm a threat. But you? That makes no sense. No offense, but your clients could always hire another lawyer."

Melanie had tried to keep up a brave front, but from the tremors of her lips he could see she'd been silently crying. She had nothing more to say and was quiet until Leonard's stomach rumbled loud enough for her to smile.

"Do you mind?" He stretched his free arm for the bowl.

She shook her head. “Knock yourself out.”

He listened for the dog, heard nothing, and then pulled the bowl to his face. The strawberry goo tasted better than anything he could remember. He dug the plastic spoon in greedily as ice cream dripped from his face onto the surfboard.

Shoving the spoon into the bowl to get every last drop, he heard a snap and pulled out a white plastic shiv. Frustrated, he threw it against the wall. A thin, cheap piece of plastic would do him no good against a hundred-plus pound dog built of muscle and teeth. But it did give him an idea. A cunning smile spread across Leonard’s face as he lifted the bowl as high as his arm could reach and slammed it on the floor.

“The dog’s up,” Melanie said.

His heart pounded and he froze.

“He’s sitting down again.”

Leonard felt safe enough to breathe.

“What are you doing?” Melanie asked.

He smashed it onto the floor again.

“The dog’s looking at you weird, but he’s not getting up.”

“I’ve got a plan,” he said.

“I hope it’s better than the last one.”

“Not nearly, but it’s the only one I’ve got and I think we’re running out of time.”

On his third try the bowl cracked. On the fourth it shattered. Shards of glass littered the floor and the surfboard. He picked up the sharpest piece he could find out of the shards. It fit nicely in his hand.

“How many binds do you think I can undo before the dog reaches me?”

Melanie thought. “Maybe half of one.”

“Sir Knight,” Leonard shouted. “What’s he doing now?”

“Looking at you like you’re nuts.”

Leonard paused. “Not exactly what I was hoping for. Anyway, I’m going to start on these straps. When he charges, you yell Sir Knight. If that doesn’t stop him I’m going to stab him.”

Her eyes grew as wide as when the psycho put his hands on her throat. "Are you crazy? He'll kill you."

"Yeah, maybe. But I can't stand this anymore. That monster has no intention of letting us out of here."

Leonard touched his hand to the Velcro snap that now secured his head. The dog didn't exactly growl, but the sneer and the drool escaping down his chin made the effect equally frightful.

"Sir Knight," they yelled in unison.

Perplexed, the dog stopped, cocked its head and quizzically looked at each of them.

Hout yanked the strip off of his arm; a slight wisp of freedom as he reached for the next strap.

"Sir Knight!" Melanie shrieked. "Look out!"

Leonard lifted his head and reached under his chin.

"Look out!" Melanie screamed.

S.K. aimed for his throat. Leonard's arm barred a clear path and as the dog pounced, Leonard jabbed the glass shard into the dog's neck. For the first time, the doctor finally felt luck on his side as blood shot from the dog's throat. Then S.K. sank his fangs into the doctor's free arm. Leonard stabbed him again.

The dog didn't yelp but violently shook his head, spraying blood in all directions. Blood ran down Leonard's arm as he thrust the glass shard again and again. The dog released his arm and darted its head in and out trying to dodge the jabs. Leonard heard a pop as the point of his weapon pierced into the dog's eye.

He hardly felt the weapon slice the skin in his palm. Thankfully, S.K. weakened with every fresh wound he inflicted. Still, the dog kept up its silent attack. S.K.'s feet slipped out from under him as his blood pooled. He dodged a blow and found an opening. The dog sank his fangs into Leonard's shoulder, inches away from the carotid artery.

Leonard screamed as the dog clamped his jaws even tighter. The makeshift weapon dropped from his hand as he lifted his arm. The dog slipped again and loosened his grip. Leonard grabbed the dog's snout and slammed its chin onto the floor.

"Kill him!" Melanie screamed. *Kill Him!* Her voice failed her the second time.

Blood splashed Leonard as he bashed the dog as hard as he could against the floor. S.K. tried to get to his feet but kept slipping on the blood, his legs flailing as his head kept getting jerked and smashed. The dog tried to stand one last time, teetered for a moment, and then dropped.

The only sound came from Leonard's heavy breathing. His arm stung, but the adrenalin made it almost painless. He'd won.

"I used to love dogs," Melanie rasped.

"Me too." Leonard lay on the board trying to catch his breath.

Melanie struggled in her own binds. "Hey, you want to give me a hand here?"

Leonard didn't move from the surfboard.

"Hey, Doctor!" she croaked as loud as she could. "I don't mean to rush you, but if he comes back and we're still here, he's going to kill us."

"Oh God." Adrenalin rushed a new supply of energy through his veins. With his back muscles screaming and his shoulder ready to pop out of its socket, Leonard was able to reach just far enough to free his other arm. A muscle pulled in his back as he undid the remaining straps. His bones creaked as he went from his knees to his feet, and staggering over to Melanie, untying the rope binding her wrists.

"You're going to need rabies shots," Melanie said.

Blood oozed through his sleeve. He laughed.

"I think you're the first person I've ever met that thought getting rabies shots was funny."

"That's the best news I've ever heard." Leonard untied the bindings around her ankles. "I'm going to be alive long enough to need rabies shots."

Melanie pulled him upright and hugged him tight. "Thank you," she whispered in his ear.

"Your voice is getting stronger," he said.

"It's okay. It'll get a lot better once I'm out of here."

The dog lay in a pool of its own blood. Leonard shut his eyes. "We've got to get out of here."

"How did you figure that clue, Sherlock?"

Leonard chuckled. "Yeah, you're recovering quite well.

She gave his hand a squeeze and steadied him as they climbed the steps. Leonard thought of his wife and took back his hand. At the top of the stairs he froze.

"What is it?" she asked, her eyes darting nervously to his.

An eerie sense wrenched at his gut. "I have this sick feeling he's standing on the other side, waiting for us."

"Don't you dare think that."

Hout shrugged. "What if he's in the other room watching TV or something?"

"Then we'd better be damn quiet," Melanie whispered.

Leonard put his hand on the knob. His nerves began to tingle. He slowly twisted the handle. His shoulders slumped as he looked at Melanie.

"It's locked," he whispered.

She stared at him, wide-eyed, and placing her hand over his she twisted.

"How can it be locked?" she whispered back. "What the hell was he thinking? What kind of fucking idiot would lock the door with two people tied up and being guarded by a demon dog from Hell?"

Leonard laughed in spite of himself. He tried the knob again, more forcefully this time. Definitely locked. Stymied, they turned away from the door. Melanie helped him back down the stairs.

"I can't look at this," he said.

Melanie couldn't keep her eyes off the dog. Red still oozed from wounds, bathing it in its own blood.

"It's not him, it's that thing," Leonard said, pointing at the surfboard. "And that." He pointed at the stocks. Melanie grabbed Leonard's arm as S.K. twitched for a moment then lay still. Leonard clenched his teeth to keep from screaming as Melanie released her grip.

"Sorry. So now what?" Melanie asked.

Leonard cast a glance around the room and focused on the locked cabinet. "Over there," he pointed. "How are you at picking locks?"

"What's in there?"

"If he was telling the truth there should be a scalpel, maybe other medical supplies. If I can surprise him I can slash his throat before he knows what's happened."

Melanie walked over to the cabinet and inspected the lock and chain. "Have you still got that spoon?"

"The handle or the spoon part?"

"Whatever is the thinnest," she answered.

The doctor shivered as he went to the dog. In the blood he picked up the broken utensil and limped over. He wiped the blood off with his shirt before handing it to the lawyer.

She re-wiped more of it off on her blouse and stuck the spoon in the groove of the screw fastened to the hinge. It looked new. "It should give way easy enough. Piece of cake." The tip of the plastic snapped off. "Damn." She tried to wedge the plastic into the groove. It fit nice and snug. Melanie smiled. Within a minute she had the hinges off. Carefully she lifted off the door and let it dangle on the chain.

A rush of relief engulfed Leonard at the sight of the scalpel that lay inside. Other medical supplies included forceps, a straight razor, a plastic bottle of rubbing alcohol, and a rag blotted with dried blood.

"Damn," Leonard said.

"What?"

"I was hoping there'd be some bandages or something."

Most of the punctures in his arm had clotted but a couple still seeped some pus and blood.

Melanie took bottle of alcohol and the razor and cut a part of the sleeve off of her blouse. "This is going to hurt." She uncapped the bottle.

The doctor bit his tongue to keep from screaming as she doused the wounds. "You're as sadistic as he is."

"Don't be such a baby." Melanie wrapped the sleeve tightly around Leonard's wounds. "That should hold for a little while. Now let's say we get out of here."

"I say that's a good idea."

They headed back up the stairs and paused once again. "You really think he might be here?" Melanie asked.

"No, I don't think so. I think he would've heard us if he were."

He banged his good shoulder against the door and his back screamed in response. "We're not getting out this way. This door is solid."

"You don't suppose he keeps a phone down here, do you?"

The psychiatrist forced a chuckle through his pain. "I highly doubt it."

They dragged back down the stairs and searched for any other way of escape. Boards of plywood were screwed tight over windows. Melinda took the straight edge and fit it in one of the grooves. The first screw finally loosened.

The board creaked as the last screw became undone. Melanie lifted off the wood panel. "Shit."

Block windows let a little light in the room but nothing else.

"Son of a bitch! Now what?"

"I don't know." Leonard's voice cracked with defeat.

"Wait a minute." Melanie ran back up the stairs with hope in her gait. "Goddamn it," she swore and plodded back down the steps.

"What?"

"I was getting so good with screws and hinges. I thought I could undo the door."

"It swings out," the doctor said. "The hinges are on the other side. I noticed that before."

She glared at him. "Now what do we do?"

Leonard thought for a moment. "We wait. We stand by the

door and when he opens it we charge him. I've got the scalpel. You've got the straight edge. Between the two of us we should be able to take him."

"Do you think you've got the strength?"

Hout gave a grim smile. "When I hear that door unlock I'll have so much adrenalin running through me, I'll plow him down." He hoped she believed him. He wished he believed it himself.

Melanie thought the plan over. "Maybe we should wait at the bottom of the stairs. Stay out of sight behind the wall. When he sees his dog he's going to freak. We might catch him off balance on the steps."

"Good idea," Hout said. "In the meantime, what do we do?"

Melanie smiled. "Let's get you prepped for that deposition. I really want to nail that bastard. Gillespy. Now it's personal."

All prepped, they exchanged life stories, and waited.

"Do you think he's coming back?" Melanie asked.

"Oh yeah, he wouldn't leave his precious dog."

Light no longer filtered in from the window. Melanie yawned.

"Stop that." Leonard stifled his own yawn. "Why don't you get some sleep? I'll take watch for a couple of hours. If I hear anything I'll wake you."

"Are you sure?"

"I don't think I could sleep anyway."

"I don't think I'll be able to either," Melanie said.

Within five minutes Leonard listened to her soft snoring.

Sixteen

Friday 1:30 p.m.

Louise was in a relatively decent mood until Handley called her person-to-person over the radio. A couple of speeding citations were issued, but otherwise it had been a nice day of cruising through the neighborhood.

"I heard you were at the scene." His voice came over crisp and clear.

"I was there," Louise answered.

"Any clues we can follow up on?"

Louise spit out a sarcastic chuckle. "Brass has their head so far stuck up their ass on this one. They're having the detectives handle it like it's a racial thing."

"You don't think so, huh?"

"Every bone in my body tells me it's not."

Louise braked at a four-way stop. To her left, a Chevy Nova rolled past the sign, saw her, slammed on its brakes, backed up, and stopped again. Louise drove in front of the vehicle and shook her finger at the driver, but let him go without a stop.

"Did you mention it to the Captain?"

"Been that route before," Louise answered. "I find it works out best when I stay out of his hair and he pretends I don't exist."

"Want me to talk to him?"

"You just worry about your retirement. They'll eventually come around. One of the Dick's is actually kind of smart."

"I just want that son of a bitch caught before I leave."

"We'll get him." Louise's face went blank as she clamped down on her anger.

"What did he look like?" Handley asked.

It took a couple of seconds for the question to register. "Huh?"

"I hear you saw Lone Bear at the morgue. How did he look?"

"He looked dead."

Louise cut off the communication and stomped on the gas. Tires squealed around the corner, before wiping away a tear. She let the wind wash the irritation off of her face as she tried to regain her composure. "What a stupid question." She smashed her palm on the steering wheel.

The dispatcher's voice came over her radio announcing that she had received a phone call from an anonymous male. "He said it was personal." Dispatch recited the number. Louise pulled over, dug her cell phone out of her purse and called the number. A young man answered.

"This is Officer Miller returning your call," she said.

"Do you know who this is?" the voice answered.

"You want to play games or tell me who you are?" Irritation rang in her voice.

"You have no sense of humor."

"I'm hanging up now."

"Wait. It's Bill Johnson."

"Do you know how many Bill Johnsons I know?" She smiled, remembering the boy.

"Do you know how much I give a shit?" Bill Johnson said.

"Hey, Injun Bill, how the hell are you?" She sounded genuinely pleased to hear him. "Pretty ballsy over the phone. Wanna show me some of that attitude face-to-face?"

"Bring it on, copper."

"Okay, punk, enough of the social niceties. Why are you wasting my time?"

"I'm hungry. Buy me some lunch and we'll talk. I think it might be important."

"Like what's so important?" Louise asked.

"I don't want to say over the phone. It has to be in person."

Louise smiled. The little bum could be a pretty smooth operator when he wanted. "You're on. But it better be worth it or you're buying. Where do you want to meet?"

"Do you know Franklin's, on Franklin Avenue?"

Louise knew of it. A dive down by the river where the dregs of the Indian population hung out and ate cheap scrambled eggs and bacon until the liquor stores opened. She wondered why the hell he'd want to meet there but decided not to ask.

"I'll see ya there in a half-hour," she said and disconnected the line. Louise pulled away from the curb. Before she'd gone a block, her cell phone rang. Flustered because she forgot to turn it off, Louise pulled her car back to the curb and answered.

"Are you nuts?" Bill Johnson's voice cut in before she said a word. "Why don't you just treat me to a dig through garbage cans? I just asked if you knew where it was. I didn't say I wanted to meet you there."

Louise chuckled. "How'd you get this number?"

"Caller ID."

His tone made it sound like she just asked the stupidest question in the world. Her number was blocked; he shouldn't have been able to get it. Then she realized she was holding one of Karla's extras. How it got in her purse, she'd have to ask. Great, so now the little punk had her partner's phone number. She'd try to remember to tell Karla it might be a good idea to get a new number.

"Then why did you bring up Franklin's if you didn't want to meet there?"

"Two blocks down there's a new place called Rupert's where they're doing that urban renewal crap. It's a white man's place. I'd like to see if your food tastes any better than ours."

"I don't know, kid. You might develop a taste for it and begin a life of crime just so you can afford it."

"It's a risk I'm willing to take," he said.

"All right, then. See you there in a half."

The sun disappeared behind a puff of clouds. Louise closed her eyes and let a cool breeze wash in through the window. She let her car idle at the curb for a couple of minutes, half expecting Karla's phone to ring again. Then she remembered that Karla had asked her to hold onto the phone last time they went out to dinner so Karla wouldn't have to bring her purse. When nothing came over the airwaves she took a deep breath of late summer air and pulled back into traffic. "At least I'm not losing my mind."

Bill sat on the smoking bench a good forty-five feet away from the front door at Rupert's when Louise pulled into the parking lot. Hard to miss her car, he jumped up and met her out in the parking lot.

"Next time, just say Rupert's. When someone asks if one knows where a place is, that usually means that's where they want to meet," Louise said.

"It's brand new. I didn't think you'd know where it was."

"I'm a cop. Give me a little credit."

Actually, Louise had no idea where some new place called Rupert's had been located and had to call in and ask. But she'd die before ever releasing that information to a sixteen-year-old.

A cold blast met them at the door. Louise took pleasure in the cool air, as did the boy. They walked to the maitre d' and Louise asked for a table for two.

"Do you have a reservation?" he asked.

Only a few tables were in use. She faced the maitre d', a forty-something year old man in the nicely pressed suit with the slicked back salt and pepper hair.

"Do we need one?"

"We usually ask that you do." The man looked up and into the mostly empty restaurant. "Tell me officer, are you doing some neighborhood outreach sort of program?" he asked, eyeing the kid.

The coolness on the outside simmered the blood that began to boil on the inside of Louise. "Something like that." The chill in her voice matched the air conditioning. The boy's face showed no emotion. He'd make a hell of a poker player, she thought.

"I'll see what we can do."

The maitre d' motioned for the hostess, whispered something in her ear, and handed her two menus. Louise and Bill Johnson followed the woman in black slacks, black vest, and white shirt to a corner table by the kitchen.

"Your waitress will be Sarah. She'll be with you in just a moment," she said sweetly.

The wood paneled walls and tables with thick plush tablecloths made Louise uncomfortable. She much preferred a more relaxed place where she could get a burger and a plate of hash browns without worrying about what other people might say when she drowned them both with ketchup.

She opened the menu and almost choked. Prime rib—$34.95. A twelve-ounce sirloin steak cost over $20. She did a mental calculation and figured date night with Karla might have to be cut back to Burger King and whatever was playing at the $2.00 theater. *God help the kid if he orders lobster.*

"Hello, my name's Sarah. Can I get you something to drink?"

The waitress wore a black dress, cut just above the knee, and black stockings. On her chest she wore a button with "Sarah" printed on it, just in case they forgot her name.

"I'll have a Heineken," Bill said.

"He'll have a Coke," Louise interrupted. "Make mine a diet."

As the waitress left, Louise laid the menu on the table. She could get a cheeseburger, with her choice of cheese, for just under $10.00.

"Okay, talk to me," Louise said.

The boy glanced warily around the restaurant. Louise did the same. The occupied tables were all white couples, all neatly dressed.

"I think it's safe here, Tonto," Louise said.

Bill Johnson smiled as the waitress set down their beverages.

"Have you decided what you'd like to order?" Sarah asked.

Louise held her breath.

"I'll have the clubhouse," Bill said.

Louise let out a sigh of relief and ordered her burger with pepper jack cheese.

"So, what's so important you have to bust my wallet?" Louise asked.

"It's about Mark Lone Bear."

"No shit, Sherlock. I would've never guessed."

The boy ignored her sarcasm. "I heard some stuff."

"Like what kind of stuff?"

"Like that he might have been supplementing his income by doing a little dealing on the side. That he might've been tipping people off that a bust was on the way. Stuff like that."

"That's bullshit!" Louise pounded her fist on the table. "Who told you that?"

The background noise that had been unnoticeable before became very apparent now that it had stopped. All of the eyes in the dining room were aimed at Louise as the maitre d' came rushing over.

"Is everything all right?" he asked.

Louise smiled. "Just a little community outreach."

After he left, Louise said to the boy, "I want to know where you heard this." Her voice edged just above a whisper, harsh and thin.

Bill Johnson shrugged. "I just heard it around. I don't know."

"It's very easy to spread crap like that around when a man is not around anymore to defend himself."

"I can't say whether it's true or it ain't, I'm just telling you what I heard."

"I want to know from who!"

"Can't say."

"Can't, or won't?"

Sarah brought over a basket of bread and two small cups of whipped butter. "Your food should be here in just a couple of minutes."

"Thank you," Louise said, her eyes glued to the boy.

Bill reached for the bread. "Ooh, still warm."

Louise ignored the comment. "I want to know who."

"I can't say." He tried to sound brave but his voice cracked.

"Then you're buying lunch. This is all bullshit, and I don't pay for bullshit."

"I don't have that kind of money."

"Then you can do dishes, or if they want to press charges, there's a cop right here."

"You're bluffing," he said. "You'd look like a bigger asshole than me."

Louise smiled and finally broke off her stare. "Yeah, you're right. But I'm still willing to be a big enough asshole to tell them to box our lunches, then take both of them home. You'll never know the fine dining of the white man."

Now Bill smiled for a moment, and then became deadly serious. Again he looked with suspicion around the restaurant. "Freddy Thunder Cloud," he whispered.

"Why should I believe any of the shit that flows out of that waste of human flesh?"

"He mentioned some guy he did business with. Called him a huge white guy, described him exactly like the guy that I saw driving Mark's car."

Sarah the waitress carried a tray and laid the sandwich in front of Bill and a burger oozing with melted pepper jack cheese in front of Louise. Bill tore into his clubhouse. Louise stared down at her plate, unable to eat.

"Sorry, kid. After lunch I'm afraid I'm going to have to take you in to look at some pictures."

Bill choked on his food. "I told you, I'd never be able to pick him out. I don't even remember what he looks like anymore."

"You just told me you did. When I find Freddy Thunder Cloud, he's going to be looking at pictures too."

Bill looked pleadingly at Louise as the appetite drained from his face too.

Seventeen

Friday 5:00 p.m.

Andrew excused himself from the table and slid his chair back. He thought he would've been safe with an egg salad sandwich, but his stomach disagreed. The pains were getting gradually worse. If he didn't start feeling better by Monday, he'd call a holistic doctor who had an office in Edina.

"You all right, New Age?" Reggie Davis asked.

"He doesn't like to be called New Age," Campbell chided.

"Since when?"

"Since Sarge here told me not to call him that no more."

"We always called him New Age," Davis said to Carlin. "What's wrong with that?"

"Oh, I don't know. What if I started calling you Eight Ball?" Carlin reached across the table and rubbed Reggie's shaved brown dome.

"You're my Sergeant. You can call me whatever the hell you want."

"Should call you Magic Eight Ball," Campbell said. "You think you fucking know everything."

"My balls have more knowledge than you'll ever know in that pea you call a brain."

"Yeah, I'm fine," Andrew said under the fits of laughter of the three men. He made his way to the restroom while popping a couple more antacids. The laughing and banter grew from his table. It gnawed at him that this wasn't the first time things seemed to liven up once he left.

Inside the men's room Andrew walked into the only stall and did an about-face. This restaurant didn't have enough disinfectant for Andrew to sit on that seat. He tried to recall gas station restrooms on the interstate that might be worse. None came to mind. He took two more antacids and stared gloomily at his reflection in the mirror above the sink.

"You need to lighten up, Miller. Fit in. Be one of the guys," his image told him.

"Maybe," he answered. "I think I'm doing okay. The new guy is always the outcast for a while."

Andrew closed his eyes and controlled his breathing until the air became a fine stream flowing in and out of his nostrils. The pain in his gut subsided and he splashed cold water on his face and looked back in the mirror. "You're doing just fine," he said as a confirmation before exiting to rejoin his pack.

Now what? Had this been junior high, Andrew would've thought he'd been a victim in the game of Ditch. The table was empty. Even the plates had already been cleared. He stalked over to the door and saw his partner outside, sitting behind the wheel of their cruiser working on a crossword puzzle.

"Thought you might've fallen in." Carlin folded the newspaper.

Andrew got into the car and rolled down the window. *Lighten up*, the voice told him. "Couldn't even get close enough. You wouldn't believe it. Shit and vomit on the rim, I don't even want to guess what else."

Rivers stared at him like he was a stranger, did a quick shrug of the shoulder and started the car. "We got a call from dispatch. Need to go to Kenowa State Bank. Some kid tried to use an ATM card that the Minneapolis cops flagged. When they tried to stop him, the kid took off. The card belongs to some missing doctor."

"Hoots or Houts or something like that?" Andrew asked. "Louise mentioned that a doctor went missing the same time as Lone Bear."

"Really." Carlin's eyebrows shot up. "Think there's any connection?"

"Anything's possible."

The sun had begun its descent as the shadows lengthened across the brownstone building of Kenowa State Bank. With the exception of the ATM built into the wall next to the door, the city council had taken great care to keep a small town feel on the outside.

Brian Gladstone, the bank manager met them at the door. The man, probably in his mid-fifties, stood no taller than Andrew's chin. He wore gold wire rimmed glasses, and had a tuft of brown hair above his forehead. It was a thinning band of gray from ear to ear around the back of his head. He wore a white shirt, brown tie, and despite the eighty plus degrees outside, and minimal air conditioning inside, he had on a brown wool suit coat. To Andrew the man looked like a stereotypical bank manager.

He introduced them to the security guard, Alvin Pervis. Pervis was a bit stockier than Gladstone and maybe ten years older, but his full head of hair was dyed black. For an old man he had a very strong grip as he shook Andrew's hand.

"Any relation to Melvin Purvis?" Carlin asked.

Gladstone looked at him questioningly.

"Famous FBI guy back in the forties," Andrew whispered to him. "Gunned down Dillinger."

"Nope," the guard said. "We spell ours with a P.E., he spelled his P.U."

Pervis laughed, Carlin chuckled, Andrew smiled, and Gladstone looked perplexed.

"Well, yes," the manager said. "Shall we adjourn to my office?"

The three men followed the manager across the bank floor into a small office. Once inside, Gladstone closed the door. The room grew stuffy.

He explained about the boy trying to use the ATM. "When he saw Mr. Pervis appear at the door, he ran."

"Wish I could've gone after him. Back in my day I would've

caught him." Pervis' voice sounded older and more forlorn then when they first met minutes ago.

"Here's the card." Gladstone handed Andrew the ATM card with Leonard Hout's name on it.

Andrew showed it to his sergeant, and they shared a barely perceptible nod.

"We got this picture from the ATM camera." Gladstone handed the photo to Carlin. "Maybe you can make copies and distribute them around."

Andrew waited for Carlin to explain to the manager not to tell him how to do his job, but his FTO only smiled. "We'll be sure to do that."

Back in the car, Carlin tore out of the parking lot.

"Where are we going?" Andrew asked.

"I know this kid. Jacob Dagin. He's just a petty vandal. Smokes a little pot, breaks curfew, and drinks in the park at night. I thought he was too smart to get into this shit."

"Maybe his marijuana habit was getting a little expensive?"

"Maybe," Carlin said.

"Maybe we should just beat the crap out him."

Carlin couldn't help but laugh. "You're going to do all right, New Age."

"Oh yeah, how much do I owe you for lunch?"

"Forget it. You buy next time."

They drove to the outskirts of Kenowa. As the duo approached a small community of trailer homes they slowly cruised the single lane roads until pulling up to a double wide. Next to it sat a rusted out Plymouth up on blocks.

"Welcome to Trailer Trash Central," Carlin said. "This is one of the more elite homes."

Carlin had hardly switched off the ignition, when the door of the trailer home flew open. A woman, between thirty and fifty, charged down the rickety wooden steps. She wore a print dress, the hem of which hung to just below the knees. Black and blue marks covered most of her shins.

"What's he done this time?"

"We just want to talk to him, ma'am," Carlin said as he stepped from the vehicle.

"Well I want him arrested. Possession of marijuana is still a crime ain't it?"

"Yes ma'am."

"Then I'll show you where he hides it. You haul his ass off to jail. Maybe I can get a decent night's sleep for a change."

"Before we go in, may I get some information from you?" Andrew asked. His sergeant nodded at him. "We'd also like your permission to search his room."

"Of course. His pot is in one of his video game boxes. I can't remember which one, but I'll know it when I see it."

Andrew bit back a grin. He wondered if mom might not be dipping into Jacob's stash when he wasn't around.

Inside the home, computer game explosions resonated in the trailer. Other than a few dishes in the sink, Andrew was impressed at the cleanliness.

They walked down a narrow hall; the gunshots and explosions grew louder.

"Jacob, I've got something for you," the mother shouted over the noise.

"What?" came a voice, feigning interest.

She opened the boy's bedroom door. Deputies entered a room littered with dirty clothes on the floor and posters of Brittany Spears sharing a lip lock with Madonna, and another poster of Mandy Moore taped to the wall.

A fifteen-year-old boy sat at his desk, his eyes taking in the explosions on the computer screen. He glanced at the direction of his mother. His jaw dropped when he saw the two deputies standing at her side. The explosions died away as the joystick dropped from his hand.

"It's in that one. Grand Theft Auto!" the mother shouted as she pointed at her son's desk.

"You're gonna narc me out?" He jumped to his feet. "You fucking bitch!"

"Don't you use that tone with me!" She threw her arms in the air. "See what I have to put up with?"

Andrew wandered over to the desk and picked up the copy Grand Theft Auto to the sound of the kid's hysterics.

"You can't do that!" Jacob screamed. "You got a warrant?"

Andrew looked at the boy square in the eye and popped open the box. "Nope."

A small baggie with a few grams of marijuana and three rolled joints fell to the floor.

"That's inadmissible!" Jacob hollered. "You need a fucking warrant!"

"You have the right to remain silent," Rivers said. "And that would be a really good idea."

"Fuck you!"

"You have the right to an attorney," Rivers continued with the Miranda recitation, ending with, "Do you understand these rights?"

"Fuck you. You need a warrant." The kid's voice had lost a little of its edge.

While the sergeant reread the kid his rights, Andrew put on the rubber gloves and placed the marijuana and the video game each in their own evidence bag.

"You can't take that." Jacob's voice shook as tears rolled down his cheeks.

"Aren't you getting tired of being wrong all the time?" Rivers asked. "Now do you understand your rights?"

Jacob slumped on his bed, defeated. "Yes," he finally said.

"Haul his ass to jail," his mother yelled as she walked over and stood above him.

"You fucking whore," Jacob shouted with renewed energy.

"You stupid little punk!" she screamed back and slapped him across the face. He yowled.

"You were witnesses! I want her arrested for assault!"

Carlin already had the woman by the arm, pulling her away from her son. "Why don't I take you into the other room? Deputy Miller, why don't you explain the other reason why we're here?"

Alone with the boy, Andrew sat next to him on the bed. Jacob dried his eyes with his sleeve. "Pretty rough around here, huh?" Andrew asked.

"What do you know about it?"

"How old are you?"

Jacob stared down at his shoes. "Fifteen. Four more months I'll be sixteen, then I'm getting the hell out of here."

"You might not have to wait. Juvenile Court is pretty good about helping kids your age. They might be able to find a nice family or group home for you to stay with."

Jacob let out a disparaging laugh. "I've been through juvi. They don't know shit. They'll probably just give me more community service and tell me I have to do whatever my mom says."

"Sometimes they get things right," Andrew said with a smile. "Who knows?"

"What are you, the good cop?"

"Always." Andrew pulled out the photo of Jacob and laid it on his bed. "Do you know where I got this?"

Jacob glanced at it. "Pretty shitty quality."

"We got it from the ATM machine at the Kenowa State Bank."

Jacob shuddered and fell back on his bed, staring up at the ceiling. Tears rolled down the side of his face, into his hair.

"Wanna tell me where you got this?" Andrew held up the card.

Jacob remained silent.

"Do you know Leonard Hout?"

Again, Jacob said nothing.

"Maybe it's time you get a lawyer." Andrew's voice held the same amount of patience and concern.

"Fuck lawyers." Jacob sat up and gave him an appraising look. "They don't give a shit about me. They just agree with whatever the judge wants."

"You don't want a lawyer? You willing to talk to me about this?"

"How much more trouble am I in?"

"Keep being honest and you won't be in any more trouble."

Jacob let out long sigh. "Who would've figured the first guy to actually treat me like an adult would be a fucking cop? Yeah, I'll talk to you."

"Smart man. Now where did you get it?"

"Some guy sold it to me."

"Who?"

"I dunno."

"Not good enough. Talk to me," Andrew's patience slipped just a little bit.

"What if I told you I was doing something illegal, would I be in more trouble?"

Andrew was really beginning to like this kid. "Did you kill anybody?"

Jacob smiled. "No."

"Then you'll be fine."

Jacob let out another long sigh. "Last night I was in the park smoking a blunt. And I'm trusting you here, I just sold a bag to a guy—and no, I'm not going to tell you who he was—when this other guy came up to me. Scared the shit out of me. He was huge, and even though it was dark, he had one of the meanest faces I ever saw. He asked if I wanted to make some instant cash. I was too scared to say no."

Andrew had his notepad out and was busily scribbling. "Did he threaten you?"

"Kinda, but not really. It was just the way he was looking at me. Crazy-like. Ya know?"

Andrew stopped taking notes and observed the boy.

"He pulls out this card and said the owner just died and wouldn't need it anymore. He said that for one hundred bucks I could pull out eight hundred dollars a day until they cancelled it. He gave me the PIN number. I asked why he didn't use it himself.

He got all pissed off and said that he was trying to do me a favor. I was afraid he might kill me if I didn't say yes. Honest."

"Did he threaten you then?"

"Just the way he looked at me. He didn't need to say nothing."

"What did he look like?" Andrew asked, trying to keep his voice under control.

"Like I said, huge, eight feet tall and built like a lineman."

"Eight feet?" Andrew asked.

"Well, maybe not eight feet, but damn, he was big."

"What else?"

"I dunno. A white guy, short dark hair. His eyes were real beady looking. It looked like he might've had his nose broke a couple of times, you know what I mean?"

"What was he wearing?"

"I don't remember. Jeans, I think. That's all I know."

Andrew finished writing in his notebook and slipped it into his pocket. "Anything else?"

"Nope."

"Okay, here's the deal." Andrew sat next to him on the bed. "Your mom wants you arrested. I'm going to have to put the cuffs on you. It's policy, plus it will probably appease your mom. When we get to the station I'm going to have you look at some pictures; see if you recognize this guy. Right now you're doing great. If you keep on this way things are going to be looking pretty good for you. I'll even testify for you, okay?"

"For a cop, you're an all right guy."

"For a punk you're not so bad yourself," Andrew smiled down at the kid. "I'll give you my card. If you ever need to talk, give me a call. And quit smoking that shit. You're a smart kid. Smoking weed is just going to make you lazy and then you'll never get out of here."

Andrew did a quick pat search then loosely placed the cuffs on Jacob. They walked out of the room and down the hall. Carlin and Jacob's mother sat in the kitchen at a cheap Formica table drinking coffee. Her eyes were red as Carlin spoke quietly.

"Mrs. Dagin, you should accompany us down to the station," Carlin said.

"I can't take any more time off of work," she said. "He's old enough to stand on his own two feet."

"Let me put it this way," Carlin's voice took on an edge. "Mrs. Dagin, you *will* accompany us down to the station."

Eighteen

Friday 5:30 p.m.

The phone rang. Gillespy checked the caller ID. With a deep sigh he put down his glass of Bacardi. "What's the good news?" he answered.

"Dr. Gillespy? Gary Warren here. How are we doing today?"

"We?" Gillespy stared at the bat logo on the bottle. He'd always been partial to bats. At the age of thirteen he caught one in his backyard. He snuck it in his room, performed his first operation, and was able to keep the heart beating for three days. That had been the turning point in his life when he decided his calling was to become a doctor. It wouldn't be until college, and the discovery of Ivan Pavlov, that he switched allegiances from surgery to psychology, then psychiatry.

"*We're* just fine and dandy."

"Me too. I haven't heard from Cartier's office. Just to let you know I'm a man of my word. I made a motion earlier today to dismiss the case. We've got an appearance before Judge Harper two weeks from next Tuesday at ten. Can you make it?"

After paying his legal bills there wouldn't be any inheritance left. His kids would love that. The thought made him smile. Gillespy took a sip of rum. "How much more is this going to set me back?"

"Listen, Doctor, if you're having any misgivings about my representation you're always free to hire another lawyer."

"Why so long a wait?" Gillespy ignored the bait.

"Papers to file, waiting for a response, then I have to respond to their response. When the wheels of justice aren't ground to a halt they move very slowly."

Gillespy refilled his glass. "Do I have to be there?" The thought of having to drive all the way to downtown Minneapolis made his stomach churn. Plus, they still wanted him on that hit and run. What better place to pick him up?

Warren paused. "Well, you don't have to be there. It's only a motion. But I thought you might like to. I thought you might like to see that bitch Cartier squirm."

"I'll think about it. Anything else?" The sound of the Warren's voice made him nauseous. The shyster was probably charging him per minute.

"I think that's all for now," Warren said.

"Good-bye, then."

Gillespy wandered into the kitchen and opened the refrigerator door. A half carton of eggs had its own shelf. Celery leaves wilted and stalks rusted with spots sat next to an open tin of herring.

"Such decisions." He pulled out the eggs, cracked three in a bowl and stirred. "What the hell do they want from me? I'm a great doctor and a good father, damn it! They think they can waltz right in and take advantage of me! How dare they suspend my license?"

His breathing grew harsh and raspy, and when he looked down he saw that egg had splashed over the counter and onto his sleeve. His heart pounded his chest. Dizzy, he dropped the fork and grabbed the counter to keep from falling. The doctor closed his eyes and waited for the nausea to subside.

When he recovered he pulled a small pan out of the cabinet, placed it on the stove and set the burner on high. He poured in the eggs then grabbed the open tin of herring and dumped that in too. The sizzling sound and smoke comforted him.

Scrambling the eggs until they were hard and dry, and chopping the herring into bite sized bits, he dumped the end result on a plate, doused it all with Tabasco sauce and ate while standing at the counter.

Sated, he took the dish and pan to the sink and dropped them on top of the others. He noticed at the mess on the counter and floor. He used to be such a neat man; an everything in its proper place man. He tried to remember when he quit caring, and concluded it didn't matter. The cleaning woman he hired would be in on Tuesday.

In the bathroom he stripped and admired his body in the mirror. He'd lost some weight. Washboard abs, he thought as he stared at his protruding ribs.

With the shower on, Gillespy waited until the room filled with steam before stepping in. The water burned, scalding his skin to a beet red. He made the shower a bit hotter, feeling the heat burn into his soul. He had scrubbed himself as if washing off the filth of the world. He turned his face up to the shower and let the water seep into the pores while he reminisced about his early days. They'd considered him an up and comer. He considered himself a savior of abused youth. He took great pride in breaking them down then rebuilding them up the right way.

"Did any of you ever thank me? No!" *The ingrates.*

Gillespy dabbed himself dry and dressed in fresh clothes, leaving yesterday's attire on the bathroom floor. He walked into his den and poured himself another shot from the liquor bottle of the day.

He found that since the kids had grown, his wife left him, and his practice had been stolen away, he missed human contact. His friends had long ago deserted him with his wife. He could call back the shyster, just to hear another human voice. No, that would be like hiring a prostitute and just as dirty.

Gillespy sat behind his desk and noticed the broken needle and syringe still lying next to the phone. He downed the rum, letting it burn his insides like the shower had done on the outside. Pulling out a piece of paper he wrote. *Codicil number 5.*

Nineteen

Friday 6:30 p.m.

Louise pulled into Lacey's parking lot ready for a brawl. She had a lot to say to Freddy Thunder Cloud, much of it possibly with her baton. The piece of slime wasn't worth bruising her knuckles. She got out of her car and squinted up into the sun. There wouldn't be many more of these kinds of days. Soon the leaves would change and the air would turn cooler.

Inside the bar she cursed herself for looking up at the sky. It would take that much longer for her eyes to adjust to the darkness of the room. More time for the dregs to hide their illegal activities.

Louise strutted up to the bar with a commanding swagger. "I'm looking for Freddy Thunder Cloud. You seen him?" she demanded of the bartender. He was the same guy she'd spoken with the other day.

The man scanned the room. "He's not here."

Louise's eyes slowly adjusted and she confirmed the barkeep's statement. "Has he been here?"

"Not since yesterday."

She cursed under her breath. "What time does he usually show up?"

The bartender shrugged. "It's not like he comes in every day."

Louise did another scan of the room. "Do you know where he might be?"

The man did a slight shake of the head and moved down

the bar to wait on a customer. After the person had been served, Louise expected the bartender to return. He didn't. Instead he pulled out a dirty towel and wiped glasses.

"Hey, you got a minute?" Louise called down.

"I'm busy." He said it with no irritation in his voice, just as a matter of fact.

"Think you'll be a little busier after the health inspector gives you a list of chores so you can keep this stink hole open?"

"That threat is wearing a little thin, officer. Every time a cop comes in here, it's the same thing, 'I'm going to call the Health Inspector.'" He didn't bother to look up as he continued drying the glassware.

"You're right. It *is* getting old. I think it's time I followed up. I'm pretty sure I can get him here by tomorrow."

The bartender sighed as he put the towel down and slowly walked back. "I don't know where he is. I don't know where you might find him."

Louise took out a card and slammed it on the bar. "Next time he drags his sorry ass in here, tell him to call me. If I have to find him before he finds me, tell him he's going to be spending the next seventy-two hours in detox before we have our little chat."

The man slid the card off the bar and into his pocket as Louise grabbed her sunglasses from her pocket.

"Should I be expecting the health inspector tomorrow?" he asked.

Louise put on her shades and became almost blind. She could make out the exit sign above the door and not much else. "Don't know. I guess it depends on whether or not good old Fred gets a hold of me before the end of the day." She took off her glasses for dramatic effect as she looked the man in the eye. She also wanted to make sure that no chairs or stools blocked her path to the door. *Nothing commands respect like tripping over a chair and landing flat on my face.*

Back out in the heat, Louise connected her cell phone to the Internet and did a search for Freddy Thunder Cloud's address.

She didn't want to go through proper channels. Not surprised, there was no listing under that name. Next she tried Mark Lone Bear and got a hit. Not only did his address pop up, but he lived in south Minneapolis, only couple of miles away.

On a lark, Louise called Karla and got her answering machine. "How would you like to come over tomorrow night and play cop and perp? Call me." She smiled as she put the phone back in her pocket.

Two cars ahead, a silver Ford Escort sped up to make a left turn through a yellow light. The oncoming car slammed on its brakes, narrowly avoiding a collision. Louise flipped on her flashers, edging around traffic and going through a red. The driver who had been cut off gave Louise the thumb's up as she passed.

She pulled up to the Ford's bumper, tailgating, and waited for him to look in his rear view mirror at the flashing lights. He kept driving; Louise began to get a sour taste in her mouth. She hit the siren, and then shut it off.

The Escort finally pulled to the curb. Louise punched the license plate number in the computer. Donald Rashy. No warrants and a valid DL. She got out of her car. The driver's door to the Escort swung open. She gripped the handle of her gun. "Stay in the car, sir."

She took a step closer. "Put your hands on the steering wheel."

The driver obeyed and she released her hold on the weapon.

"Driver's license and proof of insurance," Louise ordered.

The boy reached into his back pocket. Fear had already lined his face. "My dad is going to kill me."

The pricklies faded away as the kid pulled a folded yellow paper out of his wallet. He hadn't even gotten the plastic mailed to him yet.

"Do you know why I pulled you over?" She unfolded the paper. Paul Rashy had just passed his driver's test three days ago, the day after his sixteenth birthday.

"I didn't go through that red light. It was yellow when I entered the intersection."

"They still teach failure to yield the right of way in driver's ed, don't they? If that driver was as careless as you, you wouldn't have to be worried about your dad killing you. That would've already been taken care of."

She observed his face to see if anything that she had said might register. He looked too scared to comprehend much. "Not a good way to start a driving career," she said.

"My dad's going to kill me."

"Does he know you're driving his car?" Louise asked.

"I went to the store for my mom."

Louise noticed the grocery bag sitting on the passenger seat. "What about proof of insurance?"

"It's under my dad's name."

"Show me," Louise said.

Paul was clueless.

"You might wanna check the glove compartment."

The kid popped the door and rummaged through the maps and owner's manual. "What am I looking for?"

Louise smiled. "Never mind. I highly doubt your father would let you drive an uninsured car."

"He's going to kill me."

Louise sighed. "Wait here, I'll be right back." She took his paper back to her squad. Once inside the car Louise tried calling Karla again.

"Are you going to be a good cop or a bad cop?" Karla asked without saying hello.

"I'll be bad, very bad," Louise chuckled.

"So, what about dinner tonight?" Karla asked.

"I got something I need to do. I'll call you when I get home."

"Need some alone time, huh?"

"Maybe. I don't know. Let me call you."

"What's going on in that cute head of yours?"

"Probably trouble," Louise said. "Hell, why don't you come over tonight if you want. If I don't get arrested I'll tell you all about it."

A note of alarm registered in Karla's voice. "You're not going to do something stupid, are you?"

"Oh yeah."

"What are you planning?" Karla asked, her voice trembling.

"Listen, I gotta run. I've got a kid sitting in his car, probably shitting his pants, waiting for me to give him a ticket. Love you." Louise disconnected the call. She strolled back to Paul Rashy and leaned into the window. She could've sworn he had turned a shade whiter. His hands shook as he grasped the steering wheel.

"It's your lucky day, Paul. I'm commuting your death sentence to a warning."

Relief washed over his face. "Thank you so much."

"Don't let me down. If I ever pull you over again, no more warnings."

"You won't! I promise."

Louise got back into her car feeling good about herself. Andrew would call it good karma. She got on the computer and googled Mark Lone Bear's phone number. His address popped up on the screen. A pang of guilt stabbed at Louise. Not for doing what she was about to do, but for not knowing his address in the first place. They were pretty good buds once. She could have invited him over for dinner; they could have hung out occasionally. Hell, they didn't live all that far from each other. But once they drifted apart, Louise never followed up on her good intentions. She defended herself thinking that neither had he.

Louise pulled up to the south Minneapolis home. Not far from the Little Earth projects where a good chunk of the Native American population in the city lived, Mark's two-story stucco house stood vacant, unassuming, and hiding whatever secrets Mark Lone Bear might have had.

On the front steps, Louise shot a quick glance at the neighboring houses before revealing her lock picking kit. Before breaking and entering she noticed the doormat at her feet. Just maybe... If she got caught it would sound like a much more plausible lie than saying he had previously given her permission if anything ever happened to him. See, he even told her where he hid the key. She picked up the mat and found nothing.

"A person would have to be a moron to hide a key under the mat in this neighborhood."

Louise jumped and quickly slid the kit down her shirt, under the vest where a bulge wouldn't be seen. A Caucasian woman in her mid sixties waddled across the lawn from next door, a bundle of mail in her hands. She wore ankle socks under soft slippers that had no backs. In spite of the fact that the flower print dress hung down to her shins, Louise could tell that the woman had trouble with varicose veins. Even before the woman reached to bottom step, Louise smelled the stale tobacco. It made her want a cigarette.

"It's about time you showed up."

"Excuse me?" Louise said.

"I've been collecting his mail. Didn't know where to forward it."

"Thank you." Louise relieved the woman of the letters.

"He was a good boy. Quiet, never caused problems. Him being a cop and all, he helped keep the riff-raff out. Kept to himself pretty much, though."

Louise thought that sounded like a profile of a serial killer. "So I don't suppose you knew him very well?" Louise asked.

"Better than anyone else around here." The woman beamed, but with a sadness behind her smile. "We was good friends. He even asked me to feed his cat once when he went to visit his family. Paid me fifty bucks just to stop over a few times during the week to make sure the cat had food. I didn't even have to clean the litter box."

"Mark has a cat?" Louise asked.

"He used to. Poor critter died of that leukemia cats get. Didn't get another. Said he didn't want to go through the pain of losing another animal."

That sounded like Lone Bear. He held animals in a much higher regard than humans. *Another trait we had in common.*

"I don't suppose you still have the key?" Louise asked.

"I do. I keep it in my silverware drawer so I won't lose it. I tried to give it back to him, but he told me to keep it, that it was an extra. Said he'd probably have to leave again to see his folks and that he might have to ask me to feed Teddy again. Teddy. That was the name of his cat."

Louise wished that her collars were all this forthcoming. "I don't suppose you could get me that key?"

The woman's gray bangs hung into her eyes as she crinkled her forehead. Louise could hear the rusty wheels turning inside the old lady's head. Figuring she could have had free access to whatever he possessed, but that the thought just occurred to her now.

"As a taxpayer you'll be saving yourself some money," Louise said. "I'll have to call a locksmith. I'll be wasting my time too. I'll have to sit here and wait for him instead of being out there catching criminals."

The woman seemed to agree. "I'll be right back."

Louise watched the woman waddle back to her house. She couldn't have been taller than five foot three standing on her tiptoes; Louise guessed her weight between 210 and 220, most of it in her rear end. Louise felt self-conscious. She noticed her own gluteus maximus expanding more and more. Even though Karla told her she had a sexy butt—just like the song, Karla had a thing for big butts—Louise knew it only meant up to a certain point. "I'm going on a diet tomorrow," she said to herself.

A car cruised by slowly then turned right at the corner. Louise tried to get a license plate number but the shade thrown by the boulevard trees made it too difficult to read. She let the sun and breeze wash over her fantasizing about that being the killer and she giving chase, catching him single-handed then rubbing it in the face of the brass.

"Here you go."

Louise opened her eyes to a key dangling off of a Minnesota Twins keychain.

"Thank you." Louise reached for the keys. Mark had never

given her a clue that he might have been baseball fan, let alone any other sport. "Say, you haven't seen anybody suspicious hanging around, have you?"

The woman squinted, trying to recall. Louise knew this lady wanted to help, and would like nothing more than to suck up publicity by helping to catch a cop killer. *Hell, if she does, more power to her.*

"No," she finally said. "I don't think so. There were some neighborhood boys snooping around. But I shooed them away."

"This would've been a big guy. White."

The woman concentrated harder. "No, nobody like that."

Louise took the key out of the woman's hand. "Well, thank you for your help, ma'am."

"I've been keeping an eye on the news. They said there ain't no leads to the killer."

"Don't believe everything you hear on the news. Some things we just can't make public yet. We'll catch him. There's not a cop around who will rest until this guy is either dead or behind bars." The word dead seemed to startle the woman and Louise thought she might've gone too far. "Would you tell me your name, ma'am?"

The woman jerked, a little frightened and suspicious now. Publicity would be great as long as the killer didn't know her name. "I don't know about that," she said a little uneasily. "Why do you want to know?"

Louise thought fast. "I'd like to submit your name to my Captain for a Good Samaritan Award. You took in Officer Lone Bear's mail; you kept people away from his house. You know, there are a lot of normally good people who would've said, what the heck, I've got his keys I might as well go see what he's got. You didn't. Just for that alone you should be commended."

Louise couldn't tell if the woman smiled because her thoughts had been read, or if she were genuinely pleased. She knew Karla would give her the benefit of a doubt. Karla was the optimist of thc two. They offset each other well.

"It's Gladys. Gladys Vincenetti."

Louise wrote the name in her note pad and shoved it in her pocket. “Well, thank you for your help, Ms. Vincenetti.”

“Well, if there’s nothing else—”

“Nothing.” Louise cut her off, hoping the woman would take the hint.

“Okay then. It was nice meeting you, officer.”

“You too, Ms. Vincenetti.”

Gladys walked away; Louise slotted the key in the door. She’d been in public view way too long. Confident that anyone who saw her would think nothing suspicious, still, all it would take is one phone call to her Sergeant and she’d be looking for another job.

“Oh.” Gladys turned back around. “If you’d like to come over after you’re done, I can tell you what I know about Mark.”

Louise still liked the woman, but that would end quickly if Vincenetti didn’t go away now. “Thank you. I will want to talk to you but it will have to be some other time. I’ll contact you.” Louise slipped through the door before Mark’s neighbor could dredge up any more conversation, and quickly shut it behind her.

The shades were drawn, the house dim and dusky and smelling dank with a faint trace of cat urine that would never go away. “Not going to be a strong selling point, Mark,” Louise muttered.

Greeted with silence, Louise thought the hell with it and flipped on a lamp. She stood in the living room. A couch sat in front of a TV set. A wooden TV tray with rickety legs stood on each side of the sofa. The pillow on one end of the couch, the cushion closest to the television set, had an indentation the size of his rear end permanently set. In front of that pillow was a third TV tray. The room could use a dusting, but otherwise appeared quite neat.

Above the fireplace was a print of an Indian warrior riding his horse through the forest. On the mantel were three black and white photos taken at a powwow. One of the boys, dancing in a circle and wearing full Indian regalia, looked like a very young Mark Lone Bear. On the wall above the couch, Louise studied a print of an Indian maiden sitting in the woods next to a fire.

Three wolves were curled around her. Was that supposed to represent Mother Earth?

Louise thumbed through the mail and sorted the bills from the junk. There were no personal letters; nothing marked, from the killer. She plopped the mail on the couch putting the bills on top just like she did at home. She used to throw out the junk but Karla enjoyed going through all the crap a police officer gets. She especially liked the weapons catalogues, which made Louise wonder which of them might be crazier.

In the kitchen, the coffeemaker still had half a pot of coffee, now covered with mold. An empty cup sat in the sink.

"Well, I might as well do what I came here to do," she told Mark's spirit. "If you are involved in drugs, God help you." She laughed at her own joke. *Being that you're already with Him, I mean.*

She methodically searched every cabinet. Starting with the one under the sink, Louise checked the cleansers and other boxes for false bottoms. In the cupboard with food she found mouse turds. Either he didn't know that he had a rodent problem, or didn't care. "They eat through your wiring, ya know," she muttered, then answered herself in a ghostly voice. "I don't care anymore." A quick look at all of the undisturbed grease under the stove hood, she instantly concluded he didn't hide anything there.

Moving down the hall and into the bathroom she continued the search. She checked the drain in the shower to see if he might have tied anything to the stopper. Only strands of black hair were attached, tied to nothing.

In the bedroom, Louise saw herself very much like an intruder. Now it felt too personal. Mark slept on a twin bed. "Drug dealers don't make their beds every morning," Louise said. She admired the colorful bedspread and wished he were around so she could ask him about the symbols decorating it. "Back to business."

She scoffed at the sight of a weight bench and bar bells that occupied a large corner of the bedroom. "What a turn-off. Didn't get a lot of women, did ya, Mark?" and again she answered for him. "More women than you."

Louise walked over to his dresser and rummaged through the drawers. "I've always figured you for boxers."

She lifted his briefs and on the bottom of the stack laid a passbook. Cautiously looking around the room, Louise chastised herself for being paranoid. "Miller, you're losing it." She took out a pair of rubber gloves and pulled them on with a snap. Definitely didn't want to leave her prints on any evidence. "Why didn't I do this when I first got into the house?" she whispered. "Where was my head at?"

Afraid of what she might find, Louise opened the book. He had $729.28 in his account. Certainly not a drug dealer amount; more in line of a cop. "A frugal cop." There were no unusual transfers and a wave of relief washed over her. Granted, he could be dealing in cash only and maybe he had another account, but then why would he hide this passbook?

Louise carefully put everything back the way she found it and continued her search. The closet seemed almost military in its neatness. Shirts and slacks hung unwrinkled and spaced far enough apart not to tangle. Louise didn't shudder until she saw a highly polished wooden box sitting on a shelf above the hangers. She slid the box down and set it on the bed. A gold clasp held it shut. She rubbed her gloved hand over a surface almost glass-like in its smoothness. It was beautifully made, most probably by hand. She would love to own one like it.

Louise held her breath as she undid the clasp and opened the box. Inside laid a single eagle's feather. The box contained no note, no explanation at all. With a small gasp, Louise realized that she had crossed a line. Whatever the feather meant, it had been extremely personal. Louise had invaded a territory she had no business being in. Biting her lip, she gently closed the box and put it back on the shelf in the closet. She sat on the bed as guilt overwhelmed her. She mourned for the friend she hardly knew.

"Get over it Miller. You've got a job to do." She closed her eyes and took a deep breath. With effort Louise pried herself off the bed and resumed her search.

Between the kitchen and the living room she found the door to the basement. Louise repressed a shiver as she entered the cool, humid, and moldy smelling air. She had to pull out her flashlight to find the light switch. She flipped it on and a fluorescent bulb in the middle of the ceiling flickered.

The only things in the basement were a hot water heater, washer, dryer, wash tub, and furnace. Louise thought it odd that Mark hadn't used any of the space for storage. But if she lived in this house, she wouldn't want to go in the basement either.

She peeked inside the washing machine and checked the lint trap in the dryer. Clean. She wondered if he even used the machines. Feeling claustrophobic, Louise slipped the flashlight back onto her belt but misjudged the loop. The flashlight clattered to the floor. As she bent down to pick it up, she noticed the drain cover under the sink. The cover had edged up over the lip. It lifted off easy enough. Louise flipped on the light and aimed it down the hole. Her heart sank.

"Oh, Mark."

Twenty

Friday 7:00 p.m.

Elias felt good. Driving had cleared his head. *They must be very hungry by now.* He had driven down into Iowa, spent the night at a hotel, and then drove back. He had a telepathic conversation with Doctor Gillespy and knew the time had come for them to meet face-to-face once again.

Back in his own neighborhood, feeling like the king in his realm, Elias thought it sad that there had been no opportunity to unload his captive's credit cards. He thought about using it at the hotel but he sensed the message from Gillespy saying it would have been a very stupid thing to do. For now he drove around the park, considering which of the kids might look good on a milk carton. Unfortunately, the days of approaching children in the park were gone, at least during the day. For reasons he didn't quite understand, they all seemed afraid of him. Besides, there were always adults around to interfere. They all had cell phones now. He wouldn't get two blocks before the donut eaters would be swarming.

He pulled into his garage, making sure the wide door had closed before getting out of the car. Nothing new had aired over the scanner regarding Dr. Gillespy. Still, after he saw to his guests, he'd monitor the radio in the house.

"Yup, I bet they're starving," he said as he entered the kitchen. Elias filled two glasses of water, slathered peanut butter on two pieces of bread and put them on a tray. Feeling in a playful mood Elias hocked a wad of spit and snot on the top of one of the sandwiches. *I'll let the shrink choose first. Will he be gallant or selfish?*

He unlocked the door, stepped into the stairwell, and instantly sensed something very wrong. He hesitated a moment, before realizing S.K. was not at his post. *Where is he?* He paused, waiting for the dog to come trotting back. No S.K. He took one step down and saw the blood. Another step and he saw fur.

"S.K.!" he screamed, and pounded down the stairs.

~

The lock clicked. Leonard opened his eyes. He'd fallen asleep. Melanie was also asleep, her head nestled on his shoulder. He 'pssst' her awake as the doorknob turned.

"Ready?" His lips formed the word silently.

Melanie's grip tightened on the razor. Leonard curled his hand around the scalpel. They slipped into position when the door opened. Ducking low behind the wall on the side of the stairwell, he saw Melanie disappear across from him. He tensed, holding the scalpel so tightly his knuckles were white. A pause, then the first step creaked. The second step creaked.

"S.K.!"

The madman's feet thundered against the stairs as he came roaring down.

With the first sight of the giant, Leonard lunged, aiming for the neck. Melanie attacked at the same time, swinging the straight edge for the monster's gut. Leonard's arm lunged upward and slammed into the lip of the tray, flipping it into the big man's chest. The tip of the scalpel lodged into the bottom of the metal. Melanie fared better, slashing across through the skin of his belly.

The sadist screamed, swatting Leonard away with the tray. Leonard lost his grip. The scalpel flew across the room along with the peanut butter sandwiches. Melanie swung again and sliced him in the arm. Leonard dropped to his knees and hugged the man's thighs, trying to pull him down. A fist crashed on the top of his skull but he still held tight. The tray clattered to the floor.

Snarling, Melanie aimed for the face but the captor caught her hand and bent her arm backward, twisting her wrist until she cried out and dropped the blade. Leonard released one arm and drove his fist into the man's crotch. The monster let out a groan as his knees buckled and he toppled onto Leonard, pinning him flat.

Leonard couldn't breathe. Crushed by a huge slab of muscle and fat, he struggled to get free. Melanie let go a banshee shriek. She was able to reach under his shirt and dug her nails into and down the man's back. He screamed, arching himself. Leonard squirmed and wriggled out from underneath the behemoth. Bringing himself to his knees, the top of Leonard's head crashed into the monster's chin snapping his head back. Melanie jumped on the giant's back, her hands hooked into talons scratching and clawing, trying to dig her nails into his eyes.

The captor grabbed her arms and flipped her over his head. Leonard bent down and grabbed the tray, not noticing the lawyer fly past him. With his remaining strength he brought the metal plate up, swinging a home run swing connecting to the side of the big man's face. The metal bent and the sadist slipped on dog blood and toppled onto his side. Leonard swung again and screamed. His bad shoulder popped from its socket.

Melanie shot to her feet, ran over and landed a brutal kick to the man's face. In mid kick she slipped on the blood rink and went down too. Leonard took the tray with his good arm and slammed it on top of the fallen man's head. Melanie drove her fist into his nose. She heard a satisfying crunch as his nose broke. Blood flowed, adding to the pool they had all bathed in.

Leonard couldn't take the pain. He dropped the tray. The trance broke and Melanie looked up, her chest heaving. The big man didn't move.

"We did it," the psychiatrist panted.

Melanie grinned, and the grin became a laugh. She bent over and hugged the shrink. Leonard flinched and muffled a scream. When he recovered enough to talk, he said, "Pull my arm."

"Is this like that pull my finger joke?"

"Almost." Sweat beaded his forehead as he held up his dangling arm. "When I count to three, pull it straight and as hard as you can."

"Isn't that going to hurt?"

The doctor looked at the woman with blood-matted hair and red streaks like finger paint across her face and stomach. Her torn open blouse, now mostly red, formed a tight seal around her sides. He smiled grimly. "Yeah, it's going to hurt."

They walked outside the circle of blood to avoid slippage. She took hold of Hout's arm. "One…two…" She yanked hard.

The doctor let go a shout then sagged in relief. "I said at three!"

Melanie shrugged. "You paused. You were supposed to say three just as I pulled."

"Most people wait until they hear the word three, not just presume it's coming."

"Well pardon me! How's your arm?"

Leonard rotated it in a circular motion. "Good as new."

"Then quit complaining."

They stared at the giant lying motionless in the carnage.

"What do you think?" Melanie asked.

"I think that we should get the hell out of here."

"I mean about him."

"You mean to…" Leonard paused. "Kill him?"

"Better than he deserves," Melanie said.

"I can't do that," Leonard said, his breathing labored. "Tell you what; if he moves we'll knock him out again…and again… and again."

"Then we'd better hurry." Melanie glanced up at the exit. "First one to the door gets the first shower."

She skipped over the big man and raced up the steps. With too many hours of being bound and too much abuse to the body, all Leonard could do was limp along behind her.

Melanie glanced back and saw him struggle to keep up. She came back and helped him up the stairs. "Looks like it's going to be a tie," she said as they fumbled up the stairs. "Maybe we'll have to shower together."

"You know I'm married, right?"

"You know I'm joking, right?"

Even though he knew nothing would ever happen between them, unexplainably, Leonard felt a little let down.

"Oh my God. I cannot believe it." Melanie's voice shook.

"What is it? What's wrong?"

He watched as she tried the knob again. "Locked."

"It can't be!" Hout attempted to turn the knob himself. "How can that be?"

A menacing voice from down below answered. "It automatically swings shut and locks."

The couple froze.

He stood at the bottom of the stairs. Blood and spit ran off of the scratches on his cheeks and around his eyes, blood from his nose splattered his chin and torn shirt. The smile he wore could not camouflage the murderous hatred in his eyes.

"You need this." He dangled the key in front of them. "Ready for round two?"

He left them no choice but to fight again.

~

Elias watched them fumble down the steps. They wouldn't surprise him this time. The female was in better shape but she slowed her attack to wait for the male. When he got close, the shrink leapt. But Elias stood ready. In mid air he grabbed the doctor's shirt and flung him into the wall. He crumpled. The lawyer dove into his legs, but with his weight centered Elias didn't move. He grabbed her by the hair and pulled her up. Eye to eye he saw her terror. He did a quick head butt and she dropped.

His mind raced as Elias thought about the things he could do to two unconscious bodies, the tortures and torments he could inflict. "No. You need to be conscious."

The male moved, groaning. Elias drove a boot into his ribs.

A fresh surge of anger rose and he kicked again and again.

The woman moaned. Elias stopped his tirade and grabbed her neck, pulling her to her feet. He shoved her hard into the wall. A welt had already formed above her right eye. Her eyes fluttered open. He relished the terror he saw there.

"If you're going to kill us, just do it," she said.

He caressed the hair away from her ear, leaned in and licked it. "Oh, don't you worry. I will."

He pounded his fist into her stomach, following with an uppercut when she buckled. She landed on top of Hout. With a snort of disgust, Elias hoisted her over his shoulder and carried her back to the X. He tied her tightly this time. It didn't matter if he cut off the circulation. She wouldn't need her hands for much longer. He secured the shrink back onto the surfboard and tried to rouse him so he could knock him out again, but the asshole refused to cooperate. Still, he kicked him once more, hard, in the ribs.

Elias looked down on S.K.'s battered body and choked back a sob. He knelt beside his companion and stroked his fur. Blood still trickled from the wounds. Tears rolled down Elias' face as he wrapped S.K.'s body in a blanket. He sobbed aloud as he carried the dog upstairs.

"You deserve a decent burial."

Elias sat in his quiet room on the second floor. In a rocking chair facing the window, S.K. lay in his lap. Elias stared outside as the sun set. When it disappeared he would venture out and find a gravesite for his best friend.

Twenty-One

Saturday 3:30 p.m.

Tiffany Saangvold impatiently sat playing on her computer while waiting for her mother to come home from work. *It isn't fair. How many times does a person's birthday fall on a Saturday? Not many.* Nevertheless, her mother had made an appointment and gone to the office. They were supposed to go blueberry picking that afternoon. Her mom had promised. But when the phone rang and Tiffany saw her mother's face, she knew.

"It's just for a couple of hours," her mom had said.

Four hours ago! For now Tiff practiced Tetris until she heard the hum of the garage door opening. She ran from the game to the door and struck a pose, one elbow against the wall, her other arm in front of her, staring at an imaginary wristwatch. As she heard the car door open Tiffany thought of a better idea. She ran back to her Tetris; best to look nonchalant. *"Hi, Tiff. I', so sorry I'm late."*

"Whatever."

Nope. The waiting at the door would make her mom feel more guilty. She ran back and almost made it when the door opened and her mother walked in.

"Hi, Sweetie. I'm so sorry I'm late."

Two good plans ruined by timing. Tiffany decided it would be best to just get to the point. "Can we still go blueberry picking?"

"Oh, Honey, it's getting late. Wouldn't you rather go tomorrow?"

"But you promised we would do whatever I want for my birthday. You promised."

"If we go tomorrow, we can spend more time there. If we go now, we'll only have an hour or so."

"That's enough time," Tiffany pled.

"Oh, Honey, I'm really tired."

"C'mon Mom, it'll be fun. If you take me today you don't have to get me any more presents."

"When I got you the Wii for Christmas you said I didn't have to get you anything for your birthday. Remember?"

Tiffany slumped her shoulders and stuck out her lower lip. "All right, I guess. We can bond some other time." She moped out of the room.

Janet Saangvold's heart broke a little bit more as her daughter walked away. Way too smart for her age, the kid knew how to push the right buttons. The psychology job at the clinic had been taking far too much time away from her daughter. "Tell you what," Janet said. "Give me a half-hour to unwind then we'll go."

Tiffany perked up, ran over, and wrapped her arms around her mom. "It'll be fun, Mom. You'll love it."

Yeah, the little imp knew how to push all of the buttons—good and bad. Janet hugged her little girl back, not wanting to let go.

Tiffany switched to mine sweepers while watchfully timing her mother. When the half-hour was up, she threw the mouse down and went to get her.

Janet stood in the doorway smiling at her little girl.

"How long have you been standing there?" Tiffany asked.

"About an hour," Janet answered.

"Oh Mom, you have not."

Janet laughed. "I just got here. Do you have the bags?"

Tiffany raced past her mom and into the kitchen. "Paper or plastic?"

"Plastic," her mom called back.

Janet followed her daughter into the kitchen. Tiffany had already pulled a handful of supermarket bags.

"How many you got there, Tiff?"

"Ten. You think we need more?"

"I think you're overestimating our haul," Janet chuckled.

"What does that mean?"

"It means two should be plenty."

Tiffany eyed her mom suspiciously. "Do you mean two for each of us or two altogether?"

Janet sighed in resignation. "Fine, two for each of us. But don't you dare complain that you're sick of blueberries."

"We can have blueberry pancakes for breakfast, blueberry sandwiches for lunch and blueberries on macaroni and cheese for dinner."

The damn thing was that the kid would probably eat it, Janet thought. "Get in the car, Blueberry Queen."

~

On the wooded side of Perch Lake hiking and bike trails cut through the trees and looped around making a one, two, or three mile trail depending on how much exercise one desired. Where the one and two mile trail separated, Tiffany Saangvold had celebrated her birthday by exploring with her best friend Jenna. They wandered off the trail and discovered wild blueberry bushes hidden from sight. After being scolded by her mom to never ever leave the path—and what was she doing riding her bike out by Perch Lake without an adult—Tiffany dragged her mom to where she called "Blueberry Hill," even though the closest hill was a mile away.

Every birthday since then mother and daughter rode up to Perch Lake and picked blueberries. This would be their third trip. Janet told her daughter they had started a tradition that Tiffany thought was the coolest thing in the world.

"It's already late, Tiff. What say we drive to the trail, then bike in? It'll give us more picking time."

"Good idea, Mom."

They loaded up their bikes in the minivan and drove off. Already tired from work, Janet was grateful not to pedal the extra couple of miles.

Tiffany gazed up at the thickening clouds. "Do you think it's going to rain?"

"Who knows? It'll probably pour when we're farthest from the car." Janet didn't mean it but her voice came out cross.

"Well, we won't let a little water ruin our fun," Tiffany said.

"No we won't," Janet answered matching her daughter's enthusiasm.

The minivan pulled up to the beach parking lot. With the clouds rolling in there were plenty of spaces to choose from. Mother and daughter unloaded their bikes and hit the trail. Tiffany led the way as she knew where on the path to turn off.

They rode in silence as the wind picked up and far away thunder rumbled. The temperature felt as if it had dropped ten degrees. Janet followed her daughter hoping she'd say, let's go back home. On the other hand, if they didn't get the blueberry picking out of the way today, Janet would find herself doing this same thing again tomorrow.

A clap of thunder, much closer now, rattled the ground. The wind died and Janet felt a drop of rain. "Tiff, maybe we should do this tomorrow."

Tiffany stopped her bike and looked back at her mother. "We're here. Do you think we'll need to lock the bikes?"

I give up, Janet thought. *The sooner we start, the sooner we'll finish, and the sooner I can get home and soak in a hot bath. Maybe I'll make her eat her macaroni and cheese topped with blueberries.* That afterthought made her smile.

"I think the bikes will be fine." Janet couldn't imagine anyone hiking through the woods wanting to take a girl's pink bike or an old ten-speed Schwinn showing signs of rust.

Another drop of rain splashed Janet as they walked the bikes off the trail and into the woods. They laid them on the ground when the bikes were out of sight. Tiffany took her mother's hand and expertly led her through the brush.

A flash of lightning lit the sky. The two counted in unison. They got to three-one-thousand before the boom.

"Maybe this isn't such a great idea. Wouldn't you rather do this tomorrow?" Janet asked.

Tiffany stopped and her lower lip pouted out and began to tremble.

"We don't have to. It was just an idea." At the moment Janet would rather risk a lightning strike than deal with one of Tiffany's tantrums.

"Someone's been here," Tiffany said.

"How do you know?" her mother asked.

Tiffany's pouty look formed into a smile of guilt. "I was here a couple of days ago, ya know, to make sure there were lots of blueberries. They're gone."

Janet focused her gaze on the bushes. "There's plenty."

"Not as many as before."

A light rain sprinkled through the trees. A bolt of lightning strobed through the leaves.

"One one thousand, two one thous..." BOOM.

"That's close," Tiffany said.

"Then let's get to picking."

They plucked the ripe ones and put them in their sacks as the rain began to pour.

"What's wrong?" Janet asked.

"Nothing," answered Tiffany. "It's just that I thought we were the only ones that knew about this place."

"It's a public place, hon."

"I know. But I always wanted it to be ours."

"Well, look at it this way. About twenty-five hundred people live in Kenowa, and four hundred thousand in Minneapolis. Over a million people in the metro area. Out of all of those people, only me, you, and maybe a couple of other people know about this place. What are the odds? If even one percent of the population knew of this place there wouldn't be any blueberries left for us. This place would've been picked clean. We're the best of the best."

"Yeah, we are aren't we?"

The two silently filled their bags as the rain pounded down.

Soaked, contentment enveloped Janet, almost communing with nature like back in her pot smoking days, before Tiffany was born. She looked up at the dark sky and let the droplets cleanse her face.

A scream shattered the illusion.

"Tiffany!"

"MOM!"

Janet searched for her daughter. Didn't see her.

"Tiffany! Where are you?"

Thunder drowned out the answer.

"MOM!" Tiffany shrieked.

Janet raced to the far side of the bushes. She saw the top of her daughter's head poke above the other side. Branches raked at her skin as Janet cut through the underbrush. Scratches marred her arms and legs by the time she finally reached Tiffany and saw the horror on her face.

"What is it?" Janet grabbed her daughter by the shoulders.

"The ground. It moved." Tiffany pointed to a small mound of dirt in between two trees. Her voice shook as she spoke.

Heavy drops splashed on the ground. Janet let out a sigh. "Honey, that's just the rain. It's just making it look like…"

She stifled her own scream as the plot of earth definitely did move. She grabbed her daughter and jumped back. The mound looked as though it were breathing, rising and falling as water rolled off. Something poked through.

"What is it?" Tiffany asked.

They watched as a nose followed by a paw clawed its way free. "It's a dog." Tiffany broke her mother's grip and ran toward heap of mud.

"Tiffany, get back here. Now!"

The girl ignored her mom's order and began shoveling away the dirt with her hands. Janet ran after her. She wanted to drag her daughter away but when she got there Tiffany had already dug down to the fur.

"Oh my God."

Tiffany had brushed the dirt off of its head. The dog's eye had been severely damaged. Crusted blood had formed around its nose and broken teeth. The rest of its body hadn't fared much better. Blood had matted the fur as mud clotted many of the wounds.

"Oh, the poor baby. Why would anyone do this to a poor defenseless animal, Momma?"

"I don't know, sweetheart. Some people are just cruel, I guess."

"Then they buried it alive." Tears mixed with rain running down Tiffany's face. "We have to get it to a hospital."

"Oh, honey, the thing is almost dead. I don't think there's anything we can do except maybe make it as comfortable as we can."

"We can save it, Momma. I know we can."

Janet knew better than to argue with her daughter. When it came to helpless animals Tiffany might eventually forgive but she would never forget. Besides, she'd called her momma. How could Janet turn down her kid when she called her momma?

"We'll try honey, but don't get your hopes up too high. It's in pretty rough shape. Let's go."

"I want to stay here," Tiffany said.

Janet knew Tiffany would slow her down, but she also knew that not long ago there were some sadists roaming around and didn't want to leave her daughter alone in the woods. "It's not safe here alone, sweetie. I want you to come with me."

"No. He needs me."

This argument could easily take another hour. Time would eat away at the dog as much as its wounds now.

"Mom, I've been here alone before; hundreds of times. I'll be fine. Tell you what. If I hear anything suspicious, I'll hide."

Janet rubbed her eyes with her thumb and forefinger. "I give up."

She ran through the woods wondering who might actually be the parent here, ignoring the wet branches slapping at her as she went past. One day she'd have to come down on her kid, but as of yet she hadn't found the right battle.

The rain had abated, slowing to a gentle dousing as she got to her bike and peddled frantically to her car. The faster she rode the madder she got at the punks who would do such a thing. Siding more with her daughter, she really wanted to save the dog.

She figured it wouldn't survive the ride to the vet, but at least she could tell Tiffany they did everything that they possibly could.

One of the positives about modern day crime was its prevention. Although no motorized traffic was allowed on the trail, the path had been paved and was wide enough for an occasional police car to cruise through. Unfortunately, one hadn't been around when the bastards had done this to the dog.

Janet threw her bike in the van and sped down the trail, praying that because of the weather there were no bikers or joggers around the turns. She quickly reached the spot where the hidden blueberry path lay, grabbed a blanket and left the van with the motor still running. She saw the tears on her daughter's face and feared that she had been too late.

"Are you okay, sweetheart?" Janet asked.

"He tried to bite me," Tiffany said. "I just wanted to comfort him and he snapped at me."

"That's what dogs do, honey. You're a stranger to him. If strangers did this to you, well, you wouldn't be too trusting either, would you?" The dog's breathing was shallow and along with all the blood on its coat, his snout had been smashed.

She knelt and placed the blanket on the dog. It put up no resistance as she wrapped the blanket around him and lifted him up. Tiffany kept a safe distance.

Janet's arms ached by the time they reached the van. "Get the door for me, hon."

Tiffany slid open the side door and shoved her mom's bike over as far as it would go. Janet gently placed the bundle down and unwrapped the blanket to see if the dog was still alive. She'd be damned if she'd drive all the way to the emergency vet in Golden Valley with an already dead dog.

"Ready?" she asked her daughter.

"What about my bike?" Tiffany asked.

Janet grabbed the bike and threw it on top of her own. She waited for her daughter to protest, but noticed Tiff's complete attention on the dog.

"Ready?"

"Thanks, Mom!"

Speeding all the way, they arrived at the Emergency Pet Hospital in less than one-half an hour. Under the circumstances Janet didn't think a cop would ticket her. In fact, she'd hoped one would pull her over then give her an escort, complete with lights and sirens. Fortunately, or unfortunately, she made it without incident.

The two walked in, Janet carrying the dog. The nurse behind the counter saw them and without questions, led them to a small examining room. Janet rested the dog on a metal table.

Within a minute the doctor walked in. "I'm Dr. Logan." He shook hands with Janet then put on some surgical gloves.

"We found him," Tiffany said.

"Someone beat him then buried him alive," Janet added.

The veterinarian opened the blanket and after a quick gasp started his examination by putting his stethoscope over the dog's heart. The dog didn't protest.

"I don't know if there's a lot I can do. I think the most humane thing to do would be to put him down."

Janet had expected that answer but Tiffany burst into tears. "You have to save him."

The doctor continued examining his patient. "He's got multiple puncture wounds and slashes. He's got a broken jaw and a punctured eye. He'd lose that for sure."

"But you can save him, right?" Tiffany asked.

"Interesting," the doctor said as he lifted a paw. "This dog's been declawed."

"Why would anybody do that?" Janet asked.

"Unfortunately, I've seen it too many times. It's not that uncommon in dogs owned by drug dealers. Mostly pit bulls and rottweilers, like this one. They can sneak up on someone without being heard."

Dr. Logan gently took the dog's snout making sure it wouldn't be able to snap and checked its throat. Under the fur an old scar puckered the skin. "His vocal cords have been severed too."

Janet felt uneasy about Tiffany hearing this. She placed her hands on Tiffany's shoulders and pulled her close. Drug dealers might have done this to the dog, maybe sending a message. Janet wanted no part of that world and she'd be damned if she let Tiffany anywhere close.

"All the more reason to put him down," the doctor said.

"No!" Tiffany shouted. "You can't do that."

"Now Tiff." Janet hugged her tight.

"Even if we did save him—and that's a very big if—the surgery would be at least fifteen hundred dollars."

"We can pay for it, can't we, Mom?"

"Sweetie, you know I don't have that kind of money."

"Maybe Dad will pay," Tiffany sobbed.

"You're father won't even pay for new shoes for school." As the words escaped her lips, Janet felt a mixture of regret and anger. Anger because the bastard was late on child support, and regret because she promised herself she'd never talk bad about Tiffany's father.

"Let me talk to him." Tiffany suddenly sounded very adult. It scared Janet. "I know he'll listen to reason."

Janet closed her eyes and let out a long breath. "Fine. Save him. We'll come up with the money somehow."

"All right, Mom! You never have to buy me another birthday present ever again."

One of these days I'll start acting like a mother.

"It'll be hours," the doctor said. "There's no reason for you to stick around. Why don't you drop off your phone number at the front desk, and we'll call you as soon as we're done."

"Thank you, doctor." Janet held her daughter tight. "C'mon, Tiff. Let's go."

The veterinarian put a hand on Tiffany's shoulder. "We'll do everything we can, but don't get your hopes up too high. He's in really rough shape."

"He'll be fine. I can feel it," Tiffany said.

"We gotta go, Tiff. Let's call the police and tell them what we found. Maybe they can catch the people who did this."

Twenty-Two

Saturday 4:15 p.m.

Andrew stood in front of the bathroom mirror and shaved while Corwin purred and wove figure eights in between and around his legs. In some ways it had been a long first week, but in others it had flown by. He had no problem working six days in a row, and then getting three off. As he nicked his chin he thought about what it would be like to have his weekend being Tuesday, Wednesday, and Thursday. A good time to do errands—less crowds. Then he wondered why he was shaving on a Saturday. Just because he'd be at his sister's for dinner? He figured, what the heck, she was worth it.

He walked down the hall and measured exactly ¾ of a cup of cat food. He poured it into Corwin's bowl careful not to spill, and then cleaned the litter box. He checked his watch; fifteen minutes before leaving. Taking up the lotus position on the floor, Andrew began his meditation with Corwin curled up in his lap.

After fifteen minutes Andrew's mental alarm went off. He opened his eyes and lifted a purring Corwin off his legs. "You be a good guy, okay? No shredding the furniture or I'll declaw you myself." A good-natured, but idle threat.

He opened the door and as he stepped out the phone rang. He debated letting the answering machine pickup. Had it been important they would've called on his cell. "Oh heck." He raced to the phone and got it on the third ring.

"Hello?"

"Hey Deputy Dawg, glad I caught ya before you left. Pick up a bottle of rose or merlot, whichever one goes with brats and tofu burgers."

"Will do," Andrew said. "See you in about twenty."

Corwin started to hack. Andrew bent down and scratched the cat behind his ears but Corwin ignored him as the heaving grunts got louder. There was nothing else Andrew could do so he patiently waited for the hairball to come up. After a five-minute bout, Corwin finally vomited on the linoleum floor. Grateful it hadn't been on the carpet, Andrew grabbed a paper towel before Corwin started eating the glob, something he was prone to do.

"See ya in a few hours, Cor. Be good."

The cat was already marring the smooth landscape of the kitty litter.

~

Karla let herself into Louise's apartment, made her way to the kitchen, set the groceries on the counter and looked out the back door. Louise stood on the balcony pouring charcoal into the Weber. Karla snuck up behind her and massaged Louise's neck and shoulders. Louise dropped the bag of coals and sank back against her lover's body.

"Are you going to tell him tonight?" Karla asked.

Louise tilted her head back as far as it would bend, pulled Karla's head forward, and kissed her. "Or maybe just show him."

Karla grinned as she pulled away. "I couldn't find any tofu burgers, but I did get soy. I hope that's okay."

"I didn't know there was a difference. Anyway, just so long as it isn't red meat, he'll eat it."

Louise doused the charcoal with starter fluid and tossed in a match. Flames leapt nearly to the balcony above.

"Pour enough fluid in there?" Karla asked.

"Aw, if their deck ignites it'll just give our dinner that smoked hickory flavor."

The flames died back to a normal barbeque fire.

"He's not even my brother, and I'm nervous," Karla said. "I don't know him, but I'm afraid of what he might think."

"We can stay in the closet if you want."

"Of course not. Well, maybe. I don't know."

Karla walked into the living room and plopped onto the couch. Louise rolled her eyes and followed Karla. "It'll be fine," she said in a voice a little sterner than she meant.

"What does that mean?" Karla asked.

"What do you mean what does 'that' mean? It means everything will be fine."

Felix the Cat chimed five. Grateful for the diversion Louise glanced at the clock. "That's odd. Andrew is never late. In fact, he's just about always early."

Karla looked relieved.

"Sorry. I guess I'm a little anxious too." Louise went to the stereo cabinet and opened the doors. "What are you in the mood for?"

"Hmmm, how about George Winston?"

"Good choice. Andrew will like that." She pulled out the CD and slid it in the player. Melodious piano filled the room as Louise sat next to Karla and torched a cigarette. Karla took the pack out of her hand and shook one out for herself. Louise raised her eyebrows but lit the smoke for her anyway.

"I had no idea," Louise said.

"I can't tell you everything. There'd be no mystery left in our relationship."

They sat quietly and smoked, waiting for Andrew. Louise lit another cigarette with the tip of her old one and pulled out her cell phone. Karla closed her eyes and lost herself in the music. She seemed oblivious to an ash that grew longer and longer, coming closer to burning her fingers. Louise thought about nudging her but she looked so damned cute. Just like waking up next to her and watching her sleep. Instead, Louise placed the ashtray under Karla's smoke.

Finally, she couldn't stand it anymore. Louise got up and dialed Andrew's number. Karla opened her eyes, leaned forward and flicked her ash on the table where the ashtray sat just a minute ago. “Where are you?” Louise said into the phone while trying not to laugh at Karla’s mishap.

“Running a little late. Got stuck at the liquor store. Wasn’t sure what kind of wine went with tofu,” Andrew answered.

“The charcoal is ready. When will you be here?”

“In a jiff,” Andrew said.

“See ya when you get here.” Louise disconnected the line.

~

Andrew flipped his phone closed and shoved it in his pocket as he reached the top stair of his sister’s floor. He raced to her door and knocked.

“Who is it?” Louise called from the other side.

“Did somebody here order a merlot?”

“Door’s open, asshole.”

Andrew entered the apartment and was surprised to see a stranger rise from the couch.

Louise beat her to the door, hugged him and took the wine. He saw in her eyes something very wrong, more than her usual personality quirks. Despite putting on a good front, he could swear she was hiding something.

“Andrew, I’d like you to meet my very special friend, Karla Spires. Karla, my brother Andrew.”

Karla held out her hand and Andrew took it.

My God, she fixed me up.

“Pleased to meet you.” Andrew’s hand smothered hers, but her soft skin felt nice.

“Louise has told me so much about you.” Her smile radiated.

Andrew blushed; now knew he had shaved for a reason.

“Why so late?” Louise closed the door behind him. Something about her voice seemed a little off, too.

“Corwin wasn’t feeling too well.”

“Corwin is his flea-ridden bag of decayed meat with fur.”

“He’s actually a very good cat,” Andrew said. “He’s only eleven. He’s still got another ten or so years to go.”

"I'm amazed every morning he wakes up," Louise said.

"I love cats," Karla chimed in. "But I think I'm more of a dog person."

Louise shuddered. "Not those little yippy mops with legs, I hope."

"No, beagles, cockers mostly—ones that aren't too big, but not too small either."

"I like the tough ones. Pit bulls, Dobermans and rottweilers. Especially rotts." Louise suddenly became sullen.

"Oh, Louise, you're so butch. What about you, Andrew?"

"She was quite the tomboy." Andrew leaned over and whispered, "She used to have a rott. Someone stole it."

Karla nodded. "She told me."

Louise lit another cigarette.

"I mean about dogs," Karla said.

"I like dogs just fine. But cats are much cleaner and are far more independent. They don't take up nearly as much of your time—"

"Speaking of dogs," Louise cut in. "Karla, how many brats you want?"

"Just one for me."

"Deputy Dawg, how many burgers for you? Just to let you know they're soy and not tofu."

Andrew rolled his eyes at his sister. "Tofu is soy, sis."

Louise smiled at Karla and they shrugged in unison.

"I think I can handle two." Andrew didn't want to appear like a pig in front of Karla. Also, with his stomach acting up after every meal, three would probably activate whatever was wrong.

"Andrew, why don't you pour us all some wine and I'll get dinner on the grill," Louise said.

Karla took a seat on the sofa while Andrew headed toward the kitchen and Louise, the balcony. As the two walked down the hall together, Andrew whispered, "Not bad, sis. I wish you would've told me, though."

Louise grabbed her brother's hand. "Oh Andrew, you don't

know how many times I wanted to."

Andrew eyed his sister quizzically. "What are you talking about?"

"What are you talking about?" Louise responded, the shock turning to suspicion. She let go of his hand.

"Karla. She's beautiful. I had no idea you were going to fix me up."

Louise burst out laughing. This laugh sounded genuine. "Oh, Andrew, you are so naïve."

"What? I think we're hitting it off."

Louise renewed her laughter, shaking her head. "Pour the wine, idiot. I have to put the meat on."

She left Andrew alone in the kitchen, laughing as she went down the hall. He poured three glasses and took the first one to the living room for Karla. When he found her not there, he made his way to the balcony. Obscured by the partially open vertical blinds, Andrew saw Karla had joined his sister. When he got to the door, Andrew froze, stunned to see Louise and Karla locked in a kiss. A very intimate kiss.

"What the hell."

The women quickly disengaged, embarrassment on Karla's face, surprise from Louise. A little embarrassed himself, and unable to find the words, Andrew walked away.

Surprise shifted to anger as Louise started after her brother. "What the hell does that mean? Say something."

"Let him be for a moment," he heard Karla tell his sister.

Andrew went into the living room and sat on the couch, his brain racing in all directions. He needed to empty his mind so he grabbed the remote, shut off George Winston, and clicked on the TV.

"I'm sorry. That was uncalled for; I apologize. That was no way for you to find out."

The news flashed on the screen showing a female reporter interviewing a little girl. It looked as though the girl was trying hard not to cry.

"I saw her the other day," Andrew said.

Louise stared at the screen. "That girl?"

"The reporter. She was covering the Lone Bear story out at the lake."

"She's a bitch."

Andrew finally looked at his sister. "You know her?"

Louise shifted her focus from her brother to the TV set when the word rottweiler came over the air. She snatched the remote from Andrew's hand and turned up the volume.

"Anyway…"

"Shhh." Louise cranked the volume higher.

At the bottom of the screen, Tiffany Saangvold's name appeared. "He was hardly alive and he was trying to climb out of this hole." The camera zoomed to a clod of earth.

The two watched in silence as the child described the scene. Heat radiated off his sister as her anger rose.

A big smile broke out on Tiffany's face. "My mom said we can keep him."

The camera switched back to the reporter. "If anyone has any information, they're asked to call the Kenowa Police department. From Perch Lake, Bianca Skylar, Channel Six news."

At the mention of Perch Lake, Andrew and Louise stared at each other.

"For thirty years I've never heard of Perch Lake. Now it's a damn Mecca for violent crime. What gives, baby bro?"

Andrew shrugged. "It's just been kid stuff 'til now. Late night partying, some drugs, nothing ever major before."

Louise turned off the television. "That's your neck of the woods. Promise me you'll track down those sons of bitches."

I'll do what I can, but I'm off until Tuesday. Hopefully, whoever did this will be caught by then."

"Do you think…"

"Don't even say it," Andrew snapped. "I'm sure it wasn't your dog."

They sat in silence staring at the blank screen. The dog story had been a good diversion but Andrew knew there were personal matters to discuss. "About you and Karla."

"It's a nice night for a drive," Louise said. "I'd like to go to Perch Lake and see what the Kenowa cops missed."

"Are you crazy?" Andrew glared at his sister.

"They're idiots. If they were any good, they'd be Minneapolis cops."

"I know 'em; they're excellent officers." Andrew knew his sister was goading him, but in his mind he still needed to defend them.

"I think it's a good idea." Karla stood at the foot of the hallway holding a glass of merlot. "It'll give you two a chance to talk."

Andrew conceded defeat. "I guess I'm not that hungry anymore, anyway."

They still had a few more hours of daylight as Andrew hit the interstate. He could see Louise, always the impatient one, gnashing her teeth, willing him to go over fifty-five. As a good will gesture he eased it up to sixty. Still, cars flew past them. He'd waited for her to start the conversation, but when it became clear that she wouldn't, Andrew broke first. "You're gay, huh?"

"Yup."

"How long?"

"Oh, I made the choice about a month ago."

Andrew rolled his eyes. "I mean, how long have you and Karla been going out?"

Louise smiled. "I don't know. I guess a few months."

"Why didn't you tell me?" The hurt in Andrew's voice came through.

"I always wanted to. I don't know. It just never seemed like the right time. I wasn't comfortable talking about it."

Four lanes narrowed down to three as they hit the outskirts of Minneapolis. Three lanes quickly became one because of road construction. Traffic slowed to forty.

"So, you think I have a chance of stealing Karla from you? She seems to like me."

"She only likes you because of all the nice things I've said about you. Wait until she gets to know you. She won't even want to talk to you." Louise stared out the window. "Seriously though, she's great. She keeps me sane, Andrew."

"I thought that was my job."

"That's why she's so amazing. She keeps me sane in spite of you."

They both smiled as one lane became two. Even for this early on a Saturday evening there were a lot of cars. Andrew wished he had the squad so he could use the lights and siren.

Louise was staring out the window. He knew something more was wrong when she they passed one strip mall after another and she didn't complain about suburban lifestyle. "Talk to me," Andrew said.

Still gazing out the side window, she said, "I did something very wrong. I can't shake the guilt."

"What did you do?" Andrew grabbed his sister's shoulder, making her look at him.

"I heard some rumors about Mark Lone Bear."

He released his grip. "Since when did you ever start paying attention to rumors?"

Louise shook her head. "I don't know. I just couldn't stand the thought of anybody slamming him, especially now that he can't defend himself."

"What did you hear?"

"That he was dealing. That the guy who killed him might've been an associate or something."

"You've got to report that. Let the detectives sort it out."

"I know." She stopped and took a few deep breaths before she could talk again. "It gets worse." She waited for a reaction and got none. Andrew wore a purely professional face.

"I went into his house and—"

"How did you get in?"

"A neighbor gave me the key."

"That sounds suspicious in itself."

Louise ignored the jibe. "I found some money hidden in his

basement. Ten thousand, total. Crisp hundred dollar bills."

"What are you going to do?"

Louise turned her back on her brother and stared out the window again. "No one knows that it's there."

"No!" The car drifted into the next lane as Andrew glared at his sister. "Don't you even think what I'm thinking you're thinking."

A car horn blasted and Andrew swerved back into his lane. Louise wanted to laugh but didn't dare when she saw the seriousness of his look. *What am I thinking you're thinking I'm thinking?* She couldn't say it out loud.

"I'm not going to take the money, but damn, it would come in handy."

Andrew sighed in relief as he concentrated on his driving. "If you need money I can loan it to you."

"I don't need your money," Louise snapped. "It's just that it would be nice to see what it's like to be out of debt and actually have a little money to play with. Go on a cruise and not worry about how you're going to afford it. I was fantasizing, okay?"

Andrew frowned. "What are you going to do?"

"I don't know. I wish I could walk away. Unfortunately I had a nice long chat with his next door neighbor. As soon as the investigators come around I'd be sunk."

The limit had gone up to sixty; the needle edged past seventy-five. Fewer cars were passing him, but he still failed to pass anybody else. He let up on the gas until the speedometer showed under seventy. They got off the interstate just shy of Medina. The city was an odd mixture of farmland, townhouses, and plots of land that had sprung up houses during the 1990s.

"Any headway on Lone Bear's murder?" Andrew asked.

"They're idiots. They seem to be convinced it's an Indian related thing."

"You don't think so?"

"Not a chance."

"Did you talk to them? Maybe they know something that you don't."

"Of course I talked to them. They don't know squat."

"What did you say?" Andrew asked.

"I told them they had their heads up their ass. What else?"

She was back to sounding like the sister he knew and loved.

"They didn't insist you head their team?"

Louise smirked. "They generously offered me the prestigious position of property room clerk if I didn't shut my dyke mouth and get back on the street."

"They know? Does everyone know but me?"

"They're detectives, Andrew. They're trained to spot things like that."

"Am I that stupid?" Andrew asked.

"You're not stupid at all, just a little naïve, especially when it comes to family."

"Maybe. Still, I'm surprised you let them get away with saying that."

"Lone Bear's funeral's on Tuesday," she muttered.

"Are you going?"

"You'd think that for all of the hoopla and crapola, which he'd absolutely hate, by the way, there should be at least one person there who at least knew him and will mourn for him. Yeah, I'll be there."

"What about his family?"

"I don't even know if anyone got a hold of them or not. It was made pretty clear to me that I'd better butt out."

They reached Perch Lake and drove past the area where Lone Bear and his car had been pulled from the water. Even though the crime scene tapes had already been taken down, there remained an eerie emptiness around the beach.

~

Andrew pulled over and used his cell phone to call in and find out the exact location of where that little girl found the dog.

Louise looked across the lake to the horizon where the bright blue had faded into azure. A star had already emerged; something that wouldn't be noticeable in her neighborhood for at least another hour. For just a fraction of a moment, she thought that life out in the boonies might not be that bad.

A tidal wave of relief had washed away a great weight off of Louise, actually a double weight. Not only did Andrew now know about the money, but he now knew about her lifestyle. After the initial shock, it didn't bother him! He had made no judgments about either one. She hadn't felt this close to her brother since their parents' funeral.

The car pulled out into minimal traffic. Andrew parked in a small lot on the northwest part of the lake where the walking and jogging trails started.

"It's a bit of a walk," he said.

Louise got out of the car and instantly slapped a mosquito that landed on her arm. As they started their trek into the woods, the air became heavy with the humidity the sun couldn't reach. The afternoon's storm had left puddles on the sides of the path that sometimes spanned across where the path dipped.

Louise led the way. She walked through a cloud of gnats that became interested in her hair. A few strides behind, Andrew seemed to be in his element. She couldn't tell if the gnats and mosquitoes were harassing him, but if they were, he didn't seem to mind.

"I can't wait for fall," Louise said, ready for a fight.

"That's a beautiful time of year, too," Andrew answered.

"I hate you."

Andrew blew her a kiss.

With the trees blocking so much of the light, the crime scene reminded Louise of a set on a horror movie. The trees cast eerie shadows over the trampled mud. Sharp sticks from the brush seemed to jump out from nowhere to jab at her legs and arms.

"Blueberry bushes," Andrew said with glee.

"How can you tell?"

Andrew picked a blueberry and popped it in his mouth.

"Maybe this was a mistake." Louise swatted at gnats swarming around her head. "The place looks like it's been trampled. And it's getting dark."

"Hey, this was your idea." Andrew pulled a flashlight out from his back pocket and flicked it on.

"You always carry a flashlight?" Louise was half stunned, half in awe.

"Keep it in the glove box. Never know when it might come in handy."

"Fucking boy scout," Louise mumbled.

The shallow grave was easy to identify, but the rain had washed away blood and fur and probably anything else that might be considered evidence. Louise walked on the far side of the hole, out of the glade and into the woods. "Andrew, get your flashlight over here a minute."

He walked through the brush to where Louise stood. She pointed to the ground and Andrew aimed his flashlight. "That's one big footprint."

Andrew lined up his size eleven next to the indentation in the ground. His was a size, if not two, smaller.

A chill crawled over her skin. "A kid I was talking to said that a giant of a man was driving around in Mark's squad the day he disappeared. I have a sick feeling the same guy might've thought he killed the dog. Look at the proximity."

"Wanna hear something scarier? A kid who had Leonard Hout's ATM card said a giant sold it to him. That kid doesn't live too far from here, either."

"What the hell is going on?" Louise looked with concern to her brother, then back down at the footprint.

Andrew shook his head. "I think we've got a Perch Lake monster."

Twenty-Three

Saturday 6:55 p.m.

What started off as a cruise to ease his troubled and depressed mind, became elation after he heard the news on the radio. The speedometer needle edged past 95 miles per hour. Elias stared straight ahead, his mind reeling. S.K. was alive! That's what the radio said. At least he prayed it was S.K. The radio only said that a badly beaten rottweiler had been found alive near Perch Lake. How many badly beaten rottweilers could there be around Perch Lake? An eleven-year old girl found him. When he went to pick up his dog he'd have to give that little Saangvold girl a reward.

His mind shifted to the cause of S.K.'s pain. That doctor and lawyer would be begging for death before he finished his work! They would feel tenfold everything they put S.K. through.

He still felt the gouges digging into his back. "I'll break your knuckles then pull your fucking fingernails out, you bitch." That made him smile. That smile transformed into a wider grin as he thought about goo in his fingers as he gouged out then squished the doctor's eyes in his fist. Then S.K. could feast on whatever was left of the shrink. He pushed the speedometer past 100.

The wind against his face calmed him. He could only think of the days ahead, driving at high speeds and S.K. again hanging his head out of the window. That's it, he thought. "I'm coming, boy."

Elias pulled down the visor and gently touched the scratches around his eyes. He couldn't breath right; his nose crooked.

That could be fixed easily enough, but later. Retrieving his dog became priority number one.

In the middle of nowhere, he pulled off the highway to a little oasis to get gas and check the phone book. How many Saangvolds could there be? As the gas tank filled, Elias went to the corner of the lot where a teenage boy in a gray T-shirt and blue jeans yapped away in a phone booth. Only in the middle of nowhere would they still have a phone booth. And only a stupid-assed rube would be talking on it. Probably yapping to his girlfriend about nothing anyone else in the world would give a rat's ass about.

The kid had his back toward him when Elias rapped on the glass door. Without a glance, the teen flipped him off. Elias shoved open the door; the boy spun around.

"Hey—" He stopped when he saw what squeezed in with him.

"Don't you have a cell phone? I thought all you kids had cell phones these days." Elias yanked the receiver out of the boy's jittering hand. "He'll call you back." Elias slammed it down on the hook. "Tell me why I shouldn't break this finger." He grabbed the kid's middle finger, the same one he used to give Elias the bird.

Between fear and being crushed into the glass, the boy couldn't speak.

"If you can't tell me, maybe I'll have to break all your fingers." Elias felt something wet against his leg. He stepped out of the booth. A stain spread across the boy's groin. "You little puke!"

Grabbing the kid by his shirt collar, he flung him out of the booth and into the parking lot. The boy rolled. Elias pounced after him. Before the teen could get to his feet, Elias hauled him up by the chin and looked around. They were alone. "Give me your wallet. Now!"

Raw fear ignited the boy's face as he tried to get the wallet out of his pocket. Elias eyed his surroundings. The highway and cornfields surrounded the empty parking lot. At this distance he couldn't see the clerk through the window. Still, even if he were on the phone calling the cops, Elias would be long gone by the time they got here.

On the third attempt the boy's hand stopped shaking just enough to get it in his pocket and pull out the billfold. Elias snatched it from his hand. Seventeen dollars lay crumpled in the cheap imitation leather. Elias took it. "That's for dry cleaning." He pulled out the kid's driver's license and studied it.

"Well, Mr. Ethan Brian Hayes, who lives at one-oh-four-four-seven Barkley Curve Road, if I hear anything from the police I'll be back to pay you a little visit. No one is going to find out about our little run-in, are they?" He tossed the wallet on the pavement.

Ethan finally stuttered "N-n-no sir." He bent down to pick up his wallet and Elias snatched Ethan by the hair, mashing his face into the damp spot that his pants had absorbed.

"That's the smell of fear, Ethan Brian Hayes. Next time you're not going to be so rude, are you?"

Elias' hand gripped the top of the boy's head. He helped Ethan shake it no before releasing, then shoving him away. "Get out of here. You disgust me!"

Ethan dashed and made it to the far side of the parking lot before Elias stepped back into the phone booth. On the other side of the glass he saw a bicycle leaning against a pole. "Hey, Ethan Brian Hayes, you forgot your bike."

The boy kept running, never looking back.

Elias pulled out the White Pages, grateful it hadn't been ripped off. They actually had three phonebooks; one was Minneapolis and its suburbs. He searched, hoping the family didn't have an unlisted number. There were only two Sangvolds, one in Minneapolis and one in Apple Valley, a southern suburb. Neither made any sense. What would they be doing all the way up in Kenowa? He'd just have to ask them when he paid them a visit.

He began to tear the page out when the bold lettering caught his eye. Sangvold, also see Saangvold. He flipped a few pages back and smiled. Only one Saangvold lived in Kenowa. Elias tore that page out and stuffed it into his pocket.

A little while later, the bottom of the sun touched the horizon as Elias circled the block. As excited as he was about seeing

S.K. again, he wanted to wait until it got a little darker, and the traffic thinned a little bit more.

All his life he'd made it a practice to hide in the shadows. With the exception of driving to clear his head, he only went out in the daytime if he had a specific purpose. Even as a young boy his size made him stand out. When he stood out, he got blamed whether he did something, or not.

Feeling satisfied there would only be minimal witnesses, and dark enough that he wouldn't stand out, Elias pulled into J. Saangvold's driveway. The white vinyl sided rambler had a built in the seventies feel to it. The garage door was open, a dark colored minivan parked inside. A gas lamp radiating a soft glow sprung up from a neatly manicured lawn, the address, decorated on a plaque, hung by hooks underneath. The blinds to the front window were drawn, but Elias could see that lights were on inside.

He scanned the area once more before getting out of his car and approaching the front door. On the second ring of the doorbell a good-looking woman in her mid-thirties answered. She was petite with dark hair and a few strands of gray. Her gasp and startled look made Elias remember the bruises and scratches on his face.

"Excuse me, ma'am," he said as genteel as possible. "I heard on the news that you found my dog. I'd like to take him home now." He reached into his back pocket and pulled out his wallet. "I'd like to give you and your child a reward. Would twenty dollars be okay?"

The woman never took her eyes from his face. Her jaw still hung down.

"As you can see, my dog got the worst of it, but I didn't walk away unscathed either."

She finally blinked her eyes and gave her head a quick shake. "I'm sorry. You said the dog is yours?"

"Yes ma'am."

"The police are looking for you. Have you talked to them yet?"

The mention of the police made him shudder and she noticed.

Why were the police involved? "I really just want to put this episode behind me, ma'am. Now if you'll just bring me my dog, I'll be out of your hair."

The door stood open less than a foot. Fortunately for him, Elias wedged in his foot before she could slam it shut. With one shove he pushed the door wide open. The woman flew backward, landing on her rear. Elias scanned left and right down the street, before stepping in and closing the door behind him.

The woman scrambled, trying to get to her feet and to the phone. Elias shoved the bottom of his boot into her ass. She sprawled forward, her chin catching the corner of the end table next to the couch. The table went down along with a lamp and the phone. The dial tone sang as she grasped the receiver. Elias' foot came down on her wrist. The phone dropped.

The woman screamed for only a second before Elias kicked her in the gut. He hoisted her up by a handful of hair and flung her onto the sofa.

"Nothing stops a scream like a kick in the gut." He picked up the table and placed the lamp back on top. It was still on.

She glared up at him with hate and fear, both arms covering her stomach, one hand holding her injured wrist. A cut on her chin opened up from her fall, sending a trickle of blood down her neck.

"I really am sorry for this, but I can't have you calling the police." Elias grabbed the cordless phone and pressed the button for the dial tone. After a moment came the loud warning beep, and then silence. Now any incoming calls would get a busy signal.

"S.K.?" He glared at the woman. "Where's my dog?"

She tried to talk but could only gulp air. Elias waited patiently. "I brought him to the vet," she finally gasped.

"Which one?" He looked around the room admiring the décor. Two prints of roses in fancy vases, one picture red, the other yellow, hung behind the couch. A flat screen TV sat on the wall opposite. In the corner were two matching chairs, upholstered in red, with a reading lamp set between them. On the wall behind them were pictures of her and her little girl.

"Golden Valley Emergency Clinic."

Elias froze. "Where's your daughter?" A tinge of panic came out with the words.

A new fear spread over the woman. "A-at a friend's house."

Elias sank onto the couch, wedging the mom. He whispered in her ear. "Call her. Tell her to come out, and that everything is fine."

"Tiffany, honey, it's okay. Come on out."

Elias relaxed. The woman did as she was told with no hesitation. No mother would do that if her kid had actually been there.

"You must be Mrs. Saangvold. Or would that be Ms.?"

She didn't reply.

"What's your first name?"

Again she said nothing.

"I see photos of you, and I see photos of your girl, but I don't see any pictures of a daddy."

Beethoven's Ninth sounded in electronic notes from her purse sitting atop the coffee table. Elias reached in and grabbed it. Holding it up to her face he asked, "Who is it?"

She shook her head. "I don't recognize the number."

He placed the phone on the floor and stomped. Shattered pieces scattered across the carpet. Then he went in her purse again and got out her wallet. Opening it up he pulled out her driver's license and twenty-eight dollars. The cash he stuffed in his pocket, the license he tossed on the table.

"Oh, Janet, now what to do, what to do?" Elias said, his lips just inches from hers.

A new terror spread across her face. She struggled to get up, but he put his arm around her shoulders, holding her down.

"Why don't you leave now? I promise I won't call the police."

"Oh, Janet, if only I could believe you."

"I promise."

"Janet, I got an idea. Why don't you give me a tour of the house? Let's start with the bedroom." He held her down while boosting himself to his feet. Before she could scream again, he grabbed her by the throat.

She panicked. Instead of compliance, she stomped as hard as she could on his foot. The pain and surprise made him release his grip. Janet reached up and gouged for his eyes. When he grabbed her wrists, she jumped up, head-butting him in the nose. A new searing pain flashed through Elias' head and blood poured once again from his nose.

This time she did run. She ran and screamed as Elias gave chase. He followed her into the kitchen. Next to the sink stood a butcher's block. One of the knives was missing. He grabbed her shoulder and she swung around.

Elias saw a glint of steel clenched in her fist and raised his arm defensively. The serrated blade missed slicing into his arm by a millimeter. He grabbed her fist in his, and used the bulk of his weight to push her against the counter. He twisted her wrist so the tip of the knife now pointed at her while the lip of the counter top pressed into her lower spine bending her backward. The knife inched closer and closer to her throat.

Janet's head now touched the counter. Elias could sense her strength ebbing away. He leaned down, his face hovering above hers. "Those God damned self defense classes for women. All they do is make things worse." With a shove he plunged the blade into her neck, still squeezing her wrist over the handle.

Shock registered on her face; she gagged. Together they pulled the knife out. Blood oozed through the wound.

"Try it again?" Elias asked. "How about a couple degrees to the left?"

They plunged the knife in again. This time blood shot up to the ceiling and across the room. Janet's legs buckled. Elias stepped back to let her fall to the floor.

"Oh no. I sank your battleship."

The blood quit spurting but a growing mass of red spread around her head. Elias stepped back to avoid getting his shoes contaminated. He grabbed a paper towel and shoved wads up his nose while holding his head back to try and stop his own bleeding. His heart raced when he heard the sound of the garage door going down. Breathing as quietly through his mouth as he could, Elias heard a door open.

"Hey Mom, what's wrong with the phone, and whose car is in the driveway?"

Why can't I ever catch a break?

Elias grabbed another knife from the butcher's block.

Twenty-Four

Sunday 8:30 a.m.

Gillespy dampened a sponge to seal the envelope. He addressed it to his probate attorney and laid it on the table. He decided against letting it sit in the mailbox; instead he'd give it directly to the postman tomorrow. His children would be gratified to know they would each get one dollar, and there would be a small trust fund of fifty thousand dollars for each of his grandchildren. The rest of his estate would be donated to the NRA. His pacifist kids would love that.

The phone rang just as he placed the stamp on the envelope. He looked at the caller I.D. and cursed. The damned Sheriff's Department again. *It's Sunday, for God's sake!* For once being sober was a plus; otherwise he might have called them back to complain.

As the ringing stopped, the doorbell chimed. *Damn, it doesn't rain, it pours.* He walked to the window and peered past the curtain. His heart did a quick leap at the sight of the same red car from other day. He shielded himself behind the drapes as the doorbell chimed once more.

At least it wasn't the law again. It might be the press, but he didn't think the lawsuit, or the hit and run, had made the news. He stuck by the window peeking out, hoping for a glimpse of the persistent busybody when they left his front door for their car.

The ringing switched into a pounding on the door and Gillespy jumped, nerves prickling down his spine. It seemed forever before the pounding stopped. The doorbell remained silent too, yet whoever was at the door still hadn't come into view.

Gillespy peeked a little further around the curtain when he heard the crash of broken glass coming from somewhere in the back of the house.

"Oh my God," he whispered. Without thinking, he ran to the phone and pressed 9-1 then stopped. He could no longer involve himself with the police.

The sound of crunching glass, an intruder invaded his sanctity. Quickly, silently, the doctor ran up the stairs to the bedroom. He opened the drawer of the night table on his wife's side of the bed. One of the few things she hadn't taken with her was the gun. He'd bought it for her to use as protection while he was away at those out-of-town meetings and conventions. She'd hated it, swore she'd never touch it. As far as he knew she never did.

There sat a .22 caliber pistol, gleaming and unused. He now regretted buying her such a small gun, but he thought it would fit nicely in her dainty hand. He picked it up and rubbed the shiny barrel. He checked the clip. Fully loaded he flipped the safety off. Gillespy's hand began to shake as he left the bedroom and back down the stairs.

On the bottom he paused. He heard the kitchen faucet running. Gillespy edged around the corner. Gripping the pistol with both hands, he leveled it at the back of a giant. The man was enormous! Six-seven or six-eight, and built solid as a tank. *Dear God. Would a .22 even puncture the man's skin? Maybe if I get him in the head.*

Gillespy took aim and began to squeeze the trigger. Suddenly it clicked in his brain. The giant was washing his dishes. *What the hell*? He lifted his finger off the trigger, watching as the man meticulously scrubbed each plate, dried them, and carefully stacked them next to the sink. Gillespy thought he might have even heard him humming underneath the sound of the water.

Who is this fool? I should wait until he's done before a confrontation. "No," he whispered. Instead, with jittery hands, he leveled the gun and in a shaky voice he said, "Put the plate down and turn around slowly."

The water shut off. The man stretched his arms above his head. They almost touched the ceiling. He glanced over his shoulder, smiled, and turned around, keeping his hands in the air.

The doctor shuddered at the sight of the man's face. Scratches seamed the bruised skin around his eyes. Crusted blood formed ridges around his nostrils, and his nose twisted off to the side. A split lip, a gash on his chin, one cheek bruised and swollen, a couple of lumps on his head, he looked like a jack-o-lantern a week after Halloween.

"Who are you?" Gillespy asked.

The big man said nothing. The doctor gripped the gun tighter.

"What are you doing here?"

"You called me," the stranger said.

In his mind, Gillespy panicked. Could he have called this guy during a blackout? A wrong number? Who knows what conversation might have been exchanged? He obviously had given the man his address.

"And you felt it necessary to come and break into my home?" the doctor asked.

"Yes," the man answered as he lowered his hands and wiped them on his jeans. "You told me we had to meet."

The doctor shuddered. He had no memory of the event. None at all. "What exactly did I say?" He kept the gun leveled.

The stranger eyed him suspiciously. "Don't you remember? You told me things were getting out of hand. You said it was time to do some damage control. After we killed those two people, you told me not to go home. You said I had acted rashly, so I drove around until you called and told me to come here."

Gillespy dropped the gun his hands shook so badly. Had he helped this man kill two people? No way. No amount of alcohol could make him blackout a murder. He shivered, yes it could. But he couldn't remember even leaving the house! He had to play this very carefully.

The doctor thought back to the days when he gave up the

idea of surgery and decided to focus his attention on the mind. He started to play with all kinds of medicine, especially the psychological kind. There were a lot of holes in his psyche now; he struggled to maintain what was left of his composure.

"Tell me," the doctor said. "In your words I want to know the sequence of events and how you felt during each episode."

The giant smiled like a child. "Where do you want me to start, doctor?"

Gillespy froze. His mind raced. Did he know this giant man/child? The man/child certainly seemed to know him. The doctor had to assume this man had been one of his patients from way back when. Relief washed over him.

"Let's retire to the den. Then start from the beginning."

The giant smiled and eagerly followed the doctor. Gillespy guided him into the den—not wanting to turn his back on this stranger—and motioned him to sit on the overstuffed leather sofa while he went to the liquor cabinet and took out a bottle of Baileys. He poured two glasses and handed one to the stranger, trying to put the man at ease.

"Other than a couple of scratches, it looks like you came out of it rather well over-all."

He strolled back to his desk and took a seat. The gun still lay on the kitchen floor. Gillespy decided to trust his instincts. The man was huge, but far from an intellectual equal.

"Tell me where you're at?" the doctor asked. A familiar opening he used on his patients. A technique he found affective and satisfying.

The phone rang. The doctor held up a finger as he looked at the caller I.D. and sighed. The Sheriff's Department again. Now they were toying with him. The former client sat quietly as the doctor stared at the phone. The ringing stopped. "Nobody important."

The big man smiled. The doctor made a mental note. *He needs to feel important. Not unusual but the knowledge might come in handy.*

"You say I called you," Gillespy said. "Let's go back to the first time. How did that make you feel?"

"The very first time?" the stranger asked.

The doctor nodded as he took a sip of Bailey's. He smiled as the giant did the same, but crinkling his already crumpled nose at the taste of alcohol.

"Scared. I didn't know what to expect." He took another sip. This time his faced relaxed as he adjusted to the alcohol laced chocolate.

"Not a complete answer." Gillespy had to rein in his patience. All he knew was that this man must have been a patient of his from way back. He needed to know about the murders. Could that be why the Sheriff's Department kept calling? He quickly decided not. *It still must be about that pesky hit and run.* Had they suspected him of a murder they'd have broken down the door with a search warrant.

"Do you remember why I called you?" Gillespy made it sound like a test.

"You said I was a fuck-up. You asked if I wanted to be a productive member of society, or a leach on the butt of humanity."

"Yes, yes, yes," the doctor said impatiently. "I said that to everybody." The frustration showed as he gulped down the Bailey's and poured himself another. He was no closer to knowing who this idiot was—other than confirming he was a former patient. "What made you special?"

The man mimicked the doctor by downing his drink. He held out his glass for more. Gillespy went rigid. He didn't want to serve the man. He'd think he had an edge and the power might shift. On the other hand, he also didn't want the man to get up and approach. So, the doctor capped the bottle and tossed it over. Not very mannerly perhaps, but it served its purpose.

"My size made me special," the man said.

Getting no closer to this murderer's identity and his own involvement, Gillespy changed his line of questioning. Hell, a lot of the kids he'd dealt with were big. Who knew how many had grown up to be freakish giants?

"Let's jump ahead," Gillespy said, trying not to give away

his ignorance. "As an adult, what were you doing when I called? After all, it must have been years since you've heard from me."

The big man thought as he poured himself another glass. "Not really. We've talked a lot over the years, off and on."

The man had to be delusional. How could the doctor have blacked out years of conversations with this individual? Gillespy's patience ran dry. "This is absurd. I don't even know who the hell you are!"

His statement caught the giant off-guard. His faced darkened as they glared at each other. Gillespy broke the gaze only when the man's giant hand crushed the goblet he held. Liquor mixed with blood as shards of glass dug into the man's skin. Both dripped on the Persian carpet.

With a shriek of dismay, Gillespy grabbed some tissues and dashed around the desk over to the stranger. The man held out his hand, obviously expecting the doctor to wrap it. Instead, the doctor dropped to his knees and began blotting up the new stain ruining his rug.

Hands like vises clamped on each shoulder, hoisting Gillespy to his feet. The maniac's eyes grew wild and he began to shake the doctor, blood from his hand seeping through the doctor's shirt. "You're not nearly as strong when there aren't four orderlies standing at your side."

Gillespy's jitters disappeared as memories flooded back. Only one boy had needed four orderlies to subdue him; and only one way to keep him under control. The doctor pitched his voice for control. The doctor swung a hard slap across the man's face. "Put me down you fool! I was testing you."

The outside shaking stopped but inside Gillespy quivered like jelly.

"A test, huh? Okay, then I'll test you. What's my name?" the giant asked.

Gillespy felt the blood stick his shirt to his shoulder. "Sit down, Elias Boughton."

Cowed, the big man took his seat.

"If I still had my riding crop you wouldn't be able to sit down for a week, would you, Elias?"

Elias stared down at his feet as the doctor paced beore him.

"I invite you into my home and share my food with you, and this is how my generosity is repaid?" He smacked him across the top of his head. Elias didn't flinch. "You're still worthless. Why would I ever want to call the likes of you?"

Elias kept his eyes lowered but the doctor thought he might have seen the glimpse of a smile.

"Now, I'm going to ask you some questions. I don't care how obvious or stupid they sound to you; you will answer them. Do you understand?"

Elias nodded.

"Look at me and answer." The doctor gave him another swat across the top of his head.

Elias timidly raised his head. "Yes."

"Yes what?" Gillespy snapped.

"Yes, Doctor Gillespy."

Elias reverted from adult to the big dumb oaf twelve-year-old who couldn't control his anger. The kid had a brain like clay that Gillespy had molded into a subservient dolt, more than eager to please his superiors for any semblance of recognition. Elias' emotional scars still ran very deep.

"Now, why do you think I would ever have reason to call the likes of you?"

"I don't know." Elias shrugged his shoulders, his voice boyish.

"Not an acceptable answer. Do I need to ask it again?"

Elias squirmed in his seat.

"Do I?" the doctor yelled.

"No, Doctor Gillespy."

"Why did I call you?"

"You said you needed my help."

Another chill temporarily brought Gillespy back to the present. He still had no recollection of ever calling Elias. "Why did I say I wanted your help?"

"You said you've been following my progress and were very impressed. You said you had a job for me."

The old voice, tingeing with uncertainty, returned. "Go on."

"You said your partner was a traitor. You wanted me to teach him a lesson."

"Leonard Hout?" Gillespy asked, his voice fraying.

"Then you told me there was a bitch lawyer suing you for malpractice. You wanted me to fuck her up and make your partner look responsible. You wanted me to make sure his testimony would be worthless."

"That doesn't make any sense," Gillespy whispered to himself. From nothing to information overload evolved in just two questions. He had to sit down and control his thoughts. Bailey's would no longer do. He went for the Cutty. "What did you do?" he choked out.

"You know. You saw it all."

"Answer me!" Gillespy shouted. He took a long pull off the bottle of scotch and barely felt the burn as it sailed down his throat.

Confusion, fright, and anger reigned on Elias' face. "I did what you told me to do."

"I never told you to do anything! How could I call you? I don't even know your phone number! I'd forgotten you even existed until now!"

"Why are you testing me again?" Elias shouted.

"Because you're still a worthless piece of slime that doesn't know fact from fiction. I was not there with you! Now tell me what you did!"

A smile slowly crept across the face of Elias as a calm spread throughout his body. He stared at the doctor's throat. "I remember how that vein in your neck used to throb when you got mad. It hasn't changed. We used to make bets on who could make it throb first."

You did? Gillespy stopped his tirade and with the exception of the throbbing vein he gave the appearance of calm.

"Did you kill Leonard Hout?" he asked in a quiet voice.

"Not yet."

"The lawyer?"

"Not yet."

"Then who did you kill?" Gillespy made sure not to use the word 'we.'

Elias shrugged as he plucked slivers of glass from his palm. "A couple of whores who got in the way."

"Prostitutes?" The doctor handed Elias a box of tissues.

Again, Elias shrugged. "Oh yeah, and a cop. I did him on my own, though. That was personal business. You said it was okay, that it needed to be done anyway. It got me easy access to your partner."

Gillespy's blood turned to slush. "You said I was there?"

Elias thoughtfully watched the tissue absorb his blood. "Well, not exactly. You were there, but in my head. Watching through my eyes."

"I see." Gillespy kept his voice tranquil but inside a tidal wave of relief washed through him, like a man being pardoned from death row. He could personally certify this man as crazy. "Have our entire conversations taken place inside of your head?"

Elias eyed him suspiciously. "You know they have."

"Let's go back to the first time I contacted you. What were you doing?"

"I just finished reading an article in the paper. You messed up some bitch and she killed herself. Her family said they were going to sue you." Elias couldn't look the doctor in the eye; instead, he emptied the box of tissues and wadded them into his hand.

"What a coincidence I would pick that very convenient time to contact you."

"The world is full of coincidences, Doctor. Isn't that what you told me?"

"Yes it is." Gillespy thought about how to use this new development to his advantage. "So tell me, have all of our conversations been telepathic?"

Elias regarded his hand as he spoke. "Why do you ask me questions you already know the answers to?"

Gillespy took a sip of his drink and got up from his desk. He slowly walked over to Elias, never taking his eyes off of him and stopped just inches away so he could look down on him. "Because I am the doctor and you are the patient."

Elias shifted his gaze away, and took in the bottle of Bailey's. Not finding a glass, he took three gulps from the bottle. A thin line of tan liquid rolled out of the side of his mouth. He used his sleeve to wipe his face before it dripped onto the doctor's oh so precious rug.

He held the bottle out in front of him so he could read the label. "I think I'm developing a taste for this," Elias said.

That hadn't been the reaction that Gillespy had hoped for. The doctor's bravado melted to concern and a bit of fear as he wondered if he had pushed the big man too far. "So, you have Hout and this lawyer. What's her name—Cartier? I'd like to see them." The doctor once again used his gentle voice. "That is, I'd like to see them through my eyes, not yours."

Elias beamed and jumped up from the sofa. "It's probably best if I drive, huh?"

Gillespy let the remark pass without comment.

As they walked to the door the doctor glanced into the kitchen with its broken patio door. He paused, shrugged his shoulders and smiled grimly. He'd deal with it later. After all, this was a safe neighborhood.

Twenty-Five

Sunday 8:45 a.m.

Byron Kransky loved the smell of morning. He loved the quiet and peace by the lake before the kids crawled out of bed and littered the beaches with their presence. Kelsey loved the morning too. The golden retriever made his master stop at almost every tree and bush while he took in the smells and left his mark.

The rising sun lit the streaking clouds orange and red as the man and dog walked their usual route around Perch Lake. Coming up to their favorite part of the path, Kelsey led Byron around the curve and away from the street where only trees and lake were his personal playground.

As Kelsey walked his master down the lane, a warm breeze ruffled through the leaves on the trees. Byron kept strolling but Kelsey froze, his nose pointing up and toward the woods. Byron stopped as the leash lost its slack. He gave a soft tug but the dog stood firm. He jerked a little harder. Kelsey sniffed the air, his gaze distant as he tested a scent on the breeze.

"C'mon, boy. Let's get moving." He gave a sharp tug but instead of relenting, Kelsey tore off into the woods, ripping the leash from Byron's hand.

"Kelsey! Come!" Not worried he'd run away, Byron was more concerned that the leash would snag and Kelsey, running at full speed, would snap his neck, or maybe choke himself to death.

"Kelsey!"

Byron parted the branches and entered the woods listening. He heard a rustling to his left, moved that way and found a narrow path. He followed it past the blueberry bushes and found Kelsey busy digging into the soft mound of earth. Byron momentarily froze before throwing up.

~

Andrew sat on his couch reading Tim Laurence's "The Hoffman Process," a book about spiritual transformation. He absently scratched Corwin behind the ears. The cat purred and stretched over Andrew's lap, his head draped across his human's leg.

The phone rang. Corwin hissed as Andrew picked him up and gently dropped him on the floor.

"Hello?" Andrew cringed; the acid in his stomach roiled when he heard the voice of his FTO.

"Any big plans for the day?" Rivers asked. Before Andrew could reply, he said, "Get your uniform on and meet me at the station."

"It's my day off," Andrew said looking toward the hamper that held his crumpled uniform. "I have to take care of—"

"Take care of your business later. They're calling us in. There's been a double homicide at Perch Lake."

Andrew's stomach clenched into a knot at the words *Perch Lake,* instant memories of Mark Lone Bear's bloated body. Now there were two more?

"What do we know so far?" Andrew asked.

"Not much. Looks like mother and daughter. Some guy was walking his dog this morning and all of the sudden the dog goes all ape shit. Dashes off into the woods and when the guy follows, he finds 'em. Not a pretty sight from what I heard."

"Good God. Give me a half-hour."

"I'll be waiting." Rivers hung up.

~

A bright, cloudless blue canvassed the sky as Andrew pulled his car into the lot with three minutes to spare of the half-hour he'd promised. Carlin Rivers sat in the Crown Victoria, motor running, air conditioner on, and working a crossword puzzle. He put the paper down when he saw Andrew walking toward the car.

"Learn anything new?" Andrew asked.

"Nothing more than I already told you, other than it's a real mess. They want us for crowd control or help out however we can." Carlin put the car in drive and screeched the tires out of the parking lot.

"What's going on with this world? When was the last time there was a murder in Kenowa? And now there are three?"

"Go figure," Carlin said. "Although technically it's only two. They figure Lone Bear was probably killed in Minneapolis and his body moved to the lake."

"Don't forget the dog."

"That's the really eerie thing. The bodies are in the same place."

An involuntary gasp escaped Andrew's lips as the color drained from his face. Carlin noticed it too.

"Do you have something you want to tell me?"

Andrew searched his mind for the right words. Coming up with nothing brilliant, he spit out the plain truth. "Me and Louise were up there last night."

Carlin took his eyes off the road just long enough to give Andrew a good hard stare. "Why and what time?"

"Around six, maybe six-thirty. We think that whoever beat that dog might have killed Lone Bear. At least we think the two are related. We also think it might be tied in to that psychiatrist's disappearance."

"We? And just how did *we* come to this conclusion?"

Andrew chose his words carefully. He didn't want to come off as some sort of movie cop who did everything on his own. "One of Louise's informants, actually, an Indian boy who knew Lone Bear from the neighborhood, told her he saw a giant of a man driving Lone Bear's squad. The kid with Hout's ATM said a huge man sold it to him. And last night we found a footprint at the scene. It must've been a size thirteen, at least."

"So two kids say they saw a giant, and you found Bigfoot's

footprint that the officers, deputies, detectives, and God knows who else scoured the scene missed?"

"It was beyond the search area," Andrew cut in.

Carlin shook his head. "I've heard of crazier things."

Even though the squad car's lights were on, traffic up ahead seemed to ignore them. Carlin flipped on the siren and the cars parted a path.

"So, when were you planning on sharing your theories?" Carlin had to almost shout to be heard above the sirens. With a clear lane ahead, he flipped off the noise but kept the flashers going.

"When I came back to work. I wanted to see if we could strengthen our case, or maybe come up with another theory."

They reached Perch Lake in less than ten minutes. Andrew stared out over the water as they drove by the spot where the canoeists found Lone Bear's car. That spot would haunt him forever. At a point where the woods met the lake, news vans had taken up the majority of the parking lot. Rivers found a spot and parked next to the path that led off into the woods. A crowd of people had already gathered, mostly teens in bathing suits with a smattering of adults from nearby houses.

"News vans," Carlin spoke softly to Andrew. "Attracts people like shit attracts flies."

They shoved their way past the throng until they reached the yellow tape. Three deputies and a Kenowa police officer guarded the line as Andrew and Carlin bent under the plastic strip and made their way to the scene. Fortunately, trees barred the sight from the media.

Andrew's nausea built at the sight of activity around the bodies. A young girl, and probably her mother, lay in the hole where the dog had been buried, their faces hidden behind a mask of dirt and blood. A crime lab photographer was busy clicking away at the bodies from every conceivable angle as other techs scoured the scene; laying markers everywhere they found anything that might be relevant.

One of the detectives noticed Carlin and smiled. "Hey Sarge, didn't know you were here."

"How sick is that?" Carlin pointed to the hole.

"The son of a bitch has a real sick sense of humor."

"That's Detective Taylor. He used to be one of mine," Carlin whispered to Andrew. "A real go-getter. I knew he wouldn't be in a uniform for very long."

"What do you think they were doing out here?" Carlin asked.

Taylor examined the shallow grave. "They were already dead. Someone dumped 'em."

"Any I.D.?" Carlin asked.

The detective shook his head.

"Rivers, you old piece of shit, how's it hanging?"

Carlin smiled as the police chief of Kenowa approached. "About three inches—off the ground, you old fart. How are you, Ken?"

The two men shook hands as Andrew leaned over and whispered in his partner's ear, "The press?"

Carlin gave a barely perceptible nod, his eyes scanning for cameras and microphones.

"My trainee," Carlin jerked his head toward Andrew. "He keeps me on the straight and narrow, but I like him anyway."

"Ken Dearling," the chief said.

Andrew and the police chief shook hands.

"So what the hell is going on in this city of yours?" Carlin asked. "You trying to keep up with Murderapolis?"

"I don't know what the hell is going on. First that cop and now this. I don't get it. We're supposed to have a D.U.I. or two every week and maybe a domestic now and then, but this? It's crazy. In its infinite wisdom our chamber of commerce has been campaigning to get the big city folk out here as an alternative to the noise and violence. I think we're attracting the very element that we've been advertising to people that they can avoid."

"I think it might be just one sicko," Carlin said.

"That's one of the angles were covering, but what makes you think so?" The chief's curiosity was piqued.

"I'll let my deputy fill you in on his theory. I think it might hold some salt."

Shocked and filled with pride, Andrew watched as Taylor sidled over next to the chief to hear what he had to say. He knew Carlin's motive. If the theory held—great; Andrew would get accolades and Carlin would be happy for him. If not, Carlin would be in the clear of all the egg that would land on Andrew's face. He led the men past the clearing to where he and Louise found the footprint while explaining his thoughts.

"What would you like us to do?" Carlin asked when the chief returned. The detective stayed by the footprint.

The chief scanned the scene. "Well, seeing as how I've got all of my full-timers here, one of my part-timers on vacation, and another one out sick; that only leaves two to take calls. It would be nice if you could cruise the area and help them out."

"All five of 'em here, huh?" Carlin laughed.

"Hey, we're growing. Next year's budget might even have enough money that we can hire a sixth full-timer."

"Considering the murder rate around here, I'd ask for seven."

The mood became somber as the three men watched the two victims being loaded into body bags.

"Well, we'll be moving along. You've got your hands full. Remember, we're happy to help out. Let us know if there's anything else we can do," Carlin said.

"Just keep me in the loop," the chief said.

"Wait a minute," Andrew said as the bags were being zipped. He ran over and unzipped the bag of the daughter. "I saw her on the news last night. This is the girl who found the dog."

The entire crime scene froze as every eye focused on Andrew. In an instant Andrew could hear the breeze.

Ken Dearling fumed. "You mean to tell me no one recognized this as the..." He stopped and eyed the clearing where the police tape kept back the press on the other side of the trees. "No one recognized this girl?" he said.

Every man there looked anywhere except at the chief.

Carlin nodded as he and Andrew left the scene.

"Good going, rookie. Way to stir things up." Carlin patted him on the shoulder. As they walked the trail back to the car, they ignored the questions being hurled at them.

"Do you remember her name?" Carlin whispered.

Andrew thought. "It's Scandiwhovian. I remember it had two A's next to each other.

A new horde of news people rushed to meet them as they approached their car. A woman with a microphone squeezed her way to the front of the pack. "Excuse me Deputy, can you answer a couple of questions?"

Andrew recognized her as the reporter from Channel Six who interviewed the child.

"She's a pariah," Carlin said. "That's Bianca Skylar. Watch out for her. She actually broke into a house to get a story. To her credit, it was a crack house, but still, the owner sued. Settled out of court, but she earned herself a six month suspension. A rumor also floated around that she'd slept with some CEO before disgracing him on the air and forcing him to resign."

With her camera crew, Bianca Skylar caught up to the deputies. "What's going on back there, Sergeant?"

"Welcome back, Ms. Skylar," said Carlin. "Has it been six months already?"

"Time flies. Who is she? How was she killed? I was told it's a real mess back there. If you show me I'll make sure I get your name on the air. I'll even promise to pronounce it right."

"Oh, be still me heart." Carlin clutched his chest. "That's all we talk about in the squad room is how we all hope our names will be smeared across the news."

"Okay, how about I promise not to use your name?"

Carlin walked over and slipped his arm around the reporter. "This is what I can tell you," he spoke softly in her ear. "There will be an official press conference later this afternoon."

Skylar jerked her shoulder away from the sergeant's arm.

She nodded and winked at her cameraman as they wandered toward the scene.

"What a bitch," Carlin said as they got in the car. "She also walked on a couple of cops a few years ago. Two got suspensions, one got fired."

"What did they do?" Andrew asked.

"I don't remember. Roughed up a couple of punks, I think. Maybe one might have had a beer or two for lunch. I'm not sure. Whatever it was, they didn't deserve having their careers ruined. That's why we've got an internal affairs department."

"To ruin careers?" Andrew smirked.

"Don't be a smart ass."

Inside the squad, Andrew flipped on the computer as Carlin started the engine.

"What are you doing?" Carlin asked.

"Saangvold." Andrew punched in the name and a moment later the data popped up. "Janet Saangvold." Andrew brought up her driver's license. "Think we should check out her house?"

Carlin looked at the computer screen. "Let me tell Ken what we're doing, prepare him that the crime lab might be in for a long day." He opened the door and got out.

"Why don't you call him on the radio?"

"With all these news folk around I don't trust the radio. Especially Skylar. I wouldn't put it past her to have some eavesdropping device. She'd break in before we even got there."

Andrew opened the door to follow.

"Why don't you stay here and start working on your report. I'll be back in a couple."

Carlin closed the door, took three steps and came back and rapped on the window. Andrew lowered it a couple of inches. The sergeant smiled approvingly at his trainee. "I think you're turning into one hell of a deputy, Deputy Miller."

Carlin left him alone. Andrew beamed on the inside; he looked down and smiled. He pulled out his pad and started writing his report. All at once, a commotion by the entrance to the woods caused him to look up. Two men were shouting at one another, one jabbing his finger in the other man's chest. Andrew put down his pad and exited the vehicle, walking with a quick pace to the disturbance.

"What's going on?" Andrew asked, approaching. Both men appeared vaguely familiar.

"He stole my jacket," one of them said.

Andrew recognized Bianca Skylar's cameraman and another member of her crew. He looked back toward the squad, his heart sinking. He couldn't remember if he'd left the door open when he raced out, but it was wide open now. Then he saw the blonde hair peek up from the windshield. "Oh shit!"

He dashed back to the car. Bianca Skylar sat hunched over the computer, scribbling in her notebook. She was oblivious to him, her knees planted on the seat in front of the steering wheel, her butt in Andrew's face. Janet Saangvald's face still lit up the computer screen.

He wished Carlin had been there. He could hear him come up with something lewd and insulting and taking control of the situation. Andrew wished he could say something like that, but it wasn't him. Instead, acting on instinct only, he grabbed her ankles and yanked her out of the car. With a startled scream the reporter landed on the hard pavement scraping her knees and palms.

"What the hell?" She scowled as Andrew grabbed her under the arm and jerked her to her feet.

"That's breaking and entering. You're under arrest." He mistook the sorrow in her eyes for fear.

"Is that the victim, Janet Saangvold?" Her lips trembled as her voice cracked.

Andrew didn't know what to do. His confidence eroded to uncertainty. "I don't know what you're talking about."

"Don't treat me like I'm stupid, Deputy. It was her, wasn't it?"

Andrew wasn't going to tell her what she already knew.

"What about Tiffany?" Skylar's voice held a note of urgency.

No amount of lying would convince her otherwise. "You can't report any of this until after relatives have been notified."

"Oh my God," she whispered. Tears welled up in her eyes. She dabbed at them with the sleeve of her blazer. "Can't let a few tears ruin my makeup."

Andrew didn't know if she were putting on a show, or if the reporter really felt something for the mother and daughter. He gave her the benefit of the doubt. He decided that her attempt to act professional couldn't cover up real feelings for that little girl. "You can't report this until relatives have been notified, right?" He noticed that they had become the center of attention. Minnesota nice kept the onlookers from coming too close, but her own news crew rapidly approached.

Bianca waved them off. "Give me a minute you guys." She turned back to Andrew. "It's our station's policy."

They backed off, but another news reporter saw that there might be a story here and trotted over.

"Maybe you'd like to sit in the car and collect yourself," Andrew said.

She nodded. Andrew let her slide in. Her dress inched up to mid-thigh. The pantyhose were ruined from when he jerked her out of the car, but even that couldn't disguise a pair of great legs. He got in the car after her and closed the door as the competing reporter approached.

Andrew flipped down the computer screen and shook his head. The reporter outside raised his arms in a what's-going-on-in-there gesture. He tried to think of something to say while Bianca stared out the passenger window. "You shouldn't have broken in." It was a stupid thing to say, but at least it got a reaction.

Bianca's eyes were red, still brimming with tears. She put on a forced smile. "I just noticed the door open and no one around. I was just going to close it but I wanted to make sure you didn't leave the keys inside. That's all."

"Oh brother." The pain in Andrew's stomach bit deep. An acid belch raced up his throat, singeing every nerve along the way. "You crossed the line."

"Don't you know? I'm known for that."

Andrew took a deep breath. "You know what's coming, don't you?"

A flash of anger seared through the hurt. "You're going try and get me suspended again? Over this?"

Before she could continue her onslaught, Andrew cut her off. "I want you to tell me everything that Tiffany Saangvold told you. And I'm going to want an unedited copy of that tape."

Bianca forced out a fake laugh and dropped her head. As she rubbed her eyes Andrew knew he'd caught her off guard, and the fight had drained out of her.

"Of course." She looked up and Andrew blushed. She'd caught him looking at her legs. "You owe me a new pair of pantyhose."

Still beet red, Andrew opened his pad and started asking questions. When he finished, he saw Carlin walking across the lot. He flipped his notebook shut and Bianca handed him her card. "Please call me the second you learn anything new."

"In other words, you want the scoop."

"That's just an added perk. Now it's personal. I want to be there when you catch this bastard."

The passenger door opened and Carlin stood at the opening gesturing for the reporter to get out. He didn't look pleased.

"Sergeant." Bianca slipped past him.

"Ma'am." He nodded his head and took Bianca's seat, surprising Andrew by leaving him behind the wheel. "Well?"

"I made an executive decision. She might've been the last person who talked to Tiffany Saangvold. Thought she might be able to give some insight. I figured their identity is going to be released soon anyway, and she can't report it until after we notify relatives, so what harm could it do?"

Carlin rubbed his chin. "I don't trust her."

"She took it pretty hard," Andrew said.

Carlin fastened his seatbelt. "Okay Mr. Executive Decision, why don't you drive us to the Saangvold house?"

~

A group of boys, each wearing shorts that started halfway down their butts and ended a few inches above their ankles, skateboarded down the sidewalk as the deputies pulled into the Saangvold driveway. Across the street, an electric lawn mower hummed as its owner took great cares to not run over the cord. Down the street, the four skateboarders stood at the corner staring back.

Carlin rang the bell. When no one answered, he knocked. "Hennepin County Sheriff. Anyone home?" He turned the knob; the door was unlocked.

"It doesn't look like forced entry," Andrew said.

"That doesn't mean anything. She could've answered the door and somebody could've forced their way in." Carlin opened the door. He peeked in and spoke in the radio attached to his collar. "Send backup and a team." He recited the address.

Andrew saw a cell phone shattered on the carpet. Smears of blood were on the couch. Both men drew their guns. Carlin motioned for Andrew to go in first. As soon as Andrew crossed the threshold he sensed the negative aura. Carlin followed using hand signals for Andrew to go into the next room.

The kitchen looked like a slaughterhouse. Dried blood on the ceiling had dripped onto the floor. Blood splatter had reached all four walls and speckled the countertops. The acid in Andrew's stomach churned; he swallowed hard to keep the vomit back. A massive reddish-brown puddle on the floor in front of the sink hadn't completely dried yet. From that spot a wide swath of streaked brown led a path to the garage door. Two knives—one with a serrated edge—rested in the sink. Both were spotlessly clean.

"Jesus God Damned Christ." Carlin stopped at the foot of the kitchen door.

Andrew wondered if his sergeant might lose it too, and

followed him out. In the distance sirens blared, getting louder by the second.

"Nothing in the bedrooms. Blood in the bathroom, though. We might've caught a break there. Looks like he took a shower. The tech boys might be able to grab a hair sample." Carlin motioned toward Andrew's waist.

Andrew noticed that he still held his gun. He closed his eyes, took a deep breath, and put the weapon back in its holster.

Two Kenowa police squads pulled up to the house. Carlin met the officers at the door and told them of the grisly discovery. He told them it was their city, and they could take it from here. "We'll find out if the neighbors saw anything."

One of the officers went to his car and pulled out a roll of crime scene tape; a sight Andrew had seen way too much of the last couple of days.

"Why don't you start with that side of the street?" Carlin said.

Grateful, Andrew stepped out of the house.

Out of the nine houses Andrew canvassed, five who were home neither saw nor heard anything unusual. The others had not been home last night, or as one teen so eloquently put it, "Dude, who stays home on a Saturday night?"

Twenty-Six

Sunday 8:55 a.m.

Elias maintained a cautious vigil as he drove down the street, keeping the car within the speed limit. Gillespy had been targeted by the police, and Elias had made it his job to protect him. He kept glancing over at the doctor. The doctor stared back, never taking his eyes off him. *Like I'm being studied*, Elias thought uneasily.

A band of clouds rolled in front of the sun, partially blocking the light. It made the cornfields look like those pictures used on gospel music albums. Elias flipped down the visor wishing the sun shone through the passenger window so he could put the divider between him and Gillespy. Then he noticed that it wouldn't turn that way anyhow. He tried to break the tension with conversation.

"S.K. is alive," Elias said.

"Is that right?" The doctor's voice lacked interest. "Who's S.K.?"

Elias glanced over to see if he was being tested once again. Getting more irritated with every mile, Elias finally pulled to the side of the road and parked, twisting his massive frame so he could face the doctor. "Two things. One, S.K. was my best friend. And two, I think you'd better start treating me with a little more respect." He put on his intimidation face.

"If he's still alive wouldn't he still be your best friend?"

"What?"

"You said *was* your best friend. You spoke of S.K. in the past tense. If he's still alive then it stands to reason that he'd continue being your best friend. You speak of respect. To get respect you have to earn it. To earn it, a good start would be to speak proper English."

"Like you've earned the respect of the psychiatric community?"

The doctor failed to respond. Elias' mouth distorted into a grin—he'd hit a nerve. Satisfied for the small victory Elias pulled back into traffic. They remained silent the rest of the trip.

"We're here." Elias pulled into his driveway.

"So it seems," replied Gillespy.

"What do you think?"

The doctor stared at the modest split level for a moment. "It looks like the cheapest house on the block. That should be good, if you decide to sell."

Elias's temper bubbled to the surface. He pulled the car into the garage and pressed the button on the remote, waiting until the door closed before turning off the engine. He'd never thought about doing in the doctor, at least as an adult, until now. How easy it would be to punch his smug little face into unconsciousness and let him die of the exhaust fumes. The thought scared him and he tried to bury it, but the idea kept popping back. *I'll just save it for later.*

He unlocked the door and led the doctor into his home. "Walk this way," he said thinking of the old Marx brothers' movie. He wanted the doctor to respond but Gillespy remained silent, just looking at his surroundings.

"If I could walk that way…oh, never mind." Elias slumped his shoulders and led the way.

They reached the basement door. Elias pulled out a key, noticing a dab of blood on the knob. He half-expected the doctor to tell him he missed a spot. Gillespy seemed oblivious, just staring at the heavily reinforced door.

The lock clicked. The door swung open. A sudden chill ran through Elias as he looked down the stairs. He was so used to seeing S.K. sitting guard on the bottom step. Now, only the blood remained as a silent reminder. He bit back on his sorrow, making sure not to give Gillespy any more ammunition than he already had.

~

Gillespy followed his ex-patient down the stairs. The stench stunned him. Feces, urine, and body odor flooded his nostrils so fast his eyes started to water. Blood was everywhere. He jerked his hand off the railing, thinking of the god-awful germs that must be on it.

He wanted, no, *needed* a drink. He reached for his flask but his hip pocket held nothing.

"Where are your manners, Elias? I offered you my hospitality when you were in my home. Shouldn't you reciprocate?" Gillespy didn't want to go into the basement, yet it held a horrible fascination, nevertheless.

"What do you mean?" Elias frowned.

"It means that when you invite a guest into your home you should offer them—" He broke off at the sight of his ex-partner strapped belly down onto some torture device that held him firmly in place. Dried blood had saturated his shirt and matted his hair. Fresh blood drooled out of the corner of his mouth. "Oh my God," whispered Gillespy.

A long lost feeling of compassion overwhelmed him. He wanted to race down the stairs to help but the giant blocked his way. Fear now gripped him as he witnessed firsthand how sadistic this psycho had become, and how years of his amazing therapy had done absolutely nothing.

"What?" Elias asked.

Gillespy looked up. "Huh?"

"You were lecturing me about manners."

"Scotch, straight up."

"I've got beer or orange juice."

"Christ." It would take a keg to wash away the fear and nausea. "Beer will be fine."

Elias squeezed past the doctor as he went back up the steps. With a clear path, Gillespy raced down the stairs toward Hout. He dropped to his knees and placed his fingers on Leonard's neck, seeking a pulse. Hout was unconscious; his pulse weak but steady.

"Oh my God. Leonard, my dear boy, I had no idea. I'll get you out of this. I had no idea."

Behind him, Elias clomped down the stairs. The crazy giant carried one bottle of beer in each hand.

"He's bleeding internally," Gillespy said. "He's going to die if we don't get him to a hospital." He had no idea if that were really the case, but he had to try anything to get his ex-partner out of this hell.

"So he dies." Elias handed Gillespy a beer. "We don't need him anymore."

"You!" came a voice from the far wall.

Gillespy's heart jumped. How could he not have noticed before? Tied spread-eagled on a giant X, he hardly recognized the lady attorney. She glared at him with the one eye that hadn't swelled completely shut. Still, he couldn't take his eyes off of her small breasts cupped in a blood soaked bra.

Elias twisted off the cap on his bottle of beer and nonchalantly took a sip. "You can do her if you want."

Gillespy drifted over to Melanie. "I'll think about it." He stared absently at the woman, and for the first time in years he felt a stirring in his groin when he focused his attention up from her breasts and noticed the bruises decorating her throat.

"You'll burn in Hell for this," Melanie said, although it was hard for Gillespy to understand because her lips were as swollen as her eyes.

"She used to be okay to look at." Elias chuckled at his handy work.

Gillespy continued the ruse. "She's still okay."

Dear God, what a mess. Sure, he wished his ex-partner dead; a hundred times over, but not like this. *I just wanted you to disappear along with all of my other problems.*

Gillespy had been accused of being evil before, but his accusers hadn't known the meaning of the word. He now stared into the face of evil. And that face stared right back at him. *Get a hold of yourself, William. You're losing control.* Chills crawled down his spine as the tester became the testee. He felt out of his realm of power and now he had to tread very carefully. He thought of the gun still lying on his kitchen floor.

"What do you think?" Elias asked. "Did I pass your test?"

Gillespy looked up into the expectant face of the psycho whom he had helped create. "A plus. In fact, you've done everything I've expected from you, and more."

Elias beamed.

"I knew it. You son-of-a-bitch," Melanie spat.

He needed to control Elias. Outside interference would make that job all the more difficult.

Gillespy knew Elias' eyes were upon him. Before pulling his head back, the doctor nuzzled his face into her neck. Through the stench he smelled the remnants of perfume. Before pulling away, he whispered in her ear, "I'll get you out of this." He said this while cupping her breast in his hand, then gliding his hand down past her stomach and between her legs. Melanie writhed against her binds, but her squirming stimulated his perversion even more.

Gillespy tried to convince himself he did it because of Elias staring, but he felt disgust at himself as his excitement grew; more ashamed that his growing cock had nothing to do with sex, but total control over another human being. He stepped back before he got too carried away.

"I could set up a camera if you want something for posterity." Elias' eyes gleamed. A spot of drool escaped his lips.

"That would add to the excitement, wouldn't it, Ms. Cartier?" Gillespy became aware of the heat as the woman's eye burned into him. He sidled up next to the attorney and pressed his lips into her ear and traced her curves with his tongue.

"What kind of sick fucker are you?" she screamed, trying to squrim away.

"Elias, go get the camera," he said over his shoulder.

Melanie hocked a wad of phlegm on the doctor's cheek.

Elias giggled like a schoolboy as he bounded up the steps. The basement door clicked shut. Gillespy pulled away from the woman eying her with an apologetic look. "I'm so sorry, but I had to do that. I know you don't believe me, but I swear to God I had no idea of this until just this morning." He walked over and knelt down next to a still unconscious Hout.

"Leonard, my boy, I am so sorry." His hand shook as he spoke. He needed a drink as badly has he needed to remain sober. The bottle of beer sat less than ten feet away calling to him. He ignored it.

Melanie clamped her good eye shut and twisted her head as far away from him as she could.

"We don't have much time. He'll be back in a minute," he told her. "I can control him but it won't be easy. He can be extremely volatile."

Puzzled, she opened an eye to peek at him.

The basement door opened. Elias clamored down the steps carrying a camcorder and tripod. Melanie squirmed against her ties as the giant set up the camera. He pressed the button and the red light came on. "Ready, and action." He peered into the viewfinder.

Gillespy stared at Elias. "What are you doing?"

Surprised, Elias said, "I'm your camera man."

"No, no, no!" Gillespy shook his head. "I refuse to conduct a rape in front of an audience. You'll have to leave."

"But I want to watch," Elias whined.

"Who do you think you are?" Gillespy boomed. "Get out of here and let me do my work."

Elias looked as if he'd been slapped. He turned from Melanie to the doctor. Shaken, Gillespy met his gaze. He didn't dare turn away. The stare down wore on for almost fifteen seconds. Finally, Elias surrendered and slowly made his way up the stairs. "Call me when you're done."

When the door clicked shut Gillespy let out a shaky breath. He picked up the beer and downed half the bottle before noting the confusion on the lawyer's face.

"I'm not going to hurt you, but this is going to be a hard sell. I'll need your help. This will have to look convincing." He walked over, thinking to release her, and she screamed, shattering the air. Gillespy jumped back covering his ears. "What the hell…"

"Convincing enough?" Her smile split open a cut on her lip but she didn't seem to notice.

From behind him, Leonard Hout moaned. Gillespy rushed over. "I'm going to get you to a hospital soon, lad. Hang on just a little while longer."

Gillespy's transformation had come full circle. He'd started their relationship as a father figure, and then became mentor, and finally partner. It turned to betrayal and hatred and now, seeing him in this condition, he wanted to be like Leonard's father again.

"How is he?"

Gillespy felt no more disdain for the lawyer. No, he was going to be her savior. He was going to rescue her and the good Doctor Hout. How could anyone sue him after that?

"He's not good," Gillespy said. "We'll have to do this quickly."

"Do what quickly?" Blood dripped off of her chin and splashed onto the floor.

Gillespy raced over to the attorney and started picking at the rope.

"Are you crazy? What are you doing?"

"Getting you out of here, Ms. Cartier. Do you have a problem with that?"

"How are you planning on getting past that monster? I guarantee you he's standing just on the other side of that door. I don't think he's going to let me go just because you order him."

Gillespy stopped. She was right. How stupid was he? He had to think this through. "I hope you're not modest. This is going to have to look convincing." He grabbed her slacks at the waist and yanked them down. "Don't worry, I'm not going to hurt you."

"You bastard," she screamed.

He understood her confusion but couldn't understand why he reveled in it. Because she was tied spread-eagle he could only pull her slacks down to mid thigh. He stepped back like he was examining a patient. "It's hard to look like you've been raped if your pants are still on."

She stopped thrashing. He saw her now and nothing stirred between his legs. "Turn off the camera," she demanded.

Gillespy went to the tripod. "I'm not sure which button turns it off. Better not risk breaking it."

"I want that tape," Melanie snapped.

"Don't worry; no one will ever see it."

"They'd better not."

"Now, how good are you at playing dead?"

She looked over at Hout and winced. "Not very good, I'm afraid. He caught me once already."

"Then I'm sorry for this, but I can't take a chance of you interfering." Dr. Gillespy drove his fist into her face. Her head bounced off the wall and she was out. Gillespy rubbed his knuckles, then placed his fingers on her neck and checked her pulse. Once again, his cock became hard. "Sorry, you opening your mouth at the crucial time could ruin everything. Now the stupid oaf won't be able to tell the difference."

He finished his beer and mussed his hair, and then the self-proclaimed superhero yelled for his idiot. Soon Gillespy the superhero would make sure Elias spent the rest of his life in prison.

~

Elias sat on the couch in front of his television, his pants around his ankles, a beer in one hand, his flaccid cock in the other. Betrayal welled up inside his body turning to anger and hatred as he watched Gillespy on closed circuit.

The doctor disappeared from view. A moment later Elias heard a pounding on the basement door. Elias stood and pulled up his pants. He would not keep the doctor waiting.

~

The door opened and Elias stomped down the stairs. "I want to look at the tape."

"Later. I need your help now. I'm afraid I got a little overzealous. She's dead."

Elias ignored the woman as he lifted the camera and placed it carefully on the floor, then folded the tripod. "I leave you alone for five minutes—"

"Watch your mouth. Now listen. Your service to me has been exemplary. After one more task it will be over. We'll move these bodies to my house. I will take over from there."

"Did you kill the doctor too?" Elias asked.

"No, that was your work. At least it will be. I give him another half-hour, tops."

Elias grasped the tripod tighter and tighter as he stared at Gillespy. "I think I saw her move."

Gillespy spun around and looked at the lawyer. She still seemed to be unconscious.

"Stupid oaf, am I?"

Before the doctor had a chance to turn back, Elias swung the tripod with all of his strength to the back of Gillespy's head.

Twenty-Seven

Sunday 2:20 p.m.

Louise stormed out of the Captain's office, contemplating going back in and slamming her badge on his desk and telling him where he could shove this job. The door to the men's room opened just as she walked by and Todd Huffman knocked into her. When he noticed who he bumped, Huffman gave a little extra shove sending Louise into the wall. She didn't go down, but did a slight balance-catching dance as she righted herself into a fighting position.

"Take it easy, Miller. What's your problem, did somebody shoot a dog?" Huffman chuckled at his joke and turned away.

Louise charged, crashing Huffman into the wall. She got a clean shot to his face, feeling the satisfying pain of knuckle against bone, before he grabbed her in a bear hug. They tumbled to the floor. On the way down, she got in a head-butt to his chin before three other officers jumped into the fray, pulling them apart.

"Taser the bitch, she's crazy!" Huffman jerked himself out of the grasp of two officers holding him back, but he didn't make any aggressive moves. Louise glared back, fists clenched. She smiled at the welt already rising just below his right eye. He'd have a nice shiner in the morning.

"You gonna have the guts to tell anyone that you were beat up by a girl?"

Huffman took a step toward her; one of the officers grabbed

his arm while another cop tightened his hold on Louise.

"Miller! Huffman! In my office now!" Captain Eugene Henderson stood half outside his door. His face turned visibly red. The three witnessing cops quickly resumed their duties leaving Huffman and Miller to kill each other if they so desired.

"I don't see any girls around here," Huffman whispered.

"I'll take that as a compliment," Louise whispered back.

"It wasn't." Huffman sneered. "Only you'd be stupid enough to think so."

"Now!" Henderson shouted.

The two entered his office. Each took a chair in front of his desk. The one Louise sat in was still warm from her previous visit. On the wall next to her were photographs of the captain shaking hands with the governor, the mayor, and other past and present politicians. All political parties were represented, even an independent. On the other wall were his awards and commendations. There were quite a few.

The captain's eyes burned into the back of her head. She figured she missed her opportunity to quit. Now she'd be fired, or at best suspended. She threw the first punch. Three witnesses would swear to that. She didn't think the he-pushed-me-first defense would be very effective. Of course Huffman would claim it had been an accident, if he had the balls to even admit that much.

Captain Henderson walked around the desk and sat in his red leather chair, lined with cracks from age. He picked up some reports that lay scattered across his desk and tapped them into alignment, setting them neatly next to his pride and joy; a baseball autographed by the 1965 Minnesota Twins. There used to be a photograph of his wife and daughter, but he took that down after the divorce.

He sighed at his officers. "This is the Lord's day of rest, for Christ sakes."

They both looked down at their laps in unison.

"Let me guess," he continued. "Miller, you're still upset you can't go to Mark Lone Bear's funeral. Whether you believe me or not, it was a random drawing. Your name was drawn to patrol. I can't play favorites."

Out of her peripheral vision, Louise saw Huffman glance over at her.

"So you decided to take it out on Officer Huffman. Is that it?"

Louise opened her mouth to speak, but the next words came from Huffman. "No sir. I slipped when I opened the door to the men's room. Officer Miller was walking by and tried to catch me but we both went down."

The captain's gray eyes pierced into Huffman. To Huffman's credit, he stared right back. Slowly, the captain shifted his gaze to Louise. She did her best to emulate Huffman.

"So Officer Miller, when I question those other officers, is that what they're going to tell me?"

"I don't know what they saw. I wouldn't be able to speak for them, sir."

Louise made out the faint trace of a smile on the captain's face. If so, it was only visible for a moment. The silence became excruciatingly long.

Finally, "Is there anything either of you would like to add?" the captain asked.

"No sir," Louise said. Huffman shook his head.

Henderson slapped his hands on his desk and pushed his chair back. "Well then, you're both dismissed. Get the hell out of my office. Todd, go put some ice on that eye."

"Yes, sir."

As Huffman got up, Louise asked the captain if she could talk to him once more about Lone Bear's funeral. Huffman closed the door behind him. "There's nothing more to say, Miller. The decision's been made."

"What if I find someone willing to trade with me? Would that be okay?"

Henderson's impatience grew. "Why would someone do that? This is their chance to be in full uniform and be with their fellow officers in a show of solidarity. It's a magnificent sight. It's also quite moving when the bagpipes start playing 'Amazing Grace.'"

Louise had to bite her tongue. He couldn't care less about the man being murdered. This was just a show, and he wanted to be part of the cast. She couldn't hold it in. "I thought it was to show respect for a fallen comrade."

"Of course it is." The captain recovered. "Of course."

"So if I can find someone who will take my shift, can I go?" Louise wanted to kick herself. Now she sounded like a little kid begging Daddy to go to the circus after Mommy already said no.

The captain steepled his fingers to his chin and closed his eyes as if in prayer. After a long silence he opened them, the gray looking older and less intimidating. "I personally don't think there's anyone on the force who likes you well enough to do that." He paused, "But, if you do find someone, I'll think about it."

Amen! "Do you want me to send in the other officers?"

The captain shook his head. "What's the point? I'm sure your partner in crime has already helped them get their stories straight."

Louise had no answer and went to the door. She put her hand on the knob, but before she got it open, the captain called out. She kept her hand on the door as she turned around. "I don't know why Officer Huffman lied for you, but your job is balancing on a very thin thread right now." His eyes regained their sharp intensity. "The last thing you want to do is make waves. Do I make myself clear?"

"Very clear, sir."

As she closed the door, Louise knew very well why Huffman lied. It would look like he took the moral high ground. He covered to save another cop, even one he didn't like. While his popularity skyrocketed, hers would take another kick in the crotch.

Thinking of Mark Lone Bear, Louise drove past his house, then cruised through the neighborhood of houses known at the station as the reservation. All she could think of was a line from a Malvina Reynolds song—the one about little boxes looking the same. But Reynolds had been poking fun at the suburbs, not what society considered the dregs. Still, Louise could relate as she hummed the tune while prowling the alley looking for trouble.

Usually quiet during the daylight hours, she didn't expect to run into much. She thought about Bill Johnson and hoped to see him. Their last meeting didn't end too congenially; she wanted to make it up to him by buying him another lunch. She circled the park and made a second pass through the res but found no sign of Bill.

Bored, angry, and depressed, she pulled out her cell. The only people she could vent on were Andrew and Karla. Karla offered comfort, but Louise didn't want to be comforted—not now. Andrew would listen and offer advice. She probably wouldn't want that either, but it would be sound advice. Also, they could toss around ideas about this mysterious giant. She called his home number and when no one answered she tried his cell.

~

Carlin turned left onto Highway 81. Sun reflected off the cornfields when a call came through dispatch to talk to a Dr. William Gillespy, suspected hit and run driver.

"Everyone else has tried to get a hold of this guy. You guys might as well give it a shot too," the dispatcher said. "He doesn't answer his phone or the door. Good luck."

Andrew jotted down the information while Carlin swung the car around back into Kenowa.

Still haunted by this morning's scene, Andrew popped another antacid into his mouth. He studied Carlin's face and wondered what the man might be thinking. The sergeant gave him no clues. Andrew had wanted to stay at the woman's house and search for clues, but it had been made clear that their part in that particular homicide was over. They were front line: secure the scene, talk to potential witnesses, then hand it off to the detectives and move on. Louise complained about the same thing when she first became a cop.

"The guy's a doctor? Not too many of them wanted for a hit and run," Carlin said.

"Maybe I can ask him about my stomach," Andrew said.

"Still bothering you, huh? Why haven't you gone to a doctor yet?"

Andrew glared as his partner. "If it doesn't settle down some I'm going to emergency after shift."

"So you already told me five times." Carlin chuckled as they drove past the farms and into the neighborhood of the wealthy.

They pulled up to the address they were given. The two-story mansion had similar specs as most of the others in the area. A manicured lawn with perfectly shaped shrubs surrounded the house. Small gray and white stones decorated the line between garden and grass.

Inset in the door, a small window of different shades of smoked, cut glass made seeing inside almost impossible.

Carlin used the knocker at the same time Andrew rang the bell.

"That should get his attention," Carlin said.

"How much do you think a house like this goes for?"

Carlin shrugged. "Don't know. Maybe eight hundred thousand. Move it into the cities and I bet you could get over a mil."

Andrew let out a long whistle and Carlin knocked again. Still no answer. Something about the silence bothered Andrew.

"What do you think?" Carlin asked. "We did our good deed."

"Mind if I take a look at the back yard?"

"Why, so you can know what you'll never be able to afford?"

"Just curious. I want to check out his garden."

Carlin rolled his eyes and shrugged. "I'll be in the car."

Doing your crossword puzzle. He watched Carlin return to the squad.

A fresh cool breeze caught Andrew as he turned the corner of the house. The pine shrubs smelled fresh. A flock of mallards flew in a V overhead.

"I could get used to this," Andrew muttered.

The lush backyard stretched out to a neighboring cornfield.

Patio tiles of pink and blue formed a semicircle around a sliding glass door—a sliding glass door that had a giant hole punched through it.

Andrew trembled as he spoke into the radio attached to his collar. "We've got trouble."

"Someone forget to water the flowers?" Carlin's voice came back.

"Broken window; possible intruder."

"Don't move. I'll be right there."

Andrew peered through blinds hanging on the other side of the ragged hole. Wide slats that hung vertically opened to a scenic view as the breeze clacked them together in musicless chimes. Other than the shattered glass on the kitchen floor, everything appeared to be in place. He heard nothing stirring on the inside.

"What have you got?" Carlin asked as he turned the corner.

Andrew jumped, startled by the voice. He pointed to the busted window. "Should we go in?"

"Good question."

Andrew knew his FTO was weighing the odds of risking a case getting thrown out of court, or maybe finding someone hurt inside.

"Sheriff's department," Carlin's voice echoed. "Anyone in there?" Carlin unsnapped his holster and pulled out his gun and nodded at Andrew. "Let's go. And don't touch anything." He stepped through the shattered glass door, gun raised.

Andrew pulled out his revolver and followed him in.

"So much for being able to retire with never having to pull out my gun. This is my second time today," he whispered.

"Those days are long gone, my friend. It still might be possible you can make it through your career without pulling the trigger." Carlin scanned every detail of the premises as he spoke. "If I had to bet on one guy in the force not having to use his firearm, it would be you."

"I'll take that as a compliment."

"You should."

Andrew smiled as he stepped around the counter. "Oh shit. Sarge?"

Carlin came over and saw the small .22 lying on the floor. "Don't touch it."

The scene took on a new urgency now. Their conversation ceased. They carefully peeked around corners before entering a new room. Carlin motioned Andrew to check down the hall. He pointed to himself and then pointed up. He cautiously edged up the steps, his gun close to his side.

Andrew saw a door leading out of the kitchen and opened it up. The three-car garage held only one car, a white Lincoln Continental. Andrew toured around it, noticing front end damage. He took his flashlight and shone it inside. A parking ticket lay on the front seat.

Back inside, he walked through a pristine living room. White leather furniture atop white shag carpet decorated the room, looking like it had never been used. Andrew moved down the hall and poked his head in the bathroom. Clothes were strewn about the floor; the room had a mildewy smell to it. He peeked behind the shower curtain—nothing.

Dusty black and white photos of smiling parents and children lined the hallway. It seemed to Andrew as though the amateur photographer might have also done the developing. The smiles on the children seemed forced. The woman looked tired. Even the man's smile didn't fit. Andrew would bet this family held a lot of dark secrets.

Andrew gripped the gun tighter as he moved past the bathroom and entered the den. He felt no presence of anyone else, but the room didn't mesh with the rest of the house. It had a bad aura to it. He took a step forward and heard a crunch. Shards of glass decorated the carpet amidst what he recognized as dried blood.

He decided to risk communication. "Anything upstairs?" he spoke into his collar mike.

"Materialism up the wazoo. Anything on your end?"

"Yeah. Car has damage. Probably the one we're looking for.

Also, meet me in the den. It's down the hall, third door down at the front of the house. More broken glass and it looks like someone tried to clean blood off the carpet."

"Any sign of an intruder?"

"None."

Andrew heard Carlin bounding down the stairs. "Marco."

"Polo," Andrew responded with a smile. Leave it to Rivers to break the tension.

"Smells like there's been a party in here." Carlin crinkled his nose as walked in the room, his gun back in its place.

Andrew followed suit, relaxing a little by holstering his own piece.

"Let's get the hell out of here and call it in," Carlin said. "We'll need a warrant."

"What do you want me to do?"

"Did you touch anything?"

"No."

They went down the hall and back into the kitchen.

"Do we have enough for a warrant?" Andrew asked.

Carlin nudged the gun around the corner of the counter with the toe of his boot so it could be seen from the window. "What we do now… You secure the area and I'll get an A.P.B. issued on our Mr. Gillespy."

"Doctor Gillespy," Andrew corrected.

"All the better," Carlin said.

~

Once again Andrew felt left out of the loop as he knocked on the neighbors' doors while others did the important stuff. His job was as important, needed to be done, and normally he'd have a good attitude. But with his stomach acting up, and the sight of two innocent victims, one of them being an eleven-year-old girl, and a room soaked in blood, Andrew yearned to be part of the action.

Just like this morning, no one had seen a damn thing. Andrew met his FTO in the driveway. After telling the detective that he struck out with the neighbors, he and Carlin got in the car.

"Sucks, doesn't it?" Carlin said.

The sergeant read his mind. "Big time."

"C'mon, rookie, I'll buy ya lunch."

Acid churned. Andrew reached into his pocket and pulled out lint. "Got any antacids?"

"Sorry. And damn, I was going to suggest the Bar-B-Q ribs joint. I suppose that's out?"

"Do they serve salad?" Andrew asked.

"If you want to get your ass kicked."

"You'll defend me, won't you?"

"I'll be the guy holding you down so everyone else can get in some good shots."

Andrew smirked. "I think I'll pass on food."

A blue Wrangler 4x4 sped past. Carlin clicked on the radar and clocked it at 72. "What the hell? That's just not right. We're not even hiding."

Carlin pulled out into to street, flipped on the lights and floored the pedal.

As they neared the vehicle Andrew belched as he punched the license plate number into the computer. "Excuse me. Damn, I hate those acid burps. You know, the kind that burns all the way up the throat."

"Tell you what. After I write up this asshole, take the rest of the day off. Get your ass to emergency."

"Thanks. I think I'll take you up on that."

Carlin pulled up to the 4x4's bumper. The car slowed but didn't pull over. Andrew flipped on the siren, just to get the driver's attention, and then switched it off.

The driver pulled onto the shoulder and stopped.

The information popped up onto the screen. It showed the owner as a George Garson. He had a valid DL and no outstanding warrants.

"I'll take this one," Andrew said.

"I'll do it. Your gut's bad, and you'd probably only give him a warning anyway. I'll be right back."

Andrew sat in the car. He relaxed a little when Carlin took his hand off of his gun and rested his arm above the window as he leaned in to talk to the driver. After a couple of minutes he headed back to the squad, smiling. "Wow! Do a good deed and get rewarded." Carlin slid back in the driver's seat.

"What are you talking about?" Andrew asked.

"It's his daughter, Gracie."

"Gracie Garson?"

"The family must have a fetish over the letter G." Carlin ran her license. The face of a nineteen-year-old beauty queen popped up on the computer screen. Her license was valid. "She's trying to talk her way out of a ticket without using a lot of words."

Andrew smiled. The sex-appeal ruse wouldn't work with him but he wondered if it might on his sergeant.

"As she went for her purse, she made sure that that cute little sundress that she's wearing rode up her thigh all the way to her red thong panties."

"It must be your animal magnetism."

"Must be. Either way, she's going to be pissed." Carlin began writing up the ticket. "How's the gut?"

"Actually, doing a little better."

"Hell, it's slow, you want a ride?"

"Thanks, but you can just drop me off at my car."

"You sure? I'll let you play with the siren."

"A tempting offer. But my car will be just fine."

"Okay." Carlin got out of the car. "I'll be right back. I just need to ruin someone's day first."

Andrew's stomach rumbled as Carlin approached Garson's car. Sweat washed over his face while another grenade went off in his gut.

"You're giving me a ticket?" Andrew heard Gracie yell.

A mouthful of obscenities followed including some comments about Carlin's sexual preferences. Andrew smiled through the pain as he got out of the car. He strolled over to the woman's vehicle and saw the face of the beauty queen twisted in an ugly rage.

"Who the hell do you think you're talking to?" he snapped.

Andrew wasn't sure who looked more stunned, Ms. Garson or his FTO. Gracie stopped in mid-sentence and stared. The woman's hands began to tremble and she grasped the steering wheel tighter.

"Now if you don't want to be taken in for disorderly conduct and indecent exposure, you'll be on your way."

The red in Gracie's face changed shades as the anger disappeared, replaced by embarrassment.

"Yeah, he told me about it. I told him he should take you in. If a guy did that to a female officer, his butt would be planted in a jail cell. I'm all for equal rights."

"Yes, officer," she said.

"That's better. Now have a nice day ma'am, and obey the speed limit."

"Yes, officer." Gracie Garson clipped her seatbelt in place and pulled back into traffic.

Carlin stared at Andrew, his jaw still hanging open. "Damn, you can make one hell of a bad-ass cop."

Andrew hid a grin as he walked back to the squad with Rivers following close behind.

"You continue to surprise me, kid. And impressively too."

They got in the car and Carlin wrote his report. "Maybe you should keep your gut screwed up. You might've found a new calling for the bad cop in the good cop/bad cop interrogations."

"I just didn't want you hauling her in. I'd never get to Emergency if you did."

"You don't know how close she came." Carlin slid his clipboard back under the seat and shifted the car in gear. "After you get that ulcer taken care of, you're on your own, kid."

"What do you mean? Where are you going?"

"What I mean is, you don't need a babysitter anymore. Next shift you're on your own. You've proven yourself enough that I'm comfortable letting you go solo."

Andrew's stomach gurgled and a belch popped out of his mouth. "Excuse me."

Carlin chuckled. "I'm going to miss that."

By the time Carlin dropped him off at his car, Andrew thought he might just go home and relax instead of waiting for hours in the emergency room. That wouldn't be right. "You know, my stomach is starting to feel a little better. I think I'll just wait and see my regular doctor tomorrow."

"You made me drive all this way for nothing?" Carlin slammed his palm on the dashboard. "Forget it. You're not getting back in this car until you get your stomach checked out." He winked at Andrew then burned rubber out of the parking lot.

The telephone vibrated in Andrew's pocket. Louise offered to buy him lunch, dinner, whatever he wanted to call it.

"I appreciate the offer, but I think I'll pass. It's been a long day and my stomach's been giving me problems."

"It's always about you, isn't it? Fine, I'll eat, you can drink milk, but I gotta vent, dammit."

Even with the gut ache, Andrew had to chuckle. "As long as you asked so graciously, how can I refuse?"

They met in the parking lot of the Minnehaha Falls Diner. Louise sat in her car until her brother pulled in. Her eyes widened when he stepped out wearing his uniform. "What, you didn't have any other clean clothes?"

Andrew walked over and gave Louise a hug. "Got called in."

"I thought you were off until Tuesday."

"Thus the…my being called in."

"Don't be an asshole. That's my job."

Overhead, dark clouds made their way east; the smell of rain hung in the air. Three cars were in the parking lot besides theirs. A fourth pulled in but when the driver saw them, he pulled right back out.

"We better go in. We're scaring away their clientele," Louise said.

Two of the cars must've belonged to employees. Only one table was occupied. Louise and Andrew sat as far away as possible. Still, the young man's voice carried. The one sided conversation consisted entirely about him. The girl smiled and nodded politely.

"I bet they're on their first date," Andrew said.

"And their last," Louise added.

A waitress came to their table with menus and two glasses of water. "Can I start y'all with something to drink?" The accent sounded Carolinian. She couldn't have been much out of high school, tall and anorexic like a model—all legs. She wore a white T-shirt with Minnehaha Falls Diner emblazoned on it, white tennis shoes with white anklets, and a pair of cut-off blue jeans that stopped just below her butt cheeks.

Andrew told her water was fine. Louise ordered a Diet Coke, and watched the waitress walk back into the kitchen.

When she was out of sight, she said, "I have no recollection why I wanted to talk to you."

"What? Oh hey, Louise, when did you get here?" Andrew asked his sister.

A short but noticeable silence came from the other table.

"Yup," Andrew said. "Last date."

The waitress came back with the soda. Louise asked for a burger, well done; Andrew a dinner salad. She took their menus and left them alone. They both did their best not to ogle. Louise prepared to spill her guts about the fight, the funeral, and the fuckhead. The three F's as she rehearsed it, but Andrew spoke first. "I saw a double homicide today. Two stabbing victims. A mother and daughter."

"Oh my God, I'm sorry." Louise remembered clearly the first time she saw dead bodies. The nightmares lasted about a month.

"That's not the worst of it," he continued. "It's the little girl we saw on TV last night. The one that found the dog."

A chill exploded in an ice cloud over Louise. She forgot all about the three F's.

"You know where they were found?" Andrew answered his own question before giving Louise time to think. "In the dog's grave out at Perch Lake."

If the boy at the other table were still talking, Louise didn't hear him. All she could hear was a rush of white noise building in her head getting ready to explode.

"I told Rivers my theory—"

"Who?" Louise interrupted, her head still swimming in a fog.

"Carlin Rivers, my FTO."

"Oh yeah." Louise buried her face in her hands.

"He agrees. The dog, Hout, these two—they're all related to the giant."

Louise's fog lifted so she could think. The white noise turned back into the boy's droning on about himself. Even with food on their table he kept talking. The girl seemed more interested in her fries.

The waitress came back and set the salad in front of Louise, the burger in front of Andrew. They switched plates after she left. Louise pushed away her burger, unable to eat. Andrew picked at his rabbit food, but it didn't look like he had much of an appetite either. As he lifted a fork full of lettuce to his lips, Louise grabbed his wrist and lowered it to the table. "I'll keep the dog."

Andrew didn't try lifting the fork again. "What are you talking about?"

"The giant wants that dog dead. Who knows why, but if I have it, he has to go through me to get it."

"Are you crazy? That makes no sense at all. And even if it did, your bosses will never go for it."

"That's exactly why I'm not going to tell them."

"And what makes you think they'll just hand over the dog to you?"

"They were going to hand it over to that little girl. Now she's dead. Who else are they going to give it to? Better than having him sit in some shelter until they put him to sleep." Louise saw her brother formulating arguments in his head. "Listen, I'll call the vet, tell them that the dog is a witness and I've been assigned to take care of him. What's the big deal?"

The waitress came over. "Is everything okay here?"

"Just fine," they both said, never taking their eyes off each other.

She glanced quizzically at the barely touched food, then at them before walking away.

"The big deal is, what if they come looking for the dog and the vet says we already gave it to an Officer Miller? You can get arrested. Is that a big enough deal for you?"

Louise noticed that the yapping from the other table finally ceased. The couple were staring at her and Andrew. "What?" she shouted.

They both returned their attention back to their plates.

She turned back to her brother. "Look, Minneapolis isn't going to want him. All this shit's going on in Kenowa. As far as MPD cares, it's out of their jurisdiction. I'm sure the Kenowa cops would be happy to lead a murderer out of their city; lead him where we've got the manpower and resources to deal with him. And hell, have they got the budget to try him? That trial is going to have one big price tag."

"Manpower and resources meaning you!"

"Well, yeah."

"I'll tell you what," Andrew said. "Let me talk to Rivers. If they haven't already, I'll suggest they put a guard on the dog. If he thinks the idea has merit, you pull your scam and pick the dog up. I'll tell him you volunteered to be bait." Andrew stopped and grinned. "He'll like that part."

Louise nibbled on a French-fry and mumbled.

"I can't understand what you said."

Louise looked her brother in the eye with the most pleading expression she could muster. "I want that dog."

Twenty-Eight

Monday 3:00 p.m.

Gillespy tasted blood even before he opened his eyes. His head throbbed and he had no idea where he was. Bent from the waist at an angle, he tried to stand erect but couldn't. He couldn't drop to his knees, either. Drops of blood on the floor were presumably his. A dried rivulet crusted on his cheek. "Where am I?"

"Welcome to Hell," a familiar voice came back.

It took Gillespy a moment to recognize the lawyer. He tried to stand again. This time the bar running across the back of his neck stopped him. His shoulders hurt too. As his faculties reemerged he realized his arms were locked in place also.

"You're in the stocks," Cartier said.

Gillespy twisted a little and saw Leonard still immobile. He lifted his head up as far as he could and was only able to peek as far as the top of Cartier's pants, still down around her thighs. Straining harder he saw as far as just under her bush before pain made him drop his gaze along with his head. "How long have I been out?"

"Hard to say," Melanie answered. "He doesn't keep clocks down here. I'd guess maybe four hours…ten, I don't know."

"Where's Elias?"

"I have no idea where that psycho is. He doesn't tell us his schedule."

"Save your sarcasm for the courtroom. It doesn't suit you here, Ms. Cartier."

"Oh really? I thought it fit pretty well."

By the stairs Gillespy saw the bottle of beer. God, how he needed a drink.

"So, Mastermind, what do we do?"

Gillespy laughed but that only made his head hurt worse. He flinched instead. "Mastermind? I wasn't lying when I told you I had nothing to do with this. He came to me this afternoon and told me what he had been up to. I came here to rescue you."

"I'm guessing it's probably yesterday afternoon by now, and you're about as successful as your friend there. He tried to rescue me too. Twice. And look where it got him."

Gillespy wondered if Leonard might still be alive. Despite the hatred he felt just hours ago, he had to admit that Hout had a sharp mind and made a hell of a psychiatrist.

"Maybe it's you," Gillespy said.

"What did you say?" Anger spewed from her mouth.

"I can be sarcastic, too."

"All right Mr. Sarcasm, how do we get out of this?"

Gillespy chuckled. Had he not been in so much pain, and probably about to die, Gillespy would have been enjoying himself. He couldn't remember the last time he had such an inane conversation. He missed it. *If we do get out of this alive, maybe she'll go out with me*, he thought. *I feel a connection. Kids, I'd like to introduce you to your new mom. She's probably a few years younger than you, and she'll be getting all of your inheritance.* The thought made him smile.

"Are you still there?" Cartier asked.

Gillespy jerked his head and twisted his neck. The daydream burst as he remembered this was the bitch that wanted to sue him for everything he was worth. "Sorry. Wandered off for a second. What did you say?"

"I asked you, how do we get out of here?" Agitation echoed in her voice.

"He's a giant child," Gillespy answered. "We'll have to treat him like that. Anything to let him know he doesn't have power over you. The worst thing you can do is beg for mercy. He'll get off on that and probably kill you."

"That's good to know," Melanie said.

"It's a fine line, though. Push him too far and he'll murder you in a rage. You have to know when to back off and patronize him."

"In other words, we're probably dead either way."

"Probably," Gillespy answered.

~

Elias drove, feeling his world fall apart. He had no idea what to do. The one person he looked up to most in the world had betrayed him. Gillespy's voice no longer came to him. There was now a void in his psyche. The people he held in his basement were now worthless. Killing them would be easy enough, but what would he do with the bodies? Both that cop and the mom and her brat had been found too quickly. The cop surprised him at how soon they dragged him from the lake. Mom and kid? He should have dug the hole deeper. Maybe he should've left them in the house, but he thought buried in the woods would take longer to find. It didn't matter anymore. He would need to hide his captives' bodies much better. With no one left to tell him what to do, Elias knew he had to think for himself. That's when he always seemed to get into trouble.

"Why does everything bad always have to happen to me?" he shouted out the window.

He drove on, not knowing or caring where. Tasks awaited him when he got back. Two pleasant, one not. The lawyer would be first. That would be fun. He'd fuck her while Gillespy watched. Show him how it was done. The question he had to answer was, should she be dead first or not? "Maybe I'll do her twice. Once alive and once dead, then compare." He sent that message to Gillespy but wasn't sure if it would be received. Just in case he could hear, Elias told him he'd be next. That would be a hard one but it needed to be done. Betrayers weren't allowed to live. Out of respect, though, he'd do it quick. The one who almost murdered S.K. would be last, if he was still alive. Elias hoped so. That bastard deserved so much more pain.

How could S.K. still be alive? I held him in my lap! He didn't move. It didn't look like he was breathing. But he was alive. For the first time in quite a while, Elias smiled a genuine smile.

He slammed on the brakes and pulled a U-turn on the two-lane highway, heading back toward the city. Keeping an eye on the road signs to get his bearings, Elias formed a new plan. He'd find S.K. no matter what. He'd let S.K. get his revenge to the shitfucker on the surfboard.

The mom had said they took him to the hospital. Did she say where? He couldn't remember. How many veterinarian clinics were there around Kenowa? There couldn't be that many. The speedometer crept up as Elias headed home. They would've taken him to the emergency clinic.

~

Elias held his ear against the metal door to the basement. He heard nothing. He thought about going down to harass them but playtime would come later. An overwhelming need to find S.K. became top priority. His prisoners could wait. He pounded on the door to let them know he'd be down soon.

Only three emergency hospitals were listed in the yellow pages: one in Golden Valley, one in Coon Rapids, and one in Eden Prairie. They would've gone to the one in Golden Valley. He then remembered the woman saying that.

He hung up the phone before he finished dialing the number. He didn't want to tip them off. He sat in his den and turned on the TV. After watching two hours of mindless crap, the news finally started. The lead story was the murder of Janet and Tiffany Saangvold, found in the exact spot where they had found the miracle dog. He recorded the segment and watched it three times trying to learn anything new. Like always they had their priorities screwed up. The whole story was about the murders with just a passing mention about the dog. The anchor asked the reporter on the scene if the murders and the dog were related. The reporter said the police were looking into that. Meaning, they didn't know shit.

~

William Gillespy had a cramp in his side. It got worse when he jumped at the pounding on the door. Along with the cramp, he thought he might also have a concussion. He'd already thrown up once and might again.

"Are you okay?" Melanie called from across the room.

"No, I am not okay. I need a drink."

"Pardon me for showing concern."

"You don't give a good God damn about me. No one does."

"Oh, poor you." Melanie's voice feigned sincerity.

"The only reason you want me to live is so that you can get my money."

"Sounds like you've had too much to drink already."

Gillespy listened to himself as if he had drifted out of his body. He could feel the rage but couldn't stop it, and unfortunately for Ms. Cartier, no one else to direct it at. Lawyers, judges, even other psychiatrists had tried to make him feel helpless. None of them ever could. As of this morning Gillespy would have sworn that nobody could. Then some dumb, giant, psychopath comes along, and poof, the doctor couldn't even wipe his own ass now.

"How can you not be irate?" Gillespy asked. "Some big tough attorney in the courtroom, but when she faces real adversity she folds like a kitten."

Cartier exploded. "Who the hell do you think you are? Have you seen my face? If you'd take your fucking eyes off of my pussy long enough you might notice it's been beaten to a pulp. You think I'm a willing participant here? Fuck you! Look at your partner. I don't even know if he's still alive. He risked his life trying to get us out of here. You get a little bump on the head and you think the world came down on you? Go fuck yourself!"

A loud and furious sob followed the tirade. When it quieted to a whimpering, Gillespy asked, "Do you feel better now?"

"Fuck you!"

Properly chastised, Gillespy felt like the wind had been punched out of him. "I tried to kill myself last night. Maybe it was the night before. I don't really remember anymore. All the days seem to blend together now." He spoke quietly. "I wish I succeeded."

"So do I."

Maybe he deserved that. Maybe not. Still, she had no right to bring the weight of the world down on his shoulders. Perhaps she had accepted her fate. Had he? Was he truly ready to die? Now that he very well might, he discovered he wanted to live. More than anything else, he wanted to see his grandchildren again. It would be up to him to get them out of this alive. He was the only one who could control Elias. He could still become the super hero.

~

Elias scoped out the parking lot at the emergency pet hospital. There weren't many cars, none of them police, at least regular police cars. He searched for possible unmarked cars by looking at the side mirrors. Most of the unmarked had the double mirror, one being a search light. Not finding anything suspicious he drew in a deep breath and decided to risk it. Despite the sign banning guns on the premises, he decided to bring his own anyway. He patted his pocket satisfied with the added security as he stood by the doors inside the lobby. The only person in sight sat at the front desk. Elias walked up to the receptionist, whose nametag read Nancy.

She let out a small gasp when she saw his face. "Can I help you?" She tried to recover but still couldn't look him in the eye.

Elias decided on the shy and polite approach. "I hope so, ma'am. I was told somebody brought my dog in a couple nights ago. That he was really beat up bad."

"What kind of dog is it?"

"He's a rottweiler, ma'am. Somebody left the gate open at my house and he got out. Maybe you saw the story on the news."

The receptionist's face softened. "You're the owner of the

miracle dog! That's all we've been talking about around here. Have you talked to the police yet?"

"Yes, ma'am. It's all straightened out. They know I'd never hurt my dog. They talked to the people up in Duluth."

She eyed him suspiciously. "What are you talking about?"

Elias slapped his palm against his forehead. "Too many blows to the head. I just got back into town this morning. I had a boxing match up in Duluth. A buddy was staying at my house and was supposed to take care of him."

Nancy's face lit up. "My brother used to box. There were a couple of times he came home looking like you. He had to give it up, though, when a punch loosened his cornea."

Because of the mutual interest in boxing, Elias sensed the receptionist forming a bond between them.

"He's here?"

"Yes, well, no. I mean he was." The receptionist's smile faded into a puzzled frown as she pulled out a logbook and thumbed through the entries. "It seems someone else has claimed him. They transferred him to the University Animal Clinic for convalescence."

"What?" Elias stared at her, aghast. "How could somebody else claim him? He's my dog."

"I don't know. That's just what it says here."

"Who claimed him?" Elias' voice turned menacing.

Nancy shuddered. "I'm sorry. We're not allowed to give out that information. What we can do is contact that person and let them know the real owner has been found. Of course you'll have to produce proof he's yours. But that shouldn't be a problem."

"I want to know the address." The polite façade vanished.

"The University Hospital?"

Elias glared, watching as her pale skin faded even more. She reached for the phone. Elias shot his arm over the counter and grabbed her wrist, twisting until she dropped the receiver. Pain spread across her face. "You're hurting me!"

She drew in a deep breath and Elias knew that if he didn't do something instantly, her piercing scream would echo throughout the building. Jerking her up off of her chair, he drove his fist into her mouth. Her head snapped back and, because of the awkward way Elias had to reach over the counter, he lost his grip. She fell back into the chair and rolled two feet into the wall behind her. Dazed, she lifted her head. Blood flowed down her chin, staining her white cotton blouse. She staggered to her feet but fell back into the chair. Elias raced around the counter and grabbed her by the throat before she could try and scream again. He had entered the hospital with no intention of harming anyone, but this woman had brought it on herself.

"Why does it always have to end this way?" he hissed as he squeezed tighter. "Do you think I enjoy hurting people?"

As blood bubbled from her lips, Elias scanned the room hoping to find a more private area—and that his luck would hold out. Faint voices came from another room—the sound of things being wrapped up. Nancy's eyes bulged; blood vessels inside them broke. He squeezed harder, until he could feel no life left in her. Just to be sure he laid her face down on the floor and stomped on the back of her neck.

He didn't hear the satisfying crunch and was going to pound his boot on her again when a door opened and voices drifted down the hall. "Just go up to the front desk. Nancy will take care of you."

In a panic Elias used his foot to shove her under desk. They'd find her far too quickly, but that couldn't be avoided now. He grabbed the book with S.K.'s information and tore out of the building, veering away from the door's line of sight. He didn't dare look behind him. At worst they only saw his back. At best he made it out of there before anyone had stepped around the corner.

As he slid into his car, Elias chanced to look toward the door of the hospital. Seeing no faces in the doorway eased his racing heart and the rush from the kill wore off as he sped out of the parking lot. Anger welled up inside. He'd had no intention of killing that girl. Other than the three in his basement he had no intention of killing anyone. *Someday people will do as I say. Then they'll be fine.*

Keeping the car at the speed limit, Elias began to relax. He even smiled when he saw the flashing lights racing toward him. "That was quick," he said to himself. He then felt a pang of regret that Gillespy had turned traitor. He would've been proud. Too bad, also, that he had to kill the receptionist. She might've been fun.

The smug arrogance melted into anxiety as more lights sped at him. These weren't cop lights; these came from an ambulance. *She can't be alive. Could she? Impossible.* Elias began to sweat. If he hadn't completed his task, there wasn't a worse place for her to be. Even though it was an animal hospital, those were still doctors and they had all the emergency equipment on hand.

"Goddamn you!" He pounded the steering wheel, sending the car onto the shoulder. He quickly swerved back into his lane and checked the rearview mirror for cops. "Stay calm."

He needed Gillespy to tell him what to do next, but no voice came. *Maybe the damn shrink is right. Maybe I am worthless.* He shivered from the idea of his own inefficiency. He needed to think. Hungry, and very tired, Elias pulled off the highway and into a Wendy's Drive-Thru. He ordered a triple burger, fries, and a Coke and drove the car to the far end of the parking lot.

"I am in control," he repeated like a mantra in between bites.

After he finished his meal, Elias wiped the grease off of his hands and opened the book. He scanned through the entire thing without finding S.K.'s name anywhere. He laughed at himself for the stupid assumption that they knew the dog's name. He felt lighter as a plan formulated in his head. He went through each entry until he found notes on a rottweiler with multiple injuries.

"Louise Miller, hmm?" Elias checked the address, opened his glove compartment and pulled out a map. He didn't like the idea of driving into Minneapolis, but at least it wasn't St. Paul. In Minneapolis the streets were in alphabetical order. In St. Paul—

who knew what they were thinking when they laid out that city?

He found the street and cross section with no problem. Soon, he'd go back home and finish his business with the two now-worthless prisoners, and the traitor. It would take days, if not weeks for those bodies to be discovered. By then he and S.K. would be far away, maybe Seattle. He'd often fantasized about starting a new life but never had the courage before. Now, he realized, he had the power to do anything.

Before the recreation, he had to pick up S.K. He sat in his car and watched through the window until only a few people remained in the restaurant. Getting out of his car, Elias trotted up to the door. Like most of the fast food chains, next to the entrance a short hallway led to the kitchen and restrooms. Amazingly, this place still had a pay phone between the men's and women's rooms. Unfortunately, there was no phonebook.

He called information and dropped in enough change for the operator to connect him to the University of Minnesota Animal Hospital. He almost tore the phone off of the wall when they told him it was located in St. Paul. Before he drove out he wanted to make sure S.K. was still there.

He fought to make his voice sound calm. "I'm calling for my wife. She was going to pick up our dog and I was just wondering if she's been there yet. Her name is Louise Miller."

Elias got more information than he expected. She had already called and planned on stopping by after work. The dog was doing better than expected.

"Thank you so much. I tried her at work and she already left. I wasn't sure if she was going to get him or if she wanted me to. I guess it's just another case of the left hand not knowing what the right hand is doing. You don't have to bother telling her I called."

Elias banged his palm into his forehead. *What did you say that for, you moron? That's going to make them think.* He'd been pushing his luck, especially with that cute little bitch at the pet hospital. Now, he raised suspicions at the other place. "How fucking stupid are you?" He hurried out of the exit before he made another scene.

Inside his car, Elias counted to ten and took deep breaths until he could think clearly again.

It would be best to let her get S.K. then meet at her place and deal with her in the privacy of her own home. There he'd teach Miller a lesson as to the consequences of stealing.

Twenty-Nine

Monday 3:30 p.m.

Feeling drained from all the blood they took, and a little claustrophobic from the CT scan, Andrew sat in his underwear on the examination table waiting for the doctor to return. The sheet of paper crinkled beneath him as he shifted his position. Corwin would have a field day with this, Andrew thought as he placed his hand on the giant roll of paper at the head of the table. Getting impatient, he got up and went over to the acupuncture chart and began studying the charkas, and all the different areas to stick needles, trying to correlate why if a needle was placed in one area of the body, it helped relieve a totally different area. Why would a needle in the ear lobe help pain in a person's knee? He regarded a diagram of a human body's nerve network when the door swung open.

"I'm sorry, I told the nurse to tell you, you could get dressed."

Dr. Aaron Gorstein, a man of small stature, wore an air of authority than reminded Andrew of Napoleon. Maybe it was the way he tucked his stethoscope between buttons of his white coat. When he reached in to pull it out, he struck the same pose. Even though he'd been practicing medicine for over ten years, Gorstein could pass for a college intern. Andrew liked that about him, it meant the doctor followed the same advice he gave to his patients.

Slightly embarrassed, Andrew reached for his trousers. As he pulled them on, the doctor spoke. "I've got some good news and some bad news. Which would you like first?"

Frowned upon years ago, but now highly regarded, Gorstein became one of the premiere doctors in Minnesota to focus on holistic healing and herbal remedies to accompany traditional medicine, not to take the place of it. "Give me the good."

"You don't have an ulcer."

"Okay. What's the bad?"

"You've got diverticulitis."

Andrew had his tee shirt half on, his head just below the opening. Like a shy turtle, he peeked just above the top. "What's that?"

"In a nutshell, it's inflamed pouches on the wall of the intestine. You're a little young for it, but otherwise it's not at all uncommon."

Andrew popped his head the rest of the way through his shirt. "So, how does one get this diverticulitis, and, more importantly, how does one get rid of it?"

Gorstein pulled out his prescription pad and started scribbling. "Usually by pressure on the intestine wall. I'll have the nurse give you a pamphlet." He tore off a sheet from his tablet. "There's a danger of infection. If so, we'll have to do a little surgery."

Generally optimistic, Andrew's heart sank. Just a week on the street and he'd have to start using his sick time already. Who'd take care of Corwin while he was in the hospital? Soon, Louise would bring home her own full time patient. Carlin? No way. He didn't seem to be a cat person. Maybe Karla? As an emergency. She'd probably want to be with Louise.

"When do I have to go on the table?" He expected the answer to be 'right now.'

"Who said anything about surgery?"

"You just did."

Gorstein handed Andrew the slip of paper. "IF it gets infected. Take this to the pharmacy. Antibiotics will hopefully take care of it."

Andrew closed his eyes in relief and took a few healing breaths.

"And knock off the nuts and acorns for a while. Otherwise,

you've got a pretty healthy diet."

"You're the doctor." By now Andrew would take steroids if it would get rid of the pain.

The two men shook hands. Andrew headed down the hall for his antibiotics fix. Knowing what was wrong, he already felt better.

Driving home, Andrew switched off the air conditioner and opened the window. Grateful he wouldn't need surgery he let the wind wash over him as if it were cleansing his soul. His thoughts drifted to Bianca Skylar. Maybe he'd give her a call. She did seem like a nice person once he got past that pushy personality. He also liked her independence. And she really did have nice legs. It had been so long since he had a relationship that all of a sudden he became nervous. *Maybe I'll call her tonight, ask her if she wants to meet for coffee and talk about the case. She's got to have a boyfriend. How can a person be that good looking and that smart and not have someone else? Maybe she's gay. Where did that come from?* Ever since Louise confessed, he'd spent far too much time contemplating who might, and who might not, be gay. He concluded it was wasted energy and vowed to ignore it whenever it entered his mind.

Feeling totally flustered, Andrew tried to shut off his mind and flipped on the radio to the only New Age station in the Twin Cities. Anything to take his mind elsewhere. He caught Enya singing the tail end of *'Orinoco Flow'* before the news came on. As he reached to switch the station, a late breaking news story grabbed his attention. Another murder. This one at the Golden Valley Emergency Pet Hospital. Andrew turned up the volume. A receptionist who worked there had been found dead. Authorities were withholding her name until relatives could be reached. There were no suspects and no known motives at this time, although, police were looking for her estranged husband.

A shiver raced down Andrew's spine. That's where the miracle dog had been. The news switched to weather and Andrew turned off the radio. He drove with only the sound of the wind blowing through the car.

~

Louise knew she should go to her sergeant. She also knew, if her sarge knew what she'd done, she'd probably get fired, let alone arrested. There had been no reason for her to be in Mark Lone Bear's house. *Why did I have to be so goddamn thorough?*

She switched her train of thought. On the up side, in just a little while she'd be picking up her new dog. Better yet—her new special needs dog.

Andrew had called her last night with the update. He had talked to Carlin, and Carlin talked to his superiors. They had called her superiors. As long as it didn't interfere with her job, they didn't care what she did. Louise had been right about MPD not wanting to get involved, claiming they had no jurisdiction. They thought the Hennepin County Sheriff's Department should coordinate with the Kenowa police.

Because the dog was now recuperating in St. Paul—Ramsey County—Hennepin Sheriff's Department and Kenowa Police no longer had jurisdiction. The Ramsey County Sheriff's Department and St. Paul Police agreed that once the dog was released from the U hospital, he'd be back in Minneapolis and out of their jurisdiction.

Louise couldn't stop laughing as Andrew tried to explain the situation. They were all more concerned with covering their own asses than trying to catch a murderer. The only thing that ended up getting accomplished was Andrew called the pet hospital and asked them to put extra security around the dog. Their response had been, "We'll see what we can do."

Louise pulled out her cell and pressed 2, the speed dial for Karla. "Feel like coming over tonight and playing nurse?" she said by way of hello.

"Are you going to be the naughty patient?" Karla asked, her voice mischievous.

"I called the pet hospital. I'm picking him up as soon as I get my street clothes on."

"How's he doing?" Karla asked.

"Good enough to be coming home."

"What are you going to name him?"

"Haven't given it much thought. The vet said they couldn't save the eye. Maybe we can call him One-Eye Jack?

"Kind of long," Karla said. "I used to have a cocker named Peanut. He was a great dog."

Louise thought for a moment. "I like it."

"I'll see if I can get some time off work."

"Don't worry about it. I've got a few days sick time saved up and I think I'm going to use it."

"I thought you were going to Mark's funeral tomorrow."

"I thought so too, but brass said I couldn't go. They want me on the street."

"You've got to be kidding!"

"So I figure I'll call in sick. I don't know, maybe I'll go as a civilian."

The shadows were long by the time she refueled her squad and pulled into the precinct parking lot. In the locker room, Louise changed back into her civilian clothes, her usual brassy bitchiness noticeably subdued.

Todd Huffman had his back to Louise, bending down to take a drink from the fountain.

"Hey, I just wanted to say thanks for not ratting me out."

Huffman whipped around, water dripping off of his chin. Although not swelled completely shut, his eye glistened in a myriad of colors, a pronounced dark purple had a smattering of yellow, green, and blue. The eye itself had a splotch of red from a broken blood vessel.

"Wow, I'd hate to see the other guy," she said.

He glared down at her, his fists clenching and unclenching. "I didn't do it for you," he said.

"I know why you did it, but I still appreciate it anyway, okay?"

Huffman took a deep breath and relaxed a bit. "Yeah, you should see the other guy. Her face is uglier than sin." He bent down over the drinking fountain and slurped water.

Louise shook her head, but smiled. She had to admit, it was a pretty good dig.

Norah Jones sang "Come Away With Me" on the radio as Louise pulled out of the parking lot. She thought about the stack of one hundred dollar bills, one hundred of them, wrapped tightly in a plastic bag and hidden in the drain in a police officer's home. *Well, an ex-police officer.* What legal way could that be explained, especially after the accusation? She'd have to turn the money in, but how? What if she did it before the funeral, how would the rest of the force look at her? A hero? Yeah, right. She needed time to think. In the meantime, the money stayed hidden where she found it.

Pulling into the hospital parking lot, Louise put Mark and his money on a back burner and thought about Peanut. The small parking lot to the clinic was full, so she pulled into the parking ramp across the street. *Damn University.*

As Louise got out of her car she had developed doubts about the dog. How would he deal with a stranger? Nervous anticipation gripped her as she walked in the door.

"I've come to pick up my dog," Louise told the tech behind the counter.

"The dog's name?" The tech, "Jane" on her name tag, looked like she might be a freshman. Her fingernails had been professionally done by an artist. White swirls against a navy blue background showed off curlicues, a different design on each finger. Her jet-black hair had a wide gold stripe down one side.

"Peanut," Louise answered. "But you'd know him better as the miracle dog."

"The miracle dog," the tech beamed. "His recovery is close to miraculous. Such a gentle guy too." She called to the back for someone to get the miracle dog, his new owner was here. "He'll be right out." She looked Louise over. "They said he was going to be released to a cop. Are you a cop?"

Louise dug in her purse and flipped open her badge.

"Wow. Cool. This is going to be billed to the city of Minneapolis, right?"

A lump caught in Louise's throat. "Well, not exactly. Minneapolis, Kenowa and Hennepin County are all fighting over who gets to pay the bill. In the meantime it's coming out of my pocket."

"Let me get you the total."

Louise cringed as the computer spit out sheet after sheet of paper. "I have a feeling I'm going to be living on Ramen Noodles for a while."

The tech gave a perfunctory smile as she spread the sheets out on the counter. "There's some medications too." She put a plastic canister on the counter. "Antibiotics. The directions are on the label." She added a tube of gel next to the meds. "This one here you're going to have to rub around the hole where his eye was. They couldn't save it."

Louise could only stare at the designs swirled across Jane's fingernails.

"He gets two of these a day, one in the morning and one in the evening." Jane added another canister.

"Nice nails," Louise said.

"Thank you." Jane seemed genuinely pleased. "This one is for pain. You can give him one whenever you think he needs it. And these here…"

The door opened and a dog led the way lugging the veterinarian behind him. Peanut had a patch over his missing eye, something Louise was grateful for. He also wore a cone around his head. Dozens of patches of shaved flesh patterned his body and accentuated the stitches.

"I understand that the City of Minneapolis is picking up the tab on this one," the vet said.

"They'll reimburse me." Louise pulled out her credit card and handed it to Jane. "It's a long story."

The vet eyed her suspiciously.

"Better throw in a bag of food, too," Louise said.

"Keep him on the soft stuff for a few weeks and see how he's doing," the doctor suggested.

"Doctor?" Another young tech popped her head out from the back.

"I'll be right there."

"The instructions are self-explanatory. If you have any questions at all, don't hesitate to give us a call."

He handed Louise a thin rope with a clip on the end, and disappeared out the back. The dog wore a collar that matched the leash.

As Jane left to get a carton of soft food, Louise squatted down and put her hand in front of Peanut's snout. The dog sniffed, licked her fingers a couple of times then eased down on the linoleum floor.

"Ready for your new home, fella?" She checked his paw for the star, grateful there was nothing there.

The dog looked disinterested.

"I can already tell you're going to love Karla more than me. But hey, I'm pretty nice too."

The dog ignored her.

"One hundred and fifty-four stitches," Jane said. "Counted nine slashes and twelve puncture wounds. All missed vital organs. It was the one on the neck that almost did him in." She put a case of canned food on the counter. "He's amazing."

"He is at that," Louise agreed.

"Don't give him the dry stuff for awhile. We had to pull a few broken teeth. He also has a hairline fracture in his jaw."

Weren't you here when the doctor said the same thing? Louise winced as her credit card approved the bill. She thought about the money in Mark Lone Bear's basement.

"I'll be right back. I'm just going to throw this in the car." Louise slid the case of dog food off the counter and headed toward the parking lot.

It would be so easy to keep the money. No one would miss it, at least no one I give a damn about. It didn't really belong to anybody. Not anymore. "Why shouldn't I take it?" *Because it's wrong.* "Why?" she answered back. Her conscience didn't respond.

Louise knew herself well enough that she wouldn't be able to resist the temptation without help. Karla would put up a small argument, but in the end Louise knew that she'd be able to convince her partner. Even if she didn't, but took the money anyway, Karla would still love her. Louise needed someone stronger. Andrew.

Peanut still lay on the floor, his chin resting on his front paws, when Louise came back inside. Jane was on her knees scratching the dog behind the ears. "I want to hear a good report about you." She touched her nose to his. He raised his head enough to lick her on the mouth but Jane didn't seem to mind.

"He's pretty doped up so he might seem kind of loopy for a while."

Louise picked up the leash and gave a barely perceptible tug. Very slowly and deliberately Peanut got to his feet. She didn't know if his movements were caused by pain, or he didn't want to go, maybe a combination of the two. But once he was upright, Peanut wobbled up next to her.

Louise noticed a slight limp from the dog as they walked to the car. She opened up the back door for him. Peanut had no qualms about getting in a stranger's car. He crouched, ready to jump, but he favored his back leg and decided against it. Louise tried to coax him by patting the seat. After a bit of a struggle, Peanut got his front paws on the seat. Louise was able to push his rump the rest of the way up. Once inside and out of view from the vet, Louise took off the cone.

"If you promise not to bite at your stitches, I promise not to put this ridiculous looking thing back on you. Is it a deal?"

Peanut licked her hand.

The temperature dropped as the rain came down. She thanked the Gods for letting her get to her car first. Off to the west were clear skies, and figured by the time she got home it would probably be over. Louise glanced in the rear view mirror at her new adoptee. He craned his neck higher to be closer to the window and the cooling breeze. With a press of a button she let the back window down. If a little water didn't bother him, she wouldn't worry about her upholstery.

Louise couldn't shake the guilt about taking the money. If she didn't talk to her brother now, she never would. At the first red light she pulled out her cell and punched in Andrew's number.

He picked up on the first ring.

"I'll be right there," she said. "Oops, green light." She disconnected and smiled. The only thing he hated worse than her cryptic calls was her phoning while driving. Two digs in one shot. The day kept getting better.

The closest parking spot Louise could find was over a half block away from Andrew's apartment. She cursed his management for not having guest parking. On the plus side it had been a very brief shower.

"No way in hell I'm going to leave you in the car alone. That's how Sparky got stolen." She switched to her baby voice while scratching him behind the ears. "But he was just a puppy. You're a big strong dog, aren't you?"

She also wanted Andrew to meet the newest member of the family. "Wanna meet your uncle Andrew, Peanut?" Louise opened the back door.

Without prompt the dog hopped out of the car, his limp more pronounced than before. Louise grabbed his leash with one arm and slung her purse over her shoulder with the other.

Taking it slow, Louise and Peanut finally reached the front stairs of the apartment building. Peanut gingerly treaded up the three steps to the front door. The stairs inside were steeper. Louise knew that the dog wouldn't be able to get up one flight let alone three. She carefully wrapped her arms around the dog, trying to avoid all of his injuries. With an ummph she hoisted him. As she trudged up the stairs, Louise swore at her brother for not moving into a place with an elevator. Between the second and third floors, her arms began to ache. The dog seemed perfectly content. Then Louise remembered she'd have to do this again at her place. Maybe she should have left him at the vet for another couple of days. What's another hundred bucks after what she'd already spent?

Sweat stained the back of her shirt and under her arms as Louise put the dog down on the top of the landing. As she bent over, placing her hands on her knees, Louise coughed. She checked her purse, then pockets, for cigarettes. Finding none she cursed again. "Maybe Andrew will have a pack," she said to the dog, then laughed at her own joke.

Peanut cocked his head and Louise mimicked him playfully, and then carefully patted him on the head, mindful of his stitches. He seemed to fancy getting tickled under the ear. When she hit the right spot she could've sworn she heard him purr. "Maybe I should have named you Puddy Tat."

Peanut had no opinion one way or another, so Louise simply led him to Andrew's door. "Do you know how to knock?" she asked, looking down at the dog. He drooled but didn't knock. Before Louise could raise her arm the door opened. Andrew's smile quickly faded when he saw the dog.

"Peanut, this is your uncle Andrew. Andrew, meet Peanut."

Louise tried to enter the apartment but Andrew blocked the entrance.

"He can't come in here. I've got a cat," Andrew said.

"Oh, c'mon. You've been watching too many cartoons. They'll get along fine."

A menacing hiss came from behind him and out the door. Louise peeked around her brother and saw Corwin at the far end of the room, fur standing straight up on an arched back.

Louise patted Peanut on the head. But if the dog noticed, it didn't register.

"I'll be right back." Andrew closed the door on his sister.

Something didn't seem right about Andrew but she couldn't figure it out.

Louise's knee joints crackled as she stooped to look Peanut in the eye. She scratched him under the ear and he nuzzled his head into her chest. He smelled like antiseptic.

"If you're good, two hot babes will give you a sponge bath when we get home."

She could hear Andrew approach and as Louise stood up she gave Peanut a gentle caress under his chin. The dog snapped at her when she brushed against some stitches. She had been slow to react but due to the drugs Peanut was slower. Had he been healthy, Louise wondered if she'd still have all of her fingers.

"No sponge bath for you."

"Excuse me?" Andrew asked, frowning.

"I wasn't talking to you." She slipped past him and Peanut followed. "Where's the flea bag?"

"Standing right next to you," Andrew answered.

"You're not a flea bag." Louise spoke in a baby voice as she scratched his haunches. She thought it best to stay as far away from the teeth as possible.

A constant meow came from down the hall, trapped on the other side of Andrew's bedroom door.

"So, what brings the surprise visit?" Andrew asked.

"What surprise? I called first."

Louise plopped herself on the sofa. Peanut released a pleasure grunt as he sank down to the floor at his new master's feet.

"Can I get you something to drink?"

"Got any beer?" Louise asked.

"Water or orange juice?"

Louise struggled to her feet and followed her brother into the kitchen. She glanced back to see if the dog might follow, but he didn't. He lay next to the couch, his eye on her.

"You can stay there if you want," Louise told him.

Andrew poured himself a glass of water from the faucet. Louise opened up the refrigerator door. Lying on its side, next to a half empty carton of orange juice, sat a sparkling a bottle of cabernet. She whipped around to stare at her brother, who wore a shit-eating grin. Now she understood why Andrew seemed off when he came to the door. His usual attire of worn out jeans and a T-shirt had been replaced with dark jeans and a button down shirt.

"I've got a date," Andrew said sheepishly.

"You're kidding. Who? Anybody I know?" Her smile matched Andrew's in intensity.

"Well, it's not really a date. We're just getting together to exchange information."

"Sounds romantic as hell," Louise said. "The wine is to loosen her tongue, right?"

"Something like that."

"Who is she?" Louise asked again. She took out the orange juice and drank from the carton.

"Nobody you'd know. She's straight."

Louise nodded her head as she wiped her mouth with her sleeve. "Yeah, I've never met any of *those* people."

Andrew gulped down the water and poured himself another.

"Take it easy there, cowboy."

Andrew grinned. "She's supposed to be here in about fifteen minutes. So before I throw you out is there any real reason for this visit other than to freak out Corwin?"

Louise bit her lip and placed the juice back on the shelf. "My evil conscience is taking over. Andrew, I need you to be my good conscience for a minute." She spoke softly and very seriously.

She hardly dared to look at her brother's face. When she did, she saw that his smile had disappeared as fast as hers.

"What's going on in that head of yours?"

Louise couldn't help but grin. Karla used that phrase, too. A knock at the front door echoed down the hall and into the kitchen. Andrew's head perked up like a deer hearing a twig snap.

The tension faded. "Ooh, I get to meet Andrew's date." Louise clapped her hands together and she darted in front of him out of the kitchen.

"Sorry you had to leave so suddenly." He grabbed her shoulder and pushed her behind him.

"I bet she's going to be dreamy," Louise chided.

Andrew ignored her as he happened to glance down the hallway on his way to the door. "Corwin!" He tore toward the bedroom.

Light from the room spilled out of a wide open door. "Oh, shit!" Louise raced to the front door and flung it open. "He'll be right with you," she said, and dashed after her brother.

On the other side of the living room Louise skidded to a stop and did a double take at the woman standing in the doorway. "You've got to be kidding."

No sound came from the bedroom. Louise pictured a half-eaten Corwin lying next to a dead Peanut, his skull smashed in by Andrew's boot. Then, of course, she'd have to shoot her brother for killing the dog. The girlfriend would shoot Louise and then feel so grief stricken that she'd have to do herself in so it would make a nice tidy package for the police.

Instead she met Andrew hogging the doorway. She pushed in past him.

A very satisfied Peanut lay on the floor. Lying between his paws, Corwin purred in ecstasy as the rottweiler tongue-bathed the top of his head.

"That would make a great fluff piece." Bianca squeezed herself between them.

Andrew recovered enough to introduce the reporter to his sister. Bianca held out her hand.

"We've got standing orders at MPD to shoot any cop seen talking to this woman," Louise said.

Bianca withdrew her hand. "I've got a job to do too."

"Like hanging cops out to dry?" Louise asked.

"Gee, sis, sorry you've got to run." Andrew bent down and Corwin let out a disgruntled meow as he was picked off of the floor. Andrew handed Peanut's leash to Louise and ushered them both to the door.

"We'll talk tomorrow," Andrew whispered to Louise before pushing her and the dog out into the hallway. "Are you going to be okay?"

"I'll be fine." As the door shut behind her, Louise scratched Peanut's ear. "I can tell when we're not wanted. Let's go meet your other mom."

Thirty

Monday 6:00 p.m.

Karla set the bag of pet supplies on the floor in the hallway and searched through her purse for Louise's apartment key. After a minor meltdown she found it wedged inside a carry-size package of tissues.

She had stopped at the pet store and picked up bowls, a stuffed fleece sleeping mat and a book on rottweilers. Shocked at all the different brands of dog food, she decided Louise had to be responsible for that.

Inside, Karla put a Tori Amos CD in the player and searched Louise's cupboards for dinner. She doubted Louise would be home any time soon so there seemed no point in making anything fancy.

As Tori sang about love, Karla pulled out a package of frozen sausages, sharp cheddar cheese and a couple of eggs. She danced around the kitchen as she fried the sausage and shredded the cheese, and rhythmically swayed to the music as she beat the eggs.

~

Elias circled the block three times before pulling into the apartment parking lot. He was a stranger here, out of his realm. He had questions but Gillespy no longer answered. How could he get past the security door? Should he do a frontal assault and kick in the glass? Wait for someone to leave and sneak in? Call with some excuse and hope that they buzz him in? As soon as he made one decision doubts crept in and he'd come up with reasons why he should try another tact. Was Miller even home yet? If not, she would be in for quite a surprise. Maybe he'd greet her sniffing a pair of her panties.

Too much traffic, too many people littered the city. All Elias wanted to do was to grab S.K. and get out, back to where there was enough room to breathe. The ideal situation would be to go in and out unseen. It had worked at the pet hospital, but trepidation haunted Elias. How long would his luck last? Like always, he'd be prepared. He patted his pocket for the security of the gun, relieved by its solid presence.

Through the glass doors he saw an elderly couple walking gingerly down the stairs. He jumped out of his car and hurried and ran.

"Oh, you poor dear." The woman sympathetically held open the door as he sailed through. He mumbled his thanks in return. Confusion reigned as Elias opened the door and looked down the hallway. The doors all had numbers, but none had names.

"Sir Knight?" Elias murmured in front of each door, hoping to hear the rustling of paws inside.

He received one answer but not from S.K. The shrill yippy bark came from a dog much smaller. A snack for S.K.

With no luck on the first floor, Elias made his way to the next level. As he opened the door on the second floor landing, a woman stepped out of her apartment carrying a basket full of dirty laundry. Elias slid back into the shadows of the stairwell. He needed a new plan.

"I can help you." It was Gillespy.

Excitement and doubt surged through Elias. "How?"

"You'll have to let me go," the voice answered.

"You help me then I'll help you." Elias had to be the one in control.

"Do you promise to release me?"

"Yes," Elias lied. He tried to block out the thought of the shrink still in the stocks while letting S.K. eat his face.

"I refuse to help you."

"I'm sorry. I promise I'll let you go." Elias built a picture in his mind, concentrating on setting Gillespy free.

"Do you dare face the consequences if you're lying?"

Elias remembered the beatings, the psychological torture. He remembered his screams. "I'm not lying," he lied.

"Go down to the front door," Gillespy told him. "Her name will be on the mailbox. The mailbox will also have her apartment number."

Elias chided himself for not thinking of such a simple plan. Maybe he did. Maybe that wasn't Gillespy's voice. Just maybe he had thought of it all by himself. And maybe he *would* let S.K. eat the bastard's face. He flinched, expecting the voice to come back and protest. It didn't.

Downstairs, Elias opened the door to the entry. He froze in the doorway. *I'll lock myself out.* He wanted to share his mind again, but as the saying went, no one was home. He kept his foot in the door and stretched almost to the mailboxes. He couldn't stretch quite far enough.

Elias tapped his foot and smiled. A tidal wave of awe immersed him. Standing all by himself, a man in a strange city, Elias had hit a major breakthrough. Elias was his own master now. "I don't need you anymore, Dr. Gillespy."

His hands shook with excitement. Elias untied the laces of his boot. He couldn't stop smiling. It grew so big that the tender scab on his lip split open once again. The blood tasted sweet. He slipped his foot out of the boot that still propped open the door. No one would come and interrupt his plans. Nothing could stop the invincible Elias Boughton.

Management had done a nice job of typing the names and sliding them under the apartment number on each mailbox. Elias scanned the top row. Nerves edged into his euphoria while questions nagged at him. *What if she lives with a guy and it's under his name? What if she just moved in and the caretaker didn't change the name yet?*

"Shut up!" He clenched his eyes tight. He waited for the

questions to subside before he opened them again. His eyes refocused.

L. Miller

Apartment 307

Elias bit his lip hard enough for the blood to pour. It coated his tongue before moistening his lips. His hands shook in excitement so much that he was hardly able to re-lace his boot. S.K. was only two stories above. Soon they would be reunited and his healing would be complete.

Elias raced up the stairs three at a time. A little out of breath at the top of the third floor, Elias stood still until his breathing returned to normal, and he tried to sense S.K. Exhilaration filled the air, but not the presence of his dog.

Dark green wallpaper decorated the hallway. Even with lights attached to the wall between every apartment, because of the opaque glass shade, the hall was dimly lit. Each dark, wood-paneled door had a peephole just under its identifying number. Elias thought about putting his thumb over the hole and knocking, hoping Miller would feel safe enough in her security building to open her door. The other option would be to kick in the door. He'd have the element of surprise, but it might catch the attention of the neighbors. But he really loved to see the look of astonishment on their faces. For that slight moment, it made them seem so real.

A third option as he approached apartment 307 became readily apparent. The bitch could be stupid enough to leave her keys in the doorknob and he could silently stroll right in. His eyes grew as wide as his smile as he twisted the key and the door swung open. Prissy piano music oozed out of the speakers alongside an equally prissy female voice. A dorky looking cat clock on the wall seemed to sway its tail in time to the music. An even worse female voice from down the hall sang off key.

"Silent Kill," Elias whispered into the air. *Put that bitch out of her misery.*

Long moments passed and nothing happened. Even with

the music S.K. should have heard the command and the singing voice down the hall should have converted to shrieks. *Not that there would be a whole lot of difference.*

Elias pulled the key out of the lock and slid it into his pocket, locking the door behind him. Silently crossing the room, he lifted a pillow off the couch. "All the better to smother you with, my dear," he whispered.

With every off key note that she sang, Elias thought about ripping out her vocal chords instead. Messy, but it would send a message to every other person in the world who thought that they could sing. Of course he'd have to write a message on the wall with her blood; maybe something about not quitting her day job or 'American Idol reject.'

He slipped into the bedroom to see if maybe S.K. might be sleeping next to the bed. Nothing. Back in the hallway the singing had stopped. Elias still had a little more luck when he craned his neck around the corner and saw into the kitchen. A petite blonde-haired woman stood with her back to him, stirring something on the stove.

Still no S.K. Elias crept up behind her like a stealth bomber.

"Where's my dog?" he hissed.

Elias loved this part. The shock of a deer frozen in headlights. The woman spun around and her face did not disappoint. Then she did the unimaginable. She didn't freeze.

~

Karla's heart leapt when she saw the giant. Blood smeared across his mouth like a six-year old girl applying lipstick for the first time. How many times had Louise snuck up on her, then chided her for freezing? That first second might be the difference between life and death, she had scolded.

With one hand already grasping the handle of the skillet, Karla flung chunks of sausage and sizzling grease at her attacker. He raised the pillow like a shield. A few arrows of grease sailed over and splattered on his face. The man screamed and clutched the pillow to his face. Before he could recover, Karla swung the pan at his kneecap. He screamed again. Hot metal clanged into his leg, searing flesh.

The monster doubled over to grab his knee; Karla took aim for his head. He raised the pillow just in time to deflect the blow. The skillet flew out of her hand and arced across the kitchen, trailing the floor with the last of the grease. The fiend smiled maniacally as it clattered off the wall and bounced on the floor.

Rivulets of burned grease lined his already bloody face. He took a step toward her and his eyes grew. He realized his mistake.

Karla grabbed the pan of eggs off the stove and swung. Instead of backing away like most would have, the behemoth charged. The pan grazed the back of his shoulder, burning another patch of skin. With a scream and all of his weight, he rammed Karla, smashing her into the stove. Her back slammed into the oven handle leaving her short of breath. Her head connected hard on the metal. Blond hair ignited from the burner, crackling in the air.

Gasping for air Karla jerked forward. Singed hair stung her cheeks. A giant paw grabbed the top of her head. She wrapped her arms around his leg and sank her teeth into his already tender knee. His leg buckled and he dropped, but didn't let go of her head. She stayed on top of him, clenching her jaw, trying to bite through to the bone. He screamed. Her hand became a talon grasping his balls.

A fist connected to the side of her head. Burned eggs, burned sausage, and burned hair wafted throughout the kitchen. The room went fuzzy. Karla thought she might have seen one of her teeth imbedded in the giant's knee before everything faded.

~

Gasping for breath, Elias sat on the floor and holding his knee, his back against the counter, he stared at the unconscious woman. He couldn't help but admire her. No one, not even the orderlies at the institution, had ever hurt him like that. He plucked her tooth out of his pants leg and stared at the tiny thing with dying tendrils of hair-smoke dissipating around her head.

Soon there would be an intimate bond, a telepathic connection opening up. They would be able to communicate like he'd been able to do with Gillespy, but better. They even had S.K. in common. Startled, he suddenly remembered what he'd come for in the first place.

"S.K.?" Elias spoke louder. "Sir Knight." No answer.

He boosted himself up and limped to the refrigerator. He opened the door, pulled out a stick of butter and applied it to the burns on his face. He then plodded through the kitchen, opening drawers until he found a couple of extension cords.

"Sorry to have to do this to you, Miss Miller. One day you'll come around and then I won't need to anymore."

Elias hoisted her onto a chair and bound her with the cords. With that task done he trudged through the apartment looking for his dog.

~

Karla groaned but didn't open her eyes. The side of her face throbbed. She tasted a bloody space as she glided her tongue over her teeth. The binds ate into her wrists and ankles. Where the hell was Louise?

"Where's S.K.?"

Karla feigned unconsciousness.

"I know you're awake. I saw you move."

Goosebumps crept over Karla as his voice penetrated her throbbing head. Still, she didn't open her eyes.

"If you want me to think you're still asleep, I can play that game. Then I'll just have to take this carving knife I found in the drawer and stab you in the thigh. It won't kill you but it'll hurt like a son-of-a-bitch."

Karla opened her eyes and shivered. Sitting two feet away, the grotesque monster who broke into Louise's apartment and attacked her twirled a butcher knife on the tip of his finger. "You've got the wrong apartment, mister. There's no S.K. here." The esses came out like a hiss through the new space in her teeth.

"Then what's the dog stuff for?" Elias asked. "Or is that for your personal use?"

"My partner's a cop."

"I've killed a cop before. They die just as easy as real people."

Elias cleaned his fingernails with the knife.

A new set of shivers covered Karla's skin as she made a connection. "You killed Mark Lone Bear."

"Was that his name? He looked Indian, so that's probably the one." Elias smiled, stopped picking at his nails and cocked his head. Any sense of friendliness left his eyes. "Where's my dog?"

"I don't know. I don't have your goddamn dog." Karla kept shaking her head back and forth. *How could this be happening*?

"What did you do with him?" The monster's eyes became slits through which he glared.

"I never had him," Karla spat back.

Elias arose from his chair and leaned over Karla. "I'm losing my patience with you." He grabbed her around the neck. "I know you took him, Louise Miller. I was at the hospital. They gave me your address."

Karla's stomach knotted and bile rose in her throat. She turned her head just in time to avoid throwing up in her lap. Vomit splattered onto the floor splashing on the monster's boots. Karla felt a slight satisfaction at that. He grinned at her, unconcerned.

"Shall we play a game? Let's see if I can tell what you last ate."

The acrid taste coated her mouth as the satisfaction vanished. She spit at her captor, phlegm sticking to his shirt. He grabbed a handful of her hair and smeared the stain in her face. He squatted down to look her in the eye, and winced as his injured knee bent.

"I'm trying to be nice to you, but it's a two way street, Miss Miller. Now my patience has run out." He touched the tip of the knife to her cheek and made a thin slice into her skin. Blood dripped down off of her chin and onto her lap. He lightly ran the blade along the red stream down her neck, hooking it in her blouse, cutting the buttons on the way down to her slacks. He caressed the knife up and down her zipper. "I'll ask you one more time, Louise Miller. Where's my dog?"

"I don't know," she cried out as tears poured down her cheeks. "I'm not Louise. She's bringing home a dog but I don't know when."

Karla's heart broke as the man's eyes grew and his jaw dropped. She had betrayed Louise. Did betrayal take a back seat to survival? Maybe. But if he killed Louise, Karla could never live with the guilt. She looked in the cop killer's eyes and knew he was calculating whether or not she should live.

A pounding on the door startled both of them.

The brute held a knife to Karla's throat and whispered in her ear. "Ask who it is. Make it sound natural."

In a shaky voice, Karla called out. "Who is it?"

"Police. There's been a complaint. Open the door please."

"Apologize for the noise. Tell him everything is fine and he can go away." The tip of the knife pierced Karla's skin.

"Sorry for the noise, Officer. Everything is fine." Karla was surprised she got the words out.

"I'm not going anywhere. Open the door ma'am."

"Tell him just a minute."

"Just a sec," Karla called out.

Karla's binds loosened as the killer stepped behind her. She figured he'd stand behind the door and make her answer. That would be his mistake. She'd slam the door into him and scream for the cop to shoot while she ran down the hall. Maybe she'd survive this ordeal after all.

~

Elias cold cocked the woman who wasn't Louise Miller and she collapsed at his feet. He frantically searched around the room while taking the gun out of his pocket. He'd gotten away with killing one cop, but two? The odds weren't in his favor, especially with all the nosy neighbors. "Shoot him in the head this time," he told himself.

Walking out of the kitchen, Elias noticed the door at the end of the hall. He opened it and stepped out onto the balcony. The pounding on the front door became more insistent. "Open the door now!" the voice demanded.

Elias raced back into the kitchen, slipped the gun into his pocket, and hoisted the woman over his shoulder. She weighed hardly anything as he limped back onto the balcony. Three stories up didn't look like too far of a drop. Elias climbed over the railing, then, hanging with one hand on the wooden deck, he grabbed the back of the woman's blouse and lifted her off.

He meant to grab her arm and lower her as far as he could before dropping, but with the buttons already popped she slid out of her top and landed with a thud on the soft ground.

Still holding the blouse, Elias dangled with one hand still grasping the plank. "Oops."

"Open the door now. One way or another, I'm coming in!"

Elias let go of the deck and landed next to the unconscious woman. He bit his lip as his swollen knee with the bite mark burned. Otherwise, a perfect landing, no more harm done. Checking for witnesses, Elias swung the woman up in his arms and limped around to the front of the building. Who was he fooling? Anybody who saw him would call the police.

A police car sat unattended by the front entrance. Elias cursed himself for having parked so far away. With limited options, Elias tried to look nonchalant as he made his way to the car. He set her in the front seat and breathed a sigh of relief as he got in and started the engine.

The woman's head had slumped against the passenger window. Elias grabbed her shoulder and pulled her to him. Her head landed face first into his lap. He grinned at his body's corresponding surge of interest.

"Maybe later."

Sweat poured down his face as he pulled back onto the street. A police car, its lights flashing, was speeding in his direction. He stared straight ahead as the car flew by. He watched in his rearview mirror as the cop swerved his vehicle into the apartment parking lot.

A block from the freeway, Elias pulled his car into an alley. A driveway with a spike fence on one side and lilac bushes on the other made as good a shelter as Elias was likely to find. He scoured the area from his car, then took the woman that had intruded in Louise Miller's apartment and placed her in the trunk. He did another quick scan, got in his car, whistled as he got back on the freeway, and headed back to the world where he reigned.

Thirty-One

Monday 6:20 p.m.

Louise reached into her purse and pulled out her cell phone. She wanted to call home and let Karla know she was on the way. No dial tone, no light. Louise cursed at her dead phone.

She shook the phone hoping to bring the battery back to life for one more call. When that failed she sucked in her gut, nibbled her lower lip and timidly knocked on her brother's door. She smiled coyly when he answered. "I apologize. I was out of line."

"What do you really want?" Andrew stared at his sister but didn't open the door any wider.

Louise scratched Peanut on the head. "My cell phone died. I just wanted to call Karla and tell her I'm on the way."

Corwin slipped between the doorjamb and Andrew's foot and rubbed himself against Peanut. The dog licked Corwin's head. Andrew had seen contentment on Corwin's face a number of times but he didn't think he'd ever seen the cat smile before.

"I suppose I'd better let you in or Corwin will never forgive me." Andrew opened the door; Peanut sauntered in pulling Louise behind him. Corwin sped past Louise.

Louise gave her brother a maniacal grin. "Where's the bi—"

Andrew held up a finger in warning.

"Er, your date?" Louise corrected herself.

"She's not my date. We're just getting together to exchange information. And she's in the kitchen."

"Uh huh. Did she call you or did you call her?"

"I called her. It's funny. When she answered she was shocked. Said she was trying to find my number because she wanted to talk to me."

"Must be fate."

Andrew ignored her remark. "I wanted to know if she knew anything about the murder at the pet hospital. She said she was there, covering the story."

"Excuse me?" Louise's eyebrows shot up.

"Didn't you hear? A receptionist got murdered there this afternoon."

"Which one?" Louise looked at Peanut lying at the foot of the couch. Corwin had snuggled up next to him. Even from the distance of across the room, Louise could hear the cat purr.

"Which receptionist?"

"The hospital, stupid."

"The emergency one."

"Any suspects?"

Andrew shook his head. "They're looking for an ex-husband or something."

"That's bullshit. You know who it is."

"And get this. They've got security cameras, but they weren't on. I called Rivers when I heard. He has a sketch from Dagin's description. He already passed it around. There's not a whole lot more I can do."

"Who the hell is Dagin, and why didn't you tell me this before?"

"He's the kid who had Hout's ATM card."

"How much water?" Bianca called from the kitchen.

"Be right there," Andrew answered back. "I didn't tell you because I knew how you'd react. It's Golden Valley. You can't go charging in there."

Louise fought the urge to slug him. "What are you making?"

"Vegetable curry with rice."

Louise shuddered and tried the phone. Andrew disappeared

into the kitchen. Karla didn't answer at either of their homes, but Louise didn't feel concern until she didn't answer her cell phone. She called the number where Karla worked but got an answering machine. She pulled out her cell phone to check for messages then slapped herself upside the head.

Andrew stood at the counter dicing carrots. Bianca did the same to celery as Louise walked in. A pot of rice boiled on the stove.

Don't let that knife she's holding stab you in the back. "I don't suppose you might have an extra battery for your cell that I might borrow?"

"As a matter of fact, I do, and you may. There's one in the drawer next to the bed." He winked at Bianca. "Like the boy scouts, I'm always prepared."

"That's why Mom always liked you best," Louise said.

"Did you ever watch the Smothers Brothers on TV Land?" Andrew asked Bianca.

"Who?"

Louise rolled her eyes and left the loving couple before she threw up. As she passed through the living room, Corwin was busily at work licking his sandpaper tongue on Peanut's stitches. The dog seemed to enjoy it. *Inter species and possibly gay,* Louise thought. She left them alone and went into the bedroom. She opened up the drawer, thumbed past the box of tissues, antacids, and revolver. She paused at the unopened box of condoms.

"You really are prepared, aren't you?"

Tucked back in the corner, Louise found the battery out of its package and wondered if it was charged. Of course it would be. It's Andrew's. She inserted the small disc and her phone came to life. Louise sat on the edge of his bed and punched in the code for her messages. She recognized Paul Handley's voice. "We got a call that there's a disturbance at your place. You all right? Call me."

The second call also came from Handley. "What the hell's going on over there? I'm on my way. Call me, dammit."

The third message chilled her blood. "You've got what I want.

I've got what you want. How about we make a trade?"

A raspy voice, menacing. Louise checked the caller I.D. The call had come from Karla's cell. Louise speed dialed Karla's number again. Again, no answer. She tried Handley.

"What the hell's going on?" Louise asked as soon as he picked up.

"You tell me. I've been trying to get hold of you."

"I'm at my brother's. My cell phone died. What's going on?"

"Looks like there was a brawl in your kitchen. Tenny didn't want to enter but when I heard it was your place I got there as quick as I could and kicked in the door. Sorry about that."

"Tennyson's a pussy."

"Yeah, anyway, shit all over the place. There's some blood, too."

"Karla," Louise whispered.

"What? Anyway, report in. The Captain wants to talk with you pronto."

Louise disconnected the line. Laughing and discussion about Nickelodeon and other cable TV channels emanated along with the aroma of curry from out of the kitchen.

"Fuck it." Louise grabbed Peanut's leash. The dog slowly got to his feet. Corwin meowed in protest.

The dog could walk down stairs much easier than up. It didn't seem to cause him any pain or distress, but he still moved slow. After the first flight Louise had enough. She hefted him in her arms and carried him the next two flights. With her mind focused on Karla, the dog seemed to weigh much less.

After going through her second red light she slowed down. What was the point? Karla wasn't there, and all she needed now was to get pulled over by one of her own. She obeyed the speed limit and cursed the traffic gods at every red light until she finally made it home.

Louise didn't have the patience to coddle Peanut out of the car. She lifted him up carried him all the way to the security door. She put him down long enough to unlock the door and then hauled him up another three flights of stairs. "Next apartment is on the ground floor," she told him.

The dog seemed agitated as Louise tore off the crime scene tape. With the lock kicked in, the door swung upon. He growled and whined, walked nervously in a circle. Louise pulled out her gun. Eerie silence met her. Peanut jumped up on his hind legs and whimpered as he landed. He raced ahead of Louise down the hall.

"Get back here," Louise hissed.

The dog ignored her and swerved into the kitchen. Louise followed, the gun leading the way. Pans had been strewn about the floor. Louise slipped on a patch of grease. A chair sat in the middle of the room, drops of blood and puke splattered next to it.

"Goddamn you, Karla. What happened in here? Where are you?"

Peanut followed the scents until he located a payday of sausage bits scattered on the floor and busily lapped up the evidence.

The handle to the oven had been bent. Her comrades on the force had already been through and she didn't want to contaminate a crime scene, but Peanut found another spot of grease and contentedly cleaned the floor. She'd stop him when he discovered the blood and vomit.

Louise tried Karla's cell again. Still no answer, but as soon as she disconnected the phone rang in her hand. Louise jumped, her heart in her throat. The caller I.D. showed 'pay phone.' No number. She caught it on the second ring, her voice sounded as shaky. "Miller."

"You're home. I knew you'd get there eventually."

The same voice from Karla's cell phone.

"If you hurt her in the slightest, I will kill you." It sounded cliché, but she meant every word.

"Oh dear. I'd better be careful then."

"Is she okay?"

"She's alive. For now."

"I'll hunt you down and kill you."

"I kill you, you kill me, we're all one happy fam-i-ly. Tsk, tsk. It's up to you whether or not she stays alive."

Louise refused to give him the satisfaction of voicing another threat. Silence ate away at her already raw nerves.

The line went dead in her ear.

~

Elias rushed out of the Taco Bell. The thought of a trace hadn't occurred to him until two police cars pulled into the lot. He moved cautiously past his own car and crossed the street before looking back. Through the big picture window at the front of the restaurant, Elias saw the two Kenowa officers stand at the counter talking to the clerk. Elias couldn't breathe until he saw one of the officers reach in his back pocket and pull out his wallet. Just to be safe he waited for the cops to take their trays and sit at a table before he returned to his car.

"This is why you need me," Gillespy said.

Elias grabbed his head. "Stop it! Get out! I don't need you! Leave me alone!"

"You'll get caught."

"Oh yeah? Watch this."

Elias glanced through the window of the restaurant as he started the car. The cops took no notice of him as he pulled away.

"You do stupid things when I'm not there. Just look at the burns on your face."

"Go away!" Elias shouted.

"I'm not going anywhere! You are to come home and release me. Then I will tell you how to get out of this hole you've dug yourself into."

"I've got my own plan."

"You'll get caught. You're not smart enough to come up with your own plan."

"It will work!" Elias screamed.

"You will die."

~

Near panic, Louise stared at the phone willing it to ring.

Maybe the lines had gone down. She picked up the receiver and heard a dial tone. She quickly hung up in case he was trying to call back. After ten more seconds of silence, Louise picked up the receiver and pressed *69. The phone rang and rang. After the seventh ring someone picked up.

"Hello?"

A male voice but far different from her caller. He sounded like a teenager whose hormones were in the process of kicking in.

"I'm a Minneapolis police officer. I need to know where this phone is located."

"No, really. Who is this?"

"Kid, I don't have time to dick around. My name is Louise Miller and I'm a Minneapolis cop. I'm checking out threatening phone calls coming from this phone."

"I haven't made any threatening phone calls."

Louise wanted to reach through the wires and grab this kid by the throat. As calmly as she could, "I'm not accusing you. I'm saying it's the same phone you're talking on. Where are you?"

"At Taco Bell." The boy sounded unsure of himself.

Great. That should narrow it down to about a million. "Which Taco Bell?" She fought to keep her voice calm.

"The one in Kenowa."

His voice cracked; she was losing him. "Have you seen anyone using the phone in the last five minutes?" She tried to sound reassuring.

"No." He paused for a moment. "I gotta go, lady."

"Before you go can you get the manager? Tell the manager I have to talk to him."

She waited for a response but got nothing. On the positive side she didn't get a dial tone either. She waited over a minute, and then heaved out a discouraging groan.

"This is Russ."

"Are you the manager?" Louise asked. He didn't sound any older than the last kid.

"Yeah. Can I help you?"

"My name's Louise Miller. I'm a Minneapolis police officer. I've been getting threatening phone calls and they've been coming from your phone. Have you seen anybody suspicious lurking around? Say, in the last five to ten minutes?"

"Sorry, I've been behind the counter. The phone is around the corner by the restrooms. Hang on just a minute."

Impressed by the kid's maturity Louise stayed on the line while she assumed that he might be asking people if they saw anyone on the phone.

An adult voice came on the line. "Hello?"

"Who's this?" Louise asked.

"Officer Martell, Kenowa Police. Who am I speaking with, please?"

"Officer Louise Miller, Minneapolis PD. Fourth precinct." She recited her badge number and for the third time Louise gave her spiel, this time going into greater detail.

"Sorry, Officer Miller, I haven't seen anyone."

"Any cameras set up in the parking lot? Anything like that?"

She got a chuckle on the other end. "In Kenowa? They haven't even taken out the pay phones yet."

They exchanged numbers and Martell promised they'd keep an eye out. Louise disconnected the phone and rubbed her eyes, wondering if the kidnapper had tried calling while she'd been on the phone. She remembered the call forwarding option that came with the package she ordered, the option she never used. She would have heard a click if someone else had tried to call.

The phone rang again. Louise looked at the caller I.D. and snatched the receiver. "Karla?"

A low chortle. "Does this sound like a Karla?"

Louise swore she'd remember his menacing voice to her grave. Better yet, to his. "Where is she?" Louise spat.

"Where is my dog?" The sinister voice came back.

"Is that what this is all about?" Louise screamed. "Your fucking dog?"

"You stole him." The voice became angry.

"I adopted him, you sick freak. How do I know he's yours? What's he look like? Any identifying features?"

"He knows my voice. Put the phone by his ear."

Peanut was sprawled out on the cool tile floor. Lying on his back, his legs sprouted in the air. Louise walked over to him holding the phone out in front of her. Peanut rolled over onto his side as she knelt and rubbed his stomach between lines of stitches.

"Go ahead." She put the phone close to the dog's ear and leaned over so she could hear too.

"S.K.?"

The dog rolled instantly onto his stomach, his head shot into the air, smacking Louise on the chin. Alarmed, she placed the phone back to her ear and heard the voice whisper, "Silent kill."

The words echoed in Louise's head.

"What's he doing now?"

"Licking my hand."

"You're spoiling him!"

"At least I don't beat the shit out of him like you did!" Louise tried to control her own anger.

"What are you talking about? I'd never harm that dog, you stupid cunt. You better be there when I call back."

Louise quickly cut in. "You mentioned something about a trade. Let's talk."

The kidnapper hung up. She called her brother. Andrew answered on the third ring.

"He's got Karla!"

Thirty-Two

Monday 6:50 p.m.

Elias fumbled in his glove compartment and pulled out a roll of duct tape. *One thousand and one uses,* he thought as he tore off a long strip. He got out of the car, found a fist-sized rock and taped it to Karla's cell phone. "I'm on to you." He stood on the shore of Perch Lake and pitched the rock-phone as far as he could into the water. *Let 'em try and trace the phone there.*

As he walked back to his car he heard a pounding coming from inside the trunk. With one furious blow, he pounded back. The thumping stopped.

"What am I going to do with you? This is your own fault. You shouldn't have gotten in the way. I've got no place to put you."

"I can help you," Gillespy said.

"Leave me alone!"

"You're worthless. You'll always be worthless."

"SHUT UP! I'm not worthless. You are! I'm driving around a free man. Where are you?" Elias laughed as the voice in his head went silent. The silence fed his anger. "You can read my mind, huh? Well read this!" Elias pictured pulling out Gillespy's arms, then his legs. Then he took the head and torso and threw it in a giant vat of salt water and meditated to Gillespy's screams. "What? Nothing to say?" Elias whistled the rest of the way home.

Inside his garage he sat and watched in his rear view mirror until the door slid all the way down. Listening to the soft hum of the motor, he closed his eyes while smoke from the exhaust filled the garage with fumes. Maybe he should leave her in the trunk. Whoever she was, for such a skinny thing, she put up one good fight. He had to respect that. Maybe she deserved a painless death. It then occurred to him she still had value. He might need her until he set up the trade for S.K. He shut off the engine.

The trunk lid swung open. She gasped for air like a person who had been held underwater. Bathed in sweat, she resembled a person who'd been held underwater, too. Her terrified eyes stared back. A purple and red bruise had swollen her cheek, giving it a mutated chipmunk type of quality.

He hoisted her over his shoulder. She put up no resistance; a mild disappointment. Maybe she wasn't all that great after all. He bounced her on his shoulder to try and bolster a little life into her, but she lay there like dead weight. Well, almost, or soon to be, dead weight.

Voices filtered through the basement door, too muffled for Elias to make out the words. The chatter stopped when he slipped the key into the lock and opened the door. "Were you talking about me?" Elias called. "I hope it was nice stuff."

"You let me out of here now, Elias," Gillespy ordered weakly. His voice sounded less commanding.

Elias unloaded the woman onto the floor next to the doctor strapped to the surfboard. Her head hit his shoulder and to Elias' surprise, the man groaned.

"I thought you were dead. You smell like you're dead." Elias laughed.

Karla shivered in her new surroundings and saw the woman tied to the X. "Oh my God," she whispered and choked back a scream. She pushed herself against the wall and clamped her eyes shut.

"This has gone too far, boy. You let me out of this contraption right now." Gillespy took on and air of command again, but an undertone of panic betrayed him.

Elias ignored him for his newest captive. He caressed her cut cheek with his palm, but she jerked her head away. He grabbed her chin, forcing the girl to look at him. Karla's eyes were wide in what Elias hoped was awe. She shifted her gaze and seemed especially focused on the woman tied to the giant X.

"Stand up," he told her.

She broke her gaze from the lawyer.

"I said stand!"

She slowly got to her feet. The top of her head came up almost to his chin. Elias drove his fist into her gut. She collapsed in a heap at his feet.

"I'm sorry if I hurt you. I hope soon I won't have to do that anymore."

Holding her stomach, Karla curled up into a fetal position.

"But I can't have you running around playing hard to get while I'm busy."

"This has gone on far enough," Gillespy screamed. "You unlock me this instant!"

Elias walked toward Gillespy as if in a trance, pulling a key out of his pocket. He squatted so his face met even with the doctor's and dangled the key in front of him. His bad knee felt ready to explode, but he refused to show weakness. "Do you want me to unlock you?" He waved the key like a hypnotist in front of Gillespy's eyes.

"Don't play with me." Gillespy spit in his face. "Don't make this any harder on yourself."

Elias smirked at his audience as saliva oozed down his cheek. The lawyer stared in enthralled attention. She seemed not to care that her pants were still down around her thighs. His newest captive stopped gasping but buried her head in her arms as he stared down at her.

"Yes, Doctor Get Off Me," Elias said humbly. He squeegeed the spit off his face with his forefinger. "That's what we used to call you behind your back. Did you know that?"

"What?" the doctor boomed.

"I said, fuck you, Gillespy." An evil grin spread across Elias' face as he stuck his forefinger in his mouth and sucked the shrink's spit clean. "I am so sick of hearing your voice." A smack cracked the air as Elias slapped Gillespy across the face. "Who's in charge now, huh?" Elias screamed.

Blood trickled out of Gillespy's mouth. Elias grabbed the doctor's thinning hair and jerked his head up as far as the stocks would let him. "Call me Mr. Boughton!"

"You're sick. I can help you."

"SHUT UP! CALL ME MISTER BOUGHTON!" Elias slapped him again.

"Mister," Gillespy mumbled. "Boughton."

Elias stared wild-eyed and breathing heavily as he placed the key on the crossbar and grabbed Gillespy's head. With one hand under the doctor's chin and the other hand on top, Elias twisted.

Gillespy groaned as his shoulder tried to compensate but the bar held him snugly in place. His feet hopped up and down while his hands danced putting on quite a show while Elias applied more pressure.

Next came crackling from inside Gillespy's neck.

"Maybe I followed the wrong calling. Maybe I should have gone into chiropractics. What do you think, Doc?"

Elias put all his strength into one more twist until he heard the satisfying snap. The dancing hands abruptly stopped, the hopping feet rested on the floor, bent like a marionette. Karla screamed.

"It's harder than it looks," Elias told her.

She continued screaming.

"Shut up!" He kicked her in the back. The room became silent.

He looked at his newest captive no longer with sympathy. She had managed to crawl against the wall. Curled up in a ball she had her knees under her chin with her arms wrapped around her shins. She had become pathetic.

Elias unlatched Gillespy. The dead man slipped out of the holes and plopped on the floor.

"Well look at this," Elias said. "We just got an unexpected vacancy."

As he walked toward the girl she planted her heels on the floor and tried to push herself through the wall. Elias grabbed her by the hair and hoisted her up. Her arms and legs flung repeatedly in his direction. He held her out far enough so her punches glanced off of his arm as he dragged her to the stocks. As he readjusted his grip, Karla got in a kick that connected with his swollen knee. His leg buckled. She tore away from his grasp and fled up the stairs.

"Run!" the lawyer screamed.

From a bent position and holding tight to his knee, Elias spat at the lawyer. "She's going nowhere, you stupid cow."

A new set of sobs emanated from the top of the steps mixed with the fist pounding on the locked steel door. "Somebody help me!" she screamed.

"I'll help you, little girl." Elias limped up the stairs.

Thirty-Three

Monday 7:40 p.m.

Andrew marched into Louise's apartment with the reporter at his heels. Paul Handley and Minneapolis Police Sgt. Phil Tompkins were in her kitchen, Tomkins at the table typing into his laptop.

"Andrew, this is Paul Handley and Phil Tompkins. Phil is our communications expert."

Andrew nodded toward Tompkins, and smiled as he shook Paul's hand. "So, you're the infamous Paul Handley. Louise speaks very highly of you."

"You too," Paul said.

"What's she doing here?" Tompkins asked, angry.

"Like it or not, this is news," Bianca said.

"This is family," Louise snapped. "This is personal. It has nothing to do with the public's need to know."

"If there's a killer running around, the public has every right to know, officer. The personal family touch is irrelevant."

Louise glared at her brother. "Andrew, get her the hell out of here."

Andrew ignored the order, walked into the kitchen and spread out a map of Hennepin County on the table. Tompkins lifted up his computer and then set it on the edge of the map so it wouldn't roll up.

The dog rolled from his side onto his stomach and extended his head as an invitation to scratch his ears.

"Hello, Peanut," Andrew said.

"He's so cute." Bianca tucked her knees under her and sat on the floor next to the dog.

Andrew watched as Bianca's dress rode up her thighs. Louise elbowed him in the arm. Red-faced, he focused his attention back to the map. "Here's the Taco Bell." Andrew circled the intersection with a red magic marker.

Louise rushed over to his side. "He called on Karla's cell. We traced it to the southeast side of Perch Lake."

Andrew smiled at his sister with admiration, and circled that area on the map.

The ring made everyone jump. Louise looked at Tompkins, he nodded and she snatched the phone. She didn't recognize the number on the caller ID.

"The GPS is off on this one. You won't be able to trace it."

Louise held the phone away from her ear and motioned for her brother to listen in. "What have you done to her?" Louise growled through clenched teeth. "I swear to God, you're a dead man."

"Yeah, yeah, yeah, you've already made your intentions known. You're beginning to bore me. Now, you want to make a deal, or not?"

"Fine. You want the dog, you can have the dog. Let's trade."

Louise gave the phone to Andrew, who held it between their ears. With her hands free, Louise pressed the button and the clip popped out of her 9mm, debating whether to use two shots to the skull or an unload the entire clip and make him suffer.

"I don't know. I'm enjoying your friend's company."

Make him suffer. "I haven't grown that attached to MY dog yet. It would be no big deal for me to put him down."

The merriment disappeared from his voice. "If you touch a hair on him—"

"Yeah, yeah, yeah. You're boring me."

"All right. I'll call you tomorrow morning with instructions."

"Why not now? Quick, easy, no time to get anyone else involved."

"Because I make the rules!" the man shouted.

"Let me talk to her," Louise said.

"No."

"Why not?"

"She's all tied up at the moment." Elias chuckled.

"That's the best you can do?" Louise had enough. She slammed the clip into the gun loud enough for the kidnapper to hear. "The barrel is an inch from your dog's head. Now put her on the phone."

"You wouldn't dare." The voice sounded tentative, unsure. "Your friend will die."

"You might not know me, but Karla does. You ask her. I swear to God, your dog will just be a hundred pounds of meat. She'll understand that I had to do it." The gun shook in her hand. Andrew took it away from her. "You've got until the count of three. One…two—"

"No! Stop! I'll put her on. Just a minute."

Louise heard shuffling around and assumed he had his hand over the mouthpiece.

The lie of her life, and Louise pulled it off. Sweat rolled down her face as Andrew put the gun on the table.

After an unbearable silence, "Louise?" Karla's voice came on the line, her voice on the verge of hysterics.

Louise had to fight to keep her voice steady as her eyes welled up with tears. "Karla, Baby, are you all right? You'll be home soon."

"I'll call you with the instructions tomorrow," the man's voice returned on the line.

"His name's Elias. He killed Mark Lone Bear!" Louise heard Karla scream in the background.

The kidnapper disconnected the line.

~

Elias punched his captive in the mouth. Karla's head smashed back into the stocks hard enough that the wood creaked. Blood poured out of her mouth along with another tooth. He had held the phone to his captive's ear just long enough for her to mention her friend's name, and then took it back. He hadn't expected the added commentary.

Elias grabbed her hair and slapped her again. Closing his eyes he counted to ten. When he opened them he released his grip.

"You shouldn't have done that." Elias nudged the unconscious doctor on the surfboard with his foot. "I miss my dog."

He walked over to Gillespy and tapped him with his foot also, then came back to Karla. "She called you baby. So, does that mean you're a queer? No wonder you fought so good." Elias paced around her. "I don't think I ever met a fucking dyke before. What is it, a boob thing?" He stood behind her pressing his crotch to her rear and reached under and around and squeezed her breasts. Is it because you hardly got any and you like titties?" He let go and walked around to face her. He grabbed his knee first then stooped down to look her in the face. "Or is it because you never had a real man before?"

Karla glared but said nothing.

"What? Do you want to spit on me too? Go ahead and give me your best woogie. You saw what happened to the last guy who did."

"Fuck you," she whispered.

"Karla baby, are you all right?" He mocked Louise as he walked back behind her.

"Leave her alone you sick bastard," Melanie shouted from across the room.

"Shut up or you're next, bitch."

He yanked down Karla's pants. Underneath she wore a black thong. Elias took a deep breath to smell her fear. Karla tried to kick him like a mule but she couldn't shake her leg out of her slacks.

"Hey, look at this," he smiled as he called over to the lawyer. "She likes to floss her butt. Do you ever wear this kind of underwear?"

He slapped Karla hard on the ass. A tiny yelp escape her lips. She stopped trying to kick.

"I'll give you something to floss out of there."

"Leave her alone!" Melanie screamed.

Elias stared at her sex and licked his lips. "Don't you worry, you'll get your turn." He pulled down Karla's panties and undid his jeans. As his pants dropped to his ankles he stroked himself to get hard.

Melanie roared with laughter. "Is that all you've got? Don't worry, honey, you're not going to feel a thing."

"Shut up!" Elias screamed.

"I've got herpes," Karla said.

"Both of you shut up!"

Melanie laughed as Elias stroked harder and harder. It didn't work. The mood had been broken. "Fuck you both." Elias hiked up his pants.

"You can't. You're not man enough," Melanie shouted in between laughing fits.

"Shut up!" Elias charged at her.

"What are you going to do, kill me?" Melanie screamed. "Go ahead."

Elias halted, his face inches from hers. "Oh, I will. I've got something special planned for you."

"You don't have the guts, Elias. You're worthless."

"Shut up, shut up. Shut up!" Elias grabbed her throat.

"There's only one pussy in this room and that's you." Karla screamed. Her esses whistled from the missing front teeth.

Elias released his grip and stared in astonishment at Karla.

"You're nothing," Karla yelled. "In fact, you're less than nothing."

Elias felt the floor spinning under him. The ceiling gyrated above; he thought he might faint. He staggered to the stairs feeling dizzy. He climbed the steps and fumbled with the key but finally got the door open. He slammed it behind him.

~

"Thank you," Melanie said. Her throat burned all over again.

"I saw what you were doing. I just followed up on it."

"You're a quick study. Me and Dr. Gillespy—that's the dead guy by your feet—were talking. He reacts subserviently to people who act like superiors. He seems intimidated by them."

"He didn't seem too intimidated by the doctor," Karla said.

"They had a long history. Gillespy used to treat him in a psyche ward, or something. Years of pent up aggression. I think the doctor finally crossed the line."

"It looks like you almost crossed the line, too."

Melanie smiled. "Thanks again. I'll have to be a little more careful next time. But I have to admit it felt really good. The word is mightier than the fist."

"Tell that to my teeth."

"Hey, and good call on the herpes thing too. I think AIDS would've been a little over the top."

"Yeah, and I don't think he would've believed me if I used the pregnancy line."

"I don't think he would've cared," Melanie said.

Shock registered when Dr. Hout groaned. He hadn't moved for hours. Melanie had assumed he had died. She didn't feel very happy for him. Death would've been a more pleasant future.

"I have the feeling the next time he comes down here he's going to kill us," Melanie said.

"My lover's a cop. She'll save us," Karla said. "Plus, she has his dog."

"His dog is dead. How did you know about his dog?"

"Not dead."

"I was here. That good man strapped to the board over there killed him. See that puddle of blood by the stairs? That's from the dog."

"Well, my partner has *a* dog this maniac thinks is his. I don't think he'll kill us until he gets the dog, whether it's his or not. Louise will blow his brains out before that happens." Frustrated, she tried to think of words that didn't contain esses.

"I hope you're right," Melanie answered. "If we do live through this I know I'm going to have nightmares for years. In the back of every one of them will be that damned dog."

Karla didn't respond.

~

Elias sat on the floor gasping for air, his back against the basement door. How had his world spun so out of control? He had no special death planned for the lawyer. He didn't even have a plan to get S.K. back. All he did to deserve this was to answer Gillespy's plea when he first read that damned article. He knew that he'd never hear that voice again, and already he missed it.

~

Andrew placed his hand on Louise's shoulder. "At least we know she's still alive."

"At least she was." Louise's voice trembled.

"Keep positive," Andrew said.

Tompkins put his finger on the map. "The strongest signal bounced off of this tower, a weaker signal off of this one." He shook his head in frustration. "The call came from this part of Kenowa, or maybe the southern edge of Corcoran. Sorry, that's as close as I can narrow it."

Handley got on the phone and called Captain Henderson and told him that Lone Bear's murderer had just called Louise. They had reason to believe he lived in Kenowa. He nodded, told the captain he'd deal with it, and he'd call him back as soon as anything else came to light. "All resources are at our disposal. He wants to send over the detectives working Lone Bear's case, but I told him to hold off, we'd handle it for now. I have a feeling he's going to send them anyway."

Andrew got on his cell and called the Kenowa police. Fortunately, Ken Dearling was still in his office. He had received a fax of the sketch, but neither he nor his officers recognized the man's face.

"Does the name Elias ring a bell?" Andrew asked.

"It doesn't," the chief replied.

"I know this is asking a lot, but a person's life might be at stake. The Kenowa phonebook can't be that big. Can you have one of your guys go through it? I can't believe there can be many Eliases there."

"I have a gal just sitting by the phone aching for something to do," Dearling said.

"Much appreciated." Andrew gave the chief his number.

"The phone belongs to a Melanie Cartier," Tompkins said. "Here's her address."

Handley got on his cell and asked for a patrol to be sent to her home.

"Have you ever had any run-ins with an Elias?" Louise asked the question directly to her brother.

Andrew shook his head.

Louise grabbed her cell phone and punched in a number. "How can a goddamn giant be so invisible in a town the size of Hooterville?"

Andrew concentrated again on the map. "Here's where they pulled Mark out of the lake, and here's where they found the mother and daughter." Andrew marked both places. "Oh yeah, and here's the park where the kid who said a guy made him buy Dr. Hout's ATM card."

"This Cartier is a lawyer." Tompkins punched in a number on his phone.

"See any patterns?" Andrew asked.

He, Louise, and Handley studied the map.

"What about dog cases?" Bianca asked.

"What?" Louise wanted to punch the reporter for wasting everybody's time.

"Dog cases. You know; dog bites, noisy dog complaints, dog abuse cases. Stuff like that."

The trio looked at each other, dumbfounded.

"Why didn't you think of that?" Louise glared at her brother.

"Got a yellow pages?" Andrew asked.

He thumbed through to veterinarians while at the same time calling back Dearling. "Have you had any dog complaints? Barking, bites, anything like that?"

"Just a minute," Dearling said.

While he waited, Andrew scanned the list of pet doctors.

"Just a yapping Pomeranian," Dearling said.

"Thanks for checking." Andrew hung up. "No luck." He studied the phone book. "Five vets are in or very nearby, and about twenty or so in driving distance," Andrew said. He winked at Bianca. "You did good."

"I'm not just another pretty pair of legs."

Andrew blushed and Louise even smiled as she scanned the listings.

Tompkins got off the phone. "I called her firm. It seems no one's seen Miss Cartier since Wednesday."

The room became deathly quiet. Even the dog noticed the tension. He rolled from his back onto his stomach and planted his chin against his front legs, his eye looking up at the humans. Bianca scratched him behind the ears, away from the stitches.

Andrew's phone broke the silence.

"No Eliases in Kenowa or Corcoran. We even checked the unlisteds," Dearling said. "Anything else?"

"You going to be around for awhile?" Andrew asked. He got an affirmative. "We'll stay in touch. Thanks."

"That makes three people he's possibly holding captive," Handley finally said.

"If they're even still alive," Louise added.

"There's no reason to think they're not." Handley glared at his protégé.

Louise matched his stare. "You mean other than he's already killed three people, one of them being a cop?"

"Probably four. The Dagin kid said the guy who sold him Hout's card said the owner was dead," Andrew said.

They both stared at Andrew, their mouths open as if ready to say something, but words didn't come out.

Louise punched in a veterinarian's number. The first one she got a recorded message that they were closed for the day. "I hope the other ones are open late." She dialed the next number and gave Andrew a thumbs-up when someone answered. "Hi. I found a rottweiler and I was wondering if you knew of anyone around there who might own one? He has a tag that says S.K." Louise rolled her eyes. "Thank you, I'll do that." She hung up.

Andrew shuddered at how easily his sister could spit out a lie. "Well?"

"They suggested I bring him in so they can scan him for a chip."

"I did a story on that a couple of years ago," Bianca said. "It's a good idea."

"They should do that with people. It would make things easier, especially when a body had to be identified." She punched in the next number.

"Maybe Peanut has a chip," Bianca offered.

"I think the emergency vet would've said something," Louise answered.

"I wouldn't take anything for granted," Andrew said. "Do you have their number? I'll call them."

While Andrew talked to the folks at the pet hospital, Peanut rolled onto his back and Bianca scratched his belly. Handley got on his phone and tried the next number on the list. Louise tried the third number. In the middle of her spiel she rapped her knuckles sharply against the table for everyone's attention. "Do you have an address or a phone number?"

The excitement built as they waited. "Dr. William Gillespy. And an address?" Louise started scribbling on the map. "Thank you so much." Louise smiled as she hung up the phone.

Andrew shivered.

"Lucky break," Louise said.

"Does he live on Pennington Terrace?" Andrew asked.

Louise eyed him suspiciously. "Yeah."

Andrew let out a deep sigh. "Mark that number four on our missing person's list. We searched the place. There was a break-in and blood on the floor." He marked Gillespy's house on the map.

"They must know each other. How else would he come up with that name?" Louise said.

"Maybe this Elias was a patient," Handley said.

Bianca paused her scratching of the dog. "I've heard of him. He's a shrink that's getting sued. One of his patients committed suicide after he molested her."

"You're kidding?" Handley said. "This just keeps getting weirder and weirder." He called Henderson. "We're going to need your help, Captain. We need a patient list of a psychiatrist. A Dr. William Gillespy. Patient's first name is Elias." Handley paused and looked at the map. "He's not around to give permission. He's MIA. We think the guy who killed Lone Bear also might've killed him."

He ended with a yes sir and hung up. "He's calling the lawyers right now, but it might take awhile."

Andrew marked the vet's address on the map.

Louise studied the map and scratched her head. "What I can't figure out is how he tracked me down."

Bianca froze. "Oh my God." She stopped petting the dog. "Don't you people watch the news? I was covering the receptionist's murder this afternoon and talked to one of the doctors. She told me that their log book was missing."

"Jesus Christ." Louise dropped into a chair at the table.

She stared off into space and Andrew put a hand on her left shoulder, Handley placed a hand on her right. Peanut nuzzled his head into Bianca's thigh and whined.

"Okay, time to do some good old fashioned police work," Andrew said. "Louise, where's your digital camera?"

"What do you mean?" Bianca asked.

"Louise!" Andrew almost shouted into her ear. She blinked and vacantly looked at him. "Digital camera? Where?"

"Bedroom closet. Why?"

"Turn on your computer. I've got an idea."

She snapped back to the present and dashed off to her bedroom.

He spoke to Handley. "You still have a sketch of Elias?"

"In the car," Handley said.

"Get it."

Louise came back into the room, and gave the camera to her brother.

"Hey, Peanut."

The dog raised his head. "Smile." Andrew snapped his picture.

"What are you thinking?" Bianca asked.

"We're going to take this photo and the sketch and canvas the neighborhood."

"This is a big area," she said. "How much ground do you think we can cover?"

"I think we can narrow this down quite a bit," Andrew said as Louise uploaded the photo and sent it to the printer.

Andrew leaned over the map. Louise and Tompkins followed suit. "I think we can assume he's not in the trailer park. One, he had a big dog. Two, and more importantly, if you're holding someone captive, and in this case possibly more than one, you wouldn't do it in a trailer. Your neighbors are too close, the walls are too thin, and you don't have a lot of space." He crossed out that area on the map. Same goes for the townhouses. They share walls." He put a big red X through that area. "This section here are the mansions. I'm guessing he wouldn't live there."

"Why not?" Bianca interrupted. "There's certainly space and privacy to hold a victim."

"I just don't think he's that smooth. He bullied some kid in the park to buy a debit card. From everything I know about this guy I'm pretty sure he's not loaded."

"I wouldn't assume that," Louise said.

Andrew shrugged. Handley walked in and joined them at the table, the drawing in his hand.

"That leaves here, here, and here." Andrew pointed to three spots. "I say this one." He jabbed his finger on the map. "It's closest to the park."

Louise shook her head. "If you were bullying kids would you want to do it where people knew who you were? I'd pick the neighborhood closest to Perch Lake. It's also close to the vet and to Taco Bell."

"She makes a good point." Bianca rose from the floor.

Andrew nodded. "That's farmland. Perfect place to hide out. It's a lot of ground to cover and it will be slow. And if he doesn't answer the door, we're SOL. There's no way we'll be able to bust in without a warrant, and no way will a judge give us one."

"I grew up a farm," said Tompkins. I'm guessing this guy doesn't have family, and one person can't handle a farm by themselves. Not for very long anyway. Andrew, when you do your rounds to you see any dilapidated fields?"

Andrew shook his head. "But there's a number of hobby farms. Just a few acres."

He focused back to the map. "This last spot is single family homes and small enough that everybody should know everybody."

"Well." Louise slapped her hands on her thighs. "Should we get started?"

"Where?" Handley asked.

Andrew called Dearling one more time. He explained his theory. "If you guys could concentrate on farms and the mansions that would be great. And if you have anyone to spare, they can join us at the park area and single family homes."

"I'll coordinate it from here. I'll keep an open line," Dearling said.

When Andrew disconnected the line, they all stared expectantly. Even Peanut seemed to take an interest.

"He's only got three officers available. They'll start with the farms. Got two deputies available. They'll canvass the mansions."

Bianca looked at her watch. "It's already eight-thirty. We'd better get going."

"What do you mean *we,* white girl? You're not invited." Louise elbowed her brother.

"There's no way I'm missing out on this," Bianca protested.

Louise ignored the reporter. "Andrew, put on your Deputy

Dawg suit. I think people would be more trusting with a man in uniform."

"Good idea." Andrew nodded his head.

Louise got up and took a can of dog food out of the case. Peanut struggled to his feet then sat at attention. Louise set the bowl of food in front of him. He didn't budge.

"Go ahead," Louise said. The dog stayed at attention. "Eat. It's yummy food. Mmmm."

The dog cocked his head quizzically, but didn't move.

"Peanut."

The rottweiler looked at Bianca. She made a sweeping motion with her hand toward the bowl. Peanut charged toward the food.

Bianca smiled. "Lucky guess. We trained our dog to do that when I was a little girl. Obviously, he's been taught something similar."

"You can drop off Ms. Legs on the way." Louise gave the evil eye to Andrew.

"We should take her. I think people will be more talkative with a celebrity at their door."

"You're going to go far in this world, Deputy." Bianca squeezed his hand.

"I'll follow you guys in my car," said Handley. He looked at Tompkins. "Care to join me?"

Tompkins folded his laptop and stood up from the table. "Wouldn't miss it."

Louise rubbed her eyes. "Let's just do this."

Thirty-Four

Monday 8:55 p.m.

Wispy streaks of pink clouds hung in the air as the sun caressed the horizon. Louise stared out of the passenger window as Andrew drove through Kenowa making a pass through Main Street. Bianca sat in the back.

"My God, I think I died and went to Mayberry," Louise said.

Andrew parked the car at the outer lip of the residential section. Handley pulled up next to him. Tompkins sat the width of two car doors away from Andrew.

"Why don't you guys take the area around the park?" Andrew handed them the map, the drawing of Elias, and a picture of the dog.

"Happy hunting," Handley called over, then drove off.

"It's going to get dark really quick. Maybe we should split up. We can cover a lot more ground that way," Andrew said.

"I don't think people are going to be very cooperative, especially this late at night to a civilian telling people she's a Minneapolis cop," Louise said.

"I bet they'd be very cooperative to a reporter from Channel Six News," Bianca cooed.

"She makes a good point, Louise. Maybe you two could go together. We'll still be able to cover twice as much ground that way."

Louise shook her head. "Not a good idea to leave us alone without a chaperone."

"That was two years ago! Get over it," Bianca said. "Besides, he was a bad cop. He tarnished the entire police force. I did you guys a favor by exposing him."

"That bad cop was a friend of mine." Anger flowed through Louise.

"He couldn't have been that good of a friend if you didn't know about his martini lunches at the strip club if—and as memory serves—you said you didn't."

"That's enough," Andrew jumped in. "We're wasting time."

A tense silence lay thick in the car. It finally dissipated when Andrew opened the car door. "Fine, we'll stick together. It'll be safer that way anyhow. Besides, we only have one picture."

The two women exited the car without saying a word. As they walked up the driveway to the first house Louise asked, "How do you want to handle this?"

"Let me talk," Andrew said. "I'll show 'em the picture of Elias and the dog and ask if they recognize either." He rang the doorbell.

Through full-length side windows, the trio heard an incessant barking. Seconds later, a miniature dachshund whipped around the corner and raced to the door. About five feet away he tried to stop. Claws grappling with the slick linoleum floor, he slid all the way up to the window.

"He's safe," Louise yelled as she threw her arms out like an umpire.

The trio laughed, breaking the tension. The dog kept barking.

The outside light flashed on; a man in his early forties with thinning dark hair peeked out the window. His face darkened with worry when he saw Andrew's uniform. He opened the door. "What's he done now?"

"Sorry to bother you this evening," Andrew said, "but we're looking—"

"Bartholomew, quiet!" The dog took that as his cue that his job was done and scampered back down the hallway. "Sorry." The man glanced at Andrew, scanned past Louise and stopped at Bianca. "You look kind of familiar." His eyes stopped on her legs.

"I get that a lot. I must have one of those faces."

"Do you know this guy, or recognize this dog?" Andrew showed him the sketch and the photo. "We were wondering if you might know who he is."

"Whew! I thought my son was in trouble again." The man slowly pulled his eyes off Bianca to look at the pictures and furrowed his brow. "Ouch. Poor dog. What happened to him?"

"That's why we're trying to find the owner, sir," Louise said.

The man looked at her as if she had just appeared out of nowhere. He studied the pictures again and shook his head.

"We think he's around six foot-eight," Andrew added.

"Who's around six-foot-eight? A boy no older than sixteen came to the door. His eyes locked onto Bianca and traveled down to her legs.

"This is my son, Scott."

The kid edged past his father to look at the photo. "Hey, I know this dog."

"The owner goes by the name Elias," Andrew showed the boy the sketch.

He studied Elias' face. "Yeah, I suppose that could be him. Not a very good likeness, though. But I'm pretty sure I've seen this dog before. If it's the one I'm thinking of I seen this huge guy walking a dog like this around the lake. Always walks him at night. He wasn't all beat up though."

Louise looked at her brother. She could tell that Andrew had to concentrate to keep his hand from shaking. She shared the same sensation. "Do you know where he lives?" She had to fight the keep the excitement out of her voice.

"Yeah, a few blocks over, on Pemberton Lane."

"Do you know the address?" Louise asked.

"I don't know the address but it's the one where it looks like his grass always needs mowing."

"How do you know where he lives?" his dad asked.

"I don't know. I just seen him walking his dog out there."

"Were you following this man?"

"No, Dad," Scott rolled his eyes. "I was just riding my bike to Jason's this one time and I saw him. The only reason I remember is because the guy was so huge. I thought huge guy, huge dog, huge grass."

"Can you show us?" Andrew asked.

"I don't know if I'm comfortable with that," the father said.

"Oh, Dad."

"It'll be fine," Andrew said. "We'll just drive by the house and Scott can point it out. We won't even stop. He'll be back home in five minutes."

"You're welcome to come with us," Louise added.

"Oh, c'mon Dad. He beat up his dog. It's not like he murdered anybody."

The trio stood mum.

The father put on an air of concern, then pointed his finger at Andrew's chest. "If anything happens, I'm holding you personally responsible."

"Less than five minutes," Andrew said.

The boy followed eagerly as they walked back to the car. A look of disappointment crossed his face when he saw he'd be riding in a regular car and not a police cruiser. Louise decided she would sacrifice the front seat and sit next to the reporter so the kid could ride shotgun. But when Bianca opened the back door and got in, Scott quickly slid in next to her.

"No wonder he didn't want his dad to come," Louise whispered to her brother.

"Now I know where I've seen you." Scott pointed his finger in Bianca's face. "You're that reporter from channel six. The one who got fired for busting into that crack-head's house."

"Suspended," Bianca corrected him.

"You are so cool for doing that. The hell with what's legal. Do what's right. I was so pissed when they fired you I quit watching that news show."

"Well, they unfired me so you can start watching again."

"If you're going to be on the air, I will. Damn, wait until I tell the guys I rode in a car sitting next to Bianca Jagger."

"Skylar," Bianca corrected him again.

Louise had to bite her lip to keep from laughing out loud.

Andrew drove slowly down Pemberton Lane.

"That's the one." Scott pointed to small house on his left. It was one of only a few on the block with an attached garage.

As promised, Andrew kept driving until they got back to the boy's house. "Thank you Scott. You've been a big help."

Scott became flustered as he opened the door. "Um, Ms. Skylar? Would it be okay if I got your autograph?"

Bianca laughed gleefully as she reached into her purse and pulled out her notebook. She tore out a blank piece of paper. "To Scott, my favorite fan," she said as she wrote. Then she pulled out her compact and put on a fresh coat of lipstick, then kissed the piece of paper under her signature. She tore it out and when she leaned over to give it to him, she pecked Scott's cheek. "Explain that one to your dad."

"Whoa! Thank you!" Scott stepped out of the car and stared up at the darkening sky as if giving thanks to God.

Andrew watched and waited until the boy was safely inside.

"Can we go now?" Louise asked, her voice on the verge of hysteria.

As the front door closed behind Scott, Andrew pulled out of the driveway.

"Amazing we got a hit on our first house," Bianca said.

They pulled back up to the house Scott pointed out. The drapes were pulled over the windows and no light escaped. Even through the dying sunset Andrew could see that Scott had been right about one thing. The lawn did need cutting. Louise reached for the door handle.

"Let's wait for backup." Andrew grabbed her arm.

"That would be the prudent thing to do," she said.

Andrew called Dearling. "Deputy Andrew Miller requesting backup at one-five-four-eight-eight Pemberton Lane. Possible hostage situation."

Bianca whipped out her cell phone too. "Get a camera crew out here pronto." She repeated the address into her cell. "It's in Kenowa…I don't know. By Perch Lake. Take ninety-four to, I don't know. Mapquest it. Let's prepare for a live feed too. If this pans out, it's going to be the story of the year."

Louise jerked her arm out of Andrew's grasp and got out of the car.

"Where are you going?" Andrew asked. "Back-up will be here in less than five minutes."

She leaned over, placing her elbows on the open window, and looked her brother in the eye. "If Karla's still alive and he sees a bunch of cops storming the house, the first thing he's going to do is waste the hostages." She pushed off from the car and started for the house.

"How do you know that?" Andrew asked.

Louise didn't break stride. "Because that's what I'd do."

"Goddamn it, Louise." Andrew opened the door and said to Bianca, "Stay in the car."

~

Elias sat in the dark in his comfort room on the second floor looking out the window at the car across the street. Gillespy had been right all along. He was worthless. The walls of Elias' world crumbled around him. In a matter of minutes they would fall. A few stars glowed dim while, at the horizon, the sky managed to eke out a thin rainbow of blues.

Elias watched as the woman approached his house. The car door opened and a man got out and followed her. Elias clutched the arms of his chair tight as his heart did a leap. The man wore a uniform. That meant that he wore a gun.

It didn't matter.

Why did he have to kill Gillespy? If there was a way out of this, that damn shrink would have known. Now Elias would have to figure this out for himself. He whimpered, feeling sorry for himself.

He slowly rose from his chair. His knee ached on those first few steps. He grabbed the Glocks off the table, one for each hand. Both clips were full, twenty-six rounds in all. He strapped a Derringer .38 Special to his ankle for added security. Too bad he couldn't go to the car for his Magnum.

It was time to meet fate. He felt no regret about killing the lawyer, and the doctor might already be dead. But he really thought he might have had a chance to convert the dyke who wasn't Louise Miller. Now he would never know. But first he had one quick task to complete.

He stepped up and put his ear to the front door.

"Move off to the side. I don't want him to see your uniform when he answers the door," the female voice said.

You better be quick. With one gun tucked in his waistband, Elias held the other Glock in front of him with one hand and pulled the door open with his other. Before the door swung open, Elias opened fire. Four bullets ripped through the screen door and struck the deputy in the chest. He flew backward, his head connected with a thud against the cement pathway.

"Andrew!" Louise screamed.

Elias shifted his aim.

She reacted fast. The woman pressed herself against the house forcing Elias to step outside. He was halfway out the door before he saw the muzzle of her gun. A bullet whizzed past his face as he ducked back inside, his heart thundering. *Damn*! He hadn't planned on the woman being armed too. He slammed the door and stood behind it, sweat rolling down his face. A second blast from her gun kicked the door as Elias raced for the basement.

~

Louise kept her gun trained on the door as she knelt beside her brother and checked his pulse. Strong and steady. His eyes opened. She opened his shirt, keeping an eye at the door at the same time. For the first time she noticed the absence of blood. He'd had enough forethought to wear the Kevlar vest.

"You scared the hell out of me!"

Andrew groaned.

"Oh, shake it off, you wuss." She had trouble keeping her voice steady.

Blood pooled around the back of his head. Through the pain, Andrew smiled up at his sister.

"You'll have some impressive bruises, but you'll be okay. I'm going in."

Andrew forced his eyes open. "Wait for backup," he rasped.

"Can't. Karla's still alive. I can feel it."

Bianca ran across the street. The reporter twisted her ankle as a heel broke off her shoe.

"Get back in the car!" Louise barked.

Bianca froze before she got to the curb; she threw her hands in the air. Louise realized she had her gun aimed at the woman. She shrugged and lowered the weapon. "Sorry. Heat of the moment. He's probably got a concussion; he's wearing a vest. When the cavalry comes, tell 'em there's a female Minneapolis cop out of uniform inside. Call an ambulance."

Louise stood clear of the door, holding the screen door with her foot, and turned the knob. The oak door swung open. She peeked in, saw nothing but darkness, and stepped in.

The bastard had shut off all the lights. Listening for the slightest sound, Louise groped around for a light switch. She found one and waited for her eyes to adjust as a lamp on a small table glowed next to the door. The place reminded her a little bit like Mark's apartment. Just the essentials decorated the room. A couch with two end tables faced a blank wall. Unlike Lone Bear's, there were no pictures or decorations.

The absence of furniture made it an easy search. She made a quick peek into the kitchen and a den. He wasn't hiding on the main floor. Louise had to make a choice. To her left the stairs led up. To her right, a steel door. Faint voices came from the other side. She tried the knob. Locked. The only way to unlock the deadbolt was with a key. *Or a bullet.*

There didn't seem to be any way to keep her presence hidden. With one clean shot the lock shattered. She stepped aside and flung the door open. A flurry of bullets tore past her from the bottom of the stairs. Louise flung herself away from the opening. The shots stopped and Louise heard a series of clicks from an empty clip. She stood in the doorway, her gun held out in front of her. She took the first step, then the second.

"He's got another gun!" a screaming whistle came from below, followed by the smacking sound of fist against face.

Karla!

A blur of movement at the bottom of the staircase sent Louise to her knees. Spinning onto her back and keeping her body as rigid as she could, she slid down the steps like a human sled. The ogre jumped out and shot. A hail of bullets sailed above her. She returned fire. Her shots went high and wide. By the time Louise adjusted her aim, she'd slid all the way to the bottom. The man disappeared behind a wall next to the stairs.

Unlike her brother, Louise hadn't thought to put on a bulletproof vest. Unlike Karla's kidnapper, she only had one gun. How many shots had she fired?

A second voice, not Karla's, wracked with coughing and gagging, shouted. "Look out. He's behind you!"

Louise trusted the voice. She spun around and fired.

The man screamed as he leapt up. Blood and meat spit out of his shoulder. His gun flew across the room. He charged and she fired again. He rammed into her, shoving her against the wall. Her hand holding the gun got caught between the wall, her body, and his crushing weight.

The wind drained from her lungs. The gun clattered to the floor. The giant dropped to his knees, holding in the blood seeping from his stomach.

"Kill him! Kill him!" the woman screamed.

Louise caught him with a knee to the chin. He fell back, blood oozing from his shoulder and side. Louise bent down to pick up her gun. She couldn't. Her fingers didn't work. Pain shot like lightning up her arm. There were broken bones inside that hand. She didn't know how many. She picked the gun up with her left hand.

The man laid still, blood forming a puddle around his body. For the first time Louise searched the room for Karla. "Oh my God," she whispered. She walked over to the bloody mess of a woman tied spread eagled on the cross.

"Karla?" Her mind was playing tricks. Through the swelling and the bruises, she could tell this was another woman.

"Kill the bastard!" The woman burst into tears. "Please kill him," she whimpered. Louise looked back at the body, and the growing pool of red surrounding it. "He's dead." She tucked the gun in her pants and tried untying Melanie using only her left hand.

"Karla?" She couldn't see the stocks hidden on the other side of the stairs.

Melanie shook her head while Louise struggled with the knot. She got one arm free.

"Shoot him again. He's not dead." Melanie tried to reach for her gun but Louise pushed her arm away.

The giant's eyes were open, staring blankly at the ceiling. "He's dead, she said again." She then noticed a body strapped to a board wearing a bloody rag that used to be a shirt. Her stomach churned. "KARLA?"

"Please shoot him again."

The body was that of a man. Louise walked toward the doctor when someone called her name. Half hidden by the staircase she saw her lover bent over in the stocks. Her pants were down around her ankles; she had on a bra but no shirt. Her semi-conscious face no longer held the physical beauty Louise now realized she had taken for granted. The blonde hair Louise loved to run her fingers through was matted with blood and singed in the back. Her right eye had swelled shut above a cheek that had grown to triple its normal size. Blood caked around her split lip.

As Louise raced toward her partner, a large paw reached out and grabbed her ankle. She went down, screaming as she landed on her broken hand.

"You must be Louise Miller. It's a pleasure to finally meet you."

Melanie shrieked as Elias rolled over and rose to his knees towering above Louise. Louise kicked at him with her free leg. She caught him in the face; his grip loosened. A second boot to the face and he let go. Louise saw her gun on the floor, inches away, and reached for it, bringing the barrel up just as Elias pounced on top of her. The barrel cleared her leg just as his hand smothered hers. He tore the gun out of her grasp, twisting it so the barrel pressed into her chest. A gunshot echoed throughout the room.

Louise couldn't breathe. Elias laughed. The giant rolled off and a gush of air entered her lungs. Every nerve in her hand screamed but otherwise she seemed to be whole. She couldn't feel where she'd been shot.

"I got fuckin' shot in the butt." Elias giggled.

Louise sat up, checked her shirt for a bullet hole, then noticed her brother reeling at the bottom of the staircase. With his gun in hand he clutched his stomach; his other gripped the stair banister as he stared in horror at the carnage around him. His eyes went glossy; he dropped to his knees and threw up. Dried rivers of blood had dripped down his neck and stained the back of his shirt.

"Don't leave me now, Andrew. You stay awake." Louise feared a concussion.

Andrew got back to his feet. He used his arm to wipe away the vomit around his mouth. "Actually, I'm feeling much better."

His eyes were still red but Louise thought a little sharper.

"Untie this woman."

"He's still alive," Melanie cried. "Shoot him again!"

Elias grimaced in pain. "Did you bring my dog?"

Louise drove her boot into his face and got angrier when he smiled. She snatched the gun off the floor with her left hand and mashed the barrel into his forehead, trembling with the effort not to pull the trigger. "Your dog said to tell you to fuck off."

"Do it! Kill the bastard," Melanie screamed.

Melanie Cartier had a maniacal glint in her eye. Andrew had pulled up her pants and now worked on the knots.

"Don't do it, Louise. You'll regret it later." Andrew's voice was eerily calm.

"I don't think I will," Louise answered just as calmly. She kicked Elias in the ribs until he stirred. "But I do want some answers first. Why did you kill Mark?"

Elias opened his eyes. "Who's Mark?"

"Mark Lone Bear, the Indian cop. You killed him, you bastard!" She kicked his bloody shoulder.

Elias winced, and then smiled. "Oh yeah, him. The motherfucker ripped me off. Then I found out he was an undercover cop. Fucker was setting me up. Screwed me out of ten thousand dollars on a bogus deal."

Sirens wailed in the distance as Louise felt vindication for her dead friend.

"It took 'em long enough," Louise muttered. She tightened her finger on the trigger. "Look Mom, left handed."

"Don't!" Andrew shouted.

Louise shook her head. "He's too evil to live." Her voice held no emotion as she pulled the trigger. The blast reverberated throughout the room. Half of Elias' mouth and jaw exploded. Blood splatter ran up her leg and speckled her blouse and face.

"He's not dead. Shoot him again!" Melanie shrieked.

Death rattled in the giant's chest. Blood bubbled around the part of his mouth that was still there.

Andrew became frantic, trying to come up with something to say. "Karla needs you." His voice sounded defeated and he collapsed against the wall.

Louise paused.

"I need you too," Andrew pled.

She looked from Karla to her brother, and then down at Elias. "You son of a bitch." She swatted the handle of her gun across Elias' lifeless face before she raced to her partner. Following Andrew's gallantry Louise pulled up Karla's pants first. "Where's the key?"

"I don't know. I think it's in his pocket."

"The hell with that. Turn your head." Louise used the butt of her gun and smashed it into the cheap lock. It gave on the second blow.

"What are you doing?" Andrew yelled.

"Just picking a lock," Louise called back. She lifted the crossbar and helped Karla straighten up. They embraced and Karla burst into sobs. The sirens were very close.

"I knew you'd find me," Karla squeaked through tears.

Louise hugged her in a grip that said she never wanted to let go.

A gun blast shattered the tranquility. Two more shots followed.

"Stay here," Louise pulled away from Karla and raced around the staircase. She saw Andrew writhing in pain, hunched down against the wall grasping his stomach like his guts would fall out if he let go. Louise spun and aimed her gun at Elias. Melanie stood over the dead giant, Andrew's gun clenched in her fist.

"I told you he wasn't dead yet," the lawyer cried.

A gun lay in his hand. *Had he been holding the gun when I shot him?* She couldn't remember.

Pieces of hair, skull, and bits of brain were all that remained of Elias' head. Louise took the gun out of Melanie's unresisting hand and gave it back to her brother.

"She grabbed my gun and when I tried to get up, she shoved me down again."

"Are you okay?"

"No. She pushed me in the exact spot where I got shot. Hurts like hell."

"You keep scaring me like this and I'm going to have to kill you myself."

"Bad taste, sis."

To her left, Melanie spat in the puddle of guts.

Upstairs, the front door smashed open. A stampede rattled the house.

"In the basement," she screamed. "I'm a Minneapolis Police Officer. The situation is under control. But we need ambulances, guys. Lots of ambulances."

~

Louise had no idea how long they kept her in the basement but after a cacophony of explanations she went upstairs. Amazingly, Leonard Hout was still breathing. According to the EMTs, it might not be for long. One of the medics made a bet he wouldn't make it to the hospital.

Rigor mortis had already set in on William Gillespy.

Louise insisted everyone be taken to HCMC. Hennepin County Medical Center had one of the best level one trauma centers in the country. She refused medical treatment for herself other than letting the EMT wrap her hand. She told them she'd go to her own doctor. They told her she was crazy. She agreed.

Louise had her arm around Karla's shoulder as she escorted her partner to the ambulance. At the top of the stairs, a blinding light greeted them from outside.

"What time is it?" Karla asked.

Louise looked at her watch. "Eleven-thirty."

The light came courtesy of the Channel Six news team. Bianca Skylar was in her element standing on the murderer's front lawn giving a live news bulletin. All of her competitors were still setting up.

"Wait a minute." Louise held Karla back. "I want to wait until she's done, unless you want to be on the news." Handley and Tompkins were standing by one of the ambulances. She acknowledged Handley with a slight wave of her good hand, but still holding Karla, pressing against her body.

Karla watched the reporter, perplexed. "Why isn't she wearing shoes?"

"We're clear," the cameraman called.

Bianca thrust up her microphone in the air like the Statue of Liberty with her torch. "We did it. We scooped 'em all!"

The lights faded. Louise took Karla's hand and led her out.

The cameraman sprinted over to Bianca, whooping. "You just scooped the biggest story of the year. What are you going to do now?"

"I'm going to CNN," Bianca shouted, a goofy grin plastered to her face.

"Not a chance," Louise cut in.

Bianca stopped, unsure how to react. "I didn't see you there. Sorry, we're just releasing some tension."

Louise shook her head. "You're not going to CNN. With those legs you'll be going to FOX."

Bianca beamed. "See," she said to the cameraman. "The lesbian doesn't think my calves are too thick."

Louise smiled. "Thanks for your help. See ya around sometime."

The celebration ended when two EMTs rolled a gurney out the front door. Bianca ran over. Blood on the back of the deputy's head already oozed through the wrapping and stained the pillow. Louise and Karla joined her.

"I'm not going to let anything happen to you." Bianca brushed her hand over his cheek. "At least not until you replace the pair of pantyhose you ruined."

"What did you two do after I left the apartment?" Louise gaped at the reporter.

"I'll put that on my list of things not to do," Andrew mumbled. He struggled to smile.

"Forget it. I don't want to know."

Andrew grabbed his sister's arm. "Take care of Corwin 'til I'm better."

There were no snappy comebacks. Louise just nodded and then helped Karla into the nearest ambulance. "I got to stop home and let Peanut outside, if it's not too late already. You'll love him. He's a sweetie. Then I'll stop by your place and pick up some stuff and meet you at the hospital."

Karla faced Louise. "I don't think you can keep him."

Louise felt like Karla just punched her. "Why not?"

"I heard S.K. stories. I don't think I could ever like him."

"No honey, he's not S.K. anymore. He's Peanut. He was brainwashed for a while, but he's better now."

"I can't argue with you right now."

"Oh my God, I'm so sorry," Louise said. "Hell with it. He'll be gone before you get out of the hospital."

Karla tried to smile but the pain twisted it into a grimace. "Don't do anything yet. Let me think about it for a while."

Louise kissed Karla on her unswollen cheek and watched as the ambulance took her away. The night air felt cool with a hint that fall would be coming soon. She walked to her brother's car, praying he left the keys in the ignition.

Thirty-Five

Tuesday 12:30 p.m.

Louise sat on Karla's hospital bed, cradling her lover's head in her lap. She stared vacantly out the window. "I think I'm going to quit."

"What are you going to do?" Karla asked.

Louise shook her head and absently stroked Karla's hair with her good hand. Her right was smothered in a cast. "I don't know. Maybe we could move to Massachusetts or Iowa. They're beautiful states and we can get married."

"I've got family here."

"It's just a suggestion. I don't know."

"How's Peanut?"

Louise brushed her finger, caressing the stitches that lined Karla's cheek. She wore a patch over her eye but the doctors said she should be fine. Some dental work would fix her whistling esses. Karla reminded Louise of when she first saw Peanut.

"He's looking forward to meeting you."

"Yeah, right."

"But in the meantime, you can't separate him from Andrew's cat."

Karla smiled and Louise caressed her face. Listen," Louise said. "It's no contest. If it's between you and him, I'll get rid of him."

"We'll see. How's your brother?"

"Very lucky. There was a perforation in his intestine. He got himself a pretty nasty concussion when he banged his head on the sidewalk. They had to operate anyway, take out some of his tubing. It was very iffy for a while, but he's tough. He'll be fine. In fact, I think I'll go visit him. Do you mind if I leave you alone for a little bit?"

Karla smiled and shook her head. "I'm tired. I think I'll take a nap."

"Let me hear you say 'I need some sleep.'"

Karla's smile broadened and she flipped Louise her middle finger. "Sssally sssellss ssseashellss by the ssseashore—bitch."

Louise grinned and left the room. Karla would be all right.

~

A decorative pail full of red, yellow, and orange tulips sat on cart at the foot of Andrew's bed. He opened his eyes. Gradually the blur sitting next to him focused into his FTO.

"Headache," Andrew mumbled.

"I can imagine. You look like an Arab the way they got your head all wrapped up."

"Ha ha, you're a riot. How's my sister?"

"She won't be doing any boxing for awhile, but other than that she's fine."

"Give me the rundown, Sarge. How's everybody else doing?"

"Well, let's see." Carlin rubbed his chin. "Gillespy and Boughton are worm food."

"Boughton? Who's that?"

"Elias Boughton. Remember him? You can probably blame him for the concussion you got falling down his front steps, via the four dents he shot in your vest that ripped your guts open."

"I didn't even know he had a last name."

"Poor kid," Carlin said. "Moved in his parent's house after they died. They had put him in an institution for boys with emotional problems. Ergo, Dr. William Gillespy. As far as I know they've been pals ever since."

"What about Karla?"

"Who?"

"My sister's friend."

Carlin held up his hand, waving his thumb and pinky. "She's a little, ya know."

Andrew raised himself onto his elbows and managed to sit up. "She's a lot, ya know." He mimicked Carlin's hand gesture. "How's she doing?"

"She's a fighter. As far as I know she'll be fine."

"What about the guy on the surfboard?"

"How did you know about the surfboard?"

"Toured Oak Park Heights Prison when I was in training."

"I'm impressed. Anyway, Dr. Leonard Hout is in ICU. Critical, but they moved his progress up to stable. It's a miracle he's alive. Four broken ribs, a collapsed lung, a ruptured spleen, and God knows what else. I guess he had a reason to live or something."

"What about the lawyer?"

"Melanie Cartier? Physically she's fine, but a total nut case. She's going to be putting her therapist's kids through college with the amount of time it'll take to get her head back on straight."

Andrew laid back and stared at the white ceiling, willing his headache to go away.

"You screwed up big time out there, kid. You should have reported to me, gone through the proper channels. That was number one. And two, damn, you should have waited for backup. What were you thinking? I thought you had better sense than that."

"I did what I thought I had to do." Andrew wasn't going to rat out his sister.

"Do you know the last time a deputy got killed in the line of duty?" Carlin asked.

Andrew shook his head.

"Me neither, but it's been well over thirty years. A helicopter accident, of all things."

"Is that right?"

"The Captain's shitting barbed wire."

"He's mad, huh?"

"And I quote: 'One thing this department doesn't need is some rogue deputy running rampant through our streets.' Unquote. He's thinking about yanking you off the street and putting you back in the Government Center."

Andrew closed his eyes. He thought about the drudgery of shuttling prisoners back and forth between holding cells and the courtroom. "He's just thinking about it? He hasn't made a decision yet, right?" Andrew thought he might fink on his sister in the privacy of the Captain's office as to why he didn't wait for backup. He'd have to come up with something good as to why he didn't go through proper channels, though. Louise could help him with that one.

"He'd love to," Carlin continued. "But he's under a lot of pressure. That reporter is making you out to be some kind of super-hero."

"Hey, baby brother."

Andrew smiled as Louise walked in.

"Hello, officer," Carlin said.

"Sergeant Carlin." Louise nodded in acknowledgment. She walked over to the bed and kissed Andrew on the cheek. "How ya feeling?"

"Almost alive. Any trouble finding my room?"

"Hell, you're just a green, blue, and yellow line away from Karla."

Carlin cleared his throat and rose from his chair. "Well, I can see you two have a lot to talk about and I've got a street to patrol. Officer Miller, it was nice to run into you again. Good work. Deputy Miller, I'll stop by in a day or two. Call me if there's anything you need." Carlin Rivers walked out the door.

Louise peeked out the room and waited until the sergeant entered the elevator. "Do I make him uncomfortable?"

Andrew lifted his hand and wiggled his thumb and pinky. "Well, you're a little, you know."

Louise smiled then closed the door. She walked over and sat next to him and looked solemnly down at her feet.

"I took the money."

"You can't keep it." A tinge of regret and anger rang in Andrew's voice.

"I'm going to donate it to the pet hospital where that girl was killed."

Andrew nodded his head. "Anonymously, I presume."

Louise chuckled. "Oh no, but don't worry. I'll add your name to the card too."

It took almost a second before Andrew realized she was teasing.

"Of course anonymously, stupid."

A knock on the door startled them both.

"I guess that's better than the city coffer," Andrew said. "C'mon in!"

A wave of relief washed over Louise. She needed Andrew to be okay with her decision.

The door swung open and Bianca stepped in, barely visible behind a vase of red carnations, white daisies, and yellow orchids. Floating above her were two silver helium balloons. One said "Get Well," the other had a picture of a brown teddy bear in a police uniform. She set the flowers next to the tulips and let the balloons bounce off and settle onto the ceiling.

She sat on the opposite side of the bed from Louise and bent over, giving a kiss on Andrew's bandage. She left a perfect cherry red imprint of her lips. "Hope the nurses don't get too jealous," Bianca said.

Louise rolled her eyes. "I'm outta here. They're releasing Karla this afternoon so if you need anything call my cell. By the way, your cat prefers my place."

"I'll take good care of him," Bianca said with a wink, then cocked her head. "How come you're not at the funeral?"

"They're just putting on a show. I'll visit him later when it means something." She looked lovingly at her brother. "Besides, my family is in this hospital. I'd much rather be with them."

Louise walked away, paused, and turned back. "Oh, by the way, little brother, I apologize about the steering column in your car. Next time we're in the middle of nowhere and you decide to rupture your intestines and give yourself a concussion, don't forget to give me your car keys first."

"You should've seen it. It was great," Bianca said to Andrew. "She hotwired your car with one hand in the middle of a dozen cops. Handley had to convince her she couldn't drive one-handed."

~

Louise stepped out of the room and stood in the hallway. An orderly pushed a cart past her stacked with trays of half-eaten lunches. The cart rolled silently on the clean white tiled floor with the multicolored lines; everything so sterile, so orderly. She could see herself changing, working in this world. She could take good care of people. But then again, she'd miss her gun.

Her bond with Karla had changed dramatically in the last twenty-four hours. She inadvertently dragged the love of her life into a world she had promised herself she would never bring home. She broke the promise when she first heard about that pathetic dog.

Louise had sensed the fear in Karla's touch and knew their relationship might be irreparable when Karla balked at the marriage proposal. It felt like a stab in the heart. Karla had been the one who brought it up before.

Depression descended on Louise. She had a lot of thinking to do. She wandered absently down to the ICU. Through the glass cubicle she watched as machines blipped and hummed while a woman with tears in her eyes clung to the hand of Leonard Hout. She wanted to go over and hug the woman, reassure her that everything would be all right. Instead, she found her way back to Karla's room.

The TV was on but the sound muted. The blinds were drawn. It made the walls appear gray and tired looking. Karla's steady breathing turned into a soft snore. Louise bent down and kissed her on the forehead. She watched her lover sleep for a few minutes then quietly crept out of the room and out past the hospital doors.

About Author David Fingerman

As a student at the University of Minnesota, David Fingerman realized that if he switched his major from journalism to speech, he could graduate that quarter. It was a no-brainer.

He worked in the court system of Hennepin County for over twenty years. In 2006 he left his job to do what he loves to do—write. He has published a number stories in magazines and anthologies, and published a book of speculative fiction short stories, "Edging Past Reality." "Silent Kill" is his first novel.

David is married and presently lives in Minneapolis.

LaVergne, TN USA
07 November 2010
203867LV00001B/159/P